BESTSELLING AUTHOR COLLECTION

New York Times and *USA TODAY* Bestselling Author

SHERRYL WOODS

Miss Liz's Passion

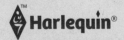 **Harlequin**®

TORONTO NEW YORK LONDON
AMSTERDAM PARIS SYDNEY HAMBURG
STOCKHOLM ATHENS TOKYO MILAN MADRID
PRAGUE WARSAW BUDAPEST AUCKLAND

PLEASE RECYCLE • THIS PRODUCT IS RECYCLABLE

Recycling programs
for this product may
not exist in your area.

ISBN-13: 978-0-373-18487-3

MISS LIZ'S PASSION

Copyright © 2011 by Harlequin Books S.A.

The publisher acknowledges the copyright holders
of the individual works as follows:

MISS LIZ'S PASSION
Copyright © 1989 by Sherryl Woods

HOME ON THE RANCH
Copyright © 2004 by Allison Lee Johnson

All rights reserved. Except for use in any review, the reproduction or
utilization of this work in whole or in part in any form by any electronic,
mechanical or other means, now known or hereafter invented, including
xerography, photocopying and recording, or in any information storage
or retrieval system, is forbidden without the written permission of the
publisher, Harlequin Enterprises Limited, 225 Duncan Mill Road,
Don Mills, Ontario, Canada, M3B 3K9.

This is a work of fiction. Names, characters, places and incidents are
either the product of the author's imagination or are used fictitiously,
and any resemblance to actual persons, living or dead, business
establishments, events or locales is entirely coincidental.

This edition published by arrangement with Harlequin Books S.A.

For questions and comments about the quality of this book
please contact us at Customer_eCare@Harlequin.ca.

® and TM are trademarks of the publisher. Trademarks indicated with
® are registered in the United States Patent and Trademark Office, the
Canadian Trade Marks Office and in other countries.

www.eHarlequin.com

Printed in U.S.A.

TM

BESTSELLING AUTHOR COLLECTION

In our 2011 Bestselling Author Collection, Harlequin Books is proud to offer classic novels from today's superstars of women's fiction. These authors have captured the hearts of millions of readers around the world, and earned their place on the bestseller lists with every release.

As a bonus, each volume also includes a full-length novel from a rising star of series romance. Bestselling authors in their own right, these talented writers have captured the qualities Harlequin is famous for—heart-racing passion, edge-of-your-seat entertainment and a satisfying happily-ever-after.

Don't miss any of the books in this year's collection!

CONTENTS

Acknowledgments

Although Dolphin Reach,
the characters and the incidents in
Miss Liz's Passion are fiction, a similarly
innovative program is currently under way at the
Dolphin Research Center in Grassy Key, Florida.
A special thanks to Dr. David Nathanson for
sharing his expertise, to the
enthusiastic Dolphin Research Center staff
and to Spring and her family for
sharing their time and enthusiasm.

Dedication

For Moira, who brings dedication, imagination
and love to some very special students.

MISS LIZ'S PASSION

New York Times and *USA TODAY* Bestselling Author

Sherryl Woods

SHERRYL WOODS

With her roots firmly planted in the South,
Sherryl Woods has written many of her more than
100 books in that distinctive setting, whether in her
home state of Virginia, her adopted state, Florida,
or her much-adored South Carolina. She's also
especially partial to small towns wherever they
may be.

Sherryl loves hearing from readers. You can join her
at her blog, www.justbetweenfriendsblog.com, visit
her website at www.sherrylwoods.com or contact her
directly at Sherryl703@gmail.com.

Prologue

The bite mark was an angry red, only one shade darker than Teri Lynn's face as she howled at the top of her lungs and clutched her injured arm. Breathless from streaking across the grassy playground to break up the fight, Liz Gentry knelt between the crying girl and her eight-year-old tormentor.

"Kevin, what is the meaning of this?" Liz demanded as she wiped away Teri Lynn's tears with a lace-edged, lavender-scented handkerchief.

The towheaded boy she addressed stared sullenly at the ground, scuffing the toe of his sneaker back and forth in the dirt. She put a firm hand on his chin and forced him to meet her gaze. "Kevin?"

She sighed as he remained obstinately silent.

"He bit me, Mrs. Gentry. For no reason, he just bit me," Teri Lynn said between sobs.

"Did not," Kevin muttered defiantly.

"Did, too," Teri Lynn insisted with a sniff as she inched closer to Liz's side.

"Kevin, if you didn't do it, who did?" Liz asked impatiently, then sighed again.

Of course, Kevin had done it. She'd seen him herself. One minute he and Teri Lynn had been tossing a ball back and forth on the playground. Seconds later he had flown at her in a rage. Half a dozen shocked classmates had stared on silently, while others, seemingly immune to Kevin's displays of temper, continued with their noisy games.

So much for her hopes for an uneventful recess, she thought as she comforted Teri Lynn. Thanks to Kevin, at the rate the school year was going, she would have had a quieter time of it in the Marines.

As the bell rang ending recess, she surveyed the combatants. Both of them had cuts and scrapes, but that bite mark on Teri Lynn's arm was the worst injury.

"Okay, we won't argue about it now. Teri Lynn, I'll take you to the school nurse as soon as I get the rest of the class inside. Kevin, you and I will discuss this after school. In the meantime, you will go to the principal's office and wait for me."

Her tone left no room for argument. Not that Kevin would have given her one. He simply nodded as he always did. Inside the building, as she watched, he walked down the deserted hall and turned into the office. She knew from experience she would find him there at the end of the school day, sitting on a bench, his expression stoic. Only the telltale traces of tears on his cheeks ever offered any indication that he'd found the recurring incidents of misbehavior or the punishment upsetting.

The last hours of school dragged on interminably. She tried to listen as the students read their English assignments aloud, but she couldn't get her mind off Kevin. Despite his troublesome behavior, something about the child's lost, world-weary expression tugged at her heart. She cared about all of her students. She loved the challenge of making them respond, of making learning exciting for them. With Kevin the challenge had been doubled because her usual methods had failed so miserably. Whether it was her own ego or Kevin's apparent need, he had gotten to her in a way that none of the other students had.

But how on earth was she going to handle this ongoing behavior problem? No matter how compassionately she felt toward Kevin, his conduct had to be corrected. There was a fight or a temper tantrum, or a sulking retreat almost every day. The child clearly needed help, more help than she could possibly offer him in a room crowded with thirty-five energetic third-graders.

It was only the first month of school and already she had repeatedly sent notes home to his father, who had sole custody for reasons not made clear in the file. No mention was made of the mother. In her first letter to Todd Lewis she had explained Kevin's behavior problems in depth, detailing her suspicions about the cause and requesting a meeting to discuss solutions. The second note and the third had been a little more impatient, a little more concise. Admittedly, the last one had been barely polite.

Todd Lewis had yet to call, much less appear, which told her quite a lot about the man's indifference to his son's well-being and left her thoroughly frustrated. Reaching him by phone had been no more successful. With an increasing sense of urgency, she had left at least half a dozen messages on his home answering machine in the last two days. If he had a business number, or cell phone number, she couldn't find it. The emergency number in the file had turned out to belong to a neighbor, who looked out for Kevin after school. Liz had been unwilling to draw the woman into the midst of the problem. She had asked her only to relay a message asking Todd Lewis to call. The woman had agreed readily enough, but admitted she rarely saw him.

Liz resolved to try just once more to arrange a meeting.

If the man failed to show up yet again, she would have to resort to stronger action. There were authorities she could ask to intercede. Filled with indignation on Kevin's behalf, she dismissed the class, asked the teacher next door to get her students to their buses, then wrote the harshest note yet, hoping to shake Todd Lewis from his parental apathy.

When she'd finished the note, she went to get Kevin. As she'd expected, he was sitting on the wooden bench in the office, his short legs sticking out in front of him, his hands folded in his lap. He didn't even look up as she sat down beside him. She was torn between wanting to hug him or shake him. He looked as though he desperately needed a hug.

"Okay, Kevin. Let's talk about this for a few minutes before you catch the school bus. Tell me what happened out there this afternoon," she began quietly.

He shook his head, his expression hopeless. That look broke her heart. No child of eight should have eyes that devoid of hope.

"Why not?" she probed.

"Doesn't matter," he said in a voice so soft she had to lean down to hear him.

"It does matter. Fighting is no way to settle an argument."

"Teri Lynn started it," he said with more spirit.

"Kevin, I was watching. I saw you knock her down."

"Only because—"

"Because what?"

His chin set stubbornly.

"Kevin?"

"She said something," he mumbled.

"What?"

He shook his head again.

"Kevin, this is not the first fight you've had. I can't help, if you won't tell me what the fights are about. I don't want to recommend that you be suspended, but that's where you're heading."

Blue eyes shimmering with tears blinked wide at her stern tone. Liz felt her heart constrict. If only she could get to the bottom of this. Her voice softened. "Honey, please, what did she say that made you so mad?"

His lower lip trembled. Liz waited as he started to speak, swallowed hard, then tried again. "She-she…said…"

"Come on, sweetheart. You can tell me."

His shoulders slumped and tears spilled down his cheeks. "She said I was a…a d-dummy."

Liz felt the sting of salty tears in her own eyes at the note of despair she heard in his voice. He believed it! This bright, outgoing child believed he was a failure because of the cruel taunts of a classmate and her own inability to find teaching methods that would reach him.

Kevin needed diagnostic testing. He needed special classes. Most of all, he needed a father who loved him enough to see that the answers to his learning dilemma were found before Kevin withdrew into himself entirely. Damn Todd Lewis!

More than ever, she was glad that this latest note had been worded so strongly. The man's indifference was appalling. Furious, she decided if he failed to respond this time it would be the last. She renewed her vow to set in motion whatever regulations were necessary to see that Kevin got the help that would enable him to learn. More important, she would see that something was done to restore his rapidly deteriorating self-esteem.

"Kevin, you are not a dummy," she said with every ounce of conviction she could manage. "You are a very smart little boy."

He regarded her doubtfully. "But you're always correcting me. That's why Teri Lynn said it. She says you don't like me, that nobody likes me because I always make mistakes." He sighed heavily. "And I do. I can't get nothing right."

"Anything," she corrected instinctively, then could have bitten her tongue. Why just this once couldn't she have let a mistake slide? "Honey, I do like you. I know this is hard for you to understand, but I believe that the reason you make mistakes is not because you're not very, very smart, but because you have something called a learning disability. That's what I want to talk to your father about. I think we should do some tests to find out why it's so hard for you to learn."

"Is that what the note says?" he asked, fingering the sealed envelope suspiciously.

She considered the note's indignant comments. For a fleeting instant she was almost grateful that Kevin had difficulty reading. "More or less," she said wryly. "Kevin, is there some reason your father hasn't been able to come in when I've asked him to?"

He stared at the floor and shook his head. "I don't know. He's pretty busy, I guess." There was an obvious note of pride in his voice as he added, "He works real hard."

"You just tell him that I expect to see him tomorrow. Okay?"

"I'll tell him." He frowned. "You're not gonna be mad at him for not coming before, are you?"

Liz struggled to keep her tone impassive. "Don't worry about that. We'll work things out and once your dad and I talk I'm sure things will get better for you. Now run along before you miss the early bus again today."

He was on his feet at once, his natural exuberance restored.

"Kevin!"

He glanced back at her. "We'll discuss your apology to Teri Lynn in the morning."

He nodded once, shot her a cheerful grin and was out the door, leaving her to ponder exactly how many years she would spend in jail if she tarred and feathered Todd Lewis.

Chapter 1

The neat, handwritten letter had all the primness of some Victorian maiden's blush. According to the indignant opening line, it was not the first such reprimand that Todd Lewis should have received in the past month. The prissy, uptight tone might have amused him had the contents not infuriated him so.

Exhausted by an endless and frustrating day under the hot Miami sun, he reached for the can of beer beside his chair. Perhaps he was overreacting. God knows, it would be understandable. He was bone-weary. His shoulders ached, his back felt like someone was holding a burning knife in the middle of it and his thighs throbbed from the strain of struggling with those damned girders since just after dawn. He had little patience left for someone who'd spent a few hours lolling around in an air-conditioned classroom and still had complaints about how tough the workday was.

He took a long swallow of beer, then slowly read the letter

again. The words and the crisp, precise, censuring tone hadn't mellowed one whit. Neither did his dark mood.

Elizabeth Gentry—he was willing to bet it was *Miss* Gentry—was sharply criticizing his son. For some reason he couldn't quite follow, she didn't seem to be too thrilled with him, either. She demanded that Todd come in the following afternoon at 3:30 to discuss the boy's "uncontrollable behavior, deplorable manners and inappropriate language."

Todd felt his blood pressure begin to soar again. He did not appreciate being chastised in such a demeaning tone by a woman he'd never even met. Nor was he wild about the labels she'd slapped on his son. Another sip of beer soothed his parched throat but not his fiery temper.

He could just picture the woman. Gray hair drawn back in a tidy little bun, a spine of steel, no makeup, rimless glasses sliding down to the end of her too-large nose, nondescript clothes in gray or brown or maybe one of those little floral prints his grandmother used to wear. He sighed at the daunting prospect. He had no idea how to deal with a sexless, unimaginative woman like that.

He took another sip of beer and read on. "Your continued refusal to take action in this matter indicates a startling lack of interest in Kevin's educational well-being and social adjustment. Should you fail to keep this appointment, I am afraid it will be necessary for me to pursue the matter with other authorities."

What other authorities? Was the woman actually suggesting that he be reported to some local bureaucrat, maybe even a state agency? A knot formed in his stomach at the insulting suggestion that he was an uncaring father, who approved of—what was it?—*uncontrollable behavior, deplorable manners and inappropriate language.*

Okay, he was willing to admit that Kevin was a handful, but what eight-year-old wasn't? He just needed a little firm discipline every now and then.

Suddenly the nagging memory of his ex-wife's endless complaints about Kevin's manageability returned with untimely clarity. He'd dismissed her rantings at the time as yet another excuse for walking out on them. Sarah had wanted to leave long before the night she'd finally packed her bags and departed. She'd been too young, too immature to accept the responsibility of marriage, much less a troublesome son. He had blamed the inability to cope on her, not Kevin.

The comparison gave him a moment's pause, but he dismissed the significance almost at once. No doubt this terribly proper and probably ancient Miss Gentry was equally inept with children. If she couldn't handle an eight-year-old boy, perhaps she'd chosen the wrong profession. Perhaps she should be teaching piano and embroidery to sedate young ladies in frilly dresses and dainty white gloves, instead of third-grade boys who got dirt on their clothes even before the school bus picked them up in the morning.

He glanced across the room at his sturdy, blond son. Kevin was quietly racing small cars through an intricately designed village he'd built from the set of Lego blocks he'd begged for and received for his birthday. Todd figured the subdued behavior would last no more than another ten minutes, long enough for his son to feel secure that this note from his teacher would not result in some sort of punishment.

"Kevin." He kept his tone determinedly neutral. Still, wary blue eyes glanced up from the toy Porsche that was about to skitter around the village's sharpest turn. A tiny jaw jutted up, mimicking all too accurately Todd's own frequently belligerent expression. That look warned him that there just might be something behind Miss Gentry's complaints.

"What's this all about, son?"

"Same old stuff." Kevin directed his attention back to the car. It whizzed around the turn and up a hill.

"What stuff?" Todd persisted. "I gather this is not the first time your teacher has written."

A guilty blush spread across Kevin's round, freckled cheeks and he continued to look down. Todd nodded with sudden understanding. No wonder the teacher had been indignant. She thought he'd seen all of her earlier notes and had intentionally ignored them.

"I see," he said wearily. "What did you do with the other letters?"

There was the tiniest hesitation before Kevin said in a whisper, "I lost 'em."

"Really? How convenient," he said, barely controlling his temper. "Suppose you tell me what they were about."

Kevin studied the miniature red Porsche he was pushing back and forth and mumbled, "She said she told you in this one."

"I want to hear it from you."

Kevin remained stubbornly silent. Todd knew from experience that getting him to talk now was going to require tact and patience. He was shorter than usual on both tonight.

"Son, she says this is the fifth note in the last three weeks. Are you sure there's not something happening in school that you should tell me about?"

Kevin's expression turned increasingly defiant. "I told you, Dad. She don't like me. That's all it is."

"School just started a month ago. Why would you think your teacher doesn't like you?"

"Everybody knows it, Dad. She's always telling me how to do stuff."

Despite himself, Todd grinned. "She's a teacher. That's what teachers do."

"Yeah, but Dad, she only tells *me*. Even when I tell her I can't do it, she makes me. The other kids get it, but I can't. I try, Dad. Really."

The tears that welled up despite the tough facade convinced Todd that his son was telling the truth, at least as he saw it.

A swift surge of compassion swept through him, blotting out for a moment his need to get to the bottom of the teacher's complaints. His overwhelming desire to protect Kevin at any cost refueled his anger at the stiff, unyielding Miss Gentry and gave substance to all of his long-standing suspicions about the school system's ineptitude. It had done a lousy enough job with him. He'd obviously been foolish to hope that things had improved.

What kind of teacher would single out a child day after day like that? He'd tried his darnedest not to interfere, to let the school do what it was supposed to do—educate his son, but he wouldn't have the boy made out to be some sort of freak because he was a little slower than the other kids. Kevin was smart as a whip. Anyone who took the time to talk to him could see that.

"Are you going to talk to her, Dad?" Kevin's voice was hesitant, the tone a heartbreaking mix of hopefulness and fear. Todd wasn't sure what response his son really wanted.

"Don't you want me to?" he asked, though he knew there was no longer any real choice in the matter.

Kevin shrugged, but his little shoulders were slumped so dejectedly it made Todd feel like pounding his fist through a wall. "She's made me stay after school almost every day this week," Kevin finally admitted. "A couple of times I almost missed the bus. I think she's real mad at both of us now."

Todd sighed. Kevin tried so hard not to let anyone fight his battles for him. If only he'd told Todd sooner, perhaps this wouldn't have gotten so far out of hand. The prospect of confronting Miss Gentry's self-righteous antagonism held about as much appeal as putting in another grueling, mishap-ridden twelve-hour day at the site of his latest shopping center.

"Then maybe it's time I have a talk with her," he said, anyway. "Don't worry about it, son. I'll get it straightened out. Tell her I'll be there tomorrow afternoon." He recalled the string of problems he'd left behind at the construction site and the imperious tone of that note, then amended, "Or the next day, at the latest."

But despite the reassurance, fear still flickered in Kevin's eyes. That frightened expression aroused all of Todd's fierce protective instincts. He remembered every single humiliating moment of his own school experience and swore to himself that Miss Elizabeth Gentry would not put his son through the same sort of torment.

Liz stared longingly out the classroom window at the swaying palm trees and deep blue sky. It was a perfect Florida day. The humidity had vanished on the breeze. She had only five more spelling papers to grade before she could leave the confining classroom and enjoy what was left of the early October afternoon. The prospect of a long swim raised her spirits considerably.

She had had an absolutely hellish day again. The school had instituted yet another form that had to be filled out, though no one knew quite why. Two of her students had been sent home with the flu, after generously sharing their germs, no doubt. She'd had cafeteria duty, which almost always left her with a headache. Today's was still throbbing at the base of her skull. And Kevin had gotten into another fight. This time he'd sent Cindy Jamison to the school nurse with a bloody lip. She herself had gotten a lump on her shin and a run in her hose trying to break up the brawl.

Now Kevin was sitting at his desk, his head bent over another assignment as they waited for his father, who was already forty minutes late. The man probably had no intention of showing up this time, either, though Kevin had vowed that he would be here.

She heard a soft, snuffling sound and looked back just in time to catch sight of a tear spilling onto Kevin's paper. Her heart constricted. Blast that stubborn, indifferent father of his.

"Kevin, bring me your paper."

He looked up, his expression so woebegone that once again she felt like taking his father apart piece by piece.

When Kevin didn't move, she said, "Aren't you finished?"

He shook his head.

"That's okay. Show me what you have and we'll do the rest together."

"It's not very good."

"No problem. We'll work on it."

Kevin approached her desk with the look of a child being told that Santa Claus was leaving him only a lump of coal. It was an expression without hope. Stoic and resigned, he placed the rumpled page in front of her. "I made a lot of mistakes."

"Then let's see what we can do about them," she said briskly. "You know everybody makes mistakes when they tackle something new. It's nothing to be ashamed of and it's definitely no reason not to at least try."

Kevin regarded her with surprise. "My dad says that, too."

Liz was startled that they'd even discussed the subject. Her image of Todd Lewis did not include supportive father-son talks. She'd been certain that he either ignored the boy altogether or pressured him by expecting perfection.

"Does your dad help you with your homework?"

"Sometimes," Kevin said evasively. "Mostly Mrs. Henley helps me." Mrs. Henley was the woman next door.

"Sometimes, if Dad's real late, she fixes dinner and helps me with my homework."

Liz felt that familiar surge of helplessness rush through her again. For the next half hour she and Kevin worked on correcting his paper. It was a tedious, frustrating process for both of them, but Kevin's glowing smile at each tiny success made the effort worthwhile. When he printed the last of the words on his list perfectly, she hugged him.

"That's exactly right. I think you deserve a reward. What would you like?"

His eyes widened. "You mean like a present or something?"

She grinned at his look of delight. "A small present."

He chewed on his lip thoughtfully, then finally said, "I'm really hungry. Could I have a hamburger?"

It wasn't exactly what she'd had in mind, but he was looking at her so expectantly, she shrugged. "Why not? I'm sure we can find someplace nearby for a hamburger and maybe even some french fries."

"Great, but what about my dad?"

Liz wasn't much in the mood to talk to Todd Lewis about anything, but regulations demanded it. "If you give me the number, I'll call him at his office and get his okay."

Kevin's face fell. "He doesn't work in an office. You can't call him."

"What about a cell phone?" she asked.

"He only uses it for work, I don't know the number."

She should have realized that the minute she'd made the first call last week and gotten only an answering machine. "Where does he work?"

"He builds stuff. You know, like shopping centers and things. He's building one now that's really neat."

Liz made one of those impetuous decisions that occasionally got her into very hot water. She didn't believe in breaking rules, but she sometimes bent them in two if she thought it would help one of her students. Right now, Kevin needed all the positive reinforcement she could give him. She'd brave a lion in his den, if that's what it took. Todd Lewis seemed only slightly less formidable.

"Do you know where it is?"

"Sure. He takes me with him lots on the weekends.

Sometimes we even go by at night, if he has to go back and work late."

It didn't sound like any sort of lifestyle for a young boy, Liz decided, and only added to her conviction that Todd Lewis was treading dangerously close to being an unfit father. Yet Kevin always spoke of his father with such obvious pride. He clearly idolized the man. That intrigued her.

"Come on, then," she said to Kevin. "Let's go see him."

When they found Todd Lewis, he was standing with one dusty, booted foot propped on a steel girder that was about to be hoisted to the third level of a future parking garage. A yellow hard hat covered much of his close-cropped brown hair and shaded his face. A light blue work shirt was stretched taut over wide shoulders. Liz found herself swallowing hard at the sight of him. He was bigger—at least six-foot-two and probably two-hundred pounds—more imposing and more masculine than she'd imagined. He made her feel petite and fragile and very much aware of her wrinkled shirt, the run in her hose and the fact that she hadn't stopped long enough to put on lipstick.

His eyes, when she got close enough to see them, sparked with intelligence and curiosity. At the sight of his son running toward him, those eyes filled with something else as well, a warmth and concern that startled her and made her wish for one wild and timeless moment that the look had been directed at her.

"Dad, this is Mrs. Gentry," Kevin blurted with a wave of his hand in her direction. Something in Todd Lewis's self-confident demeanor seemed shaken by that announcement, but there was no time to analyze it because Kevin was rushing on. "We came to see you because we're going to celebrate, but Miss Gentry said we had to get your permission and we couldn't call you, so I showed her where you are. Is it okay?"

There was another flash of amazement in those clear hazel eyes. An errant dimple formed in that harsh, tanned face. "A celebration?"

"Yeah. I got all my homework right. Mrs. Gentry helped me while we were waiting for you. I told her you were coming, but that sometimes you got really busy and forgot things. You know like you did when you had that date last week and she came to the house all dressed up and you were working on the car."

Liz noted that Todd Lewis nearly choked at that. She figured the revelation served him right.

"Sorry," he said. "I told him to tell you I'd be there today or tomorrow."

He didn't sound the least bit repentant. Before she could stop herself, she reminded him, "And I asked you to come in today. I'm sure if you'd explained things to your boss, you could have arranged for the afternoon off."

"I am the boss," he said matter-of-factly. "And I can guarantee you that I didn't get the title by walking off the job in the midst of a crisis just because of some damned whim."

Liz had to do some quick revising. She glanced around at the sprawling mall with its Spanish-style architecture, man-made lakes and fountains already bubbling. Even weeks away from completion, it promised to be spectacular. How on earth could a man in charge of all this run a business without an office? Perhaps he was one of those laid-back eccentrics who delighted in going his own way and was talented enough or wealthy enough to get away with it. She, however, didn't operate that way.

"It was hardly a whim, Mr. Lewis. If I hadn't thought it extremely important, I wouldn't have requested the meeting."

"Demanded."

"Semantics, Mr. Lewis. The point is that you did not come. Again," she added.

"I'm sorry," he said again, this time sounding genuinely apologetic. "Your earlier notes…" He gazed pointedly at Kevin. "They seem to have gone astray."

She felt some of her tension and antagonism begin to ease. That put things in a slightly different light. She should have guessed that Kevin hadn't passed them along to his father.

"And the phone messages?"

He stared at her blankly. They both turned to gaze at Kevin. He was staring at his shoes.

"Sorry, Dad. I guess maybe they got erased."

Todd Lewis sighed wearily. "We will talk about all of this later, son." He smiled at Liz and shrugged. "I guess that explains that. I really am sorry. No wonder you had such a lousy impression of me."

Liz blushed as she thought of the barely veiled charges she'd leveled at him in her last note. She probably owed him an apology of some sort. Still, he had ignored that one. He wasn't entirely blameless. Or was he?

"You did get the note I sent yesterday, didn't you?"

"Yes."

"Well…" If she'd expected to intimidate Todd Lewis with a cool stare and an unyielding attitude, she'd vastly underestimated him. Those hazel eyes pierced her without once wavering.

"It is nearly five o'clock, Mr. Lewis," she stated pointedly, not sure why she felt the need to attack rather than be conciliatory. Perhaps it was because she wasn't one bit happy about the way her pulse had been skipping erratically ever since she'd gotten within five feet of Todd Lewis.

He grinned. Her pulse leapt. She wanted to attack. Yes, indeed, that was it. An instinctive and vitally necessary response.

"Thank you for enlightening me," he retorted. He held out

his hand, displaying a forearm that was bare to the rolled-up sleeve of his shirt. "I don't wear a watch on the job. I don't like clock-watchers."

She wasn't sure whether he was referring to himself, his employees or her. Either way, if he'd hoped to rattle her, it was working. She couldn't take her eyes off that muscular forearm. If the man weren't quite so large or quite so masculine, she'd be tempted to grab it and experiment with that self-defense technique she'd learned at her last karate lesson. The prospect of flipping him onto his backside cheered her considerably.

"You know what I meant," she said stiffly. "I expected you at 3:30."

"And I had hoped to be there," he said so solemnly that she knew he was mocking her. "You know Miss Gentry…"

He made it sound as though she were some dried-up old prune. "*Mrs.* Gentry," she retorted.

He shrugged indifferently. That faint suggestion of amusement continued to play about his lips. "You may be in charge of your classroom, *Mrs.* Gentry, but I'm in charge around here. Unfortunately at a construction site things are apt to go wrong according to whim, rather than your rigid schedule. If you can think of some way to make these girders do your bidding, more power to you. I've had a helluva time with it."

This time he waited expectantly. Liz felt her insides quiver. Possibly with fury. More likely with something entirely less rational. The man was positively maddening. And far too attractive. She suspected the two characteristics were probably related. She realized she was gripping the handle on her purse so tightly the leather was biting into her flesh. She tried to relax. When that didn't work, she went for the jugular.

"You've already explained that you run the company, Mr. Lewis. You don't strike me as the sort of man who'd be foolish enough to believe he's either indispensable or indestructible. I'm sure you have assistants who could handle any crisis that occurs in the brief time it would have taken for you to keep an appointment with me."

He simply scowled at the note of censure. "That's not the way I do things," he said with finality. "Now what was so all-fired important that it couldn't wait another twenty-four hours?"

She glanced at Kevin and hesitated. She'd already said far more than she should have in front of him. What on earth had gotten into her? "I don't think this is the time or place to be discussing this."

"You picked it," he reminded her.

"Mr. Lewis!"

He stared at her intently, then finally nodded. "Kevin, go into the trailer and ask Hank if he'll take you to the top of the garage. It's another story higher since the last time you were here."

"Oh, wow! Great, Dad. Thanks." He bounded off without a second glance at either of them.

Todd Lewis watched Kevin until the door of the construction trailer slammed behind him. Then once again he propped his foot on a pile of girders, put his elbow on his knee and said, "You were saying..."

Liz sighed at the challenge and tried very hard not to stare at the way his jeans stretched across his hips. "Mr. Lewis, I did not come here to argue with you. I came to ask permission for Kevin to have a hamburger with me as a reward for working so hard this afternoon."

"Are you sure you didn't just want to check out his irresponsible father firsthand?"

The teasing glint in his eyes unnerved her. Again. "I'm sorry for some of the things I suggested in the note."

"But not all?"

"Kevin is a problem."

"Maybe you just don't know how to manage him."

The cool, unexpected taunt struck home. Liz practically

shook with indignation. It was a welcome relief after all those other feelings she'd been experiencing.

"Don't you dare try to turn this into my failure, Mr. Lewis. Since you are so cognizant of your responsibilities, I'm surprised you don't pay more attention to Kevin. Surely he counts among them. If you had, you would have noticed long ago..."

Her furious tirade faltered as his expression suddenly became all hard angles. She'd seen pictures of cold, merciless dictators who looked less severe. His eyes glinted dangerously. She actually shivered as he took a long stride to tower over her. For an instant she regretted the impulsive tongue-lashing.

"I do know my son. He's a good kid. Maybe a little high spirited, but that's all to the good in a boy. Kevin and I do just fine," he said in a voice that chilled. "We don't need some high-minded do-gooder interfering in our lives. If he's having a problem with his schoolwork, we'll talk about it. Otherwise, you stay the hell out of our lives."

She flinched under the attack, then dared to glower right back at him. This was too important for her to back down now. "I can't do that. Kevin is in trouble in school and that's my responsibility."

"Fine. I said I was more than willing to talk about his schoolwork. I'll be there tomorrow afternoon, no matter what the damn girders do. Now, if you don't mind, I'll be getting back to work."

He strolled away without a backward glance. Before Liz could fully recover from the unnerving confrontation, she saw the burly, redheaded man who'd accompanied Kevin to the top of the skeletal structure join Todd Lewis. Hank, that was his name, she recalled as she watched them. For some reason, she couldn't tear her gaze away from the encounter between the two men. She couldn't shake the feeling that she was seeing a drama of some sort unfold. Suddenly, with a sinking sensation in the pit of her stomach, she realized that

Kevin wasn't with them. Even from a distance, she thought she could see Todd Lewis's complexion turn ashen.

Unaware that she had even begun to move, she found herself not more than a few feet away. She heard Todd Lewis's harsh oath and Hank's apology.

"I swear, Todd, I thought he was coming right back to you. You want me to get the men together?"

"Not yet. What exactly did he say?"

"He asked me for some quarters for the soda machine, then he took off. That's it. Last I saw him, he was in the trailer getting a drink. If he's not there and he's not with you, I don't know where the hell he could have gone."

Hesitantly, Liz touched Todd Lewis's arm. "You think he heard us arguing, don't you? You think he's run away."

He turned on her, his shoulders tense, his jaw tight. That furious stance might have frightened her, if she hadn't looked into his eyes. There was the expected flash of anger, but there was also panic and a touching vulnerability.

That glimpse into Todd Lewis's soul removed forever any lingering doubts she might have had about the depth of his love for his son. It also left her shaken in a way she couldn't begin to understand.

Chapter 2

Todd felt like strangling somebody. Right now it was a toss-up whether it should be Hank or Elizabeth Gentry. He glowered at both potential victims, then muttered a curse under his breath. There was no point in blaming them. They looked every bit as worried and dismayed as he felt. Besides, he was the guilty one. He knew how sensitive Kevin was, how easily hurt. He should never have been discussing him where Kevin might overhear the argument. The kid had a way of popping up when you least expected it. Sending him off with Hank had been no guarantee he wouldn't be back ten seconds later.

"Hank, you take your car and head east," he said finally, fighting to think clearly through the haze of self-recriminations. With great effort, he kept his voice calm and reasonable. "I'll go west on foot. He can't have gotten too far."

Hank, the most easygoing man he'd ever known, looked downright uncomfortable.

"What is it?" Todd demanded impatiently.

"Don't forget he had those quarters. He could have taken a bus."

The already tense muscles across Todd's shoulders knotted. Only the quiet presence of Elizabeth Gentry kept him from uttering a whole arsenal of swear words. He closed his eyes and imagined shouting every one of them at the top of his lungs. Even the imagery had a restorative effect.

"Okay," he said with the careful deliberation of a man battling hysteria. He clung to his businesslike ability to remain calm in a crisis, to put his emotions on hold until every last detail had been handled. "Then we'd better take both cars. We'll meet back here in an hour. If you find him, call me."

To his amazement he sounded decisive and controlled. He felt as though he were splintering apart.

"What about me?" a soft voice interrupted. "What can I do?"

Todd stared at her. "I think you've done enough for one afternoon," he said in a cutting tone that brought Hank's head snapping up. Elizabeth Gentry stared back at Todd. She appeared serene and unfazed by his bark, but there was fire in her eyes. That look challenged him to put aside his animosity for Kevin's sake or further establish her impression of him as a jerk.

"Oh, hell," he said finally. "Come with me."

"Wouldn't it be better if I took my own car? I'll drive south toward the school. He might have gone back that way."

"I think school's the last place he's likely to head," Todd retorted, wondering why the hell she'd bothered to ask his opinion, since she had every intention of doing exactly as she pleased.

Her cool demeanor slipped just a bit at his pointed sarcasm. Then her chin jutted up. "Fine. I'll go north. Let's just stop wasting time."

With that she stalked off, her head held high, her back as

ramrod straight as he'd once imagined it to be. The effect, though, wasn't at all what he'd anticipated. Thoroughly bemused, he stared after her.

How had he gotten it so wrong? Kevin's teacher was no prim, dried-up Victorian maiden. Far from it. She was all ripe curves and passionate indignation. Even with his son missing and his anger fueled, he'd still had the most overpowering urge to tangle his fingers in that flame-red hair of hers and hush her with a breath-stealing kiss. Desire had slammed through him with the force of a hurricane sweeping across the Florida keys. Its unexpectedness had stunned him.

Her amber eyes had challenged him in a way that made his heart pound louder and faster than any jackhammer. Her derision had irked him. Her sensuality had provoked him. The hell of it was, she was also married. *Mrs. Gentry.* The combination was enough to set off warning bells so loud only a man stone deaf could ignore them. Elizabeth Gentry spelled trouble and it had very little to do with her threats about Kevin.

One good thing had come of the encounter: he knew with absolute certainty now that she would never turn her disagreement with him into a public squabble with the authorities. She'd only used the threats to assure Kevin's well-being. He'd seen the genuine concern and affection in her eyes, the caring that ran as deep and true as a mother's fierce protectiveness. It was a look that could make any man less wary than he fall in love. It was a look he couldn't ever recall seeing in Sarah's eyes, at least not toward the end.

With a disgusted shake of his head, he snapped his attention back to Kevin's disappearance. Still muttering apologies, Hank had already followed the teacher to the parking lot. Todd sprinted to his own mud-streaked, battle-scarred pickup. Gravel flew as he spun out onto Kendall Drive, forcing his way into the stream of rush-hour traffic. Locked into a slow-moving crawl, he kept his eyes peeled for some sign of a small, proud boy walking dejectedly along the edge of the highway.

His impatience mounted with every block. Horn honking, he tried weaving through traffic, but it was a wasted effort. No lane was moving any faster than a snail's pace. With each quarter mile he covered, his panic deepened. So many terrible things could happen to a kid, especially in a city the size of Miami. Kevin was all he had, all that meant anything in his life. If anything happened to him… He couldn't even allow himself to complete the thought.

His heart thudded heavily as dismay settled in. This was pointless. He'd already covered miles without seeing any sign of Kevin. If he had gotten on a bus, he could be anywhere. If he hadn't and if he'd come this way, Todd would have found him by now.

Praying that Hank or Elizabeth Gentry had had better luck and just hadn't called, he finally turned the truck around and went back to the nearly deserted construction site. The crew, unaware that there had been any sort of a crisis, had left in his absence and only one car remained in the lot—hers. In an odd way it reminded him of her. It was an ordinary, small blue Toyota, sedate and practical. Only the sunroof hinted at her sense of daring.

Had she found Kevin, he wondered as he hurried toward the trailer. If she had, he thought he might be able to forgive her anything.

He swung open the door of the trailer and saw the two of them—laughing. Her laughter was low and full-bodied. Kevin's high-pitched and raucous. Her arm was around the boy's shoulders as they studied a drawing done in red marker. The quiet intimacy of the scene, the suggestion of family, made Todd suck in his breath. For an instant an irrational fury clouded his vision, overriding his relief. He'd been out searching, his stomach knotted by worry and they were in here laughing like two thoroughly happy conspirators.

"Where'd you find him?" he asked. His curt tone drew startled glances from both of them.

"Hi, Dad," Kevin said cheerfully, obviously oblivious to his father's mood. Todd regarded him suspiciously. He was not behaving like a child who'd run away in anger.

"We've been waiting for you. See what I did. Mrs. Gentry says it's pretty good."

A surge of righteous outrage burst inside him. "Go to the truck," he said, his voice tight.

"Dad?" Kevin's voice was puzzled, his expression confused. He stared up at his teacher, which only infuriated Todd more. Since when had Kevin turned to someone other than him for instructions.

"Now!"

Shoulders slumping and lip quivering at the shouted command, Kevin started toward the door.

"I think you'd better let me explain," Elizabeth Gentry said. She spoke quietly, but there was an edge of steel in her voice. He knew instinctively it was her classroom voice. It probably terrorized the kids. He ignored it.

"Kevin, you heard what I said." His voice was calmer, but no less authoritative.

She stepped closer to Kevin and put a protective hand on his shoulder. She glared defiantly at Todd, the look meant to put him in his place. He had to admire her spunk. Under less trying circumstances, he might even find it a turn-on. Right now, it was only an irritant. He scowled right back at her.

"Save your attempt at intimidation, Mr. Lewis. When I found Kevin, I realized that in my desperation to find him, I forgot to get your number. Kevin did not run away. Don't take your frustration out on him or, for that matter, on me."

He stared from her to his son and back again. Swallowing hard, he tried to regain control over his temper. "I don't understand."

"Tell your father what happened," she urged. When Kevin

appeared to be hesitant, she smiled at him. "It's okay. Tell him what you told me."

"I went to get a drink. Hank gave me the money. And there was this cat." He regarded Todd hopefully. "It was a great cat, Dad, but he'd gotten all wet. I guess he fell in that big mud puddle in back of the trailer. Anyway, I tried to get him so I could clean him up, but he ran. I chased him across the field. When I came back, you were all gone. I must have been gone longer than I thought, 'cause Mrs. Gentry says you all were worried. I'm sorry I scared you."

Relief rushed through Todd. A cat! Kevin had been chasing a stupid, wet cat. He massaged his temples. The pounding in his head began to ease as his tension abated. He stared at Elizabeth Gentry and gave a small, apologetic shrug before grinning sheepishly at Kevin. "Did you catch the cat?"

"No," he said, obviously disgusted. "He was too fast. Anyway, he ran inside a garage. I guess he must belong to somebody."

Suddenly exuberant, Todd picked Kevin up and swung him in the air. "You want a cat that badly?"

"Not really. I'd rather have a dog, but you said we couldn't have one, 'cause we're not home enough." He recited Todd's old argument without emotion. "I just wanted to play with this one."

"Maybe we'll have to rethink that," Todd said. He caught Elizabeth Gentry watching them. She was smiling, but there was something about her eyes that got to him. She looked sad. He couldn't imagine why. Everything had turned out just fine. His son was safe. He felt like celebrating.

"I'd better be getting home," she said, the flat declaration tempering his mood.

Suddenly uncertain, he said with awkward sincerity, "Thanks for helping with the search."

"I'm glad it wasn't really necessary. I will see you at the school tomorrow, won't I?"

The woman had the tenacity of a terrier with an old sock. He grinned. "I promise not to stand you up again." He took her hand, holding it just long enough to confirm the solemnity of his commitment. Her grip was firm, her skin like cool silk, but she trembled. That tiny hint of vulnerability set off warning bells again. He released her hand, but not her gaze. The air sizzled with electricity.

"Hey, you guys, what about my hamburger?"

Todd glanced away at last to stare blankly at Kevin. When he looked back at Elizabeth Gentry, her cheeks were flushed, her eyes hooded.

"I don't think today is…" she began with surprising uncertainty.

Kevin's face fell. Todd was torn between his son's disappointment and his own need to escape the confusing emotions this redheaded firebrand raised in him.

"I'll take you out for a hamburger, son. Mrs. Gentry probably has to get home to her family."

"No, she doesn't. She doesn't have a family. She told us her husband died," Kevin announced ingenuously.

Todd's heart took an unexpected lurch. Glancing over Kevin's head, his eyes met hers. "I'm sorry."

"So am I," she said quietly, but with a surprising lack of emotion.

Todd felt guilty at the relief that swept through him. He had not wanted Elizabeth Gentry to have a husband. He was equally glad to see that it didn't appear she was living with ghosts, though why it mattered was beyond him. He didn't date women like the one standing before him. He ran like crazy from innocence and vulnerability and commitment.

"See, Dad, I told you," Kevin was saying. "Besides, she promised. She should come, too. She's probably really hungry by now."

Suddenly bolder, Todd surveyed her from head to toe with lazy deliberation, then felt renewed guilt at the look of confusion his teasing aroused. For some reason he wanted to provoke her into a mild flirtation. Perhaps he merely wanted to prove to himself that she was as unfeminine and boring as he'd once imagined her. Maybe he just wanted to shake her cool facade. Either way he knew he was playing with fire.

"Are you?" he asked in a voice thick with innuendo.

Startled eyes blinked at him. "What?"

"Hungry?"

As if she suddenly guessed the rules by which he was playing, she returned his impudent look with a touch of defiance. "Starved, actually."

Todd laughed at the prompt response to his challenge. "Then the two of you go on. I'll meet you there in a few minutes. I just want to finish up a little paperwork and give Hank a call to tell him not to worry."

"Dad, it's already late. Couldn't you just phone him on the way?"

"It won't be long."

Kevin's forehead creased with a worried frown. "You won't forget or something, will you?"

The question told Liz all too much about his tendency to get caught up in work. He caught the quick flare of concern in her eyes. Todd's gaze locked with those serious amber eyes. "No," he promised softly. "I won't forget."

With an odd tightening in his chest, he watched the two of them walk away from the trailer. She bent down to listen to something Kevin was saying, then the two of them laughed, the happy sound rippling through the evening air. How long had it been since he'd shared laughter like that with a woman? He hadn't trusted any of them since Sarah. Something told him, though, that he could trust Elizabeth Gentry. He wondered if he'd have the courage to try.

Before he could immerse himself in wasted philosophical musings, Hank came back. He gazed after the departing woman, noting the child by her side, then directed a searching look at Todd.

"Everything okay?"

"Fine."

"Who's the looker?" The interested query was made with Hank's usual lack of tact and reflected his appreciation of all things feminine.

Todd bristled. "Kevin's teacher," he said stiffly, not sure why he felt so resentful of the innocently appraising remark.

"Why didn't I ever have a teacher who looked like that?" Hank said wistfully. "I might have learned more."

"You have an engineering degree now. What more would you have learned?"

"Life, my friend. A woman like that could teach you all about life."

Todd groaned. "Does your libido ever take a rest?"

"Not since junior high," Hank retorted with an unrepentant grin.

"Go heft a few girders, then. Maybe it'll wear you out." He picked up a folder of papers and stuffed them in his briefcase.

"Not a chance. Let me know if you're not interested in that one. Maybe I'll take a shot at her. I have a real thing for redheads."

Todd looked up, incensed. "She's Kevin's teacher, dammit. Not some floozy you saw in a bar. Stay away from her."

Hank stared at him consideringly. "So, then, you are interested."

Todd slammed his fist on the desk, scattering papers. "I am not interested. I am just trying to see that my son and I get through the school year without being responsible for his teacher's downfall."

His outburst didn't seem to faze Hank. "Don't worry about that," he said easily. "I'll absolve you of all responsibility.

Just give me her name and I'll take it from there. I won't even mention I know you."

"Hank!"

"Yes, partner?"

Todd recognized that innocent tone all too well. He shook his head. "Take a hike, buddy."

"Right."

Todd heard him chuckling as he left the construction shed. One of these days a brave and daring woman was going to come along and capture Hank Riley's outrageously fickle heart. Todd just hoped he'd be around to watch the fireworks.

Less than an hour later Todd Lewis slid into the booth across from Liz, his long legs immediately and sensuously tangling with hers. He did it deliberately. She knew it. She sat up straighter and tried to draw away, but there was no way to escape, not when the man was dead set on rattling her. She recognized that perfectly innocent gleam in his eyes for exactly what it was. Temptation! A flat-out dare, which no lady would take and every woman dreams about.

Liz returned his gaze evenly, determined not to let him see that his touch was affecting her in the slightest, that it had been driving her crazy all afternoon long. Beneath the table, though, her fingernails were probably cutting right through the booth's bright blue plastic seat covers.

"Where's Kevin?" Todd asked, glancing around the crowded restaurant. Sound echoed off the glass walls and tiled floors. It was one of those places that had apparently been designed on the theory that the more noise there was in a restaurant, the more convinced people would be that they were having fun.

"He made a dash for one of the video games the minute we walked through the door."

"And you didn't dash with him?"

"I told him I'd order."

"After making such a fuss to get you to come, he shouldn't have left you alone. I'll go get him."

"Mr. Lewis—"

"Todd."

"*Mr. Lewis*, I'm used to being on my own. Kevin's with a friend. Let him enjoy himself. Besides, it would probably embarrass him to have anyone catch him with his teacher."

Her easy acceptance of being abandoned amazed him. A lot of women would have been insulted, even if the male who'd left them was only eight. "You really understand kids, don't you?"

"Don't sound so surprised. It is my job," she said, then added, "but if what you're really saying is that I genuinely seem to like kids, the answer is yes. I think they're great. They usually say exactly what's on their mind and they're open to new experiences."

"What about you? Are you open to new experiences?"

He was doing it again, lacing the conversation with enough innuendos to disconcert a saint. "I'd like to think so," she managed to say without stumbling over the response.

Todd settled back in the booth. "Then I think we should get to know each other better, don't you?"

"I suppose," she said cautiously, making the mistake of meeting his steady gaze. Her heart somersaulted. Those eyes of his could lure a woman into forgetting all reason, to say nothing of professional ethics and quite possibly her name. Her hands slid right off the seat. She clasped them tightly in her lap, drew in a shaky breath and added quickly, "For Kevin's sake."

He nodded. "Of course. Why don't we start by using first names?"

"I really don't think it would be appropriate, especially not in front of Kevin."

"But he's not here right now. Let's compromise. You call me Todd and I'll call you Miss Liz."

She grinned despite herself. "You call that a compromise?"

"You'd rather call me Mr. Todd?"

A faint smile playing about his lips mocked the seriousness of his tone. Liz frowned at his determined impudence, but she couldn't bring herself to look away. Retreat now would give him a victory in a battle she'd almost forgotten how to fight. Instead the tension built just as it had earlier, crackling through the air like summer's lightning.

It was Kevin who broke it, joining them with a huge grin on his face.

"Hey, Dad, guess what! I beat Joey Simons at Battle of the War Lords!"

"That's great, son," he said without taking his eyes from her mouth for one single second. Her lips were parched and she wanted very badly to run her tongue over them, but knew perfectly well that would only inflame the situation. She grabbed her glass of water and drank the whole thing. Todd grinned with unabashed satisfaction.

"Will you and Mrs. Gentry play with me?" Kevin pestered. "Joey had to go home."

With obvious reluctance, Todd tore his gaze away from her and looked at Kevin. "What about your hamburger? It should be here in a minute."

"Oh, yeah." He slid in next to his father. "I forgot."

Watching Kevin and his father together, Liz felt a lump lodge in her throat. Suddenly she wanted to cry. There was so much adoration in Kevin's eyes, such a sense of camaraderie between them, it almost reminded her of… Closing her eyes against the surge of pain, she sealed off the thought before it could form.

"I think I should be going," she said suddenly, just as the meal arrived. "I'll pay the check on my way out."

"No!" The protest was voiced by father and son.

"Really, it's late." She needed to escape before the threatening tears embarrassed her.

"We just got here. You haven't even eaten your hamburger," Kevin said.

"I'm not really hungry. Your father can have it."

"A little while ago you said you were starving," Todd reminded her. His penetrating gaze seemed to see right through her flimsy excuse.

"Besides, it won't be the same," Kevin said. "You promised me a celebration."

At the mention of the promise, her determination wavered. Kevin might be manipulating, but he was using the truth to do it. She had promised. However, if she'd had any idea what sitting in this booth across from Todd Lewis would be like, she would have devised some other reward for Kevin. She would have seen to it that it didn't require being crowded into such close quarters with a disturbingly masculine parent who insisted on toppling all barriers between them, starting with the informal way he meant to address her. *Miss Liz, indeed!*

Kevin was gazing at her now with wide, hopeful eyes. His father's eyes had a speculative gleam in them, as if he'd guessed that he was the reason for her desire to run and was wondering how to capitalize on his advantage. That decided her. She would stay. She would eat every bite of her hamburger, even if she choked on it.

She gave Todd Lewis her most defiant, go-to-hell glare and picked up the ketchup. Her gaze never wavered as she shook the bottle. Kevin's sharp gasp drew her attention. She glanced down. Her hamburger had virtually disappeared in a sea of thick red ketchup. She groaned. How could she have done something that stupid?

"I'll order you another one," Todd said, reaching for her plate.

She grabbed it back. "This one's fine. I like a lot of ketchup." Her tongue nearly tripped over the flat-out lie. Still, she refused to admit to her foolish mistake.

"Don't be ridiculous. I'll take it and get you another one."

"I'll just scrape a little of this off," she said stubbornly.

He shrugged finally. "Suit yourself."

Liz determinedly scraped off enough ketchup to serve all the fans in the stadium during next Sunday's Dolphins game. She took her first bite, then forced a smile as Kevin and Todd watched her expectantly.

"You're sure it's okay?" Todd asked, his expression doubtful.

"Just fine," she said with forced cheer.

To herself, she vowed to get through the next half hour without coming unglued, if it was the last thing she ever did. She also swore that she would not under any circumstances ever admit to either of the males across from her that she absolutely never ate ketchup. It gave her hives.

Chapter 3

Todd pulled his pickup into the lot behind the elementary school. The dusty playground was empty, except for a forgotten soccer ball. The swings shifted slowly in the hot stirring of humid air. The cloudless sky burned a merciless reminder that Miami was still weeks away from the first cool nights and gentle days.

As if the weather weren't enough to sap energy, Todd felt an age-old feeling of intimidation squeezing his chest as he walked around the corner of the low, brick building. When he'd finally graduated from high school two years late, he'd vowed never to cross the threshold of another school. He was here now only because of Kevin. And one feisty teacher who wouldn't let well enough alone, he reminded himself.

As he neared the entrance, he heard the faint ringing of a bell and a moment later the quiet erupted into a scene of absolute chaos. Several hundred noisy, rambunctious students began pouring through the doors like salmon frantic to get upstream. He stood out of the way and watched, hoping to catch a glimpse of the determinedly staid Mrs. Gentry in the midst of the pandemonium.

It took him only a few minutes to spot her. Her red hair was pulled tautly back. Curly strands, indifferent to her efforts at restraint, had escaped to create a halo that glittered a coppery gold in the sunlight. In her slim beige skirt, emerald green silk blouse and sensible beige pumps, she was solemnly leading a perfectly formed line toward one of the bright yellow Dade County school buses. The impression of rigidity returned with a thud, correcting a night of more alluring dreams.

Then he saw a small girl of six or seven lift a laughing face toward her. Elizabeth's—Miss Liz's—generous mouth curved into an answering smile. With fingers that seemed somehow hesitant she reached out and lovingly brushed a strand of hair back from the child's face. There was an odd sense of yearning in that fleeting touch that wrapped itself around Todd's heart.

Contradictions! So many contradictions, he wondered if he'd ever understand them all.

There's a lifetime to try.

The unexpectedly wayward thought careened through his head, slamming into his consciousness with the impact of a fullback charging at full speed. His breath rushed out, followed by a colorful, resistant oath. There was no way in hell this woman—any woman—was going to get to him again. Not after Sarah.

But his palms were sweating like a lovestruck teen's and his heartbeat skittered and danced in a way he'd all but forgotten. He seized on past hurts and entrenched bitterness to chase away the symptoms of an imagination gone awry. They did a damn poor job of it, he noted wryly as he waited at the entrance for Elizabeth Gentry to join him. He rubbed his palms on his denim-clad thighs and hoped the heat in his loins would cool.

While he waited, she stood watching—a lone sentry—until

the last school bus pulled away. Again he caught that flash of yearning on her face, the subtle droop of her shoulders when the children were out of sight. An aching need built in his chest, a need that made no sense. A tender wondering filled his soul with questions he wanted to ask, but didn't know how, didn't even know if he had the right to ask. Worse, he couldn't even imagine where all these thoughts were coming from. He covered his confusion with a smile meant to tease away the frown on her lovely face.

"Why so glum?" he asked softly, stepping from the shadows as she neared the front door.

Startled eyes met his. He thought there was the beginning of a smile, but it ended before it could brighten her face. She merely nodded in satisfaction.

"So, you came."

"I told you I would. Right on time, too," he noted as if seeking approval.

That did earn a full-blown grin. "Are you expecting a gold star for attendance? If so, it will hardly make up for all those zeros."

Despite her teasing tone, his voice and his mood went flat. "I stopped worrying about report cards long ago."

"Even Kevin's?" she queried briskly, chasing away any last remnants of the light mood.

Disappointed and unable to figure out why, he snapped, "You're all business, aren't you, Miss Liz?"

She scowled disapprovingly. The prim set of her mouth wasn't all that far removed from his original image of her. With an urge of pure devilment, he felt like kissing those lips until they were bruised and swollen and parted on a sigh of pleasure.

"It's Mrs. Gentry," she corrected with that familiar snap in her voice. "And I do try to act like a professional when I'm having a business meeting. Shall we go inside?"

"By all means," he said, responding to her cool demeanor

with a touch of sarcasm he couldn't have stopped if he'd wanted to. The woman infuriated him. Worse, something told him she enjoyed it, that she liked watching the barriers go up. He wondered why. Did she need them there to protect her heart? Not from him. He wasn't interested. Perhaps he should tell her that.

As soon as they reached room one-twenty-two, she grabbed an eraser and attacked the blackboard as if the day's lessons had offended her by lingering on display. Chalk dust filled the air with a fine mist and a scent that dragged Todd back nearly twenty years.

He pulled a too-small chair up beside her desk, turned it around and sat down straddling it to wait. With each moment that passed, his impatience grew. Only when the blackboard was cleaned to her satisfaction and the chalk lined up neatly and the papers on her desk straightened into tidy piles, did she sit down. It took several more minutes for her to lift her gaze to meet his. Only then did he realize that she'd been gathering her composure, not putting him in his place.

"Tell me about Kevin," she suggested, idly scratching at a blotchy red spot on her arm. When she pushed up her sleeve, he saw the marks went all the way up.

"Are you okay?" he asked.

She regarded him blankly. He reached over and touched one of the raised blotches. "What happened?"

Red flamed her cheeks. "Hives," she said curtly. "About Kevin…"

Hives, hmm? Generally caused by allergies or nerves. He wondered which had caused hers? He decided not to ask. It would give him something to speculate about later, when her image was plaguing him.

"I thought *you* wanted to tell *me* about Kevin," he said instead. "Isn't that why we're meeting?"

"We'll get to my observations. I thought it might be helpful if I knew whether his behavior in school reflected his behavior at home. Does he give you any discipline problems?"

Sarah's complaints sprang to mind, but he shook his head. "No more than any kid his age."

She seemed surprised by that. "Are you sure?"

"I know what I was like at Kevin's age. He's no different."

She smiled. The effect was like the sun emerging on a cloudy day. It warmed his heart, even as she said, "But I suspect you were a holy terror. That's hardly a fair comparison."

"I turned out okay," he countered, responding to her amusement. "For a holy terror, that is."

"Don't you want more for Kevin?"

He sighed. "I assume you're thinking ahead to college."

She shook her head. "Right now, I'm thinking ahead to passing third grade. He won't at the rate he's going."

Her somber prediction had the desired effect. It shook him up as none of her vague warnings had. "It's that bad?" he said skeptically. "Surely—"

"Mr. Lewis, he can't read."

"He struggles over a few words."

"The simplest words."

"Then why did he pass second grade?"

"I can't account for another teacher's decision. All I can tell you is that the situation cannot continue without doing irreparable harm. Once a child has lost the chance to acquire solid reading skills, everything else becomes almost impossible. History, geography, science, even math. Kevin is bright, but he's frustrated and angry. He takes it out on his classmates."

The scenario had an all-too-familiar ring to it. "Boys like to fight," he said defensively. "It's perfectly normal."

"He's clobbered two girls in the last week," she said bluntly.

Todd was genuinely shocked at that. He found he could no longer cling to the hope that this was all a tempest in a teapot. He'd scattered blame and defenses since the conversation began and Liz had countered every one of them. "I'll see that he's punished."

"I've already seen to that. More punishment is not the answer."

"What then?"

"Testing. Maybe special classes."

Todd felt his stomach knot. "I will not have my son made out to be different."

"But he is different," she said with surprising gentleness. "Denying it won't help him."

"Dammit, he's just a little boy," he snapped, frustration and anger on Kevin's behalf making his head pound. So much about this was familiar. Familiar and painful. He closed his eyes against Elizabeth Gentry's patient, compassionate expression. He rubbed his temples, but the throbbing kept on.

He loved Kevin, just the way he was. Why hadn't Sarah? Why couldn't Liz Gentry? He didn't expect him to scale intellectual mountains. He just wanted him to grow into a man who could take pride in whatever skills he had. His unquestioning love and support should be enough. It was more than he'd ever had. He had no idea how to explain all of that to the woman who was waiting so quietly for him to reach the right decision. Whatever the hell that was.

He studied her, wondering what made her tick, why she fought so hard for one little boy when there were dozens more needing her attention. Far more about her puzzled him. When had a woman so full of feminine promise become so wary around men, so determined to keep the focus of her life on her classroom? Or did he have that wrong, as well? Perhaps he was the only man who seemed to throw her.

"Why are you so uptight around me?" he asked suddenly.

She paled and said staunchly, "I am not uptight."

"Oh, really? Do you always destroy paper clips that way?"

"What way?" she said, staring at him blankly.

Liz recognized a desperate attempt at distraction when she saw one. Unfortunately, though, Todd Lewis was right. He was pointing toward her desk, smirking in satisfaction, mischief making his eyes sparkle. She glanced down. There was indeed a pile of twisted bits of metal in front of her. She sighed. Okay, so she was uptight. It didn't mean anything. Admittedly, though, it was usually the parents who got nervous about these conferences.

She took a closer look at Todd Lewis. He did not seem nervous. In fact, he looked every bit as overwhelming and lazily self-confident as he had the previous afternoon on his own turf. He'd obviously gone home to change before the meeting. His jeans were pressed. His shirt was crisply starched and open at the throat to reveal a tantalizing swirl of dark brown hair. His hair was damp and recently combed. He smelled of soap and the faintest trace of after-shave. It all added up to raw masculine appeal. Not even the fact that he was sitting on a scaled-down chair meant for third-graders diminished him. If anything, it simply emphasized his powerful build.

"I'll ask you again," he said. "Why do I make you nervous?"

"You don't make me nervous, Mr. Lewis." These flat-out lies were getting to be a habit around him. She scratched harder at her hives. "You make me mad." That, at least, was the truth.

It also made him tense up. "Meaning?"

"You and I seem to agree on one thing, that Kevin is a bright child. His IQ scores are well within the normal range, at the high end of the scale, as a matter of fact. Despite that, he is failing in school. His behavior is deplorable. In the last week he has bitten one classmate and bloodied the lip of another one. Is that the way you're rearing your son to respect girls?"

His distress seemed genuine. "I wish I had known about this sooner. Why didn't..."

"Don't even think about finishing that sentence. When was I supposed to tell you? When it first started happening? I wrote you a note after the first incident. I wrote you again after the second and third. You know that. You also know that my phone messages were intercepted."

"Which should tell you that Kevin knew exactly how upset I'd be. I don't tolerate that kind of behavior."

"Kevin's behavior is not the real problem."

"But you just said..."

"It's a symptom of his frustration. His self-esteem crumbles more each day that he can't keep up. From what I've observed and what little testing I am competent to do, I would guess that he has a learning disability. I think if you'd agree to testing, we could identify the problem and get Kevin the help he needs. Right now, he needs some positive things to start happening for him. Without the right kind of motivation, he'll just give up."

"Look, I love my son. I want him to have the best of everything, but I won't baby him," he said with that stubborn jut of his chin that was so often mirrored on Kevin's face. "He just needs to try harder. I'll have a talk with him."

Liz could see she wasn't getting through to him. "In Kevin's case, it's going to take more than talk. Please, let me have him tested."

"You said he needs the proper motivation. I'll see that he gets that."

There was an edge to his voice that told her exactly what Todd would consider proper motivation. Liz's heart sank.

"Why are you being so ridiculously stubborn about this? Your son's entire future may be at stake and you're acting as though it's a personal insult to suggest he have help."

"Maybe that's it," he retorted unreasonably. "Maybe I don't see where you get off telling me how to raise my son. You can't even keep your classroom under control. These fights are happening while he's under your supervision."

"I can't prevent your son's disruptions unless I put him in a straightjacket," she reminded him tightly. "I could suspend him. Is that what you'd prefer? That would take care of my problem, but it would do nothing about Kevin's."

"I've told you I'll take care of that."

"How? By punishing him? Pressuring him with expectations he can't possibly meet? How exactly do you plan to take care of it, Mr. Lewis? Are you capable of teaching him yourself? From what Kevin has told me, you don't even help him with his homework."

He stood up. For a moment she had forgotten how tall he was, how impressively built. She felt her heart catch as he towered over her, his expression cold and unyielding.

"And that's *my* problem, isn't it? He's my son. What's the old saying about teachers? Those who can, do. Those who can't, teach. That's why you're in the classroom, isn't it? You don't know the first thing about raising a child of your own. You've never had to stay up through the night worrying whether a cough would turn into pneumonia or how you could make up for some terrible hurt. I spend every day of my life trying to make up to that boy for the mother he lost, the mother who didn't want him, didn't want either of us. I won't have him thinking that I don't believe in him."

Liz felt the sharp sting of tears. For an instant she wasn't sure if they were for Kevin and Todd Lewis or for herself. How dare he talk to her of loss as if she'd never experienced one of her own! How dare he suggest that she knew nothing of mothering and worrying and loving!

"You don't know what you're talking about, Mr. Lewis," she said coldly. She tried to tell herself that he was angry, that he was only lashing out because of what he perceived as an attack on his child. Still, the cruel comments hurt.

"I think I do know exactly what I'm talking about. I was wrong about you yesterday when I said you understood kids. You don't know the first thing about real kids and their needs. You learned it all in some textbook, but when it comes to kids who don't conform, who fight and get dirty and make mistakes, you can't handle it."

A memory, as sweet and clear as it was painful, skittered through her mind. Laura looking angelic in her new Easter dress. Then, moments later, the bow in her golden hair askew, a smile of delight on her face—and chocolate streaked from head to toe.

Todd's accusation was true. She had yelled at Laura over a silly dress. She had been upset. And it had all been over nothing. Today she would give anything to take back the words. She would barter with the devil himself to hold her child one more time, to feel those plump little arms around her neck, to kiss that chocolate-sticky cheek.

She lifted eyes that shimmered with tears to stare at Todd Lewis. In a voice that shook with fury and anguish, she said, "Don't patronize me, Mr. Lewis. I know exactly how hard it is to be a parent."

The words lingered in a moment of stunned silence before he said slowly, "You have a child?"

He sounded as if the very thought of it were mind-boggling. If she hadn't been hurting so at the flood of memories, she might have smiled at his startled expression. Instead, she simply shook her head.

"But Kevin said—"

"I *had* a child. She died when she was three. My husband

died in the same accident. So don't tell me about loss, Mr. Lewis. Or guilt. Or worrying. Or loving. I could write the textbook on every one of those emotions myself."

Chapter 4

If Liz's quietly spoken words stunned Todd, the stricken expression on her face was almost his undoing. She reminded him of a wounded doe. Her eyes turned bleak as her anger faded. As he watched, shadows of fear and dismay dimmed the sparkling amber to a dull, lifeless brown. He felt her loss as sharply as he'd once felt his own, recalling in vivid detail the emptiness of those painful weeks and months after Sarah had walked out of his life, the awful sense of betrayal, the hurt of rejection.

But he'd had Kevin and, oblivious to his father's grief and anger, four-year-old Kevin had filled the house with laughter and tears and impatient demands. For the last four years Kevin alone had kept the memory of love alive in Todd's aching, embittered heart. Kevin had been the one thing left worth fighting for. That much had never changed. He would still fight tenaciously for his son.

Liz had lost both husband and child. Todd couldn't imagine anything to compare with that.

"I'm sorry," he said softly, wishing he knew more comforting words. For the first time in many years he cursed the inadequacies that had kept his vocabulary unpolished, his manner rough. He knew all the right words to keep a crew of a hundred or more men in line and on schedule. He knew just what to say to difficult suppliers or demanding tenants. He even knew the glib and easy words necessary for a casual seduction. But in the presence of this kind and wounded lady, he knew a fierce longing to be a truly gentle man with a gift for mending.

He doubted, though, if she even heard the simple expression of regret. She seemed to be lost in some faraway place where no one could reach her. A single tear slid down her cheek. She didn't seem to notice that, either, but his insides twisted at the sight. A woman's tears had never affected him so before. Sarah had cried often and loudly, using tears as a weapon. He thought he'd become immune. But not now.

With a tenderness of which he'd always thought himself incapable, he reached over to brush that lone tear away. To his astonishment, his calloused fingers trembled as they encountered silken warmth. Another tear slid down to join the first, pooling against his fingertips.

"Don't cry," he pleaded, kneeling down beside her. The tears flowed more rapidly than ever, leaving her cheeks damp and his fingers helpless. He bit back an instinctive oath and said instead, "Please."

She looked at him then. She swallowed hard and blinked against the flood of tears, but the raw emotions held her captive. He saw the flare of determination in her eyes, the desperate appeal. Then he heard the tiny sigh of resignation as she wept on, as if the tears had been a long time coming and could no longer be denied.

Todd prided himself on being cool and distant and controlled. He'd hardened his heart against women when Sarah had said goodbye and no one since had come close to melting his icy reserve. Until this moment. Until tears had spilled down Liz Gentry's cheeks. Now he found to his amazement that his heart ached for her, wrenched by the awful loss that had bruised her very soul. He wasn't wild about the circumstances, but he was as helpless to turn his back on her as she was to cease the crying.

With a ragged sigh of his own, he gathered her to him. Settling awkwardly on the classroom floor, he was unmindful of the surroundings or their earlier, hateful exchange. He cradled her as he might have a brokenhearted child. It was an instinctive response to her need. Ironically, he found that it answered a pull deep inside him, as well; a yearning to protect and cherish that he'd felt for no woman since the early days with Sarah.

The sensation troubled him, but no more than the wild urgency of desire that zinged through him at the feel of her body in his arms. Yesterday's flash of hunger had been little more than a prelude to this. Her elusive, flowery scent fired his senses. Her fragility took him by surprise, reminding him in some purely primitive way of his own power and masculinity. She fit snugly against him, her reluctant arms held stiffly at her sides. He stroked and soothed, until her shoulders relaxed and her head rested against his chest. As her tears dampened his shirt, he murmured nonsensically, his voice low and tender. The scene was all wrong. It felt incredibly right.

She inflamed him. Innocently, unexpectedly, she set his skin on fire and turned the rhythm of his pulse to something hard and swift and dangerous.

Guilt swept through him, accompanying the passion. He hadn't meant for his touch to become anything more than a gesture of comfort and compassion, but he knew the instant that she responded, the second that his own muscles went taunt. Too many nights of longing and too many years of loneliness had crept up on both of them. Her pink lips parted on a startled sigh, the hand that had rested lightly against his chest moved restlessly, halting when fingertips touched the heated column of his neck. God, how he wanted her! How he wanted that tentative touch to explore and burn across his flesh! His body throbbed with the wanting.

It was the look of bewildered confusion in her eyes that stopped him. He struggled to match the overwhelming power of their unexpectedly unleashed desire with something more rational, something they wouldn't regret. He cupped her face in his hands and gently kissed away the last traces of tears. Anxious eyes watched him…and waited, wanting, it seemed, what he wanted.

It took every ounce of control he possessed to move away. It took every last bit of strength to quiet his uneven breathing, to meet her gaze steadily as he lifted her back to her chair, settled her there and with a last tender touch let her go.

His arms felt empty. So damned empty. The sensation was oddly reassuring. It reminded him and perhaps even her that life went on. He knew then that he would not apologize. He would not pretend to regret the first honest emotion he had shared with anyone in years. Not normally one to analyze, he preferred to act. His withdrawal had caught him as much by surprise as had the desperate need he'd felt to have this woman. They were on a course that was unfamiliar to him. For the moment he left it to her to show the way.

"What do you want me to do?" he asked softly.

"Do?" she repeated, her expression puzzled. Her lower lip trembled and he wanted badly to still it with the touch of his own lips, to taste the salt of the tears that glazed her cheeks with a lingering dampness.

"About Kevin."

"Oh. Of course."

Her face, softened by the crying, carefully assumed its professional mask. Her voice, hoarse from weeping, turned crisp once more. Todd regretted that, as he hadn't regretted the rest of what had happened so spontaneously between them. Still, he turned away and paced, staring blankly out the windows, touching the pots of geraniums that dotted the sills with scarlet. His gift was no longer comfort but time. He gave her time to gather her composure around her like the protective cloak it was. His own emotions were in turmoil.

"I'm sorry," she said quietly into the stillness.

Frowning, he whirled on her, his own blood still pounding insistently. "Don't you dare be sorry," he said. His anger only seemed to dismay her more. He tried to gentle his tone, soften his fierce expression. "You…we have nothing to apologize for."

"I do. I should have stopped you."

"Nothing happened, dammit. You were upset. I tried to offer a little comfort."

"Oh, really?" Her half-formed smile bore a touch of cynicism. "It's gallant of you to put it that way, but we both know what really happened, what we almost did, and it would have been terribly wrong."

"Why?"

"You're Kevin's father. I'm his teacher."

"You're a woman first."

"Not here," she said stubbornly.

Todd sighed and shrugged helplessly. He knew when he was beat. For now. "There's no point in arguing with you when you get that high-minded note in your voice. You sound like a schoolmarm a hundred years ago, when some cowboy dared to steal a kiss."

Her face flamed with embarrassed color. "The rules haven't changed all that much," she said stiffly.

He wanted to shake her until she admitted that what had nearly happened between them had felt right, had felt good. Dear God in Heaven, he hadn't thrown her to the floor and made passionate love to her, though that's what he had wanted to do. Even now, he wanted to kiss the protests from her lips.

He moved toward her. Her eyes widened. At her look of near-panic, he muttered a harsh curse under his breath and turned back toward the windows.

"We'll just pretend it never happened," she said hopefully.

"*It* never did," he said with wry amusement.

"You know what I mean."

"I don't think so," he said softly. He turned around and smiled. "Until the next time..."

She stared at him, shocked.

"There will be a next time," he insisted. "And until then, I want to remember every delightful minute of holding you in my arms. Besides, I've never been any good at make-believe."

She appeared crestfallen by his refusal to cooperate, by the blatant taunt in his voice. He felt a momentary pang of guilt for continuing to bait her, when he knew perfectly well that flirtation was as alien to her nature as it was natural to his. Yet he would not allow her to hide from the truth, to dismiss that spark of desire as if it had never existed. He'd felt alive again this afternoon and, by God, he wouldn't change a minute of it.

She drew herself up, her chin lifting to a proud angle. "Then perhaps you should consider transferring Kevin to another class."

"Not on your life," he said, suddenly furious. "This is between you and me. We're adults. We'll handle it. I will not allow it to affect my son."

"Mr. Lewis."

"Dammit, it's Todd. Say it." He bit out the rough demand, taking a step closer. Tight-lipped, she glowered at him. He waited.

"Todd," she whispered finally, but she wouldn't look at him when she said it.

He hadn't realized he'd been holding his breath, until it

whooshed from him. He waited until she glanced up, then said, "Thank you."

She nodded. Cool. Distant. Controlled. It infuriated him.

"About Kevin," she prodded, clearly determined to get back on safer footing.

Unwilling to yield to a less personal exchange just yet, he held her gaze, trying to coax back the dangerous flare of intimacy. At last he recognized that the barriers were back in place to stay. He sighed wearily. "What do you want me to do?"

"There's a program," she began. The catch in her voice gave away her uncertainty. There was still a tiny chink in the wall. If he'd breached it once, he could do it again. If he dared. If he didn't care a whit about the consequences. If he could figure out exactly why it seemed to matter so much.

She took a deep breath and went on more firmly. "There's a really good psychologist in the Keys. She works with dolphins."

Despite everything, he found himself grinning, the hard knot in his belly dissolving as he came back to straddle the pint-sized chair beside her. "Dolphins? They need shrinks?"

To his delight, she smiled back, albeit a bit tremulously. "They do say they're almost human."

"Okay, I'll take your word for it. What about this psychologist?"

"Ann Davies. She's a good friend of mine. I'd like to have her test Kevin. Then she could recommend the next step. Maybe he'd even be qualified to be part of her program. It really is wonderful. It's innovative. If she'll take him, I just know she could help Kevin."

She sounded so hopeful, but even the prospect of testing daunted him. He seized on the one objection that seemed safe, the one possibility of preventing this whole useless process that raised hopes only to send them crashing against reality. "Are you suggesting that I send Kevin down to the Keys to live?"

"Of course not. He'd just go once a week."

"That's a long trek to manage every week. Who would take him?"

"If it turns out that's what's best for him, you would." She left him no room to argue about the inconvenience. She met his stubborn gaze with an unyielding tilt of her chin. Gone was any hint of vulnerability. The impassioned firebrand was back.

"Oh, for crying out loud," he muttered in disgust, but he knew he'd give in. He had a feeling in the end he'd find it impossible to deny this woman anything. It wasn't a realization he was crazy about.

"Just go down and talk to Ann," she urged, those wide, amber eyes beguiling him. It was like looking into the lure of whiskey and sensing salvation. It was probably twice as dangerous.

"If you're not comfortable with her and what she does, then I'm sure she can recommend someone here in Miami. Please."

He wasn't sure if it was the half-whispered plea or the eyes that implored that got to him, but he sighed heavily and surrendered. "Set it up."

Liz started calling her friend at six, while the memory of Todd Lewis's embrace still singed her memory. At first she had been horrified at breaking down the way she had. Then she realized that he hadn't been embarrassed, that he had reached out to her openly, easily. It told her a lot about his sensitivity and character, characteristics she might never have guessed at after seeing only his hotheaded stubbornness.

She also confessed to herself that she had liked being held in his arms, that she had wanted far more than she'd dared to admit to him. But it wouldn't happen again. She would not be caught alone with him again, not when they apparently set off enough sparks between them to rival the Fourth of July fireworks at Bayside.

It will not happen again, she thought firmly. It will not.

It will.

Oh, brother. She really needed to talk to Ann. Now. Tonight. And Kevin Lewis's problems, she finally admitted to herself, were the least of it.

She called every fifteen minutes, but kept getting a busy signal. When she finally got through at nine, Ann sounded cheerful but harried. Kids were arguing at the top of their lungs in the background. One seemed to be whimpering directly into Liz's ear. Probably the two-year-old. Melissa. Or was it Karen? She'd long ago given up trying to keep them straight. Besides, every time she turned around Ann was adding another one. Once in a while one of the foster kids was adopted by another family and Ann just turned right around and filled the empty bed. Her extended family grew and changed so rapidly, Liz wondered how she kept track without a scorecard and photographs posted on the oversized, industrial refrigerator that dominated the always busy kitchen.

"Pipe down, you guys," Ann bellowed, almost popping Liz's eardrum. Immediate silence descended.

"How do you do that?" Liz inquired with a familiar touch of awe.

"Don't give me that. I've been in your classroom. You're perfectly capable of achieving the same effect without even raising your voice."

"Some days I think I'd feel better, though, if I could just blast away. Doesn't it relieve the tension?"

"No. It only makes you hoarse, at least when you have to do it as often as I do around here. Jeremy, come take Melissa and put her to bed."

Melissa let out a wail of protest.

"Go," Ann said insistently. "I'll be in in a few minutes to kiss you goodnight. If you're not in bed with your face scrubbed and your teeth brushed, you won't get any ice cream for the next week."

The whimpers faded away.

"There now," Ann said. "That should give me a few minutes of peace and quiet. What's up?"

"A problem, as always."

"Hey, they're my speciality."

"I know but I tend to abuse the privilege."

"Not a chance. What's this one about? That pigheaded ex-mother-in-law of yours still giving you problems?"

"No," she said and hesitated. When she began again, it wasn't Todd she talked about. "It's one of my students." She detailed Kevin's behavior. "My guess is that he's dyslexic and that that's what's behind the hyperactivity. I also sense that he's heading for depression, if he doesn't see some improvement soon."

Ann chuckled. "Who gave you a license to practice all that psychological stuff?"

"Sorry. Just guesswork."

"Informed guesswork, my friend. I was only teasing. If you and Ed hadn't gotten married, you'd have gotten that Ph.D. and hung out your own shingle. It's still not too late for you to do it."

"Ann…"

"Never mind, I won't press. So what do you want me to do about Kevin? Test him? You could have someone in Miami do that. I can give you names."

"I know that, but I think this case needs your touch. The father is…" She hesitated.

"Ohhh, I see," Ann said at once, her inflection wry. "Just how difficult is he?"

The intuitive description was apt, but incomplete. "He's not difficult exactly. He's just worried."

"And resistant and mule-headed. What about the mother?"

"None on the scene. I'm not sure why."

"Does that have anything to do with your special interest in the case? Is this fellow attractive in the bargain?"

"I hadn't noticed."

Ann bellowed. "Then they might as well bury you now and be done with it."

"Okay, he is handsome," she admitted, knowing full well that the description was like calling the Eiffel Tower a cute little monument.

"I knew it. Sexy, too?"

There was the opening she'd been waiting for. Ann would listen. She wouldn't make judgments. She would give solid, no-nonsense advice. Liz decided that wasn't what she wanted right now, after all. She wanted to bask in the memories just a little longer, even if they were accompanied by a whole whirlwind of confusing thoughts and rampaging doubts.

"That is hardly the point," she said. "It's Kevin I'm worried about."

Ann backed off at once, but probably not for long. "Okay, bring your handsome-but-who-cares man down here and I'll work my wiles on him."

Liz hadn't counted on having to make the trip herself. "I wasn't going to come along," she protested. "I thought I'd just send him."

"Coward. Besides, if he's as unhappy about this whole idea as you say he is, he'll probably never get below Key Largo. That's where they usually chicken out. They stop for breakfast and by the time they're done, they've decided the whole trip is a waste of time. It's a long drive. They figure I really won't be able to help, anyway. The kid's complaining. He'd rather be playing baseball. Nope," she said emphatically. "I think you'd better come along."

"Okay," Liz said, laughing, ecstatic when she knew darn well she ought to be terrified. A whole day with Todd Lewis? She ought to have her head examined. "You've made your point. When?"

"Make it Saturday morning at eleven. I should be able to get this brood under control by then and meet you at my trailer at Dolphin Reach. If I'm not there, go visit Alexis. She's very pregnant and feeling put out because she doesn't think we're giving her enough attention."

"You are talking about a dolphin. What makes you think she's feeling put out?" Liz said.

"Because the fat rascal knocked me off the dock the other day, then skittered off on her tail fin. I swear she was laughing. I know the kids were."

"I'm sorry I missed the show."

"Hey, I suppose it was worth it. The man who was here to check out the center for a research grant thought the whole thing was so hilarious he approved the grant on the spot. It'll keep me in business another six months, anyway."

"Dammit, Ann, when are you going to start charging for what you do there?"

"I do charge," she said. "When the family can afford to pay."

It was an old argument and one Liz knew she had little chance of winning. Ann's soft heart would always win out over her business sense. "Well, just remember that Todd Lewis can afford it. In fact, if the price tag is high enough, he may actually take it seriously."

"You are getting devious, my friend."

"I wasn't until I met Todd Lewis," she said ruefully.

"Well, well," Ann said softly. "I thought I detected an undercurrent there."

Liz didn't like that knowing tone one bit. "Don't try to make something out of that," she warned.

The threat fell on deaf ears. "Honey, from the sound of it, I'm not the one who's in trouble here. I can't wait to meet your Mr. Lewis."

"He is not mine!" Liz bellowed.

She heard a hoot of laughter, then a soft click. She glared at the phone. How had she ever remained such good friends with such a know-it-all psychologist?

Chapter 5

Following the unanticipated Friday night arrival of a fast-moving cold front, the whole world had a surreal quality about it on Saturday morning. As Liz and Todd sped south on U.S. 1, the narrow ribbon of pavement seemed to disappear in a soupy morning mist. Cozy in the warmth of Todd's surprisingly utilitarian SUV, it was as if they were alone on a shadowy planet.

"Whenever it's foggy like this, I always think of one of my favorite poems," she said as she stared dreamily out the window.

"'Fog.' Carl Sandburg," Todd said at once.

"Amazing. You know it?" She pulled her gaze from the fog-shrouded scenery to look at the man sitting beside her.

His lips curved sardonically at her obvious surprise. He recited the brief poem, then added, "They did teach poetry when I was in school."

"Sorry."

"Besides, I had a mother who thought every day should

begin and end with Robert Frost or Emily Dickinson with an occasional diversion from one of the Brownings. Once you got beyond the one about fog, though, Sandburg was a little racy for her taste. 'Chicago' gave her palpitations."

"Naturally, that made you rush right out to read it."

His gaze slid away. "Nope," he said, concentrating on the highway. "I just took her word for it."

Increasingly curious, she prodded, "Then what is your taste in poetry?"

"Give me Bob Dylan any day."

She shot an amused glance at him. "I've never thought of Dylan as a poet."

"What are songs, if not poetry set to music?" A glint of mischief lit his eyes and her breath automatically caught in her throat. "Take 'Lay, Lady, Lay.' Now that is a great song. I've had a thing about brass beds ever since I first heard that song."

Liz ignored the innuendo and decided Todd Lewis would never know about the antique brass bed that she'd lovingly restored and now slept in. "I'm partial to 'Blowin' in the Wind' myself," she told him. "If pressed, though, I could probably make a case for 'Rainy Day Woman.'"

"Well, well, you are filled with surprises."

"As are you, Mr. Lewis."

"Todd," he coaxed, his quick glance beguiling. "Just for today, at least."

Lord, the man was persistent. She hadn't forgotten for one minute the whispered demand he'd made in her classroom and her own reluctant yielding. For some reason Todd Lewis was determined to manipulate their relationship into something personal. It had started even before he'd held her in his arms. Once they'd gotten past their initial antagonism over what was best for Kevin, he'd flirted outrageously. She was unaccustomed to such provocative teasing, but she knew enough not to think for one minute that it meant anything.

Even without the benefit of Ann's usually sensible advice, she'd known enough to lecture herself repeatedly on that subject the last couple of days.

Besides, she'd told herself staunchly, the last thing she wanted was a man disrupting her well-ordered life. After the accident, it had taken her years to reestablish some sense of control over her own fate. She would not relinquish that control easily.

He was, however, only asking her to use his first name. And, really, what could be the harm? Calling him Todd was hardly tantamount to falling into his arms. She'd already done that and though she still blushed when she thought about it the world in general hadn't come to a screeching halt. Only her own had tilted on its axis. No members of the Board of Education had called for her resignation. As long as she continued in the future to resist the sexy, come-hither glances that made her knees go weak, she saw no reason not to give in on this one little point.

Besides, she decided practically, it might help to relax him. Although he'd looked entirely too pleased with himself for being precisely on time when he'd picked her up at eight o'clock, since then he'd grown increasingly tense and withdrawn.

He looked more like a man driving to his own execution than a father going to get a little help for his son. Maybe if he knew more about what to expect, he'd ease his grip on the steering wheel and his foot off the accelerator. The wispy Australian pines along the edge of the road were zipping past at a dizzying pace.

"Okay, Todd," she said, finally. He turned a wicked, thoroughly satisfied smile on her. Her pulse took off faster than a jet trying to make up time. "Would you like me to tell you a little about what to expect at Dolphin Reach?"

The smile vanished at once, replaced by cool indifference.

"Whatever," he said, his voice flat, his gaze instantly focused straight ahead.

She tried not to feel disappointed at the lack of enthusiasm. "I think you're going to like Ann," she began conversationally. "She has a brilliant mind and she's wonderful with people. She's especially good with kids. She should have had half a dozen of her own. Not that she hasn't made up for it. She's foster mother to a whole passel of kids, mostly ones who are hard to place for adoption. A couple of them have had problems with the law. I'd be a little afraid to take on a kid like that, but not Ann. They seem to respond to all that love. Not a one has been in trouble again."

Her lengthy recitation was met by brooding silence. Still determined to overcome his anxiety, she rattled on, describing Ann's special kids, her educational background, the house she'd built along a little spit of land that jutted off one of the Keys below Islamorada.

"It started out as just an ordinary little two-bedroom, one-bath beach house, but then she started finding these kids. The third bedroom was tacked on when she took in Kelly and Michael. The fourth bedroom and the second bath came the following year. I think she's up to six bedrooms and three baths now and if there were more land, she'd probably add two or three more. She's a real pushover for a kid with a problem."

"Sounds like a generous lady."

The complimentary words had an odd, sarcastic edge to them that made her want to spring to Ann's defense. "She is," she said curtly instead and fell silent.

Todd would just have to see for himself. She knew he was uptight about this meeting, but she hoped he wasn't planning on being rude and difficult with Ann. Then she smiled. Ann would snap the arrogant starch right out of him, if he tried it. Her smile grew wider. She could hardly wait.

Suddenly he jerked the wheel and turned into a McDonalds.

"Coffee," he said when she glanced at him. From his defensive tone, she had a feeling he expected an argument.

"Sounds good," she said cheerfully, recalling Ann's prediction. The woman was an absolute, mind-reading wizard. Thank goodness, she was fully prepared to counter any argument Todd might mount to avoid finishing the journey to Dolphin Reach. She armed herself for battle.

When Todd blinked at her easy acceptance of the delay, she had to turn away to keep him from catching her confident grin. When she looked back, though, the defiant glint in his eyes hadn't quite vanished. He was pulling into a parking space, rather than the drive-through lane. "Let's go inside."

She bit back a reminder that they had another hour's drive ahead of them. "Fine."

The sun was burning away the last of the fog as they walked across the parking lot. The temperature was already climbing. Liz was glad she'd decided on shorts and a T-shirt, despite the early morning chill. Already it was too warm for the sweater she'd tossed over her shoulders at the last minute.

Inside the restaurant, Todd ordered coffee and a full breakfast for himself, then glanced at her.

"Just coffee."

When they were seated, he bit into his egg sandwich, grimaced and pushed it away. He slouched down in the booth, dominating it, his long legs sprawling. Liz had a hard time keeping her gaze off the bare, muscular length of them. Why had she told him to dress informally for this meeting? She should have known that Todd in shorts and a polo shirt would send her pulse into overdrive. She watched the play of muscles in his thick arms as he stirred his coffee, then took another bite of the sandwich. He looked as though he were being tortured. She could identify with the feeling.

She dragged her gaze away from those strong, blunt fingers

that she knew from experience were capable of incredible gentleness. She took a sip of coffee.

"How's your breakfast?" she asked innocently.

"Fine."

"Yes. I can see that."

Apparently detecting the amusement in her voice, he regarded her warily.

"Why did you order it?"

"I was hungry."

"Really?"

He finally shrugged sheepishly. "I guess I wasn't as hungry as I thought."

"Or were you just stalling?"

"I thought the woman we're going to see was the psychologist," he growled.

"She is." She grinned at him. "She'll also tell you that I frequently practice without a license. As long as I don't charge, they probably won't lock me away for it. Even so, I prefer to think of it as offering unsolicited advice. It's less risky. Now that we've analyzed my bad habits, what about yours? Why are you stalling?"

"I'm not crazy about psychologists," he admitted, the way some people confessed to a dislike of tarantulas and rats. His adamant tone startled her.

"Have you had much experience with them?"

"Enough."

The curt response was a dismissal, if ever she'd heard one. "Maybe you'll tell me about it sometime."

"Don't count on it."

The remark was said with such cold finality, Liz felt as though he'd slapped her. Over the last couple of days, she'd tried very hard to keep herself from thinking of Todd Lewis as anything more than a parent of a troubled student, but the memory of his touch had lingered. Her imagination had taken the tenderness of his comfort, the fire of his caress and soared on a less restrained journey. The man might not have much respect for her opinions, but he had desired her in a way that had stirred old, forgotten longings. For a few minutes in her classroom, she'd been reminded of what it felt like to be stirred by a woman's passions, to feel the sharp tug of yearning for a man's embrace.

Now, with those four abrupt, chilly words—*don't count on it*—he'd relegated her to an annoyance, someone he had to placate but not trust. Well, he could just take his moody, overbearing attitude and stuff it, she thought furiously. She glared at him.

He caught her expression and sighed. He ran his fingers through his hair. "Look, I'm sorry. I'm on edge. You know how I feel about all of this. If it weren't for Kevin and what you said about his failing, I wouldn't be here."

She tried to understand his misgivings, but it was as if there were some vital piece of information missing. She settled for simply acknowledging them. "I know that. Maybe you should stop thinking of this as some sort of an ordeal and consider it a chance to widen your horizons, try new things."

He chuckled. "Throwing my words back in my face, aren't you?"

"The occasion seemed to call for it."

"Okay, let's go. I'll behave. I will even try not to treat this friend of yours like she's some sort of dragon."

Liz smiled knowingly. "Oh, but Ann is a dragon, the genuine fire-breathing variety, especially when it comes to kids in trouble. Don't get any ideas about conning her with your charm."

"I never even considered it."

Her eyebrows rose skeptically. "In a pig's eye."

"Hi, Liz!" The shouted greeting came from somewhere behind a pile of yellow rain slickers. A blond—no more than twenty or twenty-one, Todd guessed—poked her pixie face above the pile and waved. "Annie called. She's running late, as usual. Tommy or one of the kids took exception to having oatmeal for breakfast and threw it across the kitchen. She's overseeing the cleanup."

"Has Alexis given birth yet?" Liz called back.

"Nope. Poor thing. She's down at the end. Go on out and scratch her belly. There's a bucket of fish on the dock. You can give her a few if she behaves."

"How will I know if she's behaving?"

"You'll still be dry."

As they wandered toward the docks behind Dolphin Reach, Todd studied her with a bemused expression. "Are we actually going to visit a pregnant dolphin?"

She grinned at him, her eyes sparkling with sheer delight. He couldn't recall ever having seen quite that look on her face before. He wished he and not some temperamental dolphin had been the one to put it there.

"Why not?" she teased, racing on ahead. The subtle sway of her hips was enough to make him forget what he'd asked. Who cared about a dolphin—pregnant or not—when a woman clad in a pair of sexy white shorts and a surprisingly provocative T-shirt was within view. He'd be willing to bet she'd thought the walking shorts sedate, the T-shirt unrevealing. They weren't, he thought with a wild skittering of his pulse as she leapt down onto the dock.

"Hurry," she was urging, just as Todd was wondering if he shouldn't dive straight into the icy waters and cool off. His libido was becoming as overactive as Hank's.

Dazed, he simply followed her, only partially aware of the dolphins who swam close, then stood on tail fins as if to bob a friendly greeting. When he caught up with Liz, she was kneeling on the end of the dock crooning to a huge dolphin. The seeming absurdity of her actions was lost on him. All he could think about was the way her attractive little butt was poking into the air. That rear would just about fit into the palms of his hands.

"Come meet Alexis," she said, as if introducing people and dolphins were an everyday occurrence. "Alexis likes company. Ann says she's been upset because she can't do as much with the kids these days. She's impatient for the baby to be born so she can get back to serious playing."

He knelt down beside her on the dock. "There's a contradiction in there, but I don't dare try to challenge it." He smiled at her. "I see that you and Alexis are old friends."

The dolphin seemed to beam in agreement, then slid into the water and swam away. A moment later, she leapt into the air with an odd sort of lumbering majesty, before diving back with hardly a splash. Back at the dock, she waited for Liz's applause and her reward.

"That was wonderful, Alexis, but don't you go getting overly excited," Liz chided as she dropped a handful of fish to the eager dolphin's mouth. She leaned down and rubbed the slick snout, then turned to Todd with a delighted grin. "Isn't she beautiful?"

"As dolphins go, I would have to say she is particularly impressive," he said dryly.

Liz turned back to the attentive Alexis. "Did you hear that, Alexis? He thinks you're impressive. That's quite a compliment from a man of his no doubt discerning taste when it comes to women."

"Sweetheart, when it comes to women, I prefer them a little sleeker than Alexis here, preferably with two legs. And," he added as an afterthought, "I definitely do not want them pregnant."

"Sssh. You'll hurt her feelings."

"Do you always get like this around the dolphins?" he inquired curiously.

"Like what?"

"Let's just say you seem to have lost all your inhibitions."

She gave him a pert smile. "Not all of them."

"Too bad."

"Don't let her kid you," a voice said from behind them. "Underneath that stern, classroom manner of hers lies the heart of a pushover."

Liz blushed to the roots of her red hair. Interesting, Todd thought, as he stood up to meet the woman who'd just joined them. Tall and raw-boned, she had short, dark hair and bright blue eyes that sparkled with intelligence. Her features were irregular but interesting. It was the warmth and humor in her expression that made her beautiful. She radiated an inner joy that was both contagious and reassuring.

"You must be Todd," she said, taking his outstretched hand in a firm, no-nonsense grip. "I'm Ann Davies. I'm so glad you and Liz were able to drive down this morning."

"So am I," he said and found, amazingly enough, that he meant it.

"Sorry I'm late, but the kids…" She shrugged. "I'm sure you know how that goes."

"Of course. We haven't been here long."

"No. We stopped for breakfast in Key Largo," Liz said and the two women exchanged a conspiratorial look.

"Am I missing something here?"

"Not really," Liz said. "Ann had warned me that she'd lost a lot of prospective clients in Key Largo."

He grinned. "I see. No wonder you were able to read my mind. You'd been coached."

"By an expert," Liz agreed. "Why don't the two of you go get acquainted and talk about Kevin? I'll stay here with Alexis."

Suddenly an old familiar feeling of dread engulfed Todd. "Aren't you coming with us?"

Ann shook her head and linked her arm through his. "I think it'll be better if you and I talk first. Liz can join us later."

Without waiting for him to agree, she turned on her heel and strode off toward the main building. Inside, she waved him to a comfortable sofa, then gestured with a pot of coffee. When he nodded, she poured two cups, then handed him one of them.

"So, Todd. You don't mind if I call you Todd, do you?"

He chuckled. "No. I only wish Liz would do it as easily."

"She has a very strong sense of what's right and wrong in professional conduct."

"I've noticed."

She glanced at him sharply. "You object?"

"Not the way you mean. It's just…inconvenient at times."

Ann's quick bark of laughter echoed off the walls. "I'm sure you find that part of the challenge."

He felt his face flame. "Maybe I do."

She looked him over assessingly. "I wish you luck," she said quietly, but with apparently heartfelt sincerity. Todd felt as if he'd passed an important test without really understanding why it mattered.

"Now, then," she went on briskly, "tell me about Kevin."

His defenses slammed back into place. Filled with reluctance, he began to describe his son. Ann listened and absorbed without comment. It was a seductive technique. Before he knew what was happening and very much to his surprise, he found himself talking about Sarah, as well.

"Kevin was only four when she left. For a long time I was terrified I'd never be able to make it up to him."

"Why did you feel the need to try? Had you caused her to walk out?"

"No. Not directly, though I'm sure there were things I could have done to make things better. But what Sarah really wanted was freedom and excitement. She hadn't expected the ordinariness of marriage. She didn't want to be tied down to running a house and taking care of a kid. Sometimes I'd get home at night and find her practically hysterical."

"Did she tell you why?"

"She said she couldn't cope—not with the marriage, not with Kevin."

"So he was a problem, even then?"

"I didn't think so," he said defensively.

"But Sarah did."

"Yes."

She paused long enough to make a few notes on the legal pad in her lap, then met his eyes with a direct, unflinching gaze. Todd realized then that in just the short time they'd been together he had come to trust her.

"I want to meet Kevin," she said. "Can you bring him down, say, the same time next weekend?"

"You're going to test him?"

"There are a few standard tests I can do to see how he processes information. Mainly I want to talk to him, find out what's been happening with him in school as he sees it. Often that tells me as much or more than the tests do."

"And then?"

She smiled at him. "Why don't we just take this one step at a time? Let's see what I learn next week and make a decision then."

Todd nodded.

She stood then and went to her desk. When she joined him again, she had several forms in her hand and Todd felt his insides twist.

"If you'll just fill these out," she said, handing them to him along with a pen.

He bent his head over the papers and read them slowly and carefully. He painstakingly went over the fine print. Finally, when he was finished, he nervously filled in the requested information and signed them with his usual bold and virtually illegible scrawl.

As he handed them back to Ann, he caught the speculative look in her clear blue eyes. "Why didn't you tell me?" she said softly.

Todd stiffened at once. "Tell you what?"

"Why didn't you mention that you're dyslexic, as well?"

Chapter 6

Shocked, Todd simply stared at Ann Davies.

"Why would you say that?"

She smiled compassionately. "I am right, aren't I? You do have dyslexia?"

Feeling utterly defeated, Todd sighed and sank back on the sofa. "How did you know?" he asked.

"I saw how you struggled with the form. Added to your defensiveness about Kevin's situation, it made sense. Did you have treatment when you were a child?"

He shook his head. "Not really. Oh, there was endless testing, but once my parents realized I wasn't the perfect son they'd anticipated they pretty much gave up on me. I struggled along and did the best I could."

"But you hated school," she guessed.

"I couldn't wait to get out. I stuck it out through high school, even though I was twenty when I graduated."

"If it was so terrible, why did you stay?"

"Because I figured I'd have to have that damned, meaningless diploma to get anywhere."

"Graduating from high school is hardly meaningless, especially under the circumstances. It was a tremendous accomplishment. You should have felt very proud."

"It is hardly an accomplishment if you still can't read worth a damn and only earned the diploma by outlasting the system."

"Liz doesn't know, though, does she?"

He shook his head. "No, and I don't want her to."

"Why on earth not? It's nothing to be ashamed of. No one knows exactly what causes dyslexia, but it is not indicative of either intelligence or character."

"No, it's not," he agreed. It was the one thing he'd worked like hell to prove, especially to himself. "I've carved out a niche in the world, proved to all those educational hotshots that I'm not the stupid kid they thought I was. That doesn't mean it's not a terrible drawback. I sure don't want it to become common knowledge that I can't even read half the contracts I sign."

"Telling Liz is hardly the same as having it become common knowledge. She'd understand."

"And I would feel like less than a man."

Ann waved that aside with a derisive snort. "That's probably the dumbest thing I've heard you say all afternoon."

His chin set stubbornly. "If you tell Liz, our deal's off."

She shook her head, her smile a little sad. "I don't think so. You'd never deprive your son of the opportunity to get a good education just because of your own ridiculous macho pride."

"Are you willing to test me?"

"No," she said easily, "but not because you're threatening me, Todd Lewis. I'll keep it between the two of us, because I think you're the one who ought to tell her. I hope you'll do it soon. Liz has had to deal with enough secrets in her lifetime."

Ann's words lingered long after he and Liz were back on the road. He wondered what she'd meant by the secrets that had affected Liz's past. Keeping his own counsel about his dyslexia seemed like such a little thing. It only mattered to him. Surely his reticence on this one thing wasn't something that would ultimately come between them.

If Liz noticed how distracted he was, she kept silent, apparently attributing it to a natural reaction to the meeting with the psychologist. He blessed her for her intuitive understanding and kept his eyes trained on the road, until he spotted the place they'd decided to stop to pick up lobsters to take home for dinner.

He wheeled into the sloped gravel driveway and slammed on the brakes. For the first time since it was the macho thing to do in high school, he felt like getting rip-roaring drunk so that he could forget all about secrets and the past.

When Todd pulled into the jammed parking lot beside the ramshackle fish house, his jaw was still set at a mulish angle. Liz had been biting her tongue all the way up the road to keep from asking him what had gone on in his meeting with Ann. It was enough that the two of them seemed to have gotten along. Even more important, Todd had agreed to come back with Kevin the following week. With their business taken care of, they were free to…to do what? The possibilities made her as skittish as a teen on her first date.

Warning herself not to start thinking like an adolescent ninny, she followed Todd across the parking lot, her steps slowing as they neared the building. Though the screened-in porch sagged and the handwritten menus were grease-stained, Liz knew the appearance of the weathered wood structure was deceptive. On weekends the place was crowded with Miamians and tourists looking for an inexpensive, informal place to sit by the ocean, sip a few beers, listen to a little music and eat some of the best seafood in the Keys. Though it was only four in the afternoon, the heavy throb of a live band filled the air. It was a sultry, provocative atmosphere.

"Let's get a beer before we pick up the lobsters," Todd suggested as he held her door open for her.

"We really should be getting back to Miami," Liz protested, giving in to her jittery nerves. "You know how this road is on Saturday nights. We'll be caught in bumper-to-bumper traffic if we wait much longer."

He shrugged off her concern with a wave toward the narrow highway. "The traffic is already bumper-to-bumper. How much worse can it get? Come, on. Just one beer. Besides, I like the group that's playing this afternoon."

"We could probably still hear them halfway home," she muttered, giving up. It was clear they wouldn't head north until Todd was ready to go. She was surprised he'd even bothered to ask her wishes, when he had no intention of complying with them.

"Smile," he leaned down and whispered in her ear. "This will only hurt for a little while."

She scowled at his back as he led the way through the restaurant to the porch in back. He found a table in a corner far away from the band, signaled a passing waitress for two beers, then sat down across from her.

"Great, isn't it?"

"Terrific." She caught the sarcasm in her tone and flinched. To be perfectly truthful, it was lovely. Sunlight set off diamond sparklers on the ocean's smooth surface. A soft, languid breeze barely stirred the air, which was fragrant with the tang of salt and the coconut scent of suntan lotion. The noise was a happy blend of laughter and music, albeit a little loud for her taste. Guiltily, she glanced across at Todd and caught the frown on his brow as he watched her.

"Sorry," she said, knowing how absurd it was to be this

nervous in the presence of a man who'd proved his kindness. He was hardly likely to seduce her in the middle of the restaurant, even if half the couples on the dance floor did seem to be engaged in some sensually explicit movements that barely qualified as dancing. Just watching them made her blood heat up and her glance skitter nervously away from Todd's. Ridiculous, she told herself sternly. How often did she get to the Keys? Not nearly often enough. She might as well enjoy it, now that she was already here.

"I didn't mean to snap," she apologized. "I like it here." Even as she said the words, she felt herself begin to relax. She smiled. "Really."

Todd nodded in apparent satisfaction. As she watched, his tension seemed to ease slightly. "Good. You need to relax more. Today with the dolphins was the first time I think I've ever seen you completely at ease."

The memory of the very pregnant Alexis lumbering into the air in a bid for attention brought back another smile. "How can you watch those dolphins and not relax? I know it's just a quirk of nature that they appear to be laughing, but it's contagious. I wish we'd brought Kevin along. He would have loved them."

"I'm glad we didn't," Todd said so softly she could barely hear him over the swell of music.

"Todd…"

"Don't say it," he said with an odd sense of urgency that sent shivers along her spine. "I don't want to talk about Kevin or his education right now. For the next couple of hours, this is just between the two of us."

Liz felt her heart slide straight down to her toes. "It can't be," she managed to say in a choked voice.

"Yes," Todd said stubbornly. "Just the two of us."

Before she could argue with him, he jumped to his feet and held out his hand. "Come on. Dance with me. They're playing our song."

"Our song?" she repeated, feeling dazed and all too intrigued. The beat was demanding, unrelenting and sensual, just like Todd. "I don't even recognize that song."

"Neither do I. If we dance to it, though, we'll make it ours. We'll never be able to hear it again without thinking of this moment and this place."

The softly spoken words were those of a romantic, but the look in his eyes was pure rogue. Despite herself, Liz responded to the pull of the words and the look. Her heart accepted the sweet tenderness of the thought. Her body throbbed to the promise of the look. She stood up and followed him to the tiny square of floor where several other couples were already gyrating to the pulsing beat.

Todd danced with a surprising lack of self-consciousness, his hips and shoulders creating a suggestive taunt that Liz unconsciously matched. As they circled and dipped, his gaze clashed with hers, holding her, teasing her. The brush of his hip against hers as he whirled her under his arm set off an explosion of desire. Whether it was that alone or merely the quick pace of the music, Liz couldn't be sure, but she was breathless and filled with an odd sense of expectation. She was almost disappointed when the music ended and Todd released her hand.

The lull in music lasted no more than an instant. Todd flashed a silent question at her and Liz found herself nodding. He laughed and the last of the shadows in his eyes fled. "I knew you'd lose yourself to this, once I got you out here."

"Don't be so smug," she retorted, but she felt too much happiness welling up inside to stay irritated for long. It had been far too long since she'd let herself go like this. The last time she'd been on a dance floor, she'd agreed to chaperon a junior-high party with a friend who taught at the school. One of the ninth graders had asked her to dance. He'd barely reached her chin and he'd moved with more dogged determination than grace. It had been nothing like this. Todd turned fast dancing into a subtle mating ritual. Heaven knows what he'd do with a slow song. It would probably be for the best if she never found out.

Fortunately, she supposed, this particular crowd was only interested in music that soared, in beats that never slowed. Her hair was a damp, uncontrollable mess and her cheeks were flushed by the time Todd finally led her back to their table. She drank her now-warm beer in a single gulp.

"Another one, please. Very cold."

Todd's eyebrows shot up at the request, but he waved the order to a waitress and the beers were on the table in icy mugs within minutes. She was just catching her breath.

Then she looked into Todd's eyes and felt the earth open up. No man had looked at her like that in years. She hadn't wanted one to. She still didn't. The heady thrill was too confusing, too dangerous. That intimate, possessive look shook her hard-won serenity the way King Kong had rattled Manhattan skyscrapers. It was an unthinking gesture on his part, probably something he indulged in all the time. A man as sexy as Todd Lewis did not sit around on Saturday nights watching his hibiscus blossom. Flirtations were probably as commonplace for him as they were foreign to her. All of which meant that she ought to stop drinking this beer at once, stay off of the dance floor and if at all possible pretend that he had the sex appeal of a turnip.

She pushed away the icy beer, regarded the dancing couples wistfully and sighed. She figured at best she had a shot at two out of three. A glance across the table assured her that Todd was no turnip and no amount of vivid imagery on her part was going to turn him into one.

"Maybe you'd better get the lobsters now," she said reluctantly.

He seemed startled by the sudden request. "Is something wrong?" He reached across the table and ran his finger across her frowning lips. The sandpapery warmth of his work-roughened touch sent tingles skyrocketing through her. "You're frowning."

Good, she thought crazily. It was very good that he couldn't tell that her well-educated brain was turning to mush and her karate-trained knees were quivering like so much raspberry Jell-O. A little more internal heat from his touches and she'd melt into a happy little puddle right at his feet.

"The lobsters," she reminded him breathily.

He still seemed puzzled, but he nodded. "I'll go get them."

While he was gone, Liz drew in enough deep breaths to restore oxygen to her apparently deprived brain. Oddly enough, she didn't seem to be thinking any more clearly by the time Todd returned with the cooler of lobsters.

"One more dance," he said, putting the cooler down on the floor and holding out his hand.

Liz nodded and got to her feet before realizing that the music had gentled to a slow, intimate caress. It whispered seductively and her pulse throbbed in awareness as Todd's arms went around her. His strength inflamed her femininity. The heat of his body enveloped her in longing. His purely masculine scent, a combination of salt and musk with a lingering hint of soap, made her thoughts career wildly to images of provocatively tangled limbs and dampened skin. She wanted to run from those images. She wanted to indulge them.

She wanted to live them.

It was the last, the desire to tempt fate, that urged her closer into his embrace. Resting her cheek against his damp shoulder, she sighed with the sheer pleasure of being held. The thunder of Todd's heartbeat matched the cadence of her own, swift and dangerous. She ignored the warning, indulging in the wild temptation, oblivious to consequences beyond this moment. She felt young and beautiful and cherished in these powerful arms. She felt even more when she looked into the hazel depths of his eyes, heard his harsh intake of breath. Desire, as demanding and insistent as anything she'd ever experienced, overwhelmed her, took her breath away.

She clung to Todd and let herself simply feel for once. She might regret the moment later, but not now. His hand, already low on her back, swept lower. Their hips fit together in an instinctive joining that shocked her with its intimacy. When she would have pulled back, Todd's whispered protest stopped her.

"Don't start thinking. Just enjoy the moment," he pleaded. "Let me hold you."

She sighed and relaxed against him. They were barely swaying to the music now, barely keeping up the pretense of dancing. She heard the warning voices begin again in her head, a whisper at first, then louder. It was only when she felt the tug on her arm that she realized the warnings weren't entirely in her imagination.

"Watch it," a couple said, pointing down as shouts and laughter erupted around them.

Dazed and bereft without Todd's arms to hold her, Liz glanced down. Lobsters—she had no doubt at all they were the ones Todd had just bought—were skittering crazily across the wooden planks in every direction.

She choked back a laugh at the startled indignation on Todd's face as he tried to round up the creatures who were making a madcap, if somewhat directionless, dash for the sea and freedom.

"Let them go," she said as laughter bubbled up. He looked at her as if she were crazy.

"Do you know how much I paid for those things?"

"Let them go. They've made a daring escape. They deserve to survive."

"But dinner?"

"I'll fix pasta. It's just as well. I'd never have been able to throw them into a pot of boiling water, anyway." She shivered. "Do you realize how cruel that is?"

"I never thought about it. I suspect if we thought too hard about killing cows or pigs or chickens, we'd never eat those again, either."

"It's not the image I mind so much, it's the action. Beef and chicken get to the stores in neat little packages wrapped in cellophane. They are not mooing and clucking in my presence. Those lobsters were going to be staring at me with their beady little eyes when I plunked them in the pot. The pasta will be much better."

"Okay, Miss Humanitarian," he said with amused tolerance, "do you want me to carry them back to sea or shall I leave them to their own devices?"

Since one of them was heading directly for the bare toes of a woman seated near the bandstand—their claws were not bound—Liz said, "I think you'd better help them along. No telling where they'll end up, otherwise."

Several of the other customers joined in the lobster chase and the whole crowd descended to the beach for an impromptu ceremony setting them free. When the last of the lobsters was out of sight, Todd turned back to her. The look in his eyes made her breath catch in her throat. He stepped closer and slid his arms around her waist.

"You're going to owe me for this," he said in a whisper that sent chills down her spine.

She lifted her face and discovered that his lips were barely a hair's breadth away.

"What?" she murmured.

"This will do nicely," he said, his mouth covering hers.

Startled, Liz's hands hung limply at her sides as those velvet lips brushed hers with fire. Her toes curled into the cool sand and her body swayed toward Todd's. As he had for those few moments on the dance floor, he became the center of her universe, the pull of gravity that drew her at will. The kiss was sweet and gentle. Though she was sure he meant it to be unthreatening, it shook her to her very core.

Romantic seductions on the beach weren't her style, especially not with the parent of one of her students. Sanity struggled against yearning and slowly but inevitably won. Determined not to let him see how deeply he had affected her, she stepped out of the embrace and faced him with a jaunty smile. That smile would earn her an Academy Award in Hollywood. It was the best acting she'd ever done.

"Next time we have a school fair, I'll know what price to put on my kisses," she said, linking her arm casually through his.

The breezy comment drew a scowl. "What the hell's that supposed to mean?"

"I'll put a sign on the booth: One kiss—three lobsters or equivalent in cash."

He regarded her disbelievingly. "You actually sell kisses at a damned school fair?"

"It's better than being dunked."

He shook his head. "I can see I've been missing a lot by skipping those fairs."

"We raise a lot of money," she said proudly.

"I'll just bet you do." He stalked off to the parking lot, leaving her to scurry along behind.

She hadn't guessed, until he spun out of the parking lot, just how mad he was. They were all the way to Key Largo by the time he spoke again. "No more."

"No more what?"

"No more selling kisses to a bunch of old fools who should be home with their wives."

Liz laughed. "They're usually with their wives. It's all in good fun, for a good cause. Some of the money is for school projects and the rest goes to the homeless."

"I'll match whatever you made in your best year, but I

will not have you sitting in a booth getting paid for granting kisses."

Liz's sense of humor began to fail her. She felt her temper begin to rise. "You don't have anything to say about it."

"Like hell," he muttered and lapsed once more into silence.

When they got to Liz's house, he sat stonily behind the wheel.

"Are you coming in for pasta?"

"I don't think so."

"You realize, of course, that this entire argument is ridiculous."

"Probably."

"Then why are we having it?"

A sheepish expression stole over his hard features. "Because I'm a pigheaded, possessive jerk."

"Agreed."

"You didn't have to agree so readily."

He looked so hurt that she found herself laughing again. "Okay. I can't say I found anything in your self-analysis with which I strongly disagreed, but I will promise not to rub it in if you'll come in for the dinner I promised you."

He still seemed reluctant.

"We can finish making plans for Kevin," she said.

Todd shook his head. "If I come in, I guarantee you that Kevin is the last thing we will discuss."

Liz swallowed hard. There was no doubt in her mind exactly what he was thinking. And wanting.

"Then maybe you'd better go," she whispered.

He put a finger under her chin and turned her to face him. "Do you really want me to?"

Dozens of conflicting emotions whirled through her, colliding like bumper cars. She blocked them all out finally and went with her heart.

"No."

He swallowed convulsively. "Are you sure?"

She gave him a tremulous smile. "Don't push your luck, Todd."

He sighed at that. Gentle fingers brushed a curl off her cheek, then lingered along the curve of her neck.

"I'd better go."

Dismayed, she stared at him. "Why?"

"You're not ready, sweetheart. I'm not ready for a one-night stand and you're not ready for anything else."

The truth of that slammed into her gut and brought her out of the sensual reverie that had led to her impulsive invitation in the first place. She leaned across and brushed a kiss on his forehead. "Thanks," she said, hurriedly opening the door as if she couldn't escape fast enough now that she'd been reminded of the stakes of the game she'd been playing.

"I'll call you tomorrow," he promised.

"Don't."

"We have to talk about Kevin, remember."

She sighed. Kevin, again. He was their link. The only one. All during the long, restless night, she tried to remember that. Instead, all she felt was the burning wake of desire left by Todd's kisses.

Chapter 7

The horrible sound of metal grinding against metal rent the air. Tires skidded and screeched on wet pavement. Glass shattered. Screams. Sirens. More screams, hers, lodged in her throat. Not her baby! No, please God, not her baby!

Heart hammering, her body soaked with perspiration, Liz awoke with a start to the sounds of thunder, rain and a frantic pounding on her front door. Before she could reconcile nightmare and reality, the doorbell rang, followed by more impatient pounding. She sat up in bed, jerked the covers around her and blinked, trying to drag herself awake and away from the pull of the familiar, haunting dream.

Even though she couldn't quite get herself moving to respond to it, that incessant pounding had been a blessing. It had ended the nightmare before she had actually seen Laura lying in the street. For weeks after the accident, overcome with guilt and grief, she had relived the horror night and day. Finally, she had been able to block it consciously during her waking hours, but not at night. Still not at night.

Her whole body shaking from the inside, she drew in a ragged breath and tried to get her act together to answer the door. She was normally a morning person, up by six, fully alert by the time she left for school at seven. The routine never varied. Even on weekends she was usually quick to waken at disgustingly early hours. Today she felt as though her brain were made of oatmeal.

She reminded herself that she also usually had more than one hour of sleep. Last night, with Todd's touches etched indelibly on her skin and in her imagination, had been the pits. It had been nearly dawn by the time she'd fallen into a restless sort of half-slumber. It was barely after seven now. It would take a powerful amount of adrenaline to convert oatmeal into functioning brain cells after that amount of sleep.

"Liz, are you in there? Dammit, open this door before I break it down."

Todd? She shook her head and tried to imagine why Todd would be beating on her door at the crack of dawn on Sunday. The doorbell chimed several more times. She'd never before realized quite how loud it was.

"Elizabeth Gentry, open this door!"

The heavy oak door rattled on its hinges. Liz flew out of bed, grabbed an oversized Miami Dolphins jersey and pulled it over her head as she ran through the house.

"I'm coming, for heaven's sake." She rolled her eyes as she caught sight of her disheveled appearance in the full-length mirrors on the dining-room wall. It was too late to do anything about that. She threw open the door. "Todd, what on earth are you doing? Trying to wake the dead?"

He simply stared at her, breathing heavily, his brown hair soaking wet. "In a manner of speaking," he said softly, his gaze covering the distance from tousled hair to bare toes in less time than it took to check out fruit for bruises. It was a quick examination for reassurance, not a leisurely survey of masculine interest.

Even half asleep, she recognized the genuine panic in his haggard face, the relief that filled his eyes. "What's wrong? Are you okay? Has something happened to Kevin?"

"No, no, we're fine. It's you."

"Me?" She might be more befuddled than usual but he was making no sense, at all. Maybe his brain was waterlogged. It was really pouring out there and the sky was pewter gray with not a glimmer of blue in sight. It was a perfect day for huddling under the covers and sleeping in. Not likely, she thought with regret.

"What's wrong with me?" she said, still trying to make sense of Todd's unexpected arrival.

"Liz, I have been calling here ever since I dropped you off last night. I thought we ought to talk about what happened. First the phone was busy, then there was no answer. I called all night long."

Liz thought of her own sleepless night and decided there was something perverse in a universe that kept two people wide awake and apart, when they could have been doing much more interesting things together. She simply shook her head and waved Todd inside. She headed for the kitchen and left him trailing along behind, dripping all over the tile floor and muttering under his breath. When she'd put the coffee on, she leaned against the counter and regarded him curiously.

No one had ever worried about her before. Not even Ed, during the three years of their college courtship or the five years of their marriage. He'd thought her capable and confident and had left her to her own devices more often than not. He'd never even opened a door for her after their first date. If Ed had called and no one had answered, he would have shrugged it off. He might have mentioned it later. He might not. There were reasons for his blasé attitude, but she hadn't known that until later. Much later. Still, it meant she didn't quite know how to handle Todd's unexpected and entirely unwarranted protectiveness.

"Liz, you still haven't answered me."

"I'm not sure I should."

"What?"

"If I explain this time, then you'll think you had the right to ask. Not that I'm not flattered you were worried, but I've been living my own life for a good many years now. I'm not used to having my activities questioned."

"Activities?" he repeated blankly. Then, "*Activities!*"

She laughed as a crack of thunder seemed to emphasize his indignant expression. "Simmer down, Mr. Lewis. Not those kinds of activities, though that wouldn't be any of your concern, either."

"I'd better sit," he said, pulling out a chair at the kitchen table. He rubbed his eyes, then ran his hand across the dark stubble that shadowed his face. He was even sexier with the unshaven look. It was odd how that worked, Liz decided. Some men simply looked like bums with a day's growth of beard. Todd was definitely not one of them.

"Do you have any idea how worried I was?" he was saying with a touch of asperity.

She dragged herself back from thoughts of sexy faces, in general, and Todd's, in particular. "I'm sorry. As you can see, you had no reason to be."

"Then why the hell didn't you answer the phone?"

He looked so bewildered that she decided to relent. "It was unplugged, at least the one in the bedroom was. I often do that, if I want an uninterrupted night's sleep."

"You get a lot of calls in the middle of the night?"

"Occasionally the kids like to play pranks, usually when one of them is having a slumber party. They think it's fun to call the teacher in the middle of the night. Last night was apparently one of those nights. The phone was ringing when I walked in. After two more calls asking whether my refrigerator was running, I decided to pull the plug."

"Your refrigerator? Some kid wanted to know about your refrigerator?"

She chuckled. "Surely, you know that one. They ask if it's running. When you say yes, they tell you to go out and catch it. It's as old as the hills. There are more. Want to hear them?"

"Spare me."

She patted him on the shoulder sympathetically as she poured him a cup of coffee. "Maybe after you've had some caffeine."

"And eggs?" he said, casting a hopeful look at her. "I never did get around to dinner. Or would you rather go out for breakfast?"

"I'd rather get some sleep," she said. "But I guess that's out of the question."

The slow, lazy grin he directed at her was pure seduction. His eyes fell to her bare legs that were only minimally covered by the loose-fitting football jersey. "Well…"

"Never mind," she said dryly, an unmistakable and infuriating catch in her voice. "I'll fix eggs. Where's Kevin?"

"He spent the night with a friend." A look of horror spread across his face. "You don't suppose…"

Liz chuckled. "More than likely he's the culprit, or at least a willing coconspirator."

"I'll wring the kid's neck."

"It's a phase. He'll grow out of it."

"If I decide to let him live that long. It's inconsiderate."

Liz pulled eggs from the refrigerator, along with milk, butter and bacon. "How do you want the eggs?"

"Done."

"Thank you. That's very helpful. For that you will get one egg scrambled and only one strip of bacon."

"I want at least three of each. I'm famished."

"Too much fat and cholesterol."

"Thanks for worrying."

"Don't mention it."

"I'll settle for two eggs, but I still want three strips of bacon."

She shrugged. "They're your arteries." She slapped the bacon into the microwave, put the bread in the toaster, then cracked the eggs into a bowl and whipped them with an easy efficiency she thought she'd all but forgotten. Big breakfasts had seemed all too lonely since… She slammed the brakes on the thought.

When the steaming food was on the table, most of it in front of Todd, she took a deep breath and said, "You want to tell me why you decided it was so important that we talk last night? You're the one who walked away from my invitation to stay."

Todd choked on a bite of egg. Odd, she thought, especially since he was the one who'd brought it up and made it seem so all-fired important. Maybe he didn't like being reminded of foolish decisions.

"Now?" he said.

"It's as good a time as any."

"Okay." He pushed his plate away and tipped his chair back on two legs. "I wanted to try to understand what's happening between us."

"And you thought that was something we could figure out on the phone in the middle of the night?"

"We sure as hell can't seem to do it when we're together. Every time I'm in the same room with you, all I want to do is make love to you."

Liz choked at that. Todd patted her on the back—none too gently—and grinned. "You asked."

She cleared her throat. "So I did."

"Anyway, I thought we might be able to talk more sensibly on the phone. Then when I couldn't reach you, I thought you might have been even more upset than I'd realized by what's been happening. I know it goes counter to your professional ethics. I know I've probably been pushing too hard. Last night you admitted that you wanted me, too, and my guess is that that threw you. Then I turned around and rejected your offer. It's all pretty confusing."

"That's putting it mildly." She regarded him curiously. "Why are you pursuing this, Todd? Because I'm not available? Is it the challenge?"

"I quit worrying about making difficult conquests years ago. I leave that to Hank now. He thrives on the chase."

"But there must be hundreds of women in Dade County who would kill for the chance to go out with you."

"None like you," he said with what sounded like total sincerity.

"Please," she retorted disbelievingly.

"Liz, you're beautiful, compassionate, intelligent. Surely I'm not the first man to be attracted to you since your husband died."

She shrugged off the compliment, unwilling to let him see that it pleased her. "I've been asked out."

"Have you gone?"

"A few times."

"Why not more?"

"No one's interested me. I'd rather spend the evening with a good book than a lousy date."

"But I do?"

"I haven't accepted a date with you yet, either," she reminded him with a teasing grin.

"Technically. But we do have a way of winding up in each other's arms. A lot of the best planned dates don't end up that way. I'll ask you again, why me?"

She looked up from her breakfast and met his gaze evenly. The daring glance cost her. She felt instantly mushy and vulnerable. She didn't like the sensation one bit. That didn't keep her from admitting honestly, "I don't know."

His smile was rueful. "And I gather you're not happy about it, either."

"Sorry."

"So, what are we going to do about it? Last night you were willing to sleep with me. Did that also mean that despite your misgivings you're ready to see if what we're feeling is real?"

"Real?" The very word made her nail-biting nervous.

"You know, the happily ever after variety of attachment."

"There's no such thing," she said succinctly and with feeling.

"I'll admit I've had serious doubts myself, but how do you account for all the couples who make it to their golden anniversary and beyond?"

"Probably sheer inertia."

She caught the momentary shock in Todd's eyes. His tone more cautious, he said, "And what we're feeling is…?"

"Lust," she said without hesitation. "It doesn't take a genius to figure it out. We don't have to spend weeks analyzing it to death. It happens to the best-intentioned people. Just remember that lust is like an itch. You scratch it, it goes away."

"And if it doesn't? Does that mean it's love?"

She shook her head and said softly, "I think love is a myth."

Todd's chair hit the floor with a resounding crash. "Okay, Liz, where did all that cynicism come from?"

"Experience," she said bitterly.

"But your marriage?"

"I don't want to talk about my marriage." She stood up and began slamming dishes into the dishwasher. She did it with such force she was surprised some of them didn't break. The fact that she'd opened up this particular can of worms annoyed the dickens out of her. Why hadn't she turned

Kevin's problem over to a school psychologist or a social worker, anyone? Why had she insisted on getting involved? Because she'd had no idea that Todd Lewis would get under her skin so, that's why. Now it was too late.

"I'm sorry you were hurt and I'm sorry if talking about it is still painful, but I don't think we have any choice," Todd persisted, ending any hope she had of being able to curtail the subject.

"Why?"

"So we can get beyond it. Weren't you in love with your husband?"

She frowned, turned on the garbage disposal and let it grind for an unnecessarily long time. When she clicked it off, Todd was still waiting. "You might as well answer," he said softly.

"Okay, dammit. Yes, I was in love with my husband."

"He didn't love you?"

She was flattered by his shocked tone. Suddenly resigned, she found herself letting the words pour out.

"Oh, I thought Ed loved me," she said. "Maybe he did at first, while we were still in college and in love with all the possibilities of life. He respected me. He treated me well. Laura and I never wanted for anything that really mattered. There were no huge fights. In fact, there was very little passion, at all."

Stacking the pans and utensils in the sink, she tried very hard to keep her tone indifferent, her manner cool.

"I can't believe that," Todd protested. "You're one hell of a sexy lady."

Once more, the compliment seemed to give her the courage to go on. "At the time I would have argued with you," she confessed. "I thought I was probably frigid, that I didn't make sex interesting enough. It wasn't until the day he died that I realized that the reason our relationship was so lukewarm was because Ed had been seeing another woman for almost the entire time we'd been married. Even his family knew it, but none of them told me. When I accused them of covering up for him, they didn't deny it."

He muttered a curse under his breath. "How did you find out?"

"Laura, our daughter. You know how three-year-olds are. They say the first thing that comes into their heads, even when they've been sworn to secrecy."

Todd's shock registered in the widening of his eyes. Honest eyes, eyes that could never conceal secrets. "Your three-year-old child knew her father was having an affair?"

"She hardly knew the details, but she had met *Aunt* Caryn. She told me all about her. She had no idea that the woman wasn't a real aunt or that in telling about her she was tearing out Mommy's guts. Poor naive Mommy."

Todd moved to stand beside her, his expression sympathetic. She couldn't bear that look. Pity was the last thing she wanted from Todd. She just wanted him to understand why she would never again trust a man, why she didn't believe in love, why there would never be anything serious or permanent between them.

"When I confronted Ed, he admitted everything. He said she meant nothing to him, that she was simply good in bed, that I was the woman he wanted to be married to, the woman he wanted as the mother of his children. I guess I was supposed to feel flattered that he trusted me in this important role, sort of a glorified brood mare and hostess for the rising young doctor."

"You said you found all this out on the day he died. What happened?"

"Laura told me all about her Aunt Caryn when she and Ed came home from what was supposed to have been a trip to the grocery store. They'd made a detour by her apartment. Apparently it was her birthday. He'd taken her a diamond necklace."

She picked up the skillet in which she'd cooked the eggs and scrubbed it with a vengeance. The scouring cleaned the pan, but did nothing to wash away the memories of her incredulity when she'd discovered the full extent of his treachery.

"Can you imagine? We were still struggling to pay for Ed's medical education and his office setup. It was a big deal for me to get a cubic zirconia pendant on our budget and he bought her a diamond necklace." She slammed the pan in the drainer.

"So you confronted him."

"You bet your life I did."

Even now she recalled her fury as she'd cornered Ed in the family room and questioned him until he'd admitted everything about the relationship.

"Had it been a fling I might have been able to forgive him, but after five years it could hardly be called that. I told him to get out, that I wouldn't play second best to a whore, that I wouldn't have a woman like that around my daughter. Do you know he was actually offended that I would call her that? He defended her. Then he went and packed a suitcase. I sat in here with a glass of Scotch, which I hate by the way, and tried to get myself under control." Her hands stilled in the soapy water. Her voice shook. "It wasn't until he was out the door that I realized he had Laura with him."

If possible, Todd looked even more horrified by that than by anything that had been revealed before. "He was taking your daughter?"

She nodded and felt the tears beginning to well up. "I tried to go after him, but by the time I grabbed my car keys, he had a pretty good head start. He was always an irresponsible driver and apparently the knowledge that I was coming after him made him even more reckless than usual. I was about a mile from here when I heard the crash." She buried her face in her still wet hands as the sounds echoed in her memory for the second time that morning. Tears mingled with dishwater.

"You have no idea what it was like. I knew it was Ed, even before I got to the accident scene. In my heart I knew it. It was as if I'd died."

Leaning against the counter, she felt Todd's arms go around her. She leaned back against the solid comfort of his chest. Her tears flowed unchecked.

"They were both dead when you got there?" he asked.

"Laura was. He hadn't taken the time to make sure she was fastened into her car seat. She'd been thrown from the car. She was just lying there… Oh, God," she whispered, as the remembered horror engulfed her. "My baby was just lying there."

When Todd turned her around in his arms, she fought to regain control. "I'm sorry. I don't know what's gotten into me. I haven't cried so much over this since it happened." She had just relived it, again and again, ridden with guilt, convinced that if she'd left it all alone, if she'd ignored Ed's adultery the way so many other wives did, her baby would still be alive.

"Maybe you should have cried long ago."

She shook her head. "It wouldn't have changed anything. At least you can see now why teaching is so important to me. It's all I have left. It's what I'm suited for. Each year those kids become my family. I won't do anything to put it at risk."

"And you think a relationship with me would do that? Or is it just that you're afraid to risk another relationship? I know all about fear, Liz. I know what it's like to be betrayed and angry and determined never to let it happen again. I went through it when my wife left."

Her spinning emotions seemed to still as Todd's words sank in. "Your wife left you?"

"She didn't want to be with me. She couldn't cope with Kevin. I'm just beginning to understand that her complaints about Kevin's behavior might have had some basis in fact, but

I still can't forget what she did. She abandoned a four-year-old boy."

"How horrible. I can't imagine a woman doing that. I'd give anything, anything, to have my baby back again."

"The point is we can't change the past, Liz. I'm just beginning to see that we have to go forward, to take risks or we might as well give up on life. I've protected myself ever since Sarah left, steered clear of emotional involvements, but I can't seem to do it with you. Maybe that's the way love works. It slips up on you when you're finally ready and then there's nothing you can do to fight it."

"This is not love," she said determinedly. The word terrified her. "It can't be."

He caressed her cheek. The expression in his eyes was gentle and understanding, but equally determined. "Call it whatever you like. All I know is that you're already in my heart. Now that I've found you, I'm not going to let you go. I didn't want to have these feelings, but I do. I won't ignore them."

"If we sleep together, it will end."

"No," he said, touching his lips gently to hers. "It will just be the beginning. Wait and see. I'm not Ed. I'm not going to turn to someone else."

Todd made the promises with confidence, but he worried. Not about his own feelings, but Liz's. She'd admitted she wanted him, that the attraction was mutual. But her faith in men was obviously shaky, and for good reason. What would happen when she found out that he wasn't the man she thought he was, when she learned that he was less than perfect, that things she took for granted in her life were next to impossible for him?

He had seen the shelves of books in the family room, the leather-bound editions that looked like classics, the brightly jacketed current fiction. What would she think if she knew that he couldn't read them, could barely struggle through the morning headlines? What would they do when she realized that something so important to her was something they could never share? And worse, that he'd kept the truth of it from her?

He wasn't sure if it was her fears or his doubts that, in the end, kept him from pushing for a commitment. Liz's affection for Kevin was strong, and she knew all of his problems. But that didn't mean she wanted to take them on on a permanent basis in both the child and the lover. He had been right to keep his dyslexia a secret. No matter what Ann thought about her friend's ability to understand, he didn't trust Liz's feelings enough to risk it. She could run, just as Sarah had.

Time was the answer…if she would give it to them. He was afraid to ask for himself. He asked for Kevin.

"Will you go to the Keys with Kevin and me next weekend?" he said.

She saw right through the ploy and shook her head at once. "You've met Ann now. You two will be fine in her hands. You don't need me."

"We do. I do." He grinned. "Remember, I still have to get past Key Largo."

Before he could wrangle an agreement from her, his phone rang. With a pitifully grateful expression, she got up to put some distance between them.

He answered the phone and with his other hand caught her as she turned away, catching her before she could leave the room. She said his name quietly in protest but he held her wrist tightly until he felt her relax, then slid his hand down to encompass hers. He rubbed his thumb in circles on her palm as he listened to Hank.

"Sorry to track you down, partner, but we've got a problem."

Todd was instantly alert. "What?"

"All this rain has turned the site into a sea of mud. I got worried and stopped by. It looks to me like we might be in trouble. The garage foundation could be slipping. I think you'd better get over here and take a look. We sure as hell don't need to have this garage tumbling down and injuring somebody."

"I'll be there in fifteen minutes. Thanks, Hank."

"You have to go," Liz said unnecessarily. There was no doubting the relief he read in her eyes.

"For a while. That was Hank. He thinks we could have a problem with the garage construction. He's already there."

The set of her lips indicated she still wasn't exactly pleased, but she merely nodded.

"Have dinner with us later," he suggested.

She withdrew without moving an inch. The shuttered expression in her eyes was unmistakable, even before she said, "No, Todd. I'm exhausted. I don't want to go through all this again."

"We won't. Not tonight, anyway. I'll ask Hank to join us. I'd like you to get to know him. We've known each other since we were kids. We've worked together since the beginning. I'm sure he has a date he'll bring along. Kevin will be there. You'll be properly chaperoned. No serious talk, just a pleasant evening at my house. Steaks on the grill, that sort of thing."

"More cholesterol," she chided.

"If I make it chicken, will you come?"

"It's Sunday night. I usually grade papers," she protested, but he could tell she was weakening.

"You have all afternoon to do the papers. We won't make dinner until seven."

"You aren't going to give up, are you?"

"No."

"Okay, I'll be there."

"Terrific."

He jotted the address on a piece of paper, then pressed a

quick, hard kiss across her lips before taking off. He wanted to get away before she could change her mind.

Or before he thought about exactly how little she had on under that damned Dolphins jersey.

Chapter 8

"So, old buddy, wasn't that the sexy teacher I heard in the background when I called you? I thought you weren't interested in her," Hank said the minute Todd joined him at the shopping-center site. Though his expression was cautiously neutral, his voice was thick with innuendo. It took every ounce of Todd's restraint to keep from punching him. Only exhaustion and the fact that Hank outweighed him held him in check. After all these years, he should have grown used to Hank's baiting. Today, though, because it involved Liz, it annoyed him more than usual.

"Tell me what makes you think the foundation for the garage might be slipping," Todd said tightly.

"Don't want to talk about her, hmmm? Interesting."

"Hank, don't you have anything better to do than to speculate on my love life? I assure you it's incredibly boring compared to yours."

"Hey, I'm just curious. It's been a long time since I've discovered you at a lady's house at the crack of dawn on a

Sunday morning. I thought you were the one who was worried about her reputation. Not that I plan to squeal on the two of you, of course. That's not my style. My mama taught me never to kiss and tell."

"I think the more appropriate lesson here would have to do with tattling," Todd said wryly. "Just for your information, though, I did not spend the night at Liz Gentry's place, if that's what you're implying with your usual lack of good taste. I went by this morning."

"To share a couple of sweet rolls and the Sunday paper, no doubt." The innocent words were delivered with a healthy amount of masculine skepticism. Todd clenched his fists.

"Contrary to your limited range of thinking, Riley, not every male-female relationship is based on sex," he said. Goodness knows he wished this one were, but Hank would have to subject him to torture before he'd ever admit it.

"It is possible," he told his inherently lecherous friend, "for two people of opposite sexes to be friends."

Hank poured himself a cup of coffee and regarded Todd doubtfully. "And that's what you and Kevin's teacher are? Friends?"

"Exactly." It was only a tiny white lie, aimed at protecting the lady's honor. He'd had those same kiss-and-tell lectures Hank had.

"It wasn't so many days ago the two of you were standing right here shouting at each other. Some of my best dates don't arouse that much passion. If that's what you call a friendly discussion, maybe I need to develop a new technique."

"We had a slight disagreement. Things change. If you don't believe me, you can see for yourself. I was planning to ask you to join us for dinner tonight at my place."

"Whoa," Hank said, a knowing grin spreading across his face. Todd considered once more rearranging that face. "First breakfast. Now dinner. I'm impressed. Now you'll never convince me this isn't serious."

"Hank, the only thing serious around here this morning is the likelihood that I'm going to hold you face-down in the mud until you scream for mercy," Todd snapped. He realized he was grinding his teeth. "Now do you want to come for dinner or not?"

"I wouldn't miss it, buddy. Anything I can bring?"

"A date, and a zipper for that smart mouth of yours. If you insult Liz, I'll start proceedings in the morning to dissolve our partnership. The only engineering job you'll be able to get will be in the far reaches of some very distant country that nobody can even pronounce, much less locate on a map."

The threat fell on deaf ears. Hank draped an arm around his shoulders and poked him playfully in the chest. His eyes sparked with mischief, just as they had during their hell-raising adolescence. Despite his current discomfort at being the object of it, he usually enjoyed Hank's irreverent humor.

"You are so-o-o cute when you're angry," he taunted Todd. "No wonder the teacher lady is crazy about you."

With a muttered oath and a glare, Todd stomped out of the trailer and splashed through the mud to the garage. He had a sinking feeling that tonight was headed for disaster.

Liz spent the whole day wondering how she had let Todd manipulate her into this dinner. For a woman with very definite ideas about what she did and did not want in her life, she seemed to be losing sight of that clear vision. She didn't want to go. She didn't have time to go.

She could hardly wait to get there.

Even though he hadn't asked her to bring anything, she had made a key lime pie. Crumbling the graham crackers for the crust and squeezing the key limes kept her hands occupied, if not her mind. Her thoughts reeled like so many leaves caught up in an autumn breeze.

These meetings between them, except when they had to do

with Kevin's progress, had to stop, she decided as she poured the filling into the pie shell. They were too volatile. They had her doing and saying things she immediately regretted, things that were totally out of character.

Just this morning, for instance, she had known she ought to go and change out of that provocative football jersey. She'd never thought of it as sexy, only comfortable. Then she had seen the way Todd's gaze lingered at the sweep of faded material over her bare breasts. She had felt her stomach turn inside out as he'd glanced with increasing frequency at the bare expanse of her legs below the too-short hem. And, dear God in heaven, she'd enjoyed it. Too much, in fact. She'd deliberately refused to change because Todd's masculine appreciation had made her feel sexy in a way that Ed's technically expert lovemaking never had. Lust did astonishing and dangerous things to common sense, she thought, running her finger around the inside of the bowl and licking the filling off her fingers in an unconsciously sensual gesture.

Tonight, though, she would tell him flatly that the flirtatious games, enjoyable though they were, were over. She didn't have to explain. It was enough to say that that was the way she wanted it. Todd was a gentleman. He wouldn't force the issue. And even if he tried, there was very little he could do without her cooperation. He was too busy to invent ways to spend time with her, if she wanted to be elusive.

Despite her resolve, she found herself dressing in a becoming turquoise sundress with an off-the-shoulder neckline. Her sandals were the merest scraps of turquoise leather. It took her twenty minutes to get her makeup exactly right. She balked when she found herself reaching for an outrageously expensive bottle of perfume on her dresser. Ridiculous. She'd just vowed that Todd would never get really close to her again, certainly not close enough to appreciate seventy-five-dollars-an-ounce perfume. She shrugged finally and dabbed the scent on her wrists and behind her ears. At least if she planned to say goodbye, she might as well make sure he'd remember her.

Todd's house wasn't at all what Liz had expected. It was old and like Ann's it wandered with haphazard charm. The nooks and crannies inside would be a child's hide-and-seek delight. Built of Dade County pine, it was situated on a Coconut Grove lot that was overgrown with palm trees, hibiscus and towering banyan trees. From the narrow, winding, well-shaded street it was almost impossible to tell that the house even existed.

Once inside, though, she discovered that it had been made comfortably modern without losing any of its original character. The colors were bold and practical. The clutter was exactly what you'd expect from a single parent and an eight-year-old boy. There were toys scattered over the floor of the den, papers littered the top of the huge desk, a magazine had been discarded in a chair; and a pair of sneakers was lying in front of the sofa with one sock nearby. Idly, she wondered about the location of the other sock.

It was the back patio area, though, that took her breath away. Complete with a pool that blended into the landscape, it was a lush tropical paradise. It was a setting meant for seduction and Liz shivered as she imagined swimming there, alone with Todd, on a starlit night.

When she reached the terrace, Hank was already there. There was an impertinent gleam in his blue eyes when Todd introduced them. His appreciative gaze swept over her and he sighed dramatically.

"Too bad old Todd here saw you first," he said regretfully as he took the pie and gave it an approving once-over before placing it on the redwood table that was set for five. "You're just my type."

"As long as they're over the age of consent, they're your type," Todd countered. "Watch him, Liz. He's an inveterate flirt."

She laughed. "And you're not?"

She wasn't sure which of the males was more startled by her assessment. As Todd started to launch an injured protest, she caught a spark of curiosity in Hank's expression, a closer examination. In that instant, she realized that whatever else these men might be—business partners, healthy competitors with the ladies, opponents on a tennis court—they were friends. Surrounded mostly by women at school, she hadn't spent a lot of time observing the traditional rituals of male bonding, the backslapping buddies who played cards or sports or simply hung out sipping beer and discussing life, but she recognized deeply ingrained loyalty when she saw it. With a single look, Hank had displayed a protectiveness toward Todd that she admired, even as it left her shaken.

A petite blonde in silky designer pants and a scanty bandeau top emerged from the house just then and Hank's attention slid away from Liz. The woman draped herself around Hank. His thick, powerful arm circled her bare waist in a friendly hug as he made the introductions.

"Gina here is an investment banker," he said.

Liz took another look at the woman she'd been about to dismiss as a cute bit of expensively clad fluff and caught the shrewdness in her eyes. Gina was grinning at her as if she knew exactly what Liz had been thinking. She wanted to die of embarrassment, as she gave herself a stern lecture on the dangers of stereotyping.

"Have you two been dating long?" she asked, envying the fact that they seemed so comfortable together. Perversely, after all her good intentions of the afternoon, she suddenly wanted Todd's arm around her shoulders. She felt a sharp pang of longing for the feeling of belonging it would impart, but he'd gone inside for the rest of the food.

"Ages," Hank said in response to her question about his relationship with Gina.

"You realize that to Hank anything longer than two hours

is ages," Todd commented from the doorway as he returned with a platter of chicken ready for the grill.

"Not so," Hank protested, his expression wounded. "I've known Gina for three weeks, ever since I asked her to go over my portfolio."

"And it took you twenty days to get her to go out with you," Todd reminded him, winking at Gina. "She's obviously more discerning than most of your dates."

"Cruel, partner. Are you trying to ruin this for me?"

Gina laughed, seemingly unaffected by the harmless bantering about Hank's flirtations. She patted his bearded cheek consolingly. "Don't let him get to you, honeycakes."

"Honeycakes?" Todd and Liz repeated in unison. Liz couldn't imagine anyone even daring to call the burly giant of a man by such an endearment. Hank looked chagrined.

"I will never live it down," he muttered, grabbing the chicken. "Let me tackle a manly task before my image is destroyed."

Gina turned to Liz. "Do you have any idea why it's considered manly to cook over a grill, when you probably couldn't get him to do the exact same thing at a stove? I know for a fact that he has never, ever cooked anything more complicated than a boiled egg."

"Perhaps it's simply a genetic defect," Liz suggested.

"No doubt."

The whole evening went like that, filled with fast quips and easy laughter. Kevin put in a brief appearance, long enough to eat, then went back to his room to play video games. He seemed to take Liz's presence in stride. He withstood Hank's friendly teasing, responding in a way that gave Liz an entirely new perspective on Todd's friend and business partner. For all of his pretended indifference to commitment, Hank fit neatly into Todd's small family. Surrogate uncle, pal, whatever, he belonged. Again, Liz felt a subtle yearning tug at her.

When the rain came back, the air cooled and they all

retreated indoors. Todd pulled Liz down beside him on the sofa and rested his hand lightly on her bare shoulder in a gesture that was both comfortably right and exciting. The light caress of his fingers played havoc with her good intentions.

It would be easy to get used to this, she thought as the conversation swirled around her. The warmth, the open friendliness, Todd's casual intimacy were all too alluring. It would be dangerous to believe in this, to believe it could last.

If Todd was to be believed about Hank's tendency to roam, Gina was all too likely to be replaced by next weekend. Was her own relationship with Todd any less tenuous? Not likely. No, this was definitely not something to count on for more than the moment.

It was Hank who broke up the party, mentioning an early day and the problems at the site that he and Todd had identified that morning and now needed to rectify. Liz suspected that the polite excuses had very little to do with his desire to go. She'd seen the exchange of heated glances between him and Gina. They might be leaving at a respectable hour, but she doubted that their evening would end. To her amazement, she found that she was jealous.

She glanced at Todd as he was saying goodbye, wishing that for just one night she could abandon her common sense. She'd almost done it last night, but Todd had stopped her. Would he do it again? It would be foolish to even consider finding out. By the time he came back into the living room, she had begun straightening up.

"You don't need to do this," he told her. "Sit with me awhile."

"Really, I don't mind. If you don't do it tonight, you'll be kicking yourself in the morning. With two of us, it'll take no time at all to get things in the dishwasher. Then I have to go."

"Liz."

His fingers caught her chin. As he forced her to face him, her lips parted involuntarily. Todd's face was only inches away. "I've wanted to do this all night," he said, just before his mouth closed over hers.

Her pulse leaped erratically as wishes came true with wicked accuracy. The kiss was all she'd longed for, tender and intimate, hungry and demanding. She gave herself up to it, savoring, clinging and demanding in turn. Whatever else he might be—domineering, manipulative rogue came immediately to mind—he was also one heck of a kisser. She felt as though the floor were dropping away below her feet, then realized that he'd scooped her into his arms and was carrying her. Where? Did it even matter?

Of course it did, she thought, snapping back to reality. Her eyes opened wide as he sank down onto the sofa, settling her into his lap.

"I haven't necked in a very long time," he said, as if he found the prospect both intriguing and amusing.

Liz had to admit to a certain longing to recall the sensations herself. "We can't do this," she protested weakly.

"Give me one good reason," he said.

"Kevin."

"I checked. He's asleep."

"He could wake up."

"He's a sound sleeper," he said, sprinkling quick little kisses up the side of her neck. He nipped her earlobe, then ran his tongue inside. She shivered all the way down to her toes. A kiss like that was worth a little risk. She turned her head for the full effect. How was this man able to slide past her defenses? Why did her judgment seem to fail at his slightest caress?

Todd's hand slid around her waist, then up, slowly, deliciously until it cupped her breast. The peak was already throbbing. His touch set off an aching sort of pleasure that rippled down to settle in her abdomen. Her back arched and she longed for Todd's hand to follow the downward path of those devastating ripples. Her whole body was tense with the wanting of that touch and the fear that it would lead to more than she could handle.

Thankfully—she supposed—it was not to be. Slowly, his caresses stilled. The kisses went from leisurely and passionate to quick and innocent. Her flesh burned just the same, but she was coming back to earth, back to a reality that included test papers to be graded and a long drive home.

"I have to go," she said, more shaken than she cared to admit.

"I wish you didn't. I'll follow you to be sure you get home safely."

The gentlemanly offer touched her. "You can't do that. I don't want you to leave Kevin alone in the house. I'll be fine."

He studied her intently. "Will you really?"

"Absolutely."

"I'm talking about more than the drive home, Liz."

"I know. I'll be fine on all counts."

"And you'll go with us on Saturday?"

Her smile was wobbly. Mrs. Elizabeth Gentry would never smile that way, would never even consider continuing this relationship. She had made that decision quite rationally just this afternoon. As for Todd's Miss Liz? She obviously had a reckless streak that matched the unexpected daring in his soul.

"You mount an incredibly effective campaign," she admitted, weakening.

"Irresistible?"

"Irresistible," she confirmed reluctantly.

"I'll pick you up at eight again."

She nodded.

"I'll call during the week."

She nodded again.

"Dream about me tonight," he said as he tucked her into her car.

Liz refused to answer, but she could tell from the devilishly certain look in his eyes that he knew she would.

Chapter 9

"I'm not going!" Kevin's voice rose in a wail.

Todd stared at him, startled by the vehement outburst. Just last night Kevin had been excited by the prospect of spending a day in the Keys. For the past week he'd taken the idea of meeting Ann Davies in stride, or so it had seemed. Maybe he'd just needed desperately to feel optimistic about Kevin's attitude.

"You are going," Todd said firmly, as he grabbed a striped polo shirt out of the batch in the dryer and looked it over. Thank goodness, it wasn't too horribly mussed, even though it had been left in overnight. Todd hated washing and ironing, which was why they always seemed to get done at the last possible minute when every piece of clothing and towel in the house was dirty.

"Put this on," he said, holding out the shirt.

"No." Kevin crossed his arms over his bare chest.

"Kevin!"

"No," he said again, taking off for his room. Todd heard the door slam behind him. His heart sank.

Carrying the shirt, Todd walked slowly through the house, trying to decide how to handle this tantrum. He was already fighting his own demons about the day's plans. He wasn't prepared to do battle with Kevin, as well. After a brief struggle to control his temper, he tried the door. Kevin had locked it from the inside.

"Son, I want you to open this door," he said in a low, barely controlled voice. When there was no sound from inside, his voice climbed a notch. "Now!"

"I won't do it. I won't go," Kevin whimpered tearfully. "You can't make me."

"We both know I can. Now open the door and let's talk about it."

Finally the key rattled in the lock. Todd turned the knob and stepped inside. He held out the shirt. "Put this on."

Kevin's eyes shimmered with tears and his lower lip trembled. He shook his head. Todd sighed.

"Son, put the shirt on," he said wearily. "Then we'll talk about this."

When Kevin remained right where he was, Todd tugged the shirt over his head and struggled to get his arms through the sleeves. Kevin offered limp resistance. "You know, son, when we talked about this last night, I thought you understood why we were going to the Keys today."

"I don't want to go see some dumb old psychologist," he said, his expression mutinous.

"Then tell me why you feel that way."

"No. I just won't go."

The stubborn refusal cost Todd the last of his patience. He grabbed Kevin around the waist, hefted him into the air and carried him across the room.

"Sit," Todd said, plopping him down on the unmade bed. He sat down beside him. "We've been talking about this all week. This is not some sort of punishment. Dr. Davies is going to try to help you, so you won't have so much trouble with your schoolwork."

"I'm doing better," he mumbled. "Mrs. Gentry said so."

"That's true, but you could improve even more once we know exactly what the problem is. Isn't that what you want?"

"I guess."

"Then what's the problem?"

Kevin kept his eyes downcast. Todd saw tears begin to run down his cheeks. His heart constricted. It took every ounce of his self-control to keep from going into the other room and calling Liz to say that the trip was off.

"Son, talk to me. You know you can tell me anything. Are you afraid?"

Kevin shook his head.

"Then what?" Todd asked, feeling increasingly helpless.

"Dad, aren't you proud of me anymore?" Kevin said in a tearful, scared voice that broke Todd's heart.

"Oh, Kevin," he said, his voice catching.

He should have realized how it would seem. He should have known that after a lifetime of unquestioning support even when grades slid, Kevin would see this as a sign of betrayal. He pulled him into his arms and tried to quiet his heartbroken sobs. For a fleeting moment, as he hugged Kevin close, he resented Liz for driving a wedge between him and his son; for getting them involved in this wasted exercise.

Then he thought of how different his own life might have been if someone had really worked with him. Oh, he'd accomplished a lot, more than he'd had any reason to expect, but there might not have been nearly as many scars. No matter what his reservations might be, they had to give this a try.

"Dad!" The protest was long-suffering. When Kevin wriggled to get loose, Todd gave him one last hug, then ruffled his hair.

"Sorry. I just want you to know that that is something you never need to worry about. I am very proud of you," Todd said, letting him go with a little pang of regret. Sometimes he missed the days when Kevin had been willing to cuddle in his lap and watch TV until he fell asleep. Those days had given him such a feeling of completeness, as if he'd spent his whole life just waiting to be a father. He'd vowed to do it all so differently from the way his own father had.

"I will always love you and be proud of you," he said earnestly, praying that his words were getting through. "As long as you're doing your best, I can't ask for anything more. Dr. Davies may be able to help you do that."

"But why can't Mrs. Gentry? I like her. She's made the other kids stop laughing at me. I haven't had a single fight, Dad. Not even one."

"And I'm sure she appreciates that, son. She knows how hard you're trying. But this learning disability stuff is not her specialty. She is going with us today, though. Dr. Davies is her friend. I met her last week. She's every bit as nice as Mrs. Gentry."

"Who cares if she's nice?" Kevin grumbled with another spark of resentment. "It's Saturday. Why do I have to take a bunch of dumb old tests on Saturday? If she really cared about me, she wouldn't make me do that. I wanted to play baseball."

"You can play baseball tomorrow."

As the realization that his father was not going to relent finally sank in, Kevin sighed in resignation. "Will I have to go next Saturday, too?"

"I don't know. If she wants to work with you, we'll have to work out the arrangements."

"Try to make it so I don't go on Saturday. Okay, Dad? Please."

"I'll do the best I can," Todd said, grateful that this first battle appeared to be behind them.

He could still recall exactly what it had been like for him being dragged from psychologist to psychologist, usually after school and on Saturdays. If his reading deficiency hadn't made him feel different enough, his inability to participate in other activities had only served to emphasize that difference. While other boys played Little League games, he sat in sterile waiting rooms and looked at papers he couldn't understand. It seemed as though every time he finally got to join a team, his parents heard about some other doctor, some new program.

He had actually been relieved when his parents had given up on him. At least, he'd been able to get involved in sports again. He'd become a first-class swimmer, winning meets around the state. The successes had been the only bright spots in an otherwise dreary adolescence.

Kevin was every bit as good as he had been. They swam laps together in the backyard pool most evenings. Kevin was like a little fish, already competing in local swimming meets and picking up ribbons. Todd had a feeling if things worked out and Kevin got a chance to swim with the dolphins, he wouldn't be able to keep him home from the Keys. So far, though, he hadn't told him about that aspect of the program for fear Ann wouldn't take him on as a client.

It was exactly eight, when he pulled into Liz's driveway, Kevin sitting stoically in the backseat. Before he could even cross the lawn, Liz was coming out the door carrying a picnic basket. The sight of her cheerful expression chased away the last lingering traces of resentment. She might have forced his hand in this, but she'd only had Kevin's interests at heart. He knew that with absolute certainty.

"What's this?" he asked, taking the heavy basket from her.

"Breakfast. Fresh-squeezed orange juice, a Thermos of coffee, warm Danish and milk for Kevin."

He chuckled. "Taking no chances that we'll get sidetracked in Kcy Largo, huh?"

She looked up at him innocently. "I just thought this would be so much healthier than anything we could get along the way."

"Right."

As they headed down U.S. 1, Todd was increasingly grateful for Liz's presence. While he toyed nervously with the radio, she kept Kevin occupied with an imaginative variety of games designed for car travel. There was nothing condescending about it, either. She played along with him with enthusiasm. By the time they'd passed through Tavernier, even Todd found himself relaxing and joining in.

They were almost to Dolphin Reach when Kevin propped his chin on the back of the front seat and asked hesitantly, "What's going to happen when we get there, Dad?"

"You mean with the tests?"

"Yeah. Will they be hard?"

Todd remembered only the frustration, the repeated sensation of failing. He couldn't recall anything about the actual content. Nor was he willing to admit in front of Liz that he even knew what to expect. Besides, he thought defensively, the tests had probably changed dramatically over the last twenty years or so. Ann hadn't shown them to him and he hadn't asked.

"Kevin, this is nothing for you to worry about," Liz intervened. "It's not like school, where you get a grade. Dr. Davies only wants to see why you're not doing well. That'll tell her how to go about helping you. Lots of students your age come to her with exactly the same kind of problem."

"You mean they can't read, either?"

Todd heard the amazement in Kevin's voice. Perhaps he needed to hear that he wasn't alone. God knows, it might have made a difference with him. He'd thought for years that he was the only one struggling to make sense of his assignments. Once more Liz had said exactly the right thing. If only she hadn't hinted that Ann Davies would accept Kevin into her program. There were no guarantees of that. Nor was there any evidence yet that what she offered would be the best treatment for Kevin's difficulty.

He himself had been to dozens of experts and no one had ever set out a plan for helping him. Everyone had agreed that there was a problem, but they'd all seemed more fascinated by identifying the cause than by finding a solution. The methods for correcting it had been as varied as the number of psychologists he'd seen.

First his parents were told to help him with his schoolwork. Then, they were told to make him do it on his own, even if he failed. Another one thought he should be removed from regular classes. Yet another insisted he should remain in the mainstream and be held back, if necessary. He fell two grades behind and grew angrier with each passing year.

As Liz cheerfully expounded on the excitement at Dolphin Reach, Todd's irritation with her lack of sensitivity mounted. If she kept on, Kevin would be horribly disappointed if Ann turned him down.

"Liz, let's just get through the testing," he snapped. His short-tempered comment had both Liz and Kevin staring at him. "Sorry. I just don't want Kevin counting too heavily on this."

Until he saw Kevin's face fall, it hadn't occurred to him that he'd just suggested the possibility of another failure. Silently, he cursed himself as Kevin sat back, subdued for the rest of the trip. Liz looked as though she wanted to take Todd's head off, but she bit her lower lip and kept quiet. When they arrived at Dolphin Reach, she was the first one out of the car.

Ann met them as they crossed the parking lot. She looked tired and disheveled, but she was smiling warmly. Liz hugged her and introduced her to Kevin. After hanging back for a minute, Kevin responded just as Todd had to Ann's quiet questioning and interested attention. By the time they had walked into the building, she had Kevin chattering away. At the door to her office, she dismissed Todd and Liz.

"Go see Alexis," she ordered. "She's had the calf. If she were any prouder, she'd be handing out cigars."

"But," Todd protested, looking pointedly at Kevin.

"Kevin and I will be just fine," Ann responded. "Go."

With a last reluctant glance, Todd followed Liz outside and down to the dock. He was spoiling for a fight, but she didn't even give him a chance to throw the first verbal punch. As she had the previous week, she bounded on ahead. She was kneeling down for a closer inspection of the newest dolphin by the time he arrived.

"Isn't this the most beautiful dolphin you've ever seen," she enthused, her eyes flashing with excitement. Her earlier irritation with him seemed to be forgotten.

Like babies, Todd thought the tiny dolphin looked pretty much like all the others. He knew better than to say it. "Exceptional," he confirmed, biting back his desire to snap at her, to snap at anyone.

Liz apparently caught the tautness in his voice. She glanced up at him pointedly. "Do you want to explain what's wrong or do you plan to take my head off the rest of the morning? If you can't think of something pleasant to say, maybe you should just go back inside and wait in the lobby."

He closed his eyes and sighed. When he opened them again, he dropped down beside her on the end of the dock. "I'm sorry. It just worries me to see Kevin getting his hopes up. This program of Ann's may or may not be right for him. Even if she does take him on, it's going to be a slow process. Kids tend to expect overnight miracles."

She rocked back on her heels and put her hand on his thigh. It was meant as no more than an impulsive gesture of apology, but Todd felt the blood begin to pound through his veins.

"Okay, maybe I was overselling it a bit," she admitted. "I'll try to be more careful. Just don't let your doubts rub off on Kevin. He needs to have a little hope."

He lifted her hand to his lips and kissed it. "Deal," he said, his gaze locking with hers.

Liz seemed troubled as she withdrew her hand. She started to speak, then fell silent. Before he could press for an explanation, Alexis apparently tired of being ignored. She began chattering for attention. Liz leaned over to rub her snout, then reached out to stroke the calf that was right at Alexis's side.

Todd watched the interaction with something that felt strangely like envy. She was so affectionate with Kevin, even with the dolphins, but around him there was still so much reserve. How could she melt in his arms one day and be so distant the next? Still, the idea of being jealous of a dolphin was clearly absurd. Observing them, he found himself grinning.

"Careful, Liz. Alexis seems to be a little nervous. Are you sure you should be hovering quite so close to the calf?"

"Don't be silly," she said, stretching a little further to pet the baby dolphin. "She knows I'd never..."

The words died in a sputter as Alexis tumbled Liz straight off the dock and into the icy water. She bobbed up, hair streaming and indignation written all over her face. Todd pulled out the camera he'd tucked in his pocket and began taking pictures.

"Don't you dare," she said, scrambling back onto the dock.

He chuckled. "Who's going to stop me?"

"I am," she said, her shoes sloshing as she tried to chase after him. Her clothes clung to her body, the T-shirt displaying the tantalizing thrust of her hardened nipples, her white shorts practically transparent. Todd's breath caught in his throat and his step faltered. She took full advantage of the hesitation to put both hands on his chest and shove. He stumbled backward, but caught himself just in time to prevent himself from tumbling backwards off the dock.

"You'd better be very glad that didn't work," he said softly. He shot her a look of feigned menace.

The spark in her eyes dimmed. "Oh?" she taunted right back.

"Between us I have the only dry clothes," he pointed out. "Not that I'm complaining about the way you look in those, you understand, but they are a bit provocative."

Her gaze lowered self-consciously and her cheeks flushed pink. "If you were a gentleman, you'd do something."

"Already we have a problem," he teased with a wicked grin.

"Todd, don't you have a beach towel in the car?"

"I might."

"Well, then, get it," she said. He had a feeling she was only barely resisting the urge to stamp her foot in annoyance.

Reluctantly, he went to the car and got her a towel. When he came back, he'd also taken off his shirt. He held both items out to her. Her gaze seemed riveted to his bare chest.

"Liz."

"Umm…"

"Your towel. My shirt. Don't you want to go inside and dry off?"

She still looked slightly dazed, a fact he found more than a little flattering, to say nothing of arousing. Of all the times and places to stir her senses—and his own. Shirt and towel slid from his fingers as he stepped closer. Her gaze held by his, Liz waited. She ran her tongue across her lips and his heart thudded. The woman's power to arouse him awed him. Her ability to do it at the most inconvenient times was just part of what made her fascinating.

Before he could enfold her in his arms, he heard Kevin's shout, then the thunder of feet along the dock.

"Hey, Dad, guess what? I have 'lexia. Ann says she knows

just what that is. And you know what else, Dad? She says I'm going to get to swim with the dolphins. Isn't that great? Wait till the kids in school hear about it."

He skidded to a stop and his expression changed from excitement to bemusement as he saw Liz dripping from head to toe. "Mrs. Gentry, what happened? You're all wet."

"It seems Mrs. Gentry couldn't wait for you. She's already been for a swim with the dolphins."

"In her clothes?"

Todd grinned, ignoring her murderous glance. "Like I said, son, she couldn't wait."

Ann arrived just in time to hear the tail end of the conversation. Her eyebrows rose questioningly and her lips twitched with amusement. "I don't suppose I need to ask how this happened."

Liz grimaced. "A friend would not gloat. A friend would get me some dry clothes."

"I brought you a towel and offered you my shirt," Todd countered indignantly.

"I wanted something dry," she retorted, staring pointedly at the shirt and towel in question. They were floating in the water. As they watched, one of the other dolphins approached the shirt cautiously and, after a brief investigation, swam off with it.

"That's Jacquie," Ann said. "She's the most curious of any of our dolphins."

"Terrific," Todd muttered, though he couldn't resist laughing at the dolphin's antics. Jacquie seemed as pleased with her new acquisition as any other lady who'd been on an unscheduled shopping trip and had found a bargain in a favorite color.

"Why don't you two drive over to my place and scavenge around for some dry clothes," Ann suggested. "I've promised Kevin a chance to swim with the dolphins. One of the trainers will be here in a minute to take him in."

"I'd like to stay and watch," Todd said, "That is, if you don't object."

"Of course not. Liz, what about you? My clothes will be too big, but you're welcome to whatever you can find."

"I think I'll wait, too. The sun's hot. With this breeze, I'll drip dry in no time."

Within minutes Kevin was in the water with the dolphins, who seemed delighted to have a human playmate. They tossed a ball with him. They let him hold onto a fin, while they swam with him alongside. After each stunt, they waited for him to give them their reward. The excitement in Kevin's eyes made Todd's heart flip over. His laughter was young and carefree, exactly the way it should be for an eight-year-old and all too often hadn't been for Kevin.

When Ann finally called a halt to the swim, Kevin climbed out of the water reluctantly. "I get to do it again next week, right?" he begged Ann.

"You know the rules."

"I have to write an essay about what we did today."

"That's right. I want it to be the very best you can do, okay? You have a whole week to work on the spelling. I want you to do it all on your own. No help from your dad or Mrs. Gentry. You can have them look it over when you're finished, if you want to, but you write it by yourself. Try to tell me everything that happened."

Kevin threw his arms around Ann's waist with an impulsiveness that startled all of them. "I will. I promise."

All the way home Liz listened to Kevin's nonstop chattering. She felt warm inside, as if her mission had finally been accomplished. In time, Kevin would be okay. He would learn how to cope with his dyslexia, how to minimize its impact on his life.

This was what her life was all about—helping kids. This was something that really mattered. Getting involved with a man like Todd was only a risk, an unnecessary complication.

She needed to extricate herself from the relationship before one of them got hurt. Already she was too attracted to him, already he was able to wound her far too easily. His irritation that morning, his obvious resentment of what he viewed as her interference had hurt. The more entangled their lives became, the greater the risk of emotional scars when the school year ended and Kevin no longer provided the link between them.

Lost in thought, she didn't notice until it was too late that Todd had driven to his place in Coconut Grove. Reluctantly she followed him inside as Kevin ran off to find paper and pencil so he could begin working on his essay about the dolphins. She glanced at Todd and caught the pride in his eyes. It filled her with satisfaction, knowing that she'd had a small part in their happiness.

"I've never seen him this carefree, this anxious to do any sort of homework," Todd said. "Thank you for giving him this chance."

"You're giving him the chance. I just pointed you in the right direction."

"I'm still not sure I understand the connection between the dolphins and Kevin's dyslexia."

"They're the incentive. They give Kevin a reason to succeed with the actual reading and writing exercises. He wants to swim with them again and by having him describe the experience, Ann is getting him to take auditory and visual experiences and put them down on paper. I'm not sure I understand why it works. I only know it does. I don't suppose it would have to be dolphins. It could be anything a child really loves, something that will make the struggle to put words on paper worthwhile."

"However it works, I'm grateful."

Just then Kevin came racing back to join them. He was waving a sheet of notebook paper. "Hey, Dad, look at this. What do you think?"

"You've finished your essay already?"

"Yeah. I wrote all about swimming with the dolphin and I said that you and Mrs. Gentry were there, too. Look at it. How'd I do?"

"Remember what Dr. Davies said, you're supposed to do this on your own."

"But she said I could let you look at it."

"Not right now, son. Mrs. Gentry and I were talking."

Liz couldn't believe he was putting such a damper on Kevin's excitement. She held out her hand. "Bring it here, Kevin. I'd like to see it."

Kevin gave his father one last disappointed look before bringing the paper to her. He handed it to her solemnly. "This is very well written, Kevin. Maybe you could try to put in a little more about what you did with the dolphins in the water."

"You mean like playing catch with them?"

"Exactly. And be sure to double-check your spelling."

He grinned. "I'll bet that means I made a mistake somewhere, huh?"

"Just a couple. You can figure them out."

"Okay. Thanks." He bounded off, his enthusiasm renewed.

Liz turned to Todd. "Why wouldn't you at least look at his paper?"

"Ann didn't want him to have help."

"That wasn't help. It was support. He was excited. He just wanted to share it."

"Then I was wrong. Can we get back to us for a minute?"

He reached out to take her in his arms, but she backed away a step. "I think I should go."

"Because of what just happened?"

"Of course not. I just don't think this is a good idea."

"Please change your mind, Liz. Stay here tonight. Don't

make me take you home just yet. Help Kevin and me celebrate his first lesson at Dolphin Reach."

Her breath caught in her throat. Longing swept through her, followed by determination. She could see right through his manipulation. She couldn't allow him to use Kevin to hold her. "I can't," she insisted.

Todd frowned. "Can't or won't?" he asked, obviously puzzled.

"Does it really matter?"

"Liz, what's going on here? I thought we were going to try to move ahead, take this relationship one day at a time and see where it went."

She shook her head. "I tried to make you understand. I don't have relationships. Not the kind you mean. I know how I want to spend the rest of my life. I want to teach. I want to have a few good friends, people I can count on."

"And you don't think you'll be able to count on me?"

"You and I aren't friends, Todd. We're physically attracted. We have a common bond through Kevin. That doesn't add up to friendship."

He looked as though she'd struck him. "Is that how you view the last couple of weeks? A couple of parent-teacher conferences and a few passionate kisses?"

"That's exactly what it's been," she said stubbornly.

"I see. Then I'm the one who's had it all wrong. I thought the feelings ran a little deeper. Forgive me. It's been so long since I've wanted to hold anyone in my arms, I thought it must mean something."

She winced at his demeaning tone. "I didn't mean to make it sound cheap. I'm sorry. I'm not very good at this."

"Neither am I, apparently," he said dryly. She sensed that he was struggling with his temper. She honestly couldn't blame him. She'd been sending mixed signals. That was all the more reason to clarify things now.

Todd wasn't waiting for a response from her, though. "So,"

he said with an attempt to sound casual, "what say we start over? Let's try to become friends."

She blinked. This wasn't what she'd expected, at all. She'd anticipated anger, reproach, but not this cool acceptance, this rational proposition.

He grinned. "Not what you were expecting, huh?"

"Not exactly."

"Look, I'm willing to admit that maybe everything has happened too fast. Rather than turning our backs on it though, why not start over and go about this more slowly, just get to be friends. You say you want friends you can count on. I'd like to be one."

Liz was filled with doubts. A man like Todd as a friend? Impossible. "Do you honestly think we can put limits on this?"

"We can try."

Todd watched the play of emotions on her face and held his breath. He knew this was the only way he was likely to keep Liz in his life. Unless he could persuade her that staying was safe, she would run from the more intense emotions. Quite possibly it was the only time in his life, he'd deliberately set out to turn his life into a living hell. He had no doubt that's what it would be, too. Having Liz close enough to touch, but off-limits would be sheer torment.

He watched her reaction closely. She seemed perplexed by the offer, doubtful of his sincerity. More than that, though, she seemed tempted. That alone told him that given time, he might just be able to pass through hell to get to heaven.

Chapter 10

For nearly three weeks, Liz and Todd struggled valiantly to maintain a purely platonic relationship. The vow to retreat from the intensity and get to know each other hovered over them, keeping their desires in check but not entirely forgotten.

They talked nightly on the phone, even when they'd parted barely an hour earlier. Sometimes the conversations were no more than a quick goodnight, a hurried reminder of the next day's plans. Sometimes they lasted for hours.

Todd tried to schedule every spare minute, insisting that the outings were just casual.

"It's not a date," he'd say in the midst of Liz's increasingly weak objections. "We're just going to a movie."

Or they'd go fishing, or to a football game, or to whatever he'd dreamed up to bring them together. He made each invitation seem so innocent, so persuasive that to refuse seemed churlish.

Besides, Liz told herself, they were just having fun. It had been a long time since she'd had a pal who enjoyed doing impulsive, spur-of-the-moment things. She and Todd were increasingly comfortable together. She was almost able to ignore the little zing that shot through her when his hand brushed her accidentally. She was certain that with a little more practice, she'd stop gazing at his lips and remembering them hard and seductive against hers.

She told herself it was all a question of mind over matter. If she concentrated hard enough on what they were doing, she'd forget all about what they *weren't* doing. It rarely worked.

They went to the movies, left halfway through and picked up a 1940s comedy at the video store. Sitting side by side on the sofa, a huge bowl of buttered popcorn between them, their hands repeatedly touched until Liz, feeling increasingly desperate, finally stopped reaching for more.

They went fishing. Todd caught several red snapper. Liz got sunburned because she hadn't been able to bring herself to ask Todd to spread lotion across her back. Simply touching his shoulders with the cool sunscreen had set her on fire. The thought of his hands on her, even in the most innocent caress, had left her weak and trembling.

Todd called in a few favors to get tickets for a University of Miami football game. Despite the noisy crowd, Liz fell asleep during halftime, exhausted from night after night of restless tossing and turning to avoid dreams that seemed filled with Todd.

They took Kevin to Zoo Miami, where Liz claimed to be so enchanted by the aviary that she spent the entire day there. She'd been unable to face the fact that she was growing increasingly attached to the two of them, that every excursion felt more like a family outing, the kind she'd envisioned with Ed and Laura and never really had. She was losing her heart and had no idea how to go about reclaiming it.

They walked in the Grove at dusk, ate Mexican food on the terrace at Señor Frog's, then strolled a few blocks down

Main Highway to have frozen yogurt for dessert. Her own yogurt melted and ran down her arm, when she got lost in the sight of Todd's tongue slowly licking the swirl of chocolate and vanilla.

Back at his place, he dragged out a guitar and strummed along to album after album of Bob Dylan songs, beginning and ending with 'Lay, Lady, Lay.' All Liz could think about was how it would feel to have those blunt, calloused fingers stroking her flesh with the same gentle touch as she lay across her own brass bed.

It was exactly the sort of nondemanding, friendly relationship Liz had been so sure she wanted. It was driving her crazy.

There were nights when Todd left her house that she paced the floor until three in the morning trying to figure out why he no longer kissed her goodnight. The fact that she'd set the rules only irritated her. There were days in her classroom, when she caught herself staring at Kevin and wondering what a child of hers and Todd's would look like. There were moments in the supermarket, when she found herself automatically buying food enough for three instead of one.

On rare occasions, usually in the middle of sleepless nights, she admitted to herself she was hooked. Not once, though, did she call it love. She knew perfectly well it was a silly obsession. Denial was a potent aphrodisiac. She actually considered abandoning the stupid rules and trying to seduce him, but figured she didn't know the first thing about how to do it. If he merely laughed at her, if he'd lost interest, she would die of embarrassment.

When she actually stopped to think about the amount of time she was wasting daydreaming about her relationship with Todd—or the lack of one—she wondered if perhaps she ought to go into counseling. He wasn't turning his life inside out over this. He'd amiably accepted the restrictions and gone on about his business.

His shopping center was still on schedule. In fact he and Hank were already in negotiations to build another one. He'd taken her to the top of the parking garage to get a view of this one at night with all the lights on and the fountains glistening. She'd never thought of a shopping mall—much less a parking garage—as romantic. Todd's was.

There were no puffy, dark circles under his eyes from sleepless nights, as there were beneath hers. When she'd grumpily asked how he'd been sleeping, he'd said cheerfully, "Never better." She believed him. If anything, he looked healthier and seemed happier than he had when she'd first met him.

She couldn't even goad him into an argument. She found she missed the arguments almost as much as she missed his kisses.

"This isn't working," she announced that night as she prepared dinner for the three of them at his place.

He glanced up from the blueprint he was studying at the kitchen counter. "What's wrong with it? It smells great."

She snatched the blueprint away and tossed it across the room. "I am not talking about dinner!"

"Okay," he said cautiously. "What's the problem?"

"I am not your housekeeper."

"I never suggested that you were."

"Then why am I over here every night cooking dinner?"

"We could come to your place, if that would be easier," he offered cheerfully.

She threw a plate across the room and watched in fascinated horror as it shattered. She *never* threw things. She discussed things in a quiet, rational tone. At least she always had in the past.

"You idiot," she shouted. "You are missing the point." She picked up another plate. He caught her wrist.

"If you throw any more, we'll *have* to eat at your place. I'll be out of dishes. Care to tell me what this is really about?"

"It's about us. I've known you barely a month and you're already taking me for granted."

"Liz, I do not take you for granted. I appreciate all the time we spend together. We have a lot of fun. You're a great cook."

"See what I mean. Who cares if I'm a great cook?"

"You were the one who said you didn't want to go out to dinner so much, that you enjoyed cooking."

"Would you get that pea-brain of yours away from your stomach and think about us for a minute."

"Us?"

"Yes, us. You're not exactly courting me anymore."

"Courting you? Correct me if I'm wrong, but didn't you tell me that you had no intention of ever becoming involved in another relationship? Didn't we agree to just be friends?"

"Yes, but…"

"Are you telling me you've changed your mind?" There was a gleam of satisfaction in his eyes when he said it. She barely noticed. She was too intent on expressing the rage that had been building for days now.

"No. Yes. Dammit, Todd, I can't even think with you around."

"I'd leave," he said reasonably, "but it's my place."

"Then I'll go."

To her astonishment and absolute fury, he didn't try to stop her. He did call her at midnight to whisper goodnight. He was definitely trying to drive her crazy.

Two days after Liz had stalked out of his kitchen in a huff, Todd was bent over a sheet of figures on cost overruns when Kevin came to stand beside him.

"Can it wait, son?" he asked, fighting as always to make sure the numbers were being correctly interpreted by his mind. He had less trouble with math than he did with reading, but he still didn't trust himself. A distraction was the last thing he needed.

"Sure. I guess so," Kevin said, but didn't move.

Todd glanced at him and pushed aside the papers. "Why do I have the feeling I'd better listen now? Is everything okay?"

Kevin shifted uneasily from foot to foot. "I did something in school today. I think maybe you're going to be mad about it."

Todd's heart sank. From the reports he'd gotten from Liz lately, he'd thought Kevin's days of troublemaking were behind him. "Go on."

"I volunteered you for something."

Cautious relief eased through him. "What exactly did you volunteer me for?"

"I said you'd be one of our room mothers," Kevin blurted, watching him warily.

Todd's eyebrows shot up at that.

"I mean I know you'd be a room father, but that's not what they call them. Will you do it?"

"What exactly does a room *mother* do?"

"Helps with parties and field trips and stuff."

"For the whole year?"

"Yeah. The kids all think it'll be really neat to have a father do it for a change."

Todd sensed that the real issue had been Kevin's desperate desire to be like the other kids. He didn't have a mother to offer up for service, so he'd presented his father as the logical alternative.

Todd found he was torn between annoyance and delight. "Is there something special coming up that will require my presence? You know I have to plan ahead if I'm going to be away from work."

Kevin's face lit up. "Then you'll do it? You'll really do it?" He was practically bouncing up and down in his excitement. Todd felt his heart flip over. How much had Sarah's abandonment cost his son? Would he be able to make up for all the big things as easily as he'd made up for this little one?

"I'll do it," he promised. Even if he would feel like a damned fool. Room mother, indeed. Liz had probably been chuckling all afternoon. "I'll call Mrs. Gentry and work out the details."

"Great, Dad," Kevin said, throwing his arms around his neck and hugging him tightly. A lump of unexpected emotion lodged in Todd's throat.

"Dad, can I ask you something?"

"Of course."

"Are you and Mrs. Gentry gonna get married?"

Todd swallowed hard. Out of the mouths of babes… "Son, where would you get an idea like that?"

"You see her all the time and I even saw you kiss her once. I figured maybe you were going to get married."

"And how would you feel if we did?"

Kevin shrugged. "It'd be neat, I guess. I haven't had a mom in a long time. I think she'd be a pretty good one to have. She takes real good care of us."

"Well, son, I don't know if you can understand this, but I do like Mrs. Gentry a whole lot. I'm just not so sure we're ready to start talking about marriage."

"Oh," Kevin said, looking more disappointed than Todd had anticipated.

"I'll make you a promise, though. If things change, you'll be the first to know."

"Okay, Dad. Thanks for being room mother," he said and bounded off to share the news with one of his friends.

Todd sat for a long time afterwards staring into space. Marriage, huh? He couldn't deny that the thought had crossed his mind with increasing frequency. Had Liz thought about it? Was that why she'd been so touchy lately? Had this crazy game they'd been playing finally forced her to acknowledge her feelings? He'd thought the other night that she was beginning to come around. The clatter of broken plates had actually warmed his heart. If she didn't actually admit to a change in her way of thinking of them soon, he might very well have to resort to more aggressive tactics to remind her of exactly how terrific they were in each other's arms.

With that resolution in mind, he picked up the phone and called her. As always, just the sound of her voice improved his mood. "Okay, lady, what's this room-mother stuff?"

Her low chuckle sent flames leaping through him. "I thought you'd be thrilled. Not every child is so enthused about having a parent do the job. Kevin can hardly wait."

"So I gathered. Do I have to wear an apron?"

"I think you can probably skip the apron, though you looked pretty cute in the one you wore to barbecue the chicken the night Hank and Gina came over."

"When's my first assignment?"

"Ahh, I see Kevin left the dirty work to me."

"Uh-oh. I don't think I'm going to like this."

"Oh, I don't know. How do you feel about baking cookies?"

"Baking cookies?" he asked in a slightly horrified whisper. Chicken on the grill was the height of his culinary expertise.

"Little pumpkins would be nice," Liz continued, amusement lacing through her voice. "It should be fairly simple for a man of your exceptional talents. Maybe round sugar cookies with orange icing and cute little faces drawn on them. What do you think?"

"I think you and my son have lost your minds. I have never baked a cookie in my life. I'll pick some up at the bakery."

"Store-bought cookies are not the same," Liz chided. "Especially for Halloween. Ask any third-grader."

"Then you can plan on getting your cute little tush over here to help me."

"Is that any way to talk to your son's teacher?" she inquired with feigned indignation. He heard quite clearly her stifled laughter.

"When do you want the cookies?"

"The Halloween party is next Friday, after lunch." Her tone turned serious. "Really, Todd, will this be okay for you? I know you have work to do."

"It's important to Kevin. I'll make it okay. As for you, we have a date for Thursday night to bake cookies."

"Should be interesting," she said, which he assumed was an acceptance. It was also an incredible understatement. If he had his way, the night would involve more than browning a few cookies in the oven.

"By the way," he added idly, "if you ever tell Hank about this, I will show your coworkers the pictures of you being dunked by a dolphin." He hung up on her sputtered protest.

When Liz showed up at Todd's the following Thursday at seven, she found him with flour up to his elbows and sprinkled across his nose. She brushed it away and gave him a quick kiss. A *friendly* kiss. She stiffened her spine resolutely and marched past him. "Any flour left for the cookies?"

"You really are pressing your luck," he growled as he followed her back to the kitchen. She stood in the doorway and stared. All the starch went right out of her spine. There was a white dusting of flour everywhere and one suspicious looking glob on the floor. Todd apparently caught the direction of her gaze and muttered, "I dropped an egg."

"Looks more like the whole carton."

"Okay, so it was a couple of eggs."

She found the fact that he was throwing himself into the project with such abandon a little touching. For all his grumbling, she had a feeling he was enjoying the fact that

Kevin had wanted him involved in his school activities. She hoped he also realized that it was another sign of Kevin's growing adaptation.

Looking around again at his enthusiastic efforts, she shook her head. She had a hunch she should have let him buy the cookies.

She dusted off a stool by the counter and sat down. "Since everything's obviously under control, I think I'll just watch awhile."

"Don't be sarcastic, sweetheart. Roll up your sleeves and get to work. I've already sifted the flour."

"Yes. I can see that."

He shot her a venomous look. She grinned and reached for the cookbook. "Let's see now. Two cups of sifted flour."

"I'm tripling the recipe."

"Good God!"

"Kids eat a lot of cookies, right? Besides we may lose a few until I get this right."

"Smart thinking."

"Thank you."

"Have you added the sugar?"

"Done."

"Butter?"

"Here."

"A kiss?"

His head shot up. She wondered where the devil that had come from. She tried for a nonchalant shrug. "Just wanted to be sure you were paying attention."

Before she realized what he intended, he moved around the counter, circled her waist with his arms and covered her mouth. There was no time to protest that she'd only been teasing. And there was nothing light-hearted about Todd's kiss. It was every bit as greedy and soul-shattering as the ones she'd recalled. The last of her cool resistance melted away, until she was warm and pliable in his arms. How had she survived the last few weeks of denial? When she was breathless and limp, he stepped back with a satisfied smirk.

"I think I like that ingredient the best."

"Oh, yes," she whispered, her eyes locked with his. If she had her way this was just the first of many. They would overdose on kisses. They would drop the pretenses, go with the flow, whatever the current vernacular was for admitting that she couldn't go on a minute longer without knowing what it would be like to have Todd caress her and love her. It was several excruciating, timeless minutes later when she finally dragged her attention back to the recipe.

The first batch of cookies was finally in the oven. The rest were laid out on cookie sheets waiting. Todd poured them each a cup of coffee and sat down beside her at the counter. Liz held the warm mug in both hands and sipped slowly, not liking the unexpected direction of her thoughts. Why was there always this one part of her brain that insisted on being sensible? Why did sanity have to creep in, just when she was ready to experience the glory of giving in to temptation?

She tried very hard to tell her brain to mind its own damned business. Unfortunately, it didn't seem to be listening. The nagging thought was something she hadn't been able to shake ever since Kevin had volunteered his father to be room mother.

"Todd," she began finally.

"Oh, dear. I don't like the sound of this," he said.

"I haven't said anything yet."

"But you're going to, and that tone tells me it's not good news."

"It's not bad news exactly. It's just a question."

"Go on."

"Have you ever heard from Sarah?"

The look he turned on her was appalled. "Where did that come from?"

"I just wondered. You've never really said."

"No. The divorce was handled by our attorneys. She didn't contest it. I have no idea where she is."

That was good, she supposed. Or was it? She took a deep breath and reached over to put her hand on his. He turned his hand palm up and enfolded hers.

"What's going on in that head of yours?" he asked softly.

She lifted troubled eyes to his. "Do you think maybe you should try to find her?"

He released her hand and stood up so fast the stool went spinning and crashed into the counter. "Are you out of your mind?" he exploded. "Why would I want to do that?"

"For Kevin's sake," she said simply, then went on with a rush before he could snap her head off. "Maybe he needs to know his mother. Not live with her or anything like that. Just get to know her."

"You seem to be forgetting one little thing: Sarah wanted nothing to do with Kevin."

"It's been a long time. Maybe she misses him. Maybe she's sorry she left."

"She knows where to find us."

"Todd, don't let your pride stand in the way of what might be best for Kevin."

"How can knowing a self-involved, uncaring woman like Sarah possibly be best for him?"

"She's his mother," she repeated staunchly. "He has a right to find out about her for himself."

"When he's older, I won't try to stop him. But now? No way. It would just be asking for more heartache. What the hell put this idea into your head? Was it this room-mother nonsense?"

"I guess so. It just seemed as though he wanted so badly to be like all the other kids."

Todd looked crushed. He stalked over to the oven and yanked out the trays of cookies, replacing them with the next batch. Liz waited. She could see the agony of indecision etched on his face. When he came back, he pulled her into his arms and held her close, his face buried in her hair. She could feel the steady rhythm of his heartbeat and knew that, in the end, his strength would bring him to the right decision.

"I'll think about it, okay?"

"That's all I can possibly ask."

He put a finger under her chin and tilted her head until he could look straight into her eyes. "Is this by any chance the last big barrier between us?"

She took a deep breath and nodded. "I think maybe it is."

"You don't make it easy for a guy, you know that, don't you?"

"That goes both ways. You've turned my life upside down, too."

His arms tightened around her. "God, I love you."

"Don't say that," she pleaded, but the words sang in her heart.

"She wants me to hunt for Sarah," Todd told Hank the next morning. "Can you imagine? I told her it's the worst idea I've ever heard, but she's got this crazy notion that Kevin needs his mother."

"Maybe she's right," Hank said, not looking up from the blueprints spread across the desktop.

Todd crumpled the soda can in his hand and threw it across the room. "Not you, too! Is everyone around me going crazy at once?" The can hit the wall and toppled neatly into the trash can.

"Nice shot," Hank said. "It's not such a crazy idea and not just for Kevin's sake, either. Seems to me like a meeting with your ex might put a lot of ghosts to rest, once and for all."

"I am not living with any blasted ghosts!"

"Aren't you? You've been mooning around here over Liz

for weeks now. If you ask me, the only reason you haven't asked her to marry you is because you're still scared to death that she'll dump you the way that Sarah did."

"Okay. I admit it. I'm scared. That's because Liz hasn't wanted anything more from me. She put up the barriers. It doesn't have anything to do with ghosts or living in the past."

"It does from where I sit. For some reason you're equating Liz with that creature who walked out on you. She may even sense that. Women have a way of trying to protect themselves when they see pain lurking on the horizon. If you ask me, she's been pretty smart to keep her distance. Deep down, you've always believed that every woman is just as shallow as Sarah."

"Liz is not like that."

"I believe that. I don't think you do."

"Dammit, where do you get off telling me what I believe?"

"Hey, you brought this up. I'll just ask one more thing and then I'll butt out. Have you told her about your dyslexia?"

He colored guiltily. "What does that have to do with anything?"

Hank shook his head at the blatant evasion. "You know the answer to that one, pal. Think about it."

Todd did little else the rest of the day. He didn't like the answer that kept coming up.

Chapter 11

A holiday party always seemed to bring out the worst in Liz's students. As excitement mounted, it was more and more difficult to keep their attention on their lessons. Even though she tried to keep their interest by devising holiday themes for their assignments, by lunchtime they were virtually out of control.

Losing patience finally, she stood at the front of the classroom and said very softly and emphatically, "If I don't have quiet in here by the time I count to five, there will be no party."

A stunned hush promptly fell over the room.

She nodded. "That's better. Now until our parents get here, I want you to write an essay describing your Halloween costume and why you chose it. There will be a prize for the best essay. Any questions?"

She looked around and saw that notebooks were being hurriedly opened. No hands went up. "Okay. You'll have about twenty minutes."

As she finished giving the instructions, she turned and saw Todd watching her from the doorway. He'd dressed in western garb, complete with red bandanna at his neck, cowboy boots and a hat that looked as though it had served an extended tour of duty on a dusty, lonesome trail. The outfit suited him. Her heart thumped unsteadily as she went to join him. She had an unexpected longing to desert this classroom and head west with him before sundown. An image of cool Montana nights and the glow of camp fires held an undeniable appeal to a heart that had never before yearned to roam.

"Howdy, pardner," she teased in a voice that was surprisingly steady. "I like the duds."

"You look a mite fancy for a place like this," he observed with a pretty fair imitation of a Texas twang. "In fact, you look as though you ought to be sipping mint juleps with Scarlet and Rhett."

She brushed a hand over the wide hoop skirt that suddenly made her feel delicate and feminine next to his blatant virility. "It's a little much, but it was all the costume shop had left in my size, unless I wanted to come as a robot."

His eyes blazed approvingly. "This is a definite improvement over clinking metal. I like skirts that swish. As for that neckline…"

Liz felt the heat rise in her cheeks. She'd known that darn neckline was too revealing. She'd figured no third-grader would notice. She hadn't stopped to consider how Todd would react. Or had she?

"Did you bring everything in or do you need to go back to the car?" she said.

He grinned wickedly at her nervous change of subject. "Okay, Miss Liz, but we'll get back to that neckline later. I have the cookies and the punch mix here."

"Then you might as well start setting up. It'll give the kids hope that this party is actually going to happen."

When they'd put the trays of cookies on a table set up in

the back of the room, he leaned down to whisper, "I don't suppose it would be proper for the teacher to get caught being kissed by the room mother."

"Good deduction," she said as her pulse zipped along.

"So what do we do to kill time until we start this shindig?"

Forcing herself to be matter-of-fact when her thoughts kept zooming back to the last time Todd had been in her classroom, she said, "I've put out the punch bowl. You can start mixing the juice and ginger ale. Jamey's mother should be here in a minute. She's bringing the cups, plates and napkins. Once everything's ready, we'll have the costume parade. You two get to be the judges. The principal will be the third judge."

"Are there criteria?"

"Scariest and most unusual."

"Are Jamey and Kevin disqualified? I may be biased, but I do think my son looks especially handsome in his Indy 500 jumpsuit."

"He still can't get your vote. He and Jamey get extra cookies for giving up the right to compete."

"I suppose that's fair. I'd go for the cookies myself, if I hadn't been the one who baked them. After you left last night, I must have tried one from every batch just to be sure they tasted okay. I've decided that a sugar binge is every bit as deadly as drinking alcohol. My stomach still rolls over at the sight of all that orange goo." He shuddered convincingly.

"That is not goo," Liz protested. "It's frosting. Admittedly, they may not look much like pumpkins, but they're just fine. The kids will love them."

"Hey, you're the one who drew the faces on them. Don't blame me if they look weird."

When they'd finished making the punch, Todd's expression turned serious. "Do we have time to talk before the party gets rolling?"

Liz glanced around the room. "If you can talk fast. Chaos tends to erupt without notice."

"I've been thinking about what you said last night."

Her head snapped up at that. Her hands stilled over the trays of cookies. "About Sarah?"

"Yes. I talked to Hank about it, too. He agrees that maybe it's time to try to find her, for my sake as much as Kevin's."

Liz felt her heart begin to thud. That wasn't something she'd considered when she'd made the suggestion. She hadn't been thinking of Todd, at all, only Kevin. "I'm not sure I understand," she said uneasily.

He touched her lips with the tip of his finger. "No frowns, sweetheart. Hank thinks maybe I've let the memories of the past ruin the future for me. He thinks seeing Sarah will put them to rest."

"Do you agree?"

"Not entirely, but I'm willing to look for her for Kevin's sake, anyway. I think you're both right about that. I talked to a detective before I came over here."

"What did he say?"

"That it could take awhile, that I shouldn't get my hopes up, that people who want to vanish generally cover their tracks pretty well, especially when they've had a four-year head start."

"For what it's worth, I think you're doing the right thing," she said, though her voice shook. She couldn't quite bring herself to meet his gaze. She was afraid of what she'd see there. Was he beginning to anticipate seeing Sarah after all this time? How much claim did his ex-wife still have on his heart? For her to have had the power to hurt him so badly, he must have loved her very much.

"Your opinion is worth a lot," he said, tilting her chin up until she had to face him. "I know how much you care about Kevin. That's the reason I'm doing this. The only reason."

Still filled with doubts despite the reassurance, she nodded and abruptly turned to go back to the front of the room.

"Liz."

She looked back.

"Don't say anything to Kevin. If we find Sarah, I want to talk to her first, see where she's coming from before I tell him about this. I don't want him hurt again."

"I understand. This is something between you and your son, Todd. It has nothing to do with me." She wanted so badly to be brave, to face the possibility that this could cost her everything. Instead, her tone simply came out clipped and icy.

He sighed, no doubt understandably confused by what he must view as her sudden change of heart. "You're wrong, Liz. It has everything to do with you. Because of you, Kevin may have his mother back in his life and you and I may be able to move on with our life."

Todd's words were nothing more than an empty promise, she kept telling herself as despair wrapped itself around her. Ed had solemnly repeated the wedding vows and, in the end, they'd meant nothing.

Worried and trying not to let it spoil the party for the kids, she went to help them begin getting into their Halloween costumes. Never in her life had she been more thankful of the noisy distraction of thirty-five high-spirited eight-year-olds. Never had she been more in need of those shy smiles and exuberant hugs. She felt as if her entire life was suddenly hanging in the balance. She'd never expected to feel that way again. She hadn't wanted to let any man get that close. Now it looked as though her worst fears were coming true. She was dangerously close to losing the man she loved.

It was nearly a month before Todd heard from the detective he'd hired. On the Monday before Thanksgiving, Laurence Patterson called with the news that he'd found Sarah. She was living in a small town in the Florida Panhandle. She was working as a hostess in a restaurant at a resort hotel on the Gulf coast. She'd never remarried, though there was apparently an older man with whom she'd been involved for the past year.

"I have a picture I can send you. Do you want me to talk to her or do you plan to take it from here?" Patterson asked.

Todd wanted the whole thing to go away. He'd almost convinced himself that the search was going to turn up no news and that he and Kevin would go on with their lives just as they had been for the last four years. He would convince Liz to marry him and they would all live happily ever after. The easiest thing would have been to ask for the picture, pay the detective for his time and pretend that it had all been a dead end. He had seen Liz's doubts magnified out of all proportion over the last few weeks. He could put them to rest once and for all by not involving Sarah in their lives.

But he knew he'd never be able to look either Liz or Kevin in the eyes again, if he told the lie.

"Send the picture and your bill, but I'll take it from here. Do you have a phone number and address for her?"

Patterson gave him the information, including her schedule at work. When he'd hung up, Todd turned around and stared out the window at the tropical setting he'd created in his backyard. Today it didn't have the power to soothe him. He wanted Liz. He needed her sensible advice, her gentle smile and the love that radiated from her, even as she protested that she didn't believe in the emotion. He knew, though, that he was on his own with this one. He had to make the decision, plan how he would handle the meeting. He had to live with it. Then he had to convince Liz that they were going to be just fine.

He glanced at the picture of Kevin on his desk and made up his mind. He called his travel agent and booked a flight for the next day. Putting it off would only make the prospect loom larger.

At noon Tuesday, his heart hammering, he walked through the bright, airy lobby of the Sea Tide Inn and through the French doors leading to the restaurant.

He saw Sarah before she saw him. Reed slender, blond and elegant, she was seating a family of six at a large, round table that overlooked the Gulf of Mexico. She was friendly, which didn't surprise him. She'd always been a wonderful hostess. What amazed him was that she was thoroughly at ease with the kids. She actually seemed to be enjoying their teasing boisterousness.

It was only when she came back to her hostess station and caught sight of him that her smile faded. Her eyes widened in shock. Her step faltered. She tried a tentative smile, but couldn't maintain it.

"Hello, Sarah," he said quietly. To his astonishment there was no anger underlying the greeting. In place of love-turned-to-hate, there was only emptiness. So many years of wasted energy, he thought with regret. At least he would be able to return to Liz at peace, knowing that the love he felt for her was whole, untainted by the past.

"Todd, what are you doing here?" She sounded more curious than dismayed.

He smiled faintly. "Frankly, I'm a little surprised myself."

"Then this is a coincidence?"

"No. As a matter of fact, I hired a detective to look for you."

The color drained from her face. "Why? Nothing's wrong, is it? Kevin…"

"He's fine. Do you have time to talk?"

"Actually, no," she said, then looked around, clearly distraught. "Maybe I could find someone…"

"No. It's not necessary, really. This can wait."

"Are you sure? Could you come back about two? I should be able to take a break by then."

He nodded. "I'll be back." He touched her hand in a brief gesture of reassurance. "Don't worry, Sarah. I promise everything's okay."

He spent the next two hours driving around the area, trying to understand his initial reaction to this meeting, which had been such a long time coming. He'd realized at once that Sarah no longer mattered to him, that her decision to go might very well have freed him from a relationship that had been all wrong from the first. At the time he'd been too caught up in the rejection, too furious at the apparent ease of her abandonment of Kevin to think clearly about the wisdom of what she was doing.

By the time he went back to the inn, he was in control of his emotions, looking forward to a final resolution. She was waiting for him, watching the door anxiously. Her expression brightened when she saw him.

"I thought we could have some lunch here, if that's okay with you," she said. "Even though the worst of the rush is over, I'm technically still on duty. I'll be able to keep an eye on things."

"No problem."

They settled at a comfortable table and ordered lunch. The waiter and busboy both treated Sarah with deference and she was genuinely kind to them.

"You seem to have found a niche for yourself here," he observed.

"I like it. The owners are wonderful people, the staff is great and I enjoy meeting so many tourists."

"Is it what you expected to find, when you left us?"

"Not exactly, but I'm content. I've grown up a lot in the last four years." She stirred her coffee, though she'd put nothing in it. It was the only hint now of her continued nervousness.

"How is Kevin really? You're sure everything's okay?" she asked finally.

"I'm surprised you're interested." He regretted the bitterness the minute he'd made the remark. He hadn't come to make accusations, only to move ahead.

She turned sad blue eyes on him. "I've always been interested, Todd. I just figured I'd given up the right to ask. I thought you both deserved a clean break. It was all I had to give you."

He hadn't counted on her still hurting. She was the one who'd walked away. He'd expected her to be carefree. "I'm sorry. I didn't mean to make this difficult for you. Kevin really is fine. I brought along some snapshots. Would you like to see them?"

There was a touching eagerness in her expression as she took the photos and went through them slowly, asking questions about where they'd been taken, how old he'd been.

"He's grown so much," she said with a sigh, when she'd looked at the last of them. She continued to hold them, running her fingers idly across the surface of the top photo as if she were caressing her son. She couldn't seem to drag her gaze away.

"Kids have a way of doing that. It seems every time I turn around, he's outgrown the clothes I bought."

"He's in school now?"

Todd nodded. "Third grade."

"How's he doing?"

"He's had some problems," he admitted reluctantly.

She frowned and put the snapshots back in front of him. "What sort of problems?"

"Behavior problems, at least that's what first got my attention. It seems you weren't the only one who thought he was unmanageable. His teacher this year finally forced the issue. We've had Kevin tested. He's dyslexic, just like me. A lot of his anger was caused by frustration. He's getting help now and things are better. Not perfect, but better."

"I'm glad he's getting help."

"And I'm sorry I didn't listen to you. It might have saved him some rough times. It might have made a difference for all of us."

"Don't blame yourself. Neither of us was very good at communicating back then. I was better at yelling and running. You just wanted to stick that stubborn head of yours in the sand."

"You're not the first person lately to point out that my obstinacy gets me in trouble," he said with a rueful grin. He hesitated. "Sarah, do you want to come back?"

At her stunned expression, he said quickly. "I don't mean to stay. Just to see Kevin again. I think knowing that his mother still loves him might make a big difference in his life. This isn't an impulsive decision. I've been thinking about it."

Tears spilled down her cheeks at the invitation and for once Todd felt something at the sight of them. He pitied her for all the wonderful years she'd lost with her child. "You really wouldn't object?" she said in a choked whisper. "You'd let me see him?"

"You could spend Thanksgiving with us," he said, praying that Liz would understand. "I know it's short notice, but somehow that seems like the perfect time for a family reunion."

She reached across the table and clasped his hand. "I'll never be able to thank you enough for doing this. I know how badly I hurt you. I can imagine how difficult it must have been for you to come."

"I love our son," he said simply. "I had to come." He stood up then. "I'll make the arrangements and get back to you, Sarah."

He was almost out the door, when he found himself turning back. She was sitting right where he'd left her, following him with eyes still luminous with unshed tears. He'd left the snapshots on the table and she was holding them tightly.

"You won't disappoint him, will you?" he said.

She shook her head. "Never again, Todd. I promise."

Liz felt her world shift and tumble off kilter when Todd called to tell her that Sarah would be coming for Thanksgiving.

"You've seen her, then?" she said in an amazingly calm tone. A chill seemed to settle over her.

"Today. I flew up to the Panhandle this morning. I didn't tell you before I went because I wasn't sure what I'd find. Maybe I just needed to handle it on my own."

"If she's coming here, that must mean it went okay."

"She's changed, Liz. Or maybe I'm the one who's different. I don't know. She misses Kevin. I could tell. I showed her pictures and she cried. I had to ask her to come. You understand, don't you?"

"Of course, I understand. This is what I wanted, remember?" But she hadn't wanted this. Not on Thanksgiving. She had wanted the three of them to spend the holiday together, like a real family. It was exactly the sort of dream she'd warned herself against having. It was turning into a nightmare.

"…I thought we could pick her up at the airport together," Todd was saying.

"What?" she said incredulously, certain she'd misunderstood. "What are you talking about?"

"On Thursday morning, I thought you and I would pick her up. I want you to meet her before I take her to the house. I need you to help me prepare Kevin for this."

"You want me there?"

"Of course, I want you there. We'd planned the day. Hank's coming. That should help some. Not that he's crazy about Sarah, but he'll be supportive. I know it may seem a little awkward for everyone, but I think it's the best way to handle it for Kevin's sake."

For Kevin's sake. But dammit, what about for her sake? How was she supposed to cope with being the outsider at this little gathering?

"Liz, what's wrong?"

"Nothing."

"Don't tell me nothing. You're upset. I know I probably shouldn't have sprung this on you at the last minute, but I thought this was what you wanted."

"It was. It is. Oh, Todd, I'm sorry. I don't know what's gotten into me. I guess the reality has thrown me more than I expected it to. I'll be fine by Thursday."

She was not fine. She covered her fears by wearing a dress that she knew was one of Todd's favorites, by cooking a meal that included all the traditional Thanksgiving fare, by setting Todd's table so perfectly it could have been photographed for a gourmet food magazine.

At her insistence, they warned Kevin about the surprise visitor they were having. He turned very quiet at the news and retreated to his room.

"What do you suppose is going on in his head?" Todd asked worriedly. "Maybe this was a mistake."

"You're doing the right thing," Hank said, walking in on the end of the scene. "Of course, he's going to be a little taken aback. Give him some time for it to sink in. When Sarah gets here, it'll be up to her to win him over."

In the end Todd went to the airport alone, leaving Hank and Liz with Kevin.

"Nervous?" Hank asked as she kept poking her head in the oven to check the turkey.

She let the door slam shut and paced instead.

"You don't have a thing to worry about, you know."

"Who says I'm worried?"

"Sorry," he said, grinning. "It was just a guess. For the

record, though, I've known Todd for a lot of years. I was around when Sarah made mincemeat out of his heart. He's never been happier than he's been since he met you."

She sighed and touched his hand. "Thanks for the vote of confidence." Then she resumed pacing.

"Don't mention it." He caught her wrist as she passed by him for the fourth time. "Can I make a suggestion?"

"Why not?"

"Todd will probably kill me for butting in like this, but let me stay here with Kevin tonight."

"Why would you want to do that?" she said, staring at him in confusion.

"So you and Todd can be alone. Go to your place. Go to a hotel. It doesn't matter, as long as you spend some time together. I think you'll have a lot of talking to do, once Sarah's gone."

Hank's words were innocent enough, but his implication was anything but. Liz's face flamed in embarrassment, but she felt tears clog her throat. In that instant she decided that Hank Riley had more sensitivity than anyone she'd ever met besides Ann.

"You're a fraud," she accused softly, giving him a watery smile.

"Oh?" His eyes twinkled with amusement.

"Don't even waste your time trying to deny it. I just hope I'm around when the right woman takes the time to get beyond that tough, lecherous facade of yours."

"It'll never happen."

"That's what they all say, right before they fall."

The reunion between Sarah and Kevin was every bit as awkward as Liz and Todd had anticipated. Kevin stared at his plate all through dinner, speaking only when spoken to and then only in monosyllables. He never once looked directly at his mother. He asked to be excused even before Liz served the pumpkin pie. Sarah looked as if she might cry.

"Give him time," Liz told her gently, surprised at the compassion she was feeling toward her. She'd wanted so badly to hate her, but she found that she couldn't.

"Liz is right," Todd concurred.

"I'm not so sure. I hurt him very badly. Maybe I don't have the right to even ask his forgiveness."

"Everyone has the right to ask forgiveness," Liz said. "Kevin needs to learn that forgiving and forgetting are part of growing up, too."

"You can come back tomorrow," Todd reminded her. "You have the whole weekend to try to get through to him."

After they'd called a cab to take Sarah to a nearby hotel, the three of them cleaned up the dishes, then Hank looked pointedly at Liz before making a discreet exit to play video games with Kevin.

"What was that all about?" Todd asked, staring after him. "Hank usually can't wait to go off on some date after one of these holiday celebrations. Family togetherness makes him nervous."

"He's planning to play matchmaker tonight."

"Matchmaker?"

"He's offered to stay here, so you and I can be alone."

Todd looked stunned. "He had no right," he said indignantly. "I'm sorry if he embarrassed you, Liz."

She put a hand on his arm. "He didn't embarrass me."

"He should never...what?"

She grinned, hoping her expression conveyed bold daring, rather than the jittery nervousness she was feeling. "I said he didn't embarrass me. I think he's right. I think it's way past time for us to have an entire night alone." She stood on tiptoe and wound her arms around Todd's neck. Her mouth met his in a slow, sensuous caress. "Am I getting through to you yet?"

"I'm not sure," he said with feigned puzzlement. "Could you try that again?"

"With pleasure."

It was several minutes before Todd broke free of the heated embrace. Breathing hard, he whispered, "I think we'd better leave now or we'll have a helluva time explaining to Kevin why we locked him and Hank in the bedroom."

Liz nodded with a sort of lazy contentment. "After you," she murmured, certain that she had never before felt anything to match the warm glow that had settled deep inside her.

Todd shook his head as he linked her arm through his. "Together, sweetheart. From now on, we do it all together."

Chapter 12

Halfway to her house, Liz suffered the onset of a terminal case of cold feet. If there had been any way short of declaring a medical emergency to get Todd to turn the car around, she would have done it. Todd was the right man, but this was the wrong night. Sarah's presence had triggered a decision that should have been made under less volatile circumstances. She wasn't really ready. She'd be ready in another year or two—or perhaps the next century, whenever they started handing out guarantees with relationships.

She glanced over at Todd. He looked thoroughly at ease. Confident. Though his full attention appeared to be on the busy road, a smile played about his lips. She wondered if she'd put it there, if some private anticipation of the night ahead was already giving him pleasure. Renewed panic promptly set her heart to pounding harder. As if he'd heard it, Todd turned toward her. His expression immediately grew troubled.

"Second thoughts already?"

"What are you, a mind reader?" she said lightly.

"It's hard to miss the signs. You're holding onto your purse as if you're anticipating a mugging at every intersection. If you bite your lower lip much harder, it'll be far too sore for me to kiss it the way I want to."

Powerful, sensual images suddenly captivated her. "The way you want to," she repeated weakly. She was going to faint, just from the caress of his words. One actual kiss and she would simply float happily into oblivion. She swallowed hard and tried to appear only mildly interested in the direction of the conversation.

Todd, however, was not through with the torment. In a voice that slid over her senses like silk, he said, "All I've been able to think about all day is a slow, leisurely kiss. There were too damned many people around. I wanted to taste your mouth when it was still flavored by cranberry sauce and wine. When you ate the whipped cream off your pumpkin pie, I could just imagine…"

Liz knew exactly what he could imagine. She wasn't sure she could stand hearing him say it, though. "Todd, do you think we could talk about something else?" Her own voice was no more than a husky whisper.

"Why? Is this bothering you?"

"No." The denial came out as a squeak. "It's just that there's a lot of traffic. You really ought to be paying attention. If you're thinking about kissing and…whatever else it is you're thinking about, you might be distracted. You know what the drivers are like around here. You have to drive defensively every second."

"I think you're the one who's distracted," he taunted, sounding very pleased about it.

"But you see that doesn't really matter," she insisted. "I'm not driving."

"Okay. I'll concentrate on driving, if you'll tell me what you're thinking about." There was a wicked boldness behind the suggestion. Liz's heart lurched once, then set off at an erratic clip that should have required installation of a pacemaker. "Well?"

She tried to stall for time to gather her thoughts. She needed to come up with a diversionary tactic that was far removed from the wildly sensual images that were actually rampaging through her mind.

"I, um, I was just wondering if I turned the dishwasher on before we left your house."

Weak, Elizabeth, she thought disgustedly. Really weak. She glanced over at Todd to see how he'd reacted. He was regarding her skeptically. Amusement danced in his eyes. "Oh, really?"

She persisted with dogged determination. "Maybe I should call Hank and check, when we get to my place. I'd hate to have all those dishes waiting for us tomorrow."

"I turned the dishwasher on."

"Oh."

"Anything more on your mind? Perhaps you'd like to discuss something a little less weighty? Perhaps a solution for world peace?"

She glared at him. "Don't make fun of me."

She caught him struggling with a grin. "I don't mean to, sweetheart. It's just that you're taking all this so seriously."

"It is serious."

"It's meaningful. It's wonderful. It is not life or death. Making love is a natural outgrowth of a relationship between a man and a woman. I want you, Liz. I've wanted you in my arms and in my bed practically since the first time I saw you."

"We're going to be in my bed," she pointed out irrationally.

Todd laughed. "Caught on a technicality. Want me to call Hank and have him take Kevin to his place for the night?"

"Don't be ridiculous."

"It's hard not to be, when you're acting like a giddy

teenager who's afraid her parents are going to discover that she knows all about sex."

She immediately stiffened. "I'm sorry if I can't be casual about this."

"Sweetheart, there is nothing casual about my feelings. I promise you that. Casual is a one-night stand. Casual is sex on a first date. Casual is falling into bed with someone you know perfectly well you'll never marry. This is not casual. Okay?"

She sighed. "I know," she said in a low voice, barely above a whisper. "Maybe that's the worst of it."

At the next traffic light, he turned to her, his expression grave. "Liz, do you want to change your mind about tonight? If you do, I'll understand. I want you very badly, but I can wait until you're ready."

The offer hung in the air between them. Liz seriously considered taking him up on it, then realized that not only would it be cowardly, it also was not what she wanted at all, not deep inside where emotions formed.

"I don't want to wait," she said, then added with a kind of quiet desperation, "I just want to be there."

"Me, too, sweetheart. Me, too."

The urgency and longing in Todd's voice got to her. As suddenly as they'd attacked, the butterflies vanished. She was as sure of her feelings for Todd, as sure of what she wanted as she'd ever been of anything in her life. He was a man of warmth and humor and sensitivity. When he cared, he cared with a blind and deep passion. He would always cherish those he held dear, scaling mountains, slaying dragons, if that's what was called for. A growing part of her was ready to relinquish at least some of her independence in order to bask in that loving protectiveness. He was right. There was nothing casual about the feelings between them.

Even with that reassurance, at her front door she fumbled through her purse for the key until Todd finally took over the search. He unerringly found the keys and had them inside the house in less than ten seconds.

It seemed like a lifetime.

Despite the resolution she'd come to in the car, Liz found herself at a loss again the minute they crossed the threshold.

"I think we could both use a glass of wine," Todd said.

Liz nodded. Then her heart sank. "Oh, dear, I don't think I have any."

"No problem," he said, holding up a bottle she hadn't even noticed. "An old Boy Scout is never unprepared."

"I didn't know Boy Scouts drank wine," she said, her sense of humor making a tentative comeback.

"They don't, but that motto stays with them for life. Sit down and I'll get the wine ready."

Liz didn't want to sit down. She didn't want to let Todd out of her sight. If she were alone too long, she had a feeling all her insecurities would come spinning back and take control again. When she was close to him, all she could think about was getting closer. His heat drew her like a fire on a chilly night. His scent was every bit as alluring as the tang of salt on an ocean breeze. His touch…ah, yes, his touch had the power to send her senses on a path every bit as thrilling as that of a star hurtling through a midnight sky.

Apparently unaware that she'd followed him, he turned quickly away from the kitchen counter and found her less than an arm's length away. His eyes widened, then sparked with golden fire.

"I didn't want to wait alone," she explained as he put the glasses and wine back on the counter and reached for her.

"You're not alone, sweetheart. Not anymore."

Blunt but gentle fingers tangled in her upswept hair and sent it tumbling down her back. Warm, wine-scented breath whispered a caress along her neck and turned her blood to flame that fired her body from the inside out. Held tight against his body, hip intimately fit to hip, thigh caressing thigh, she trembled and nearly wept with the joy of the sensation. By the time his lips claimed hers, her body had already surrendered, accepting finally that fate had made her his.

"Liz, should we talk?" he said, his breathing ragged, his voice hoarse.

"No more. Not now. I want to feel. I want you to love me, Todd. We've waited so long. Just love me." The last was part demand, part plea. The urgency conveyed itself to him, because he swept her into his arms and carried her through the house, guided by her murmured directions, spurred on by her unrestrained kisses.

At the sight of her brass bed, Todd's eyes smoldered. "Somehow I've always known," he said. "When I've imagined you waiting for me, it's always been in a bed like this."

"I haven't always had this bed," she said, wanting him to know he would be the first to share it. There were no ghosts here. "I bought it after..."

"Ssh. No talk of the past tonight. We're living in the present. There's just you and me and the way we feel when we're together."

With great care and evident fascination he began to remove her clothes. His hands were adept at the task, but it was the expression in his eyes that set off fireworks. There was so much adoration there, so much tenderness. Liz had never felt as beautiful. He took away her shyness and gave her back love.

He took far less care with his own undressing. She wanted to savor the slow revelations as he had with her, but it was as if he'd already expended the last of his self-control. He was bare to the waist in what seemed no more than a single urgent tug of his shirt. Belt and pants followed before she could even begin to delight in the broad expanse of his chest. Dressed only in navy briefs, he pulled her back into his arms. She felt as if she'd come home, after a long, lonely journey. She felt as if heaven might be no more than a kiss away.

The slow, sweet caresses gave way to more demanding touches. With unerring accuracy Todd discovered the secrets to her body. He teased boldly. He stroked with maddening tenderness. And when, at last, he claimed her, it was with a promise on his lips and in his touch. With passion exploding in a burst of rainbow colors, the promise was kept.

Again and again through the timeless night, they found new ways to communicate without words. Todd sighed in contentment as Liz lay curled against his side, her head resting on his shoulder, her hair streaming across his chest. He had known she would be like this. He had known that her sensuality would match his, that she would arouse him beyond his wildest dreams.

Time and again, he had watched her amber eyes darken with passion, lit by an internal flame. With breath held, he had watched her lazy, catlike stretches. Then, unable to resist the tempting curves, he had stroked her until her skin glowed and her body turned demanding. Sheathed in silken heat, he had found release. He had discovered commitment.

The only things he didn't find during the hours when they loved and slept and loved again were the words to tell her how he felt. He talked of love but not permanence. He blamed it on Liz's oft-spoken fear of marriage, but he knew it was his own. The commitment might be there in his heart, but the vows terrified him. They were too easily broken, the heart a long time mending.

It was only seven when he slid from the bed and took a shower. When he came back into the bedroom, a towel wrapped around his hips, Liz was awake, her eyes still heavy-lidded with sleep. She looked magnificent and incredibly tempting. Still. Always.

"You're up early," she observed.

He heard the regret in her voice and grinned. "Believe me,

I'd rather be back in that bed with you, but we need to get back to my place."

"Hank's there."

"True, but Sarah's coming back."

"Yes, of course. I'd forgotten." Her voice went flat and the fire in her eyes dimmed.

Todd went to sit on the edge of the bed. He braced his hands on either side of her and leaned down to press a kiss to lips still swollen and sensual from a night of passionate lovemaking. "What's wrong?"

"Who said anything's wrong?"

"Is it Sarah? You're not jealous of her, are you? There's no reason to be. She may be back in my life, but she is still very much the past, romantically speaking. You're my present, my future."

Her arms crept around his neck at that. Her kiss was a little desperate, demanding, hungry, even after so many others. "Make love to me, Todd. Again. I need you so."

His body responded at once to her urging. His head resisted. "We really need…"

Her lips were on his shoulders, his chest. Her hands provoked and teased until his protests died. He came alive to her touch, his arousal more urgent than even the first, his need as sharp and demanding as hers. She pulled him to her, crying out her need, seeking something more, luring him beyond past heights until tension shattered into a thousand bits of pleasure that shimmered forever before finally dimming into exhausted contentment.

"I don't think I'll ever move again," he said, sprawled on his back, Liz's leg draped across his.

"It's okay with me. I could stay this way forever."

"Probably not forever," he said practically.

"I suppose sooner or later we'd want food," she conceded.

"Maybe a little wine."

"A swim would be refreshing."

"Maybe a video, an old Katharine Hepburn-Spencer Tracy film."

She lifted herself to one elbow and grinned at him. "I've always said the excitement doesn't last. It's not even twenty-four hours and you want to rent a movie."

"I was thinking long-range. At the moment, I'd settle for one last kiss and breakfast."

"I can manage both of those."

"From you I'll take the kiss. I think we ought to get Hank and Kevin for breakfast. We'll even get Sarah and go someplace with an outdoor terrace and champagne and strawberries."

"Okay," she said agreeably, but her voice went flat on him again.

She was quiet during the breakfast they all shared at an oceanside restaurant on Key Biscayne. Though her smile was warm and intimate whenever he managed to catch her eye, she evaded most of his attempts to draw her into the conversation.

Kevin was slowly beginning to respond to Sarah, reluctantly agreeing to go for a walk along the beach with her. Todd hadn't thought it possible, but Liz went even quieter after that. Fortunately Hank kept up a nonstop conversation on business and the attributes of the various bikini-clad tourists wandering past. Both of them watched Liz uneasily, but neither of them seemed able to reach her. Not even Hank's intentionally blatant, sexist remarks could goad her into a reaction stronger than a mild frown.

To Todd's dismay, the minute they got back to his place she said she had to leave.

"I have a lot of papers to grade and lesson plans to complete," she insisted over his protests.

Troubled but unable to do anything except accept her excuses, Todd said, "I'll call you later."

"Whatever," she said, slipping into her car before he could even kiss her goodbye. He felt his stomach tie into knots as he watched her drive away.

"Hey, buddy, what was that all about?" Hank asked, waiting for him as he walked slowly back toward the house.

"I wish to hell I knew."

"Last night—?"

"Is none of your business," he snapped, heading for the terrace.

Hank followed silently. When they'd been seated for a few minutes, he said, "I'm not trying to pry, you know."

Todd felt like a louse. "Oh, hell, I know you're not. Nothing happened last night that should have sent her scurrying out of here this morning. Quite the contrary, I thought we were well on our way to a new understanding."

"It may be my fault," Sarah offered, coming to join them on the terrace.

Todd shook his head. "I asked her about that. She knows it's over between the two of us. I don't think she's jealous."

"Maybe not of you and me, but what about my relationship with Kevin? From what you've told me she's taken a special interest in him from the beginning. After losing her own child, maybe she's afraid of losing Kevin, too."

Todd groaned as the obviousness of the explanation struck him. "That has to be it. Why the hell didn't I see it?"

"Could be because you thought of yourself as the only important factor in the equation," Sarah chided. "Liz may be looking at the whole package."

"I'd better go talk to her."

Sarah shook her head. "Talking won't convince her, Todd. You're going to have to show her that she's still the most important person in your life and in Kevin's. Actions speak louder than words. It'll be easier when I'm gone."

Todd regarded Sarah with new respect. "You've changed."

She gave him a wry smile. "I told you I'd grown up. About time, don't you think?"

"Better late than never," he said, then stood up. "I think I'll go call Liz. She should be home by now."

He heard Hank's ribald comment as he went into the kitchen. Sarah chuckled. Then he heard Kevin calling out to the two of them to watch him dive into the pool. His world was nearly perfect.

Then he heard Liz's voice, his heart filled to overflowing and he knew the meaning of true contentment.

Chapter 13

As if he'd guessed the cause of her uneasiness, Todd set out to court Liz over the next few weeks. She recognized all the signs of a man intent on wooing a woman. She found flowers—tiny, delicate orchids, no less—on her desk at school, delivered mysteriously, no doubt by Kevin. Todd took her to romantic dinners in quiet, out-of-the-way restaurants. He took her on moonlit walks on the beach. And he made sure that Kevin was included in many of their outings. The lure of family was once again ensnaring her.

As the Christmas holidays neared, they went shopping together. Using Kevin as the excuse, they spent hours in toy stores, arguing over practicality and educational value versus sheer enjoyment. Todd insisted on a train. Liz picked out a talking computer that helped with spelling and reading. Todd chose a collection of battery-powered toy cars. Liz found picture-filled editions of classic books, as well. In the end it was clear that Kevin's growing pile of presents was probably as much for them as it was for him.

Two weeks before Christmas Kevin begged to get a tree.

"It's still early," Todd protested. "All the needles will fall off."

"The same tree will still be sitting on the lot a week from now," Liz countered, taking Kevin's side. "By then the needles will be in even worse shape from all that exposure to the sun."

"Tell the truth," Todd retorted with an indulgent smile. "You can't wait, either. I've seen the way your eyes light up at the mall displays. The next thing I know you're going to want to sit on Santa's knee."

She grinned back at him. "An intriguing notion. Think he'd bring me what I want?"

"Perhaps you ought to whisper it in my ear first."

"Hey, you guys, are we gonna get a tree or not?" Kevin inquired testily.

"We'll get the tree," Todd said, casting a look of regret at Liz.

It took hours. They finally found what they wanted at the fourth Christmas tree lot they went to.

"Hey, Dad, I think this is it," Kevin shouted as Liz and Todd examined a small, perfectly formed Scotch pine on the other side of the lot.

"Let's take a look at what he found."

"But this one's just fine," Todd protested.

"Come on, Scrooge."

When they rounded the corner of the last row, they found Kevin standing, hands on hips, staring up in awe at a storybook tree at least ten feet tall and so big around only the largest room would accommodate it. Liz's eyes widened.

"It's beautiful," she breathed softly.

"It's too big. We'd have to move half the furniture."

"Oh, Dad, please. I'll help with the furniture."

"We don't have nearly enough decorations."

"I'll buy some new ones," Liz offered.

Todd thew up his hands in surrender. He turned to the salesman. "I guess we'll take it."

"And the little one," Liz said.

Todd looked bewildered. "The little one? Why two?"

"For my house."

"But you're hardly ever there."

"It would seem too dreary without one."

"I'll go get it," Todd said.

They stopped off at Liz's house and decorated her tree in less than an hour. The efficient, emotionless process reminded her of all the Christmases when Ed had left the decorating to her and barely showed up long enough to exchange presents on Christmas morning. As much as she'd always loved the holidays, Ed had turned them into an ordeal to be gotten through stoically. Laura had been barely old enough to understand what was happening until that last Christmas. Liz treasured her memories of that day. Her family had come from Indiana, their last visit before the accident and before their own deaths a year later. Even Ed had been more jovial than usual, as they all shared in Laura's wide-eyed amazement.

This year held all the promise of matching that last year with her family. Excitement already teased at her senses as it had when she'd been growing up in Indiana. There was no wintry bite in the air, no pond frozen over for ice-skating, and they hadn't gone traipsing into the countryside to find the tree, but the spirit was there just the same.

On the way to Todd's they stopped to pick up extra strands of lights, colored balls and boxes of icicles for his tree. They turned the night into an impromptu tree-decorating party. Hank came with his latest date. Kevin invited a friend. Liz fixed a huge pot of shrimp gumbo. Carols played in the background throughout the evening as they fought over the proper placement of the colored lights, then on the best technique for adding icicles.

When everyone else had left and Kevin had gone to bed,

she and Todd sat on the sofa and stared at the blinking lights. "Silent Night" played softly around them.

"It's beautiful. If you squint your eyes, all the lights sort of blend together. It's like a kaleidoscope or maybe an impressionist painting," she said, curled contentedly into Todd's arms. When he didn't respond, she poked him gently with her elbow. "Hey, you, don't you think it's beautiful?"

"I don't know," he murmured, running his finger along the back of her neck. "I can't take my eyes off of you."

"Oh, Todd."

Her life, she decided, was just about perfect.

On Friday of the week before Christmas Liz was at the stove, Kevin at the kitchen table doing homework, when Todd came in through the garage. The mall had opened the week before with fireworks displays and sales to tempt even the most jaded shopper. He was simply finishing up the last minute work as the stores settled in. Already, a new project was underway. It would get into full swing the week after New Year's. Hank had already left town for the holidays to visit friends in Maine. Since it was unseasonably hot still in Miami, he had promised to bring back snow for Kevin. Liz knew that Todd had bought tickets for all three of them to go visit the snow instead. The trip was yet another surprise for Kevin. She worried that Kevin was likely to become spoiled, especially with Sarah now doing her best to win him over, but it was not something she felt comfortable discussing with Todd. The status of their relationship was still too uncertain, too impermanent.

"A man could get used to this," Todd said, dropping a kiss on her forehead as he reached into the refrigerator for a beer. He popped the top, took a sip, then lifted the lid of the pot on the stove. "Smells wonderful. What is it?"

"Seafood chowder."

"Any lobster?" he inquired, winking at her.

"Have you checked the price of lobster lately?"

"Oh, is that why you left it out?"

Liz laughed at his determined reminder of the night they'd set the lobsters free in the Keys. "Don't press your luck with me, Mr. Lewis. You'll be eating hot dogs all alone on the patio."

"There's a front moving through. It's cold on the patio."

"Exactly," she said, smacking his hand as it dipped into the salad bowl for another cherry tomato.

"Hey, Dad," Kevin interrupted. "Can you help me with this?"

"What is it?"

"It's a math assignment. You're great at math."

As Todd went to look over Kevin's shoulder, Liz felt a familiar warmth stealing through her. This was what she'd expected to have with Ed, the camaraderie, the laughter, the caring. The last few weeks had been just about perfect, the best she'd ever had. It was all getting to be far too comfortable. How much longer would Todd allow this casual situation to last? How much longer before he began pressing for something more permanent? She loved him. She'd long since admitted that, but every time she thought of marriage, she bumped straight into all of her old insecurities. He seemed to have his share of doubts, as well.

As she watched, Todd straightened, a shuttered expression on his face. "You'll get more out of it, if you try to do it yourself," he said, his tone curt.

"But, Dad," Kevin protested, as Todd threw his empty beer can into the trash can and walked through the door.

"Try, Kevin. If you still can't get it, maybe Liz will help you when she has a minute. I'm going to take a shower before dinner."

"Todd, there's time," she began, but he was already gone. She stared after him, wondering what on earth had gotten into him. He usually didn't press Kevin like that, when he knew how easily the child gave up in the face of school work that seemed beyond him. "Sweetheart, I'll help in a minute. Just let me stir the chowder."

Kevin slammed his book on the floor. "I'm going swimming."

"Kevin!"

Liz stared around the suddenly deserted kitchen. So much for a cozy evening at home.

Dinner was a tense affair. Todd looked guilty. Kevin sulked. And she foolishly tried to keep a conversation going despite it. She might as well have been talking to herself. After about twenty minutes of this strained atmosphere, Kevin asked to be excused.

"Go," Todd said tightly.

"What has gotten into you?" Liz snapped. "When you came in tonight, you were in a perfectly good mood. Now you're growling around like a bear with a thorn stuck in its paw. All Kevin did was ask for a little help with his homework. You didn't have to make a federal case out of it. You know he still has difficulty with math when it involves word problems."

He glared at her and said nothing. She scowled right back. "Don't try intimidating me, Todd Lewis. I can always leave," she said, proving the point by getting to her feet.

"That's why you like it this way, isn't it? When things get tough, you can still walk out."

Stunned by the harsh accusation, she ripped off the apron she was wearing and grabbed her purse. As she passed his chair, he caught her wrist.

"Don't go."

"Let go of me," she bit out, her teeth clenched.

"Liz, please."

She sighed. "Can you give me one single reason I should stay?"

"I want you here. I'm sorry for what I said and I'm sorry for spoiling the evening."

"I'm less concerned about having the evening spoiled than I am about what's wrong with you."

"I can't explain. It's just that sometimes my temper gets the better of me. It's as if our whole relationship is all tied up with helping Kevin. Sometimes I wonder what will happen when the school year ends and he's no longer your project."

"My project? Is that what you think this is all about?"

"Isn't it the truth? Haven't you set your life up so that it works in neat little nine-month cycles? No one kid gets too close for too long. June rolls around and there's a natural break, no messy emotional loose ends. This year it was Kevin. Sometimes I wonder if you'd put up with me at all, if you weren't so worried about him."

Liz was flabbergasted. "Todd, how can you even think that? How can you resent the fact that I care about Kevin? He's your son. He's not your competitor. I have enough love to go around."

"I know that," he said defensively. "And it's not that I resent Kevin. Hell, I don't know what it is. It was a long day."

"No longer than most and you were in a great mood when you came through the door. Please, tell me what's really wrong."

Todd's chair scraped the tiles as he shoved it back angrily. He threw his napkin on the table. "Just forget it. I'm going out for awhile."

"Leaving me here with Kevin? I don't think so. I'm not your hired babysitter, Todd." Once again she grabbed her purse off the kitchen counter and stalked through the house and out the front door, setting off the burglar alarm in the process. She heard the damn thing ringing until she turned off the street.

* * *

The next morning Liz set out at dawn to drive to the Keys. Suddenly she needed desperately to see Ann. She needed her friend's advice and warmth and the crazy exuberance of her household. She arrived while the kitchen seemed to be under siege. No one heard her knock, so she finally just walked in.

"Hi, Liz," Tracy greeted her without the slightest evidence of surprise. Tracy was the oldest of the current brood, a sixteen-year-old who'd been a victim of abuse. Ann had taken her in when she was thirteen, skinny and terrified. She had blossomed into a lovely young woman.

"Want some cereal? Juice?" she asked.

"Just coffee, if there's any made."

"Sure thing. Have a seat if you can find one. Josh, you're through. Move it and give Liz your chair."

"That's okay. I can stand for awhile. It's a long drive."

Josh grinned at her. Dark-haired and dark-eyed, he had been sullen and difficult when he'd arrived, sent to Ann as an alternative to becoming enmeshed in the juvenile justice system. It had taken the better part of a year for Ann to penetrate his brooding moods and show him that there were more positive ways of getting attention than breaking the law.

"You'd better sit," he advised. "Tracy's decided she's boss for the day. She gets nasty if we don't follow her orders."

Liz found herself grinning, despite the weight that seemed to have lodged in her chest the night before. "Then by all means, I'll sit. Is Ann around?"

"Last time I saw her she was trying to persuade Melissa to give up her blanket long enough for it to be washed," Josh said as Tracy handed Liz a mug of coffee. "I've got to get out of here to cut the grass before soccer practice. I'll go look for her."

"Thanks, Josh." She pushed cereal bowls and dirty glasses

out of the way, so there'd be room for the coffee mug. Once she'd been settled, the other kids still at the table seemed to forget all about her. She sat quietly and let the noisy teasing ebb and flow around her. Even when tempers flared it was all so alive, so filled with energy and joy. It made her own house seem even quieter.

A few minutes later, Ann breezed into the room, dropped a kiss on Liz's forehead and set about hurrying all the children out the door to do their various chores. "Tracy, watch the little ones. Try to see that they don't fall in the ocean and drown."

She fixed herself a cup of tea, then sat down. "So, what brings you to visit so early on Saturday morning?"

"I just felt like a drive."

Ann directed a sharp look at her. "You hate traveling on U.S. 1 almost as much as I hated living in Miami. Try another one on me."

"It's Todd."

"You're in love with him?"

Liz nodded, not at all surprised that Ann had guessed. That's what Liz loved about her. She was smart and intuitive. Also, she wasted no words, just offered a blunt summation that zeroed in on the heart of the problem.

"And that's a problem? Why? It's about time you admitted it. I've known it for weeks now."

"That's because you're an objective observer. I've been fighting it."

"Are you crazy? He's gorgeous, generous, sensitive and he loves you. Or doesn't he?" She shook her head. "I don't know what I'm bothering to ask for. He's just as starry-eyed as you are."

"He says he does."

Ann put her elbows on the table and leaned forward. "Okay, Liz, that's enough double-talk. Sweetheart, I'm a psychologist, not a mind reader. So far, everything you've said adds up to bliss. You don't look blissful."

"I'm miserable. There's something he's not telling me. We had this huge fight last night, because he wouldn't be straight with me. Maybe he's still in love with his ex-wife. Maybe he just can't figure out a way to break it to me."

"Didn't you tell me that you played hostess to her at Thanksgiving? Living with a zillion kids under the age of eighteen, I may not be up on all the current social graces, but I sincerely doubt that Todd would have had the two of you in the same room if he were still hot for his ex."

"I don't think he was...then."

"Has anything happened to suggest he's changed his mind. Is he making late-night calls to her? Has he taken off on any unexplained business trips? Found any lipstick on his collar?"

Liz laughed despite her gloomy mood. "When you put it that way, it does seem pretty farfetched. That still doesn't explain this weird mood he's been in. Last night Kevin asked for help with his homework and the next thing I knew Todd had stomped out of the kitchen. Nothing I said or did made any difference. He wouldn't talk about it."

Ann seemed to go perfectly still. "I see."

"Well, dammit, I don't see."

"Did you try to talk to him about it?"

"Yes. He just snapped my head off. He went on some crazy tirade about me making Kevin my project for the year. He thinks I'm already gearing up to get the two of them out of my life."

"Any truth to that?"

"No. It took me a long time to admit I loved him. I sure as hell don't want to walk away from him now."

"Then why aren't you in Miami working this out with him, instead of down here talking to me."

Liz managed a wavering grin. "Because you don't yell at me."

Ann grinned back. "Stick around."

"On second thought, I seem to feel this desperate need to head north."

"Smart decision." She reached over and held Liz's hand. "Talk. Don't attack. Secrets are rarely revealed when everyone's yelling at the top of their lungs."

She turned a penetrating gaze on Ann. A couple of earlier comments suddenly clicked. "Do you know something about this?"

"I didn't say that. I was speaking in generalities."

Liz shook her head slowly. "I don't buy that for a minute. And the only reason I won't press you on it is because I know all the rules about confidentiality."

She waited for some indication that her noble restraint had hit its mark. Ann only repeated, "Talk to him. He'll come around. And no matter what, remember the stakes. Good love is hard to find."

"Maybe I should just hang around here. You're supposed to see him today, aren't you? Doesn't Kevin have an appointment?"

"He did. Todd called a little while before you got here to cancel."

"Oh, hell."

Ann shrugged resignedly. "One missed appointment is not the end of the world. In fact, right now, I'd suggest you leave that subject alone. Stick to what's happening between you and Todd, for once. He may need to know he comes first with you."

Liz thought about Ann's advice all the way home. An hour later she had just gotten out of the tub, when the doorbell rang. She wrapped herself in a terry-cloth robe, wound a towel around her wet hair and peered through the peephole. Todd was standing on the doorstep, his expression subdued.

"Can you give me one good reason to open this door?" she said, though there wasn't much anger behind the taunt.

"I love you."

Her remaining irritation slid away. "Not bad," she said, swinging open the door. "What'll you do for an encore?"

He pulled her into his arms and slanted his mouth across hers. His tongue teased. His rough hands slid inside her robe and caressed her breasts, his thumbs rubbing the nipples until they hardened into sensitive buds. Liz melted. Her knees went limp and she clung to him.

"Don't ever walk out on me again," he pleaded, his voice hoarse and urgent. "Please."

"I'm sorry. It was a cowardly thing to do. I should have stayed so we could talk it out. Can we do it now?"

"Not right now, Liz. I want to take you away. I want to go someplace where it's just the two of us, someplace where we can concentrate on us."

Ann's comments echoed through her mind. "Does this sudden desire to get away have to do with what you said earlier about our needs getting all twisted up with Kevin's?"

"Partly. Mostly, though, there are things I want you to know about me, things I haven't been able to tell you before."

"And we need to go away for you to be able to do that?" she said, puzzled.

Todd's mouth curved into a rueful expression. "Maybe I just want you to be someplace where you can't run away so easily."

"There's nothing you can say that would be so awful that I'd run from you."

"I'd like to believe that, Liz. God knows I need to believe that."

"You can," she said, increasingly concerned by his odd mood. "I love you. I'm scared, especially knowing that there is some secret between us, but that doesn't mean I intend to run from my feelings or from yours."

"Wait before you say that. Wait until you know everything."

"We're all going away next week."

"That's just it, we're all going."

"Don't you think we'll be able to find time alone?"

"I suppose."

"Todd, we'll make the time. That's a promise."

He held her then, the embrace surprisingly desperate. The renewed certainty that there were emotions plaguing Todd that threatened their happiness scared her to death. Suddenly the entire holiday season, which she'd been anticipating with such excitement, seemed threatening. Would they still be together beyond the New Year?

Chapter 14

Liz's growing despair almost ruined the holidays for her. She was terrified to let herself feel too much for fear it was all going to be snatched away from her again. She wrapped presents for Todd and Kevin and went to parties with her coworkers and Todd's friends with a vague but no less disquieting sense that it was all for the last time. Her mood communicated itself to Todd and he grew increasingly quiet.

In the already tense atmosphere, it wasn't surprising that they got into frequent quarrels over inconsequential things. The bickering escalated into a full-scale battle when she asked about inviting his family to spend Christmas Day with them. She knew they lived in Boca Raton, but very little else.

"Wouldn't they like to be here on Christmas morning? They could drive down on Christmas Eve. There's plenty of room for them."

"No."

"Todd, it's Christmas. Families should be together."

"Not mine."

"Tell me why."

"It's none of your damned business why. The point is I don't want them here. Now stop bugging me about it." He stalked out of the house, slamming the door behind him.

Furious and hurt, she turned around to see Kevin standing on the terrace, his whole body shaking. "Is Dad leaving?"

Liz was shocked by the panic in his eyes, the absolute terror that radiated from him. "You mean for good?"

He nodded, still trembling. She knelt down and gathered him close. "Oh, sweetheart, of course not. I just upset him. That's all. He'll be back."

"When he and Mom fought, she didn't come back."

"This is very different."

"You asked him about my grandparents, didn't you?" he said.

"Yes." She wondered at his oddly accusing tone.

"You shouldn't have done that. He doesn't like them. They came here once and he yelled at them. They didn't ever come back."

Liz sighed. Another secret. Would they never end? Could they survive them?

Despite her doubts and fears, on Christmas Eve she gave herself a stern lecture on wasting the moment. She determinedly allowed herself to indulge in the luxury of being part of a family again. She set out to make the night special. If it was going to end, it would be with only the best of memories.

After a dinner in a favorite neighborhood restaurant, they drove to see the gigantic Christmas tree in Bayfront Park. Kevin could hardly contain himself. He'd been convinced that no tree could possibly be bigger than theirs. They followed that with a visit to a house near Todd's that put on an annual display of holiday scenes complete with animated figures and enough lights to dazzle children of all ages. Kevin was enchanted. Liz felt her own spirits rise.

The transformation was almost complete by the time they went to a midnight service. Stars glittered brightly. The air, though hardly wintry, had turned brisk enough for sweaters and jackets. At the church they were surrounded by people she had come to know or at least recognize over the past few months of being at Todd's. With the Nativity acted out in front of the candlelit altar, she found herself slowly responding to the carols and the joyous atmosphere. She left the service with a renewed sense of hope.

Getting Kevin to bed was the toughest task of the night. He no longer believed in Santa Claus, but that didn't prevent him from wanting to lurk about in the living room just in case the old guy showed up. When he'd finally been convinced that leaving cookies and milk on the coffee table would be incentive enough for Santa or whatever elves were delivering the presents, he went to bed. Todd and Liz spent the next two hours assembling the train set under the tree.

Drinking eggnog and arguing over the arrangement of the village prolonged the process.

"I'm the developer. I know all about land use," Todd grumbled.

"I want the church next to the train station," Liz insisted.

"Have you ever been to a train station? They're always in the worst part of town."

"All the more reason ours should have something beautiful nearby." She grinned. "Besides, they both need an electrical connection and we only have one."

Todd groaned. "So much for urban planning."

On Christmas morning Kevin was up by five-thirty. Todd sent him straight back to bed again, but by six, he'd given up. Half asleep, he and Liz sat on the sofa and watched as Kevin's excitement mounted with each present. Hugs were doled out with enthusiastic frequency. Squeals of delight mingled with the sound of the train whistle and cars racing across the tile floor. It had been years since Liz had heard so much noise at that hour of the morning. The nostalgia choked her. The reality made her feel complete.

Kevin had done his own Christmas shopping. He had found lace-edged handkerchiefs embroidered with her monogram. He was practically bouncing up and down on the sofa, as she opened them. "See," he enthused, "they're just like the ones you always have in school."

"They're lovely. The perfect present."

"Now mine," Todd said, handing her a large box.

When she ripped away the paper, she saw the name of an exclusive boutique in Mayfair, an elegant collection of shops in the heart of Coconut Grove.

"Todd," she protested, her fingers caressing the embossed gold foil label. Even the label was probably fourteen-karat gold, she thought nervously.

"Don't say a word until you've opened it. It's something I wanted you to have and I won't take no for an answer."

Inside, amidst layers of tissue paper, she found the most beautiful dress she'd ever seen. Ankle-length green satin, it was draped to leave one shoulder bare. The single strap was held together with a rhinestone clasp. At least she hoped those were only rhinestones glittering up at her. It was elegant, sexy and totally impractical for a schoolteacher.

"Wow!" Kevin said.

"You said it," she said in an awed whisper.

"Put it on," Kevin said. "I want to see."

She shook her head. "I can't. Todd, it's lovely, but I'll never…"

"You will," he said adamantly. "Remember we have a date in Maine for New Year's Eve and that's the dress I want you to wear."

* * *

Although Liz had worried about the extravagance, the trip to Maine was exactly the vacation they all needed. With snow on the ground, a huge fireplace in the lodge and nothing to do all day but enjoy the spectacular scenery, ski a little or simply sit back and read all the books she'd put aside during the fall school term, Liz was in heaven.

On New Year's Eve afternoon she was almost finished with a Pulitzer Prize-winning biography, when Todd came back from taking Kevin to town for a new pair of ski boots to replace the ones he'd outgrown. He leaned down to kiss her.

"Umm, nice," she observed, "but your nose is cold."

"So's the rest of me. Care to warm me up?"

"It's the middle of the afternoon and your son is in the next room."

"No, he's not. Hank and his date took him for the rest of the day."

"What a wonderful friend," she noted.

"I thought you'd think so."

"Sometimes I wonder if we'd ever have a moment alone, if it weren't for Hank."

"I think we owe it to him to make his sacrifice worthwhile," he said, pulling her into his arms. His hands were already sliding under her sweater to caress and tease.

"Absolutely," she concurred, fumbling with the zipper on his jacket.

It took far more time to disrobe in the icy climate, but the loss of time was more than compensated for with the heightened sense of anticipation. As layers were peeled away and kisses stolen, the sweet tension mounted in Liz. Even before Todd had her clothes off and cast aside, he had teased her to a shattering climax.

"Not fair," she murmured, clinging to him and seeking the

masculine nipples that were buried in swirls of dark blond hair that matted his chest.

"You didn't enjoy that?" he said, groaning himself as her tongue teased the hard little bud.

"I wanted you with me, inside me."

"It doesn't always have to be that way. Sometimes I just want to give you pleasure. I want you to take everything I can offer you and let me watch as you reach the crest."

"Then let me do the same," she said, drawing him down in front of the fire, her hands already at work, stroking the supple muscles that spanned his chest, the flat plane of his belly with its tiny, sensitive indentation. Her tongue flicked in and out in a sensual rhythm that had Todd already breathing hard by the time she reached lower. At her sure, insistent touch, he moaned with pleasure.

"I see what you mean," he said on a ragged sigh. "I want you with me."

A slow smile spread across her face. "I'm right here," she said and settled on him, riding him with wild abandon until they both reached a destination far beyond their dreams.

They were lying together on the rug in front of the fire, still bathed in the afterglow of lovemaking that grew more satisfying each time they were in each other's arms, when Todd murmured, "What did you do today?"

"You mean before this?"

"Umm."

"It wasn't nearly as interesting."

"Tell me anyway."

"I was reading." She described the biography. "The writer is excellent and the man it's about is someone I think you'd really admire. You ought to read it, when I'm finished. It's fascinating."

She felt Todd's arms stiffen at once. Twisting, she scanned his face. "What's wrong?"

He sighed heavily and released her. "I suppose now is as good a time as any to tell you."

Cold without his arms around her, she reached for a blanket. Her heart thudded ominously. "Tell me what?"

"I can't read the book, Liz," he said bluntly. "I can't read any book. At least not easily. I'm dyslexic. Ann's done a little work with me over the last couple of months and coupled with what I've managed to do myself, I'm a little better, but it will always be a struggle."

She saw the uncertainty written all over his face, the fear that his announcement was going to change something between them. That vulnerability broke her heart. At the same time, she felt betrayed. He'd kept something so basic about himself from her, something that would have told her so much about him and about his protectiveness of Kevin. The fact that he hadn't trusted her with his secret hurt. Worse, she realized now that Ann had known. That only compounded her feeling that for all the love he'd professed, Todd hadn't loved her enough.

"Why didn't you feel you could tell me?" she asked, her heart aching.

"I was afraid it would change things. When you and I met, I was still in a lot of pain over Sarah's rejection. I was convinced that she'd turned away from Kevin and from me because we were less than perfect. I know it sounds crazy, especially after the way she's been acting lately, but that's the way I felt at the time. I couldn't bear the thought of losing you the same way."

"But you told Ann."

"I didn't tell her, at least not willingly. She guessed that very first day we went down there."

That didn't make her feel any better. "My God, I must have been blind," she said pulling away and going to get a robe. When she was covered, she sat huddled in a chair and went over all the signs she'd missed before.

"That's why you never helped Kevin with his homework," she said. "Why you got so angry that night he asked you to look at his math. Those were word problems."

He nodded.

"And that's why you never looked at your mail when I was around. That's why Hank was usually the one who went over the terms of your contracts, rather than the other way around. It never made sense before that you were in charge, that you made the business decisions, but he worked on the contracts. He knows, too."

"Don't say it like he's part of some conspiracy. We grew up together. He's always known. I'm not sure I'd have gotten through high school without Hank. In his way, he coached me through it as best he could."

Liz felt numb. "I want to go home," she said. "I have a lot of thinking to do."

Todd's expression hardened. "I knew this would happen. It's the reason I didn't tell you sooner. I knew you'd walk away from me."

She shook her head. "I'm not walking away because you're dyslexic, Todd. That's something you couldn't help. I admire the way you've overcome it, the way you've gone on to make a success of yourself despite the difficulties. I'm leaving because I can't stay in a relationship without trust. It just won't work. I'm going home."

With the same stoic expression she'd seen all too often on Kevin's face, Todd nodded and left her alone to pack. No protests. No pleas. Just calm acceptance, as if he'd known all along what her decision would be.

In a daze, she called the airlines, made a reservation for the next flight back to Miami and packed her bags. She was getting ready to call for a bellboy, when there was a knock on the door.

"Liz, it's Hank. Can we talk?"

Reluctantly, she opened the door. "I'm running late. I have a cab waiting."

"If you're determined to go, I'll drive you. We can talk on the way."

"I don't think so. I'm not sure I can bear to listen to a lengthy defense of what Todd has done. Whatever you want to say, say it here."

"Dammit, what exactly has he done? He hasn't lied or cheated or betrayed you. Not really. He's acted human. He held back a part of himself that was less than perfect because he was afraid it would change the way you felt about him. Now you're proving him right. You're leaving. I thought you were different. We both did."

"Dammit, I told him I'm not going because he has difficulty reading. I'm going because he didn't trust me enough to tell me."

"If every person you'd ever really loved had abandoned you and you were convinced that they'd all done it because you couldn't live up to their expectations, would you openly admit it to the next person who came along? Especially when you could manage to cover up the flaw? Is what Todd did any different from a woman who wears makeup to disguise a birthmark for fear that it will scare off a potential suitor? Is that a lie? Or what about the woman who wears a certain style of clothes not because they're stylish but because they hide a flaw in her figure. Sure, sooner or later the truth comes out. If the relationship grows the man sees the birthmark or the heavy thighs or the small bust, but by then he's also gotten to know the person inside that flawed body."

"But if the man was so superficial that the birthmark or thighs or the size of the bustline would have scared him away, is that the sort of man she should want?"

"Liz, in the beginning most relationship are superficial. They're based on all sorts of preconceived notions of what we expect true beauty or intelligence or sensitivity to be. There are very few of us who don't try to minimize our flaws and emphasize our good qualities, when we meet people for the first time. Hell, when you go on a job interview, your resumé covers all the successes. You don't spend a hell of a lot of time discussing the classes you almost failed or the fact that four days out of five you couldn't afford to dress in the suit you chose for the interview."

"Then you think that what Todd did was okay?"

"I think it was human. Has he ever told you the way his parents treated him? Did he ever explain how his brilliant father, a man at the top of the legal profession, turned his back on him once he'd decided Todd would never be able to get through law school?"

"That's why he doesn't see his parents?" she said in a shaky voice.

"Yes. They gave up on him, too. Imagine what that does to a kid in his teens when he's already struggling with just growing up. Then his wife walks out, too. Probably not for the same reason, but it's another rejection just the same. Is it any wonder he's cautious with the truth? Just promise me you'll try to see it from his point of view. The man's nuts about you."

"You're a good friend, Hank. I'm glad he's always had you to make up for the losses, to stand by him. He told me what you did for him in school."

Hank feigned shock, allowing a tiny flicker of amusement to spark in his eyes. "He didn't. He promised he would never tell about that date I arranged for him."

Liz laughed. "Still can't admit it, can you?"

"Admit what?"

"That you're a terrific guy."

"I know *that*. I thought you wanted me to tell you what happened on the date."

"Get out of here, Hank."

"On my way."

At the door he stopped and looked back. "You'll never find a finer man, Liz. And I doubt if there will ever be one who'll love you more."

She sighed. "I know that. I'm just not sure it's enough."

All the way to the airport, she thought about what Hank had said. She recalled the look in Todd's eyes when he'd told her the truth, that mixture of hope and anxiety. And then she remembered the despair when she'd done exactly as he'd anticipated and turned away from him. The horrible lump in her throat seemed to grow larger with each mile she put between her and Todd.

"Turn the cab around," she finally told the driver.

"You forget something? You'll never make your flight, if we go back."

"I almost forgot the most important thing of all," she said. "And if I don't go back, I may lose it forever."

He shrugged, obviously used to impulsive, scatterbrained tourists. "It's your nickel on the meter, lady."

When she got back to the hotel, she made sure that Todd was out of the room before going back. Once inside, she showered and changed into the green gown he'd given her for Christmas. She was just putting the finishing touches on her hair when she heard the door to the room open.

Todd came in and sank down into the chair in front of the fireplace. She'd never seen him look quite so sad, so utterly defeated. Knowing that she was responsible made her heart ache.

Taking a deep breath, she put a smile on her face and stepped into the room. When Todd looked up and saw her, his shock registered in his eyes.

"I thought you'd left," he said cautiously.

"I had. I came back."

"Why?"

"It's New Year's Eve and I had this date I didn't want to miss."

"Anyone I know?"

"I'm not sure. He's tall, handsome, incredibly sexy and quite possibly the nicest man I've ever known."

"Sounds like a helluva guy. What happens after tonight? Do you have any plans?"

"That's up to my date."

Todd didn't even attempt to hide the anguish she'd put him through. Not even the teasing lightened his mood. "Liz, I can't take you walking out on me again. If you don't plan to stay, go now."

"Like I said, what happens next is up to you."

She saw the heat flare in his eyes, the first hint of hope. "You could start by taking off the dress," he suggested.

She allowed herself a slight chuckle. "Oh, no, you don't. I just put it on."

He stood up and came closer. He ran one finger along the low-cut neckline, leaving a trail of fire across her skin. "There's not much to it," he observed. "How much trouble could it be to take it off, then put it back on again? I'll even help."

"What a guy!"

He reached around her and worked the zipper down. The slow rasp sent shivers along the curve of her spine. "I love you," he whispered, kissing the hollow at the base of her neck. "I missed you."

"I was only gone for an hour or so."

"But it could have been a lifetime."

"I'd have come to my senses sooner or later."

"What made you change your mind?"

"Something Hank said."

"Hank came to talk to you about me? What did he say?"

"He said I'd never meet a finer man."

"Probably true," he teased immodestly.

"He said no one would ever love me more."

"Definitely true."

"He also mentioned something about a date he arranged for you."

"He what?"

"That, of course, was the clincher. Hank Riley is not going to direct your social life."

"Does that mean you're going to take me out of circulation?"

"I suppose I'll have to."

"Quite a sacrifice you're willing to make."

"Keep it in mind, when you're taking out the trash. That should even things up rather nicely."

He sighed. "I can't believe New Year's Eve is actually working out the way I'd planned. You're here. You're wearing the dress I'd imagined you in." He glanced down at the pool of green satin at her feet. "Well, almost wearing it, anyway. It seems like there was something else."

"Something else?"

"The ring. There's supposed to be a ring."

"An engagement ring? You actually have an engagement ring?"

"I have a wedding ring, too, but Hank's holding on to that. I didn't want to lose it before the wedding. Thank goodness he didn't mention that while he was trying to be persuasive."

"My head seems to be spinning here. What exactly did you have in mind for tonight?"

"Just the proposal. I figured we'd have to wait for the wedding."

"I'm glad you realized that. It takes time to plan a wedding."

"Oh, it's all planned. I just couldn't figure out how to get you to the church without telling you what I was up to."

"You were incredibly confident, weren't you?"

"Not for a minute, sweetheart. I've been praying since the day we met."

Epilogue

The late afternoon sunlight streaming in the nursery window cast a golden shadow over the room he and Hank had added to the house barely in the nick of time. Fascinated, Todd stood in the doorway feeling his chest constrict in awe at the sight of Liz seated in the old-fashioned rocker, breast bared as their baby suckled, one tiny hand resting on the creamy mound.

"How are my two girls today?" he asked softly, not wanting to disturb the age-old serenity of the intimate moment between mother and child, but needing to feel a part of it.

Liz lifted her head and smiled. The radiance of that smile lit the room, welcoming him. "Why not come and see for yourself. Your daughter is a greedy little thing. She must have gotten it from you."

"I'd trade places with her in a minute," he said in a choked voice. His eyes met Liz's and caught the smoldering heat that always set him on fire.

They had been married more than a year now and that sharp pang of desire hadn't diminished. If anything, the intensity of his feelings had grown, almost overwhelming him at times. His life was fuller, richer than he'd ever imagined possible.

As he watched, Liz put the baby over her shoulder, patted her back, then held her up for him to take. Amy smelled of talcum powder and felt a little bit like heaven in his arms. He wondered if he'd ever taken the time to enjoy Kevin as much when he was an infant and Sarah had still been there to care for him. Probably not. It was only after she'd gone that he'd grown truly close to his son.

"Maybe she'll actually nap long enough for me to get a decent dinner on the table," Liz said hopefully, fastening her blouse.

"I can think of better ways to spend the time," he said, holding the baby in the crook of his arm and grinning suggestively at his wife.

"Kevin will be home from baseball practice in twenty minutes."

"Clock-watcher," he chided.

"It's a good thing one of us is."

"There's still time for a shower."

"Only if you take it alone."

"Surely there's something we can manage in twenty minutes."

She came to stand beside him as he put the baby into her crib. Her arm looped around his waist and she leaned against him, soft and warm and desirable. "We can stand here and admire our handiwork."

He felt a familiar silly grin of satisfaction slip into place. "We did do a good job, didn't we? Amy is quite possibly the most beautiful baby ever born. She will no doubt grow up to be Miss America." He brushed a light, hopeful kiss across Liz's lips. "Want to see if we can do it again?"

"Oh, beautiful or not, I think one baby in diapers at a time is quite enough, thank you very much. Why don't we go into the kitchen and try to get your mind on other things."

"My mind has rarely been on other things since I met you."

"And here I thought Hank was the one with the overactive libido."

"Speaking of Hank, we had a meeting today. We had to make some decisions about the jobs we have lined up. We decided he'd take the one down in the Keys. He'll be down there for the next few months until the mall is complete."

"Is he going to commute?"

"Not if he can help it. It's pretty far down. He'd even be better off in Key West, if he has to commute from someplace. He's looking for a house or condo to rent for four or five months. Unfortunately, it's the height of the tourist season, so he's not having a lot of luck. Everything's either booked or outrageously expensive."

He caught a sudden gleam of mischief in Liz's eyes. "I recognize that look. What are you thinking?"

"What about Ann's place?"

"What about it?"

"It's only a few miles from the mall. He could stay there. A couple of the kids could double up for a short time."

"Hank hates kids."

Liz grinned. "So he says."

Todd began to understand the perverse scheme that was forming in his wife's devious mind. "Ann's far too independent, far too opinionated," he noted with a glimmer of satisfaction. "She'd drive him crazy. They fought all through the wedding rehearsal."

"Exactly."

"I love it. Think she'll go along with it, though? She called him a chauvinistic jerk at the reception."

"All we have to do is explain how lonely he is, how

desperate for a place to stay. Ann has never turned down a stray in her life, especially one in need of reforming."

Todd's laughter boomed through the house. The baby whimpered. He fought to control his delighted reaction to the prospect of Hank Riley and Ann Davies in close proximity.

"I give 'em twenty-four hours."

Liz shook her head solemnly, though her eyes flashed with amusement. "I'm betting on a lifetime."

* * * * *

HOME ON THE RANCH

USA TODAY Bestselling Author
Allison Leigh

ALLISON LEIGH

started writing early, with a Halloween play that her grade-school class performed. Since then, though her tastes have changed, her love for reading has not. And her writing appetite simply grows more voracious by the day.

She has been a finalist for a RITA® Award and a Holt Medallion. But she feels most rewarded as a writer when she receives word from a reader that they laughed, cried or lost a night of sleep while reading one of her books.

Born in Southern California, Allison has lived in several different cities in four different states. She has been, at one time or another, a cosmetologist, a computer programmer and a secretary. She has recently begun writing full-time after spending nearly a decade as an administrative assistant for a busy neighborhood church. She currently makes her home in Arizona with her family and loves to hear from her readers, who can write to her at P.O. Box 40772, Mesa, AZ 85274-0772.

Chapter 1

"He is not an ogre."

Belle Day flicked her windshield wipers up to frenzied and tightened her grip around the steering wheel of her Jeep. She focused harder on the unfamiliar road, slowing even more to avoid the worst of the flooding, muddy ruts.

It wasn't the weather, or the road, or the unfamiliar drive that had her nerves in a noose, though. It was the person waiting at the end of the drive.

"He is *not* an ogre." Stupid talking to herself. She'd have to keep that to a minimum when she arrived. Not that she did it all the time.

Only when she was nervous.

Why had she agreed to this?

Her tire hit a dip her searching gaze had missed, and the vehicle rocked, the steering wheel jerking violently in her grip. She exhaled roughly and considered pulling over, but discarded the idea. The sooner she got to the Lazy-B, the sooner she could leave.

Not exactly positive thinking, Belle. Why are you doing this?

Her fingers tightened a little more on the wheel. "Lucy," she murmured. Because she wanted to help young Lucy Buchanan. Wanted to help her badly enough to put up with Lucy's father, Cage.

Who was not an ogre. Just because the therapist she was replacing had made enough complaints about her brief time here that they'd found a way through Weaver's grapevine didn't mean *her* experience would be similar.

That's not the only reason. She ignored the whispered thought. The road curved again, and she saw the hooked tree Cage had told her to watch for. Another quarter mile to go.

At least the ruts in the road were smoothing out and she stopped worrying so much about bouncing off into the ditch. The rain was still pouring down, though. Where the storm had come from after weeks of bone-dry weather, she had no idea. Maybe it had been specially ordered up to provide an auspicious beginning to her task.

She shook her head at the nonsense running through it, and slowed before the quarter-mile mark. It was raining and that was a good thing for a state that had been too dry for too long. She finally turned off the rutted road.

The gate that greeted her was firmly closed. She studied it for a moment, but of course the thing didn't magically open simply because she wished it.

She let out a long breath, pushed open the door and dashed into the rain. Her tennis shoes slid on the slick mud and she barely caught herself from landing on her butt. By the time she'd unhooked the wide, swinging gate, she was drenched. She drove through, then got out again and closed it. And then, because she couldn't possibly get *any* wetter unless she jumped in a river, she peered through the sheet of rain at Cage Buchanan's home.

It was hardly an impressive sight. Small. No frills. A porch ran across the front of the house, only partially softening the brick dwelling. But the place did look sturdy, as the rain sluiced from the roof, gushing out the gutter spouts.

She slicked back her hair and climbed into her Jeep once more to drive the rest of the way. She parked near the front of the house. Despite the weather, the door was open, but there was a wooden screen. She couldn't see much beyond it, though.

She grabbed her suitcase with one wet hand before shoving out of the Jeep, then darted up the narrow edge of porch steps not covered by a wheelchair ramp. A damp golden retriever sat up to greet her, thumping his tail a few times.

"You the guard dog?" Belle let the curious dog sniff her hand as she skimmed the soles of her shoes over the edge of one of the steps. The rain immediately turned the clumps of mud into brick-red rivulets that flowed down over the steps. Beneath the protection of the porch overhang, she wiped her face again, and flicked her hair behind her shoulders. Of all days not to put it in a ponytail. She couldn't have arrived looking more pathetic if she'd tried.

She knocked on the frame of the screen door, trying not to be obvious about peering inside and trying to pretend she wasn't shivering. Even sopping wet, she wasn't particularly cold. Which meant the shivers were mostly nerves and she hated that.

She knocked harder. The dog beside her gave a soft *woof.*

"Ms. Day!" A young, cheerful voice came from inside the door, then Belle saw Lucy wheel into view. "The door's open. Better leave Strudel outside, though."

"Strudel, huh?" Belle gave the dog a sympathetic pat. "Sorry, fella." She went inside, ignoring another rash of shivers that racked through her. It was a little harder to ignore Strudel's faint whine when she closed the screen on him, though.

She set her suitcase on the wood-planked floor, taking in

the interior of the house with a quick glance. Old-fashioned furnishings dominated mostly by a fading cabbage rose print. An antique-looking upright piano sat against one wall, an older model TV against the other. The room was clean but not overly tidy, except for the complete lack of floor coverings. Not even a scatter rug to quiet the slow drip of water puddling around her.

She looked at the girl who was the reason for her water-logged trek. "Your hair has grown." Too thin, she thought. And too pale. But Lucy's blue eyes sparkled and her golden hair gleamed.

Lucy dimpled and ran a hand down the braid that rested over her thin shoulder. "It's dry, too. Come on. We'll get you some towels." She turned her chair with practiced movements.

Belle quickly followed. Her tennis shoes gave out a wet squeak with each step. They were considerably louder than the soft turn of Lucy's wheelchair.

She glanced through to the kitchen when they passed it. Empty. More than a few dishes sat stacked in the white sink. The stove looked ancient but well preserved.

"This is my room." Lucy waved a hand as she turned her chair on a dime, stopping toward the end of the hall, unadorned except for a bookshelf weighted down with paperbacks. "Used to be Dad's, but we switched 'cause of the stairs." She smiled mischievously. "Now I have my own bathroom."

Belle's gaze drifted to the staircase. "And up there was your old room?"

"Yeah, but the bathroom's in the hall. Not the same. There's an empty room up there, though. You don't have to sleep, like, on the couch or nothing."

Belle smiled. "I know. Your dad told me I'd have my own room." She hoped the two upstairs rooms were at least at opposite ends of the hall.

She walked into Lucy's bedroom. It may have been temporarily assigned because of Lucy's situation, but it bore no sign that it had ever been anything but a twelve-year old girl's bedroom. There was pink…everywhere. Cage had even painted the walls pale pink. And in those rare places where there wasn't pink, there was purple. Shiny, glittery purple.

Hiding her thoughts, she winked cheerfully at Lucy and squished into the bathroom where the towels were—surprise, surprise—pink with purple stripes. As she bent over hurriedly scrubbing her hair between a towel to take the worst of the moisture out, she heard the roll of Lucy's chair. "Is your dad around?" She couldn't put off meeting with him forever, after all. He *was* employing her. He'd hired her to provide both the physical therapy his daughter needed following a horse-back-riding accident several months ago, and the tutoring she needed to make up for the months of school she'd missed as a result.

Lucy didn't answer and she straightened, flinging the towel around her shoulders, turning. "Lucy? Oh."

Six plus feet of rangy muscle stood there, topped by sharply carved features, bronze hair that would be wavy if he let it grow beyond two inches and eyes so pale a blue they were vaguely heart stopping.

"I guess you are." She pushed her lips into a smile that, not surprisingly, Cage Buchanan didn't return. He'd hired her out of desperation, and they both knew it.

After all, he loathed the ground she walked.

"You drove out here in this weather."

Her smile stiffened even more. In fact, a sideways glance at the mirror over the sink told her the stretch of her lips didn't much qualify for even a stiff smile. "So it would seem." It was easier to look beyond him at Lucy, so that's what she did. "Sooner we get started, the better. Right Lucy?"

For the first time, Belle saw Lucy's expression darken. The girl's lips twisted and she looked away.

So, chalk one up for the efficiency of Weaver's grapevine again. Judging by the girl's expression, the rumor about Lucy's attitude toward her physical therapy was true.

Belle looked back at Cage. She knew he'd lived on the Lazy-B his entire life. Had been running it, so the stories went, since he'd been in short pants.

Yet she could count their encounters in person on one hand.

None of the occasions had been remotely pleasant.

Belle had had her first personal encounter with Cage before Lucy's accident over the issue of Lucy going on a school field trip to Chicago. Lucy had been the only kid in her class who hadn't been allowed to go on the weeklong trip. Belle—as the newest school employee—had been drafted into chaperone service and had foolishly thought she'd be able to talk Cage into changing his mind.

She'd been wrong. He'd accused her of being interfering and flatly told her to stay out of his business.

It had not been pleasant.

Had she learned her lesson, though? Had she given up the need to *somehow* give something back to his family? No.

Which only added to her tangle of feelings where Cage Buchanan was concerned. Feelings that had existed long before she'd come to Weaver six months ago with great chunks of her life pretty much in tatters.

"Did you bring a suitcase?"

She nodded. "I, um, left it by the front door."

He inclined his head a few degrees and his gaze drifted impassively down her wet form. "I'll take it upstairs for you."

"I can—" But he'd already turned on his heel, walking away. Soundless, even though he was wearing scuffed cowboy boots with decidedly worn-down heels.

If she hadn't had a stepfamily full of men who walked

with the same soundless gait, she'd have spent endless time wondering how he could move so quietly.

She looked back at Lucy and smiled. A real one. She'd enjoyed Lucy from the day they'd met half a year ago in the P.E. class Belle had been substitute teaching. And she'd be darned if she'd let her feelings toward the sweet girl be tainted by the past. "So, that's a lot of ribbons and trophies on that shelf over there." She gestured at the far wall and headed toward it, skirting the pink canopied bed. "Looks like you've been collecting them for a lot of years. What are they all for?"

"State Fair. 4-H." Lucy rolled her chair closer.

Belle plucked one small gold trophy off the shelf. "And this one?"

"Last year's talent contest."

Belle ran her finger over the brass plate affixed to the trophy base. "First place. I'm not surprised." Belle had still been in Cheyenne then with no plans whatsoever about coming to Weaver for any reason other than to visit her family. Her plans back then had involved planning her wedding and obtaining some seniority at the clinic.

So much for that.

"Won't be in the contest this year, that's for sure."

"Because you're not dancing at the moment?" Belle set the trophy back in its place. "You could sing." She ignored Lucy's soft snort. "Or play piano. I thought I remembered you telling me once that you took lessons."

"I did."

"But not now?"

Lucy shrugged. Her shoulders were impossibly thin. Everything about her screamed "delicate" but Belle knew the girl was made of pretty stern stuff.

"Yeah, I still take lessons. But it doesn't matter. If I can't dance then I don't want to be in the contest. It's stupid anyway. Just a bunch of schoolkids."

"I don't know about stupid," Belle countered easily. Most talented school kids from all over the state. "But we can focus on *next* year." She took the towel from her shoulders and folded it, then sat on top of it on the end of Lucy's bed. She leaned forward and touched the girl's knee. The wicked scar marring Lucy's skin was long and angry. "Don't look so down, kiddo. People can do amazing things when they really want. Remember, I've seen you in action. And I already think you're pretty amazing."

"Miss Day."

Belle jerked a little. Cage Buchanan was standing in the doorway again. She kept her smile in place, but it took some work. "You'd better start calling me Belle," she suggested, deliberately cheerful. "Both of you. Or I'm not going to realize you're talking to me."

"The students called you Miss Day during the school year," he countered smoothly.

"You're not a student, Cage." She pointedly used his name. More to prove that she could address the man directly than to disprove that whole ogre thing. The fact was, she knew he was deliberately focusing on her surname. And she knew why.

She was a Day. And he hated the Day family.

His eyes were impossible to read. Intensely blue but completely inscrutable. "I need a few minutes of your time. Then you can…settle in."

Belle hoped she imagined his hesitation before *settle*. Despite everything, she wasn't prepared to be sent out on her ear before she'd even had a session with Lucy. For one thing, she really wanted to help the girl. For another, her ego hadn't exactly recovered from its last professional blow.

She was aware of Lucy watching her, a worried expression on her face. And she absolutely did *not* want to worry the girl. It wasn't Lucy's problem that she had a…slight…problem with the girl's dad. "Sure." She rose, taking the towel with her.

"Then I'll change into something dry, and you—" she gently tugged the end of Lucy's braid "—and I can get started."

The girl's expression was hardly a symphony of excitement. But she did eventually nod, and Belle was happy for that.

She squeaked across the floor in her wet sneakers and, because Cage didn't look as if he would be moving anytime this century, she slipped past him into the hall. He was tall and he was broad and she absolutely did not touch him, yet she still tamped down hard on a shiver.

Darned nerves.

"Kitchen," he said.

Ogre, she thought, then mentally kicked herself. He was a victim of circumstances far more than she was. And he *had* painted his bedroom pink for Lucy, for heaven's sake. Was that the mark of an ogre?

She turned into the kitchen.

"Sit down."

There were three chairs around an old-fashioned table that—had it been in someone else's home— would have been delightfully retro. Here, it obviously was original, rather than a decorating statement. She sat down on one of the chairs and folded her hands together atop the table, waiting expectantly. If he wanted to send her home already, then he would just have to say so because *she* wasn't going to invite the words from him. She'd had enough of failure lately, thank you very much.

But in the game of staring, she realized all too quickly that he was a master. And she…was not.

So she bluffed. She lifted her eyebrows, doing the best imitation of her mother that she could summon, and said calmly, "Well?"

Interfering, Cage thought, eying her oval face. Interfering, annoyingly superior, and—even wet and bedraggled—too disturbing for his peace of mind.

But more than that, she'd managed to make him feel out of place. And Cage particularly didn't like that feeling.

But damned if that wasn't just the way he felt standing there in his own kitchen, looking at the skinny, wet woman sitting at the breakfast table where he'd grown up eating his mother's biscuits and sausage gravy. And it was nobody's fault but his own that Miss Belle Day—with her imperiously raised eyebrows and waist-length brown hair—was there at all.

He pulled out a chair, flipped it around and straddled it, then focused on the folder sitting on the table, rather than on Belle. This was about his daughter, and there wasn't much in this world he wouldn't do for Lucy. Including put up with a member of the Day family, who up until a few years ago had remained a comfortable distance away in Cheyenne.

If only she wasn't…disturbing. If only he hadn't felt that way from the day they'd met half a year ago.

Too many "if onlys." Particularly for a man who'd been baptized in the art of dealing with reality for more years than he could remember.

He flipped open the folder, reining in his thoughts. "Doctors' reports." He shoved a sheaf of papers toward her. "Notes from the last two PTs." Two different physical therapists. Two failures. He was running out of patience, which he'd already admitted to her two weeks ago when he'd flatly told her why the other two hadn't worked out; and he was definitely running out of money, which he had no intention of ever admitting to her.

He watched Belle's long fingers close over the papers as she drew them closer to read. He pinched the bridge of his nose before realizing he was even doing it. Maybe that's what came from having a headache for so many months now.

"Your last therapist—" Belle tilted her head, studying the writing, and a lock of tangled hair brushed the table, clinging wetly "—Annette Barrone. This was her schedule with Lucy?" She held up a report.

"Yeah."

She shook her head slightly and kept reading. "It's not a very aggressive plan."

"Lucy's only twelve."

Belle's gaze flicked up and met his, then flicked away. He wondered if she thought the same thing he'd thought. That Annette had been more interested in impressing her way into his bed than getting his daughter out of her wheelchair.

But she didn't comment on that. "Lucy's not an ordinary twelve-year-old, though," she murmured. The papers rustled in the silent kitchen as she turned one thin sheet to peruse the next. Her thumb tapped rhythmically against the corner of the folder.

"My daughter is not abnormal."

Her thumb paused. She looked up again. Her eyes, as rich a brown as the thick lashes that surrounded them, narrowed. "Of course she's not abnormal. I never suggested she was." She moistened her lips, then suddenly closed the folder and rested her slender forearms on top of it, leaning toward him across the table. "What I *am* saying is that Lucy is highly athletic. Her ballet dancing. Her riding. School sports. She is only twelve, yes. But she's still an athlete, and her therapy should reflect that, if there's to be any hope of a full recovery. That's what you want, right?" Her gaze never strayed from his.

He eyed her. "You're here."

She looked a little uneasy for a moment. "Right. Of course. You wouldn't keep hunting up therapists who are willing to come all the way out here to the Lazy-B on a lark. But my point is that you *could* just drive her into town for sessions a few times a week. She could even have her tutoring done in town. All of her teachers want to see her be able to start school again in the fall with her class, rather than falling behind." Her lips curved slightly. "The cost for the therapy would be considerably less if you went into town. You could have a therapist of your choice work with Lucy at the Weaver hospital. I know the place isn't entirely state of the art, but it's so new and the basics are there—"

"I'll worry about the cost." That faint smile of hers died at his interruption. "You're supposed to be good at what you do. Are you?"

Her expression tightened. "I'm going to help Lucy."

It wasn't exactly an answer. But Cage cared about two things. Lucy and the Lazy-B. He was damned if he'd admit how close he was to losing both. Like it or not, he needed Belle Day.

And he hoped his father wasn't rolling over in his grave that this woman was temporarily living on the ranch that had been in the Buchanan family for generations.

He stood, unable to stand sitting there for another minute. "Set whatever schedule you need. Your stuff is in the room upstairs at the end of the hall. Get yourself dry. I've got work to do."

He ignored her parted lips—as if she was about to speak—and strode out of the room.

The sooner Belle did what he hired her for and went on her way, the better. They didn't have to like each other. The only thing he cared about was that she help Lucy and prove that he could provide the best for his daughter.

Once Belle Day had done that, she could take her skinny, sexy body and interfering ways and stay the hell out of his life.

Chapter 2

The rain continued the rest of the afternoon, finally slowing after dinner, which Belle and Lucy ate alone. Cage had shown his face briefly before then, but only to tell Lucy to heat up something from the fridge and not to wait on him. Belle had seen the shadow in Lucy's eyes at that, though the girl didn't give a hint to her father that she was disappointed. And it was that expression that kept haunting Belle later that evening after Lucy had gone to bed. Haunted her enough that she didn't close herself up in the guest room to avoid any chance encounter with Cage.

Instead, she hung around in the living room, knowing that sooner or later he would have to pass through the room in order to go upstairs. But, either she underestimated his intention to avoid her as much as possible, or he had enough bookkeeping to keep him busy for hours on end in his cramped little office beyond the stairs.

When she realized her nose was in danger of hitting the pages of the mystery she'd borrowed from the hallway shelf, she finally gave up and went upstairs. Walked past the bedroom that Cage had traded with his daughter. The door was open and she halted, took a step back, looking through the doorway. There was only the soft light from the hall to go by, but it was enough to see that the room was pink.

He hadn't painted over the walls in Lucy's original room as if she was never going to be able to return to it.

She chose to take that as a good sign. All too many people entered physical therapy without really believing they'd come out on the other side.

Though the room was pink, it still looked spare. All she could see from her vantage point was the bed with a dark-colored quilt tossed over the top, a dresser and a nightstand with a framed photograph sitting on it. The photo was angled toward the bed.

"Something interesting in there?"

She jerked and looked back to see Cage stepping up onto the landing. He looked as tired as she felt. "Pink," she said, feeling foolish.

His long fingers closed over the newel post at the head of the stairs. He had a ragged-looking bandage covering the tip of his index finger. She'd noticed it earlier. Had squelched the suggestion that she rewrap it for him, knowing it wouldn't be welcomed.

His eyebrows pulled together. "What?"

She gestured vaguely. "The walls. They're pink. I was just noticing that, I mean."

"Luce likes pink." His lashes hid his expression. "She's a girl."

"My sister likes pink." Belle winced inwardly. What an inane conversation.

"And you?"

"And I…what?" He probably thought she was an idiot.

"Don't like pink?"

"No. No, pink is fine. But I'm more of a, um, a red girl."

His lips lifted humorlessly. "Pink before it's diluted. You fixed pizza."

She blinked a little at the abrupt shift. "Veggie pizza. There's some left in the refrigerator."

"I know. And I'm not paying you to play cook."

That derailed her for half a moment. But she rallied quickly. Anyone with two eyes in their head could see the Buchanans could use a helping hand. "I didn't mind and Lucy—"

"I mind."

She stiffened. Did he expect her to assure him it wouldn't happen again? "The whole wheat pizza and fresh vegetables, the fact that Lucy didn't want to eat that leftover roast beef you told her to eat, or the fact that *I* dared to use your kitchen? Any other rules I need to know about?"

Apparently, he didn't recognize that her facetious comment required no answer. "Stay away from the stables."

"Afraid a *Day* might hurt the horses? Why did you even bother talking me into taking this job?"

"The horse that threw Lucy is in the stable. I don't want her tempted to go there, and if you do, she'll want to, as well. And the only thing my daughter needs from you is your expertise."

"Which, by your tone, it would seem you doubt I possess. Again, it makes me wonder why you came to me, not once but twice, to get me to take on Lucy's case for the summer." The hallway seemed to be shrinking. Or maybe it was her irritation taking up more space as it grew.

"You have the right credentials."

"Just the wrong pedigree." Her flat statement hovered in the air between them.

Every angle of his sharp features tightened. "Is your room comfortable enough?"

"It's fine." She eyed him and wondered how a man she barely knew could be so intertwined in her life. "Sooner or later we might as well talk about it." His expression didn't change and she exhaled. "Cage, what happened was tragic, but it was a long time ago." She ought to know.

Finally, some life entered his flinty features, and his expression was so abruptly, fiercely alive that she actually took a step back, earning a bump of her elbow against the wall behind her.

"A *long* time ago?" His bronze hair seemed to ripple along with the coldness in his voice as he towered over her. "I'll mention that to my mother next time I visit her. Of course, she probably won't mind, since she barely remembers one day to the next."

Belle's stomach clenched. Not with fear, but sympathy and guilt. And she knew he'd never in a million years accept those sentiments from her, if he even believed she was capable of experiencing it.

She'd heard he was overbearing. But he believed she was the daughter of a devil.

She folded her hands together. Well, she'd been warned, hadn't she? "This was a bad idea. I shouldn't have come here. You…you should bring Lucy into Weaver. I will work with her there." She didn't officially have hospital privileges, but she had a few connections who could help arrange it, namely her stepsister-in-law, Dr. Rebecca Clay. And it didn't matter *where* Belle and Lucy did the tutoring.

"I want you here. I've told you that."

Belle pushed her fingers through her hair, raking it back from her face. "But, Cage. It just doesn't make any sense. Yes, I know it's a long drive to make every few days into town, but—"

His teeth flashed in a barely controlled grimace. "My daughter will have the best care there is. If that seems extravagant to you, I don't care. Now, are we going to have this—" he barely hesitated "—discussion every time we turn around? Because I'd prefer to see something more productive out of your presence here. God knows I'm paying you enough."

She sank her teeth into her tongue to keep from telling him what he could do with that particular compensation. Compensation they both knew was considerably less than she could have charged. "I'd like my time to be productive, too," she said honestly. "I have no desire to spend unnecessary time under your roof."

"Well, there's something we agree on, then."

Her fingers were curled so tightly against her palms that even her short nails were causing pain. "And here's something else we'd better agree on." She kept her voice low, in deference to Lucy sleeping downstairs. "Lucy doesn't need the added stress of knowing you detest me, so maybe you could work on summoning a little…well, *friendliness* is probably asking too much. But if Lucy senses that you don't trust me to do my best with her, then she's not going to, either, no matter *how* well she and I got along when she was in my P.E. class."

"I don't need you telling me what my daughter needs. I've been her only parent since she was born."

"And it's amazing that she's turned out as well as she has." She winced at the unkind words. "I'm sorry. That was—"

"True enough." He didn't look particularly offended. "She *is* amazing."

Belle nibbled the inside of her lip as thick silence settled over them. Should she have listened to her mother's warning that she was getting in over her head? Not because of the skill she would require to work with Lucy—as her therapist as well as a tutor—but because of who Lucy *was?*

Probably.

She sighed a little and pressed her palms together. "Lucy is a great kid, Cage. And I really do want to help her." That was the whole point of all this.

Mostly.

A muscle flexed in his jaw and his gaze slid sideways, as if he was trying to see the bedroom downstairs where his daughter slept. "If I believed you didn't, you wouldn't be here."

Which, apparently, was as much a concession as she was likely to get out of the man. For now, anyway. Fortunately, somewhere in her life she'd learned that a retreat didn't always signify defeat.

"Well. I guess I'll hit the sack." She was twenty-seven years old, but she still felt her face heat at the words. As if the man didn't know she'd be climbing into bed under his roof. She was such a head case. Better to focus on *the job*. The last time he'd come to her house—after she'd already refused Lucy's case once—he'd admitted that he'd fired Annette Barrone because of her overactive hormones. Belle had assured him that he had no worries from her on *that* score.

As if.

"I went over and checked out the barn earlier," she said evenly when neither one of them moved. "The setup is remarkable." And another indication of his devotion to his daughter. Every piece of equipment that she could have wished for had been there, and then some. The hospital in town should only be so lucky. "I rearranged things a little. If that's all right."

Now, his hooded gaze slid back over her face. And she refused to acknowledge that the shiver creeping up her spine had anything to do with his intensely blue gaze.

"Use your judgment."

She nodded. "Okay, then." The door to her bedroom was within arm's reach. Not at *all* at opposite ends of the hall from his. "Good night." She wished he would turn into his own bedroom. But he just stood there. And feeling idiotic, she unplastered her back from the wall behind her and went through the door, quickly shutting it behind her.

A moment later, she heard the squeak of a floorboard, and the close of another door.

Relief sagged through her. After changing into her pajamas, she crossed to the bed and sat on it, dragging her leather backpack-style purse up beside her. She rummaged through it until she found her cell phone and quickly dialed.

A moment later, her sister, Nikki, answered with no ceremony. "So, are you there?"

Belle propped the pillow behind her and scooted back against it. The iron-frame bed squeaked softly, as if to remind her that it had survived years and years of use. It was a vaguely comforting sound. "Yes." She kept her voice low. The house might be sturdy, but the walls were thin enough that she could hear the rush of the shower from the bathroom across the hall.

She stared hard at the log-cabin pattern of the quilt beneath her until the image *that* thought brought about faded. "The drive was hellacious in the rain."

"Well, we've heard Squire say often enough that Cage Buchanan doesn't like visitors, so there's not a lot of need for him to make sure the road is easy."

"I know." Squire Clay was their stepfather, having married their mother several years earlier. She tugged at her ear. "Anyway, I know it's late. You were probably already in bed."

"It's okay. I wouldn't have slept until I knew you hadn't been beheaded at the guy's front door."

"He's not *that* bad."

"Not bad to look at, maybe. I still can't believe you took this job. What do you hope to prove, anyway?"

"Nothing," Belle insisted. "It's just a job to fill the summer until—" *if* "—I come back to the clinic."

Nikki snorted softly. "Maybe. But I'm betting you think this is your last chance to prove to yourself that you're not a failure."

Belle winced. "Don't be ridiculous, Nik."

"Come on, Belle. What other reason would have finally made you agree to that man's request?"

"*That man* has a name."

Nikki's sudden silence was telling. That was the problem with having a twin. But Belle was not going to get into some deep discussion over her motivation in taking on this particular job. "Speaking of the clinic," she said deliberately. "How are things there?"

"Fine."

Now it was Belle's turn to remain silent.

"They still haven't hired anyone to replace you, if that's what you're worried about," Nikki finally said after a breathy huff.

"That's something, at least." And a bit of a minor miracle, given the number of patients the prestigious clinic handled. She still wasn't entirely sure it wasn't because of the position her sister held as administrative assistant to the boss that Belle had been put on a leave of absence rather than being dismissed.

"And I know you're wondering but won't ask," Nikki went on. "So I'll just tell you. Scott's only coming in once a week now."

She wasn't sure how she felt at the mention of him. A patient she hadn't managed to completely rehabilitate. Briefly a fiancé she shouldn't have completely trusted. "You've seen him?"

"Are you kidding? I hide out in my office. If I saw Scott Langtree in person, I'd be liable to kick him." Nikki paused for a moment and when she spoke, her voice was acid. "*She* comes with him, now, apparently. Has most of the staff in a snit because she's so arrogant. Not that I'm condoning what Scott did, but from what people around here are saying about his wife, it's no wonder the man was on the prowl for someone else."

Belle plucked at the point of a quilted star. "But you haven't seen her?"

"Nope. And I consider that a good thing. I'd have something to say to her, too, and then *I'd* have my tail in a sling at work, just like you."

Belle smiled faintly. Nikki was her champion and always had been. "Hardly like me. You'd never be stupid enough to fall for a guy who already had a wife."

"And you wouldn't have fallen for Scott, either, if he hadn't lied about being married," Nikki said after a moment. "Good grief, Belle. The man proposed to you and everything. It's not your fault that he left out the rather significant detail that he wasn't free to walk another aisle."

"I caused a scandal there."

"Scott created the scandal," Nikki countered rapidly, "and it was half a year ago, yet you're still punishing yourself."

Belle wanted to deny it, but couldn't. Her relationship with Scott Langtree *had* caused a scandal. One large enough to create the urgent need for Belle to take a leave of absence until the furor died down. But it wasn't even the scandal that weighed on Belle so much as the things Scott had told her in the end.

Things she didn't want to dwell on. Things like being a failure on every front. Personal. Professional. Things that a secret part of her feared could be true.

"So," she sat up a little straighter, determined. "Other than…that…how are things going at work? Did you get that raise you wanted?"

"Um. No. Not yet."

"Did you *ask* for it?"

"No. But—"

"But nothing. Nik, you stand up for me all the time. You've got to stand up for yourself, too. Alex would be lost without you, and it's high time he started realizing it. I swear, it would serve the man right if *you* quit." But she knew Nikki wasn't likely to do that. Alexander Reed ran the Huffington Sports Clinic, including its various locations around the country. He had degrees up the whazoo, and was a business marvel, according to Nikki.

Belle just found the man intimidating as all get-out, but had still worked her tail off to get a position there.

A position she *was* going back to, she assured herself inwardly.

"So, what's he like? Cage, I mean. As ornery as everyone says?"

Belle accepted Nikki's abrupt change of topic. Alex was too sensitive a subject for her sister to discuss for long. "He is not an ogre," she recited softly.

Nikki laughed a little. "Keep telling yourself that, Annabelle."

Belle smiled. "It's late. Get some sleep. I'll talk to you later."

"Watch your back," Nikki said, and hung up.

Belle thumbed off her phone and set it on the nightstand. She didn't need to watch her back where Cage Buchanan was concerned. But that didn't mean she would be foolish enough to let down her guard, either.

The bed squeaked again when she lay down and yanked the quilt up over her. Even though the day hadn't been filled with much physical activity, she was exhausted. But as soon as her head hit the pillow, her eyes simply refused to shut, and she lay there long into the night, puzzling over the man who slept on the other side of the bedroom wall.

When he heard the soft creak of bedsprings for the hundredth time, Cage tossed aside the book he was reading and glared at the wall between the two bedrooms. Even sleeping, the woman was an irritant, and as soon as she was busy for the day, he was going to oil her bedsprings.

The last thing he needed night after night was to hear the

sound of that woman's slightest movement in the bed that was so old it had been ancient even when he'd used it as a kid.

He hadn't noticed the squeaks before. Not with either therapist. Hattie McDonald with her militant aversion to smiles and her equally strong dislike for the remoteness of his ranch, nor Annette Barrone who'd made it clear she'd rather be sleeping in his room, anyway.

He climbed out of bed—fortunately a newer model than the one next door—and pulled on his jeans. He'd never been prone to sleeplessness until six months ago when he'd gotten the first letter from Lucy's mother. A helluva way to kick off the New Year. She wanted to see her daughter, she'd claimed. A daughter she'd never even wanted to have in the first place. He'd put her off, not believing her threat that she'd enlist her parents if he didn't comply. When he'd known Sandi, she'd wanted nothing to do with her parents beyond spending her tidy trust fund in any manner sure to earn their dismay.

Only she hadn't been bluffing. And it was a lot harder to ignore the demand for access to Lucy when it came from Sandi's parents. Particularly when it was backed up by their family attorneys.

Then came Lucy's accident several weeks later and his insomnia had only gotten worse. In the past week, with Belle Day's arrival pending, it was a rare night if he got more than an hour or two of sleep at a stretch. It was pretty damn frustrating.

He'd given up coffee, counted sheep and even drunk some god-awful tea that Emmy Johannson—one of the few people he tolerated in Weaver—had suggested. Nothing had worked.

And now he could add Belle Day's bed-creaking presence to his nightly irritations.

Barefoot, he left his bedroom. He could no more not glare at her closed door than he could get a full night's sleep these days.

He went downstairs, automatically stepping around the treads that had their own squeak, and looked in on Lucy. She'd kicked off her blankets again and he went inside, carefully smoothing them back in place. She sighed and turned on her side, tucking her hands together beneath her cheek in the same way she'd done since she was only months old.

There were times it seemed like twelve minutes hadn't passed since then, much less twelve years. Yet here she was, on the eve of becoming a teenager.

That was the problem with baby girls.

They grew up and started thinking they weren't their dad's baby girl anymore.

He left her room, leaving the door ajar so he could hear if she cried out in her sleep. Since she'd been thrown off that damn horse he should have sent back to her grandparents the day it arrived, she'd been plagued in her sleep almost as much as Cage.

He didn't need any light to guide him as he went through the house. The place was as familiar to him as his own face. Nearly the only thing that had changed since his childhood was the bed he'd just left behind and, if he'd had any foresight of the financial hit he would soon be taking with all manner of legal and medical costs, he wouldn't have bought the thing last year at all.

He went out on the front porch where the air still carried the damp from the rain even though it had finally ceased. It was more than a little chilly, but he barely noticed as he sat down on the oversize rocking chair his mother had once loved.

If the room at the care center would have had space for it, he'd have moved it there for her years ago. There wasn't much she hadn't done sitting in the chair here on this very porch. She'd shelled peas, knitted sweaters and argued good-naturedly with Cage's father when he and Cage came in after a long day.

But her room, while comfortable enough, wasn't that spacious.

And the one time he'd brought her back to the Lazy-B, she hadn't remembered the chair any more than she remembered him.

He leaned back, propping his feet on the rail, and stared out into the darkness. Strudel soon appeared beside him, apparently forgiving Cage for his banishment after dining on yet another pair of Cage's boots. He scratched the dog's head for a minute, then Strudel heaved a sigh and flopped down on the porch. In seconds, the rambunctious pup was snoring.

Lucky dog.

There were a lot of things Cage wished for in his life. But right then, the thing at the top of the list was sleep. He'd nearly achieved it when he heard a short, sharp scream.

Lucy.

He bolted out of the chair, leaving it rocking crazily behind him as he went inside. And he slammed right into the slender body hurtling around the staircase.

He caught Belle's shoulders, keeping her from flying five feet backward from the impact. "Lucy—" Her voice was breathless. Probably because he'd knocked the wind clean out of her.

"She sometimes has nightmares since the accident." He realized his fingers were still pressing into her taut flesh and abruptly let go. His eyes, accustomed to the darkness, picked up the pale oval of her face, the faint sheen of her skin. A lot of skin, it seemed. She was wearing loose shorts and some strappy little top that betrayed the fact she wasn't skinny everywhere.

He deliberately stepped around her and went into Lucy's room. But his daughter was already quiet again. Still sleeping, as if nothing had disturbed her at all.

He raked his fingers through his hair, pressed the heels of his palms to his eyes. God, he was tired. Then he felt a light touch on his back and nearly jumped out of his skin. He turned, pulling Lucy's door nearly closed again. "What?"

His harsh whisper sent Belle backward almost as surely as their collision had.

"Sorry." Her voice was hushed. "I thought…" He felt her shrug more than saw it. "Nothing."

He pinched the bridge of his nose. He could smell her, rainwater fresh. The sooner she went back to bed, the better. He wasn't interested in what she thought. Or how she smelled. Or why she couldn't keep still for five minutes straight in that old bed. "You thought what?" he asked wearily. He wished the moon were shining a little less brightly through the picture window in the living room, because with each passing second, he could see her even more clearly. Definitely not *all* skinny.

She tugged up the narrow strap of her pajama top and hugged her arms to herself. "Nothing. It doesn't matter."

"Fine. Then go to bed."

She laughed—little more than a breath. "You sound like my dad used to."

He knew it was an innocent enough comment, aimed at the order he'd automatically given. Knowing it, though, didn't keep him from reacting. Before he could say something that might send her straight for the decrepit Jeep she'd arrived in—and away from any possibility of helping his daughter—he stepped around her and headed upstairs.

"Cage—"

He didn't want to hear anything she had to say. She'd said the magic word, sure to remind him just who she was, and to what lengths he'd been driven for his daughter's sake.

Dad.

"Just go to bed, Belle," he said, without looking back.

Chapter 3

Belle propped her hands on her hips and counted off a slow inhale and an even slower exhale. It was far too beautiful a morning, all promising with the golden sunrise, to let annoyance ruin it already. "Cage, I need to go over a few things with you about Lucy. I wanted to last night, but we never got to it."

His long legs barely paused as he passed her in the kitchen and headed out the back door of the house. "I've got a water tank that needs fixing." His tone was abrupt, as if he begrudged providing even that small bit of information.

Clearly, that somewhat approachable man she'd encountered in the middle of the night was banished again.

She hurried after him, letting the screen door slap shut noisily after her. She darted down the brick steps and jogged to keep up with him. She raised her voice. "Lucy told me yesterday that you haven't worked with her on any of the exercises she's supposed to do on her own."

He stopped short. Tilted his head back for a moment, then

slowly turned to face her. The shadow cast by his dark brown cowboy hat guarded the expression in his blue eyes, but even across the yards, she could feel the man's impatience. "I can't be in two places at once, Miss Day."

She mentally stiffened her spine at his exaggerated patience. So much for his one slip of calling her Belle the night before. "I'm aware of that, *Cage*. But you hired me to help Lucy, and—"

"I didn't hire you to lecture me on my ability to parent my own daughter."

Her lips parted. "I wasn't suggesting—"

His eyebrow rose, making him look even more sardonic than usual. "Weren't you?"

"No!"

"You weren't so reticent before Lucy's accident when you accused me of being unreasonable where she's concerned 'cause I wouldn't let her go on that godforsaken field trip to Chicago."

She glanced back at the house where Lucy still slept. The truth was, she *had* thought he was being unreasonable. But that was half a year ago and there were more important things on the agenda than eliciting his approval for a simple school field trip. "Look, maybe we should just talk about…things." She'd thought so all along, but hadn't had the courage to do so. Hadn't had much of an opportunity, either, given their brief conversations about Lucy where Cage had firmly kept control.

His expression hadn't changed. "You're here for one reason only, Miss Day. It'd be better all around if you'd remember it."

Her jaw tightened uncomfortably. "I'm not the enemy, all right?"

His expression went from impatient to stony.

Her hands fell back to her sides. "I see. I *am* the enemy."

Of course. Resulting from long-past history neither could change.

"If you need something that strictly pertains to Lucy—whether it's her therapy or her schoolwork—I have no doubt you'll let me know. Other than that—"

"—stay out of your hair?" Her tone was acid.

"That's one way to put it." He slapped the leather gloves he held against his palm. "Excuse me." He turned on his heel and strode away.

Belle stuck her tongue out at his back, and returned to the house. She yanked open the aging avocado-green refrigerator door. Maybe it was wrong of her, but she took great delight in making breakfast out of a leftover slice of pizza.

For Lucy, however, she set out an assortment of supplements on the counter, and then prepared a real breakfast. After peeking in the girl's bedroom to see that she was still sleeping, Belle pushed her feet into her running shoes and went back outside.

Even though the sky was clear, the dawn air still felt moist from the previous day, as she set off in a slow jog. Well beyond the simple brick house stood the sizable barn, doors open. She didn't want to wonder if Cage was in there. She wondered anyway, quickening her pace and then had to tell herself that she was being a ninny. The man ran a ranch. If he was in his barn, so what? Better there than in the house, bugging her and Lucy. Might present a problem when she and Lucy went to the barn to use the equipment, though.

She didn't doubt that he wanted the best for Lucy, which she certainly couldn't fault. Nevertheless, she'd never met a more antisocial man in her life. But, then, she'd been warned well enough before she took on this job, so complaining about it now was only so much wasted energy.

She figured she'd run a good hour by the time she returned to the house. She darted up the brick steps and went in through the front door, peeling out of her sweatshirt as she went. Surely the bathroom wouldn't still hold the lingering scent of Cage's soap by now.

The bathroom was no longer steamy, true. But she still took the fastest shower in her life before changing into fresh workout clothes. Then she went and woke Lucy. While the girl was dressing—something she didn't need assistance for—Belle wandered around the cozy living room.

She peered again at the silver-framed black-and-white photos hanging above the fireplace mantel. Cage's parents. And a young Cage. She sighed faintly as she studied the Buchanan family. She knew only too well that he'd been a teenager when he'd lost his father, and for all intents, his mother, as well. She ran her fingernail lightly over the image of the solemn-looking little boy. Were there any photos of him smiling?

Did Cage Buchanan ever smile? Ever laugh?

"Hey, Belle. I'm fixing waffles for breakfast. You know the fruity kind with whipped cream? Those frozen waffles are really good that way. Like dessert."

Belle looked back to see Lucy rolling her chair into the kitchen. She headed after her, and hid a smile at Lucy's disgruntled "Oh." Obviously, she'd seen the breakfast that Belle had already set out for her. There would be *no* frozen waffles.

She stepped around Lucy's narrow chair, tugging lightly on her gilded braid along the way. "It'll be good, I promise."

"Dad calls breakfasts like this 'sticks and weeds.'"

At that, Belle laughed softly. "Well, these sticks and weeds are a lot better for you than just a frozen waffle out of a box. It's a bran mix. And the strawberries on top are plenty sweet already without adding cream or sugar. But I could fix you eggs if you'd rather." She refused to wonder what Cage had eaten.

Lucy's perfectly shaped nose wrinkled. "Eggs. Gross."

"Yeah," Belle agreed. "I used to think so, too. But they're

good for you, and there are lots of ways to fix them. So, what'll it be?"

Lucy eyed the table for a moment. Then she shrugged, and started to wheel forward. Belle casually stepped in her path and held out her hands expectantly.

And she waited.

And waited.

Finally, Lucy put her hands in Belle's. And she stood, her weight fully concentrated on her uninjured leg.

Belle winked cheerfully. Lucy wasn't the first patient she'd ever had, and certainly not the first who was leery of leaving the safety net, no matter how much they wanted to. But there was absolutely no reason why Lucy should still be depending entirely on the chair. "Stiff?"

Lucy nodded. There was a white line around her tight lips. Belle supported her as she twisted around and sat at the table. Then she tucked the wheelchair out of the way and sat down across from Lucy.

"Aren't you having any twigs?"

"Ate earlier. Not everyone sleeps in until noon."

Lucy rolled her eyes. "Yeah, right." She picked up the spoon and jabbed at her food. Gave an experimental taste. When the girl gave a surprised "hmm" and took another taste, Belle busied herself by filling a few water bottles and putting away the dishes they'd used and washed the night before as well as the stack that had already been there. She refused to feel guilty about it, either. It wasn't as if she was stealing the Buchanan family silver. She was just washing some crockery.

Lucy was nearly finished with her breakfast before she spoke again. "Did you see my dad this morning?"

"Yes, for a few minutes." Belle folded the dish towel and left it on the counter next to the sink. "He was heading out to fix a water tank."

"Oh." Lucy passed over her dishes.

Belle took them and set them in the sink. She flipped on the faucet to rinse them and glanced at Lucy. "Were you hoping for something different?"

Lucy shrugged but couldn't quite hide her diffidence. "He works the Lazy-B mostly by himself, you know."

Belle did know. She also knew that he hired on hands as needed, and that he usually didn't much want to admit to needing anything.

The man gave *loner* new meaning.

"I know." She smiled gently and moved the chair back around for Lucy. "Come on. It's beautiful outside. Let's go for a little walk."

"No exercises yet?"

Lucy looked so hopeful that Belle had to smile as she helped the girl back into her chair. She crouched in front of her. "I'll tell you a secret," she confided lightly. "Exercise comes in all sorts of forms. Sometimes you don't even know you're doing it." She grazed her fingertips over Lucy's injured leg. "So. What do you say? A walk?"

Lucy nodded. Satisfied, Belle rose and handed Lucy a bottle of water, took one for herself and they headed out the front of the house, where Lucy's ramp was located.

Before long, Belle had to push the chair for Lucy because of the soft ground. The morning was delightfully quiet, broken only by the song of birds flirting in the tall cottonwoods that circled the house.

They walked all the way down the road to the gate then headed back again. "Do you like living on a ranch?"

Lucy lifted her shoulder, her fingers trailing up and down her braid. "It's okay, I guess. I used to spend part of the week in town. During the school year. Dad pays my friend Anya Johannson's mom for my board for part of the week. She teaches me piano and takes me to my dance lessons after school and stuff. Well, that's what we used to do." She tossed her braid behind her back.

They were within sight of the large red barn before Lucy spoke again. "You grew up in Cheyenne. Right?"

"Yup. Until I took the job at your school last year, and when I went away to school, I'd always lived in Cheyenne. My sister, Nikki, still does. And my mother's been living at the Double-C Ranch since she married Squire Clay a while back."

"Were your parents divorced?"

"No. My dad died just before Nikki and I turned sixteen."

"Does she look like you? Nikki?"

Belle grinned. "Nah. She's the pretty one. Likes to shop for real clothes, not just jeans and workout gear. She looks like our mom. Auburn hair, an actual *figure*."

Lucy made a face, looking down at herself. She plucked the loose fabric of her pink T-shirt. "Yeah, well, I'm never gonna get…you know…boobs, either." Lucy's pale cheeks turned red. "Not that you don't, uh—"

Belle laughed. "It's okay. I do. But believe me, my sister got the larger helping in the chest department. And you're only twelve. You've got oodles of time yet."

"I'm gonna be thirteen next month."

Belle renewed her grasp on the handles of the chair, pushing it harder over the gravel road. "Why sound so glum about it? Are you going to have a party?"

"And do what?" Lucy thumped her hands on her chair.

"Who needs to *do* anything? You're going to be thirteen. I remember when Nik and I turned thirteen. We sat around with our friends and talked boys and makeup and music, and ate pizza and popcorn and had a blast."

"Doesn't matter. Dad's not going to let me have a party, anyway."

"Has he said that?" She would be upbeat if it killed her. "It never hurts to just ask. What's the worst that could happen? That he'd say no? You've already decided that, anyway.

And he might surprise you." Whatever she'd seen or heard about Cage, the man was admittedly doing back flips for his daughter. What was one small party?

"He doesn't want me to do anything," Lucy insisted flatly. "Ever since my accident, he's been—" she shook her head, and fell silent.

"Worried about you, perhaps?" Belle maneuvered Lucy's chair through the opened barn door.

Lucy didn't respond to that. But she did respond to the changes Belle had made inside the barn. Most particularly the portable sound system she immediately flicked on. Banging music sounded out and Belle looked past Lucy's slack jaw as she handed the girl her iPod. "Hope there's something you like on there. I downloaded a little of everything."

Lucy flipped through the playlist. "Dad would like this."

Belle glanced over. Beatles. Drat. Her own personal favorite. "Anything *you* like?"

"Classics." Lucy shrugged diffidently. "Weird, huh?"

She felt as if she'd hit a treasure chest when she leaned over to scroll down several more albums on the iPod and the girl laughed delightedly. "Beethoven. Pachelbel. Rachmaninoff. A little of everything."

Belle took the iPod and connected it to the player. She pressed the play button and the strains of Mozart soared right up to the rafters.

Cage could hear the music a mile away. It was loud enough to scare his prized heifers out of breeding for another two seasons, and certainly loud enough to put his daughter in hearing aids before her next birthday. He wanted to race hell-bent for leather to the barn the way Strudel was, but he kept his pace even for Rory's sake. He was walking the horse back to the stable, hoping Rory's lame leg wouldn't require more than some TLC and rest. He knew the vet would come if he called, but it sat wrong in Cage's belly to keep looking at the balance of his bill with the man, knowing he wouldn't have it paid off anytime soon.

Naturally, the music grew even louder the closer he got to the barn and it showed no sign of abating even after he'd tended to Rory. He strode inside, only to stop short at the sight of Belle and Lucy. His daughter was lying on the incline bench. Not an unusual sight. But she was laughing, her head thrown back, blond hair streaming down her thin back, her face wreathed in smiles.

And Belle was laughing, too. She sat on the floor in front of the bench, her legs stretched into a position he thought only Olympic gymnasts could obtain, and she was leaning forward so far her torso was nearly resting on the blue mat beneath her. The position drew the tight black shirt she wore well above her waist, and for way too long, he couldn't look away from that stretch of lithe, feminine muscle.

Neither his daughter nor Belle noticed him and he felt like an outsider all over again. He liked it no more now than he had the previous day.

Then Belle turned her head, resting her cheek on the mat, and looked at him.

Not so unaware, after all.

"Come on in," she said. And even though she hadn't lifted her voice above the music, he still heard her. Her brown gaze was soft. Open.

She didn't even flinch when Strudel bounded over to her, snuffling at her face before hastily jumping over her to gleefully greet Lucy.

Safer to look at the slice of Belle's ivory back that showed below the shirt than those dark eyes. Maybe.

He deliberately strode to the speakers and turned down the volume. "Trying to make yourselves deaf?"

Lucy rolled her eyes. "It wasn't *that* loud."

He wished for the days when she hadn't yet learned to roll her eyes at him. "I'm going in to get your lunch."

"Belle already did."

At Lucy's blithe statement, Belle pushed herself up and drew her legs together, wriggling her red-painted toes. He saw a glint on one toe. She wore a toe ring. Figures.

"We left a plate for you," she said, apparently trusting that he wouldn't lecture her about her "place" in front of Lucy.

In that, she was correct. For now, at least. He eyed her for a moment. "Then I'll go down to get the mail."

Lucy ignored him as she flopped back on the slanted bench. Belle's gaze went from him to Lucy and back again. "If you have some time this afternoon, maybe Lucy could show you a few of the new exercises we've been working on."

He nodded and resettled his hat as he left. In the seconds before someone—his daughter probably—turned up the volume of the music again, he heard Lucy's flat statement. "He won't show. He never does."

It was an exaggeration, but that didn't stop the words from cutting. But he was only one man. As he'd told Belle, he couldn't do it all. Keep the Lazy-B going and spend hours with his daughter when he'd already hired a therapist for her for that very purpose. He whistled sharply and Strudel scrambled out of the barn, racing after him. The dog might have promise, after all.

He drove the truck down to get the mail. There was a cluster of boxes belonging to the half-dozen folks living out his direction. His place was the farthest out, though. The box was five miles from the house. Usually, he swung by on Rory. Not today.

Back in the house, he dumped the mail and the morning paper on the kitchen table and yanked open the refrigerator door. Sure enough. A foil-wrapped plate sat inside. The woman made pizza with whole wheat. Whole wheat? He wasn't even aware that he'd had any in his house. Either she'd brought it in her suitcase, which was entirely possible since she had no qualms about thinking she knew best where his family was concerned, or the stuff had been lurking in his cupboards courtesy of Emmy Johannson, who periodically brought groceries out for him.

God only knew what lurked on that plate under the foil. He ignored it and made himself a roast-beef sandwich, instead. He was standing at the counter eating it when he saw Belle through the window over the sink striding up to the rear of the house. He turned a page of the newspaper and continued reading. Something about a chili cook-off.

It wasn't engrossing stuff, but it was better than watching Belle. The woman had a way of moving and it was just better off, all around, if he didn't look too close. He didn't like her, or her family, and she was there only out of his own desperation. So he needed to get over the fact that she turned him on and he needed to do it yesterday.

The screen rattled as Belle pulled it open and popped into the kitchen. His gaze slid sideways to her feet. Scuffed white tennis shoes—a different pair than the wet blue ones the day before—now hid the red-painted toes and the toe ring. He looked back at the newspaper and finished off the sandwich.

Only Belle didn't move along to the bathroom, or to do whatever it was she'd come in the house to do. She stood there, her arms folded across her chest, skinny hip cocked.

He swallowed. Finished the glass of milk he was drinking.

She still hadn't moved.

He sighed. Folded the newspaper back along its creases. Crossed to the table to flip through the mail. Too many bills, circulars advertising some singles' matchmaking network, an expensive-looking envelope with an all too familiar embossed return address. He folded the envelope in half and shoved it in his back pocket. "What is it now?"

"I noticed that Lucy is still depending exclusively on her wheelchair."

The one remaining nerve not gone tight at the sight of the envelope now residing next to his butt joined the knotted rest. He opened a cupboard and grabbed the bottle of aspirin that had been full only a few weeks ago. He shook out a few, the rattle of pills inside the plastic sounding as sharp as his voice. "And?" He shut the cupboard door again only to find her extending a condensing bottle of water toward him.

"And it concerns me, because it's encouraging her to keep favoring her injury."

"She's not supposed to use her leg, yet." He swallowed the aspirin.

"She's not supposed to use it completely," Belle countered. "But she should have been up on crutches weeks ago, yet since I've been here—"

"Twenty-four hours now?"

"—I haven't even *seen* a pair of crutches. She does have them, doesn't she?"

Cage strode over to the tall, narrow closet at the end of the kitchen and snapped open the door. Inside, along with a broom and the vacuum cleaner, stood a shining new pair of crutches. "Satisfied?"

Her lips tightened. She flipped her long ponytail behind her shoulder and brushed past him to remove the crutches. He looked down at her, clutching the things to her chest. The top of her head didn't reach his chin. In fact, she wasn't much taller than Luce.

The realization didn't make Belle seem younger to him. It only made his daughter seem older.

He pushed the closet door shut and moved across the room. "She says that she still hurts too much to use 'em."

Belle nodded. "I understand, believe me. But getting on her feet with these is a major component of her recovery. And the longer we wait, the more it's going to hurt. You're going to have to get over trying to protect her, Cage. Her recuperation is *not* going to be pleasant all the time, but she does have to work through it before it'll get better." Her hand reached out and caught his forearm, squeezing in emphasis. "And it *will* get better." Then, seeming to realize that she was touching him, she quickly pulled back.

"Easy advice," he said flatly. "You ever watch *your* child trying to straighten or bend a leg that doesn't want to do either despite two separate surgeries that should have helped it? To steel yourself against the pleading in her eyes when she looks at you wanting permission to…just…stop?" If he'd expected her to look shocked at his unaccustomed outburst, he was wrong. Shock would've been better, though, than the expression softening her eyes. It was easier to take when she figured he avoided Lucy's sessions because of the never ending needs of the Lazy-B.

"I haven't watched *my* child," she said. "Since I've never even had one, that would be difficult." Then she suddenly lifted her foot onto one of the kitchen chairs and whipped the stretchy black pants that flared over her shoes up past her knee. The scar was old. Faded. It snaked down from beyond the folds of her pants on the inside of her taut thigh, circled her knee and disappeared down her calf. "But I have dealt with it myself."

The water and aspirin he'd just chugged mixed uncomfortably with his lunch. Lucy's healing surgical scars were bad. But when they healed, he knew they would look far better than Belle's.

"Not pretty," Belle murmured, and pulled her pant leg back down. "My hip doesn't look quite so bad."

"What happened?"

It was hard to believe it, but her brown eyes looked even darker. "I thought you knew."

"I suppose that's why you went into physical therapy," he surmised grudgingly.

"Yes." She sucked in one corner of her soft lip for a moment. Her expression was oddly still. "I was with my dad that night, Cage. The night of the accident."

He'd been wrong. His nerves *could* get tighter. "I didn't know you'd been hurt." He couldn't have known since her family had been living in Cheyenne at the time.

She studied the crutches she held. "I was lying down in the back seat. I didn't have on my seat belt, which my dad didn't know. When…it…happened, I was thrown from the car. Metal and flesh and bone. Don't mix well usually." She lifted her shoulder slightly. "Which is something you know only too well, I'm afraid. I'm sorry. I thought you knew," she said again then fell silent.

She looked miserable. And damned if he could convince himself it was an act, though he wanted to.

"Look, Cage, it's not too late for me to go. I know Lucy knows about the accident between our parents and she doesn't seem to hold it against my family. But everyone warned me this would be just one constant reminder after another." Her gaze whispered over him, then went back to the crutches. "I can hold my own against those opinions." Her voice was vaguely hoarse. "But if your feeling the same way gets in the path of Lucy's progress then my efforts here will be for nothing. Are…are you sure you want me to stay?"

No. He stared out the window. Lucy was sitting in her chair just outside the barn, Strudel half in her lap while they played tug with a stick. "Lucy still needs help." His voice came from somewhere deep inside him.

He heard Belle sigh a little. "I could talk to the people I worked with at Huffington. Maybe I could find someone willing to—"

"No." He couldn't afford to bring someone else out to the ranch, to pay their full salary. Belle had been willing to agree for less than half what she deserved, and he knew it was only because of her fondness for his daughter. Something he'd deliberately capitalized on. The fact that she'd be able to provide the tutoring Lucy needed was even more of a bonus. "You came to help Lucy. I expect you to hold to your word."

"All right," she said after a long moment. She tucked her arm through the center of the crutches and carried them to the door. Then paused. "I'm really sorry your father didn't survive the accident, Cage."

"So am I," he said stiffly. He'd lost both his parents that night, even though his mother had technically survived. Apparently, the only one to escape unscathed that winter night nearly fourteen years ago had been the man who'd caused the accident in the first place.

Belle's father.

And even though he'd died a few years later, Belle was, after all, still his daughter.

Chapter 4

"I want to go with you."

Cage shook his head, ignoring Lucy's mutinous demand. "Not this time, Luce."

"Why not? I want to see Grandma."

He wished Belle wasn't standing at the kitchen sink washing up the pans she'd used to prepare Lucy's breakfast. He wished she'd stop doing things he wasn't paying her to do. She'd been under his roof for three days. He'd already warned her to stop dusting the shelves and mopping floors. They may have needed it, but when he'd come upon her doing the chores, he'd lit into her. More than necessary, he knew, but seeing her so at home in his house bugged him no end. He didn't want her being helpful. Not unless it was on his terms. "I'll take you to see her another time."

"When?"

"A few weeks."

Lucy's lips thinned. "I haven't seen her all summer."

"And nothing's changed." Her eyes widened a little at his

sharp tone. He stifled a sigh. Before Lucy's fall, they'd gone every weekend. "Maybe this weekend. When Miss Day is off."

The prospect seemed enough to satisfy his daughter. "Miss Day's day off," Lucy quipped. Her lips tilted at the corners, thoroughly amused with herself and he felt his own lips twitch.

God, he loved the kid. "Yeah."

"Don't make fun of my name," Belle said lightly over the clink of dishes in the sink. "I grew up hearing every pun you could ever think of."

"Day isn't bad," Lucy countered. "You oughta hear what people used to call my dad."

Belle leaned her hip against the counter as she turned to look at them. The towel in her hand slowed over the plate she was drying. "Oh?"

"Yeah, Cage isn't his *real* name, you know. Who would name their kid *that*?"

Cage caught his daughter's gaze, lifting his eyebrow in only a partially mock warning. "Did you make your bed?"

Lucy laughed. But she took the hint and didn't pursue the topic of Cage's first name. She lifted her arms and he automatically started to reach for her to transfer her from the chair at the table to her wheelchair. But he caught Belle's look.

How to protect someone in the long run by causing them pain now? He felt the humor sparked by his daughter drain away and instead of lifting her, he handed her the crutches that were leaning against the wall.

"Dad." Lucy pouted.

"Lucy," Belle prompted gently. "We've talked about this."

He supposed that wasn't surprising. If she'd taken him to task about the crutches, she'd probably done the same with his daughter. Understanding the reasons was one thing. Liking it another.

Lucy took the crutches. Belle set down the towel and helped the girl to her feet. With the crutches tucked beneath her arms, Lucy looked at Cage. "She told me not to pout around you 'cause you were too much of a marshmallow to hold out against me." Then she shot Belle a look before awkwardly swinging out of the kitchen.

Belle's cheeks were pink and she quickly turned back to the dishes.

Cage filled a coffee mug with the fragrant stuff she'd made earlier, damning the consequences, and watched her for a moment. She was wearing another pair of those long, curve-clinging pants. Yoga pants, he knew, because he'd had to buy some for Lucy.

Today, Belle's pants were as blue as the ocean. She wore a sleeveless top in the same color that hugged her torso and zipped all the way up to her throat.

She'd have been about Lucy's age when the accident happened. How long had it taken her to recover from *her* injuries?

He abruptly finished off his coffee. Learning that she'd been hurt in the same accident as his parents didn't change anything. Gus Day had killed his father on a stretch of highway outside of Cheyenne, pure and simple. He sat the emptied mug down with a thunk. "Marshmallow?"

"She wasn't supposed to tell you that."

"She's still young. She hasn't learned the art of discretion."

"She's learned a lot of other things. If you're worried that going with you to Cheyenne today will be too taxing, don't. She's up to the trip."

He'd told Belle and Lucy that he was making the drive when they'd both stopped in surprise at finding him in the kitchen that morning instead of already out for the day as he usually was. "It's business," he said again. True enough in a sense. Personal business. The kind he wasn't inclined to share, not even with Lucy. Not until he was forced to. "I probably won't be back until late."

Belle didn't look happy.

"I told you that I can have Emmy Johannson come over to watch her."

"And I told you that would be ridiculous since I'm staying here anyway. You want to have the argument you've been spoiling for now that Lucy's out of range?" She shot him a look, her eyebrows arched, and when he said nothing, she deliberately dried another plate. Short of yanking it out of her hands there wasn't much he could do about it. "I'm not going to twiddle my thumbs between sessions and lessons, Cage, but that wasn't what I was trying to get at anyway. Has it occurred to you that maybe Lucy wants to be where *you* are?"

"She wants to see my mother. And this discussion is over." Maybe he couldn't keep her from washing the damn dishes, but he didn't have to listen to advice unrelated to Lucy's rehabilitation.

Belle shrugged and focused on the dishes again, seeming not to turn one hair of her thick brown ponytail at his decree. But her lashes guarded her eyes. And he damned all over again the turn of events that had prompted him to bring her into this house.

A timely reminder of why he was going to Cheyenne in the first place.

He rose and grabbed his hat off the hook. "Luce has my cell-phone number," he said as he strode from the room. He thought he heard her murmur "drive carefully" after him, but couldn't be sure.

Lucy was in her bathroom when he hunted her down to tell her he was leaving. He rapped on the door. "Behave yourself," he said through the wood.

She yanked open the door, leaning heavily on her crutches. "What else is there to do," she asked tartly. "You won't let me go near the horses anymore."

"When I'm sure you're not going to go near *that* horse, I'll consider it."

"You're *never* going to let me ride Satin again, are you?"

It was an old refrain and one he didn't want to be pulled into singing. "Make sure you feed Strudel," he said. "And do the exercises on your own that Miss Day says you're supposed to be doing.

"I hate doing them. They hurt. And they're boring." Her face was mutinous. An expression that had been too frequent of late.

"I'm sorry they hurt, but I don't care if they're boring," he said mildly. "They're necessary."

Her jaw worked. Her eyes rolled. Then all the fight drained out of her and she gave him a beseeching look. "How come you won't let me go with you today?"

Dammit, he *was* a marshmallow where she was concerned. But not this time. "You got a problem hanging around here with Miss Day?"

Lucy rolled her eyes again. "Jeez, Dad. Her name is Belle. And *no* I don't have a problem with her. Not like *you* do, anyway."

"I don't have a problem with Miss Day."

"Right. That's why you watch her like you do. You oughta just ask her out on a date or something."

"I do not want to date Miss Day," he assured evenly and gently tugged the end of her braid as he leaned down to kiss her forehead. "Behave."

She grimaced. "Like there's anything else you'd let me do? Say 'hi' to Grandma for me."

He nodded as he headed out. If he did go by the care center, he'd pass on the greeting, but he knew there would be no reciprocation, which was the very reason why he would *never* want to date Miss Day.

"Have you ever been in love, Belle?"

The question came out of the blue and Belle looked up from Lucy's leg. "Is the cramp gone?"

Lucy nodded, gingerly flexing her toes.

It was evening and they were back in the barn again. Cage hadn't yet returned from Cheyenne.

"So, have you?"

Belle leaned back and grabbed a hand towel, wiping the remains of oil she'd been using from her palms. "Yes."

"With who?"

Belle flicked Lucy with the end of the towel and rolled to her feet. The song had ended and she selected another. "Howie Bloom," she said.

"Howie?" Lucy echoed.

"We were in second grade together. I thought he was the perfect man. He, however, thought Nikki was the perfect woman."

"They liked each other?"

"Nikki told him to take a hike. She'd never have poached on what I considered my territory."

"I wish I had a sister," Lucy grumbled dramatically. She flopped back on the blue mats, flinging her arms wide, before slowly moving them up and down. If she'd been in the snow, she would have been making snow angels. Belle wondered if the girl even knew she was partially moving her legs—both of them—as well, and decided not to point it out. It wasn't the first time she'd noticed Lucy unconsciously using her injured leg.

"Instead, I'm all alone," Lucy lamented. "With dad. I think he needs a woman. Then mebbe he wouldn't be on my case all the time."

Belle sank her teeth into her tongue for a moment and when

the urge to snort passed, she chanced speaking. "If your dad wants to be with someone, I'm sure nothing would stop him." It seemed a safe enough response. And Lord knew the man was attractive. For a grouch.

"I s'pose. He could'a dated Anya's mom. They were in school together when they were little. But she got engaged to Mr. Pope. Dad's way hotter than he is."

Larry Pope was a teacher at the high school. A perfectly nice man, what little Belle knew of him. She seriously doubted anyone in Weaver muttered *ogre* behind his back. But he wasn't in the same hemisphere of hot that Cage Buchanan occupied.

Which was neither here nor there, Belle reminded herself.

"Then Anya and I would be sisters. But Dad never looked at Mrs. Johannson like…you know."

"And Anya is away visiting her dad?"

Lucy nodded. "'Til next month." She exhaled, sounding utterly dejected.

Belle pushed to her feet and held out her hands. "Come on. Let's go make popcorn and watch movies." Lucy had a sizable collection of DVDs in her bedroom from which to choose. Maybe one of them would provide enough distraction that she'd stop wondering what kind of woman Cage did look at like *you know*.

Cage could see the blue-tinted glow through the living-room windows as he finally drove up to the house that night. Television was on. It was after midnight.

He parked near the back of the house. Sat there in the dark, listening to the tick of his cooling engine. Unlike the bluish light coming from the window at the front of the house, the light he could see from the upstairs one looked golden. Either Belle had fallen asleep with the light on, or she was still awake. Probably the reason for that blue glow downstairs.

He blew out a long breath and grabbed the manila envelope that had been his companion on the long drive up from Cheyenne and headed inside. His trip had been successful only in giving him some breathing room.

Hopefully.

The aroma of buttery popcorn met him. Two bowls—one empty, one nearly so—sat on the table.

He hadn't stopped for dinner before driving back and grabbed a handful from the remains. Lightly doused with Parmesan cheese. Lucy's doing, he figured. Kid liked the stuff on everything.

The low murmur of voices and familiar music from the television kept the house from being entirely silent. He went into the living room. Lucy, tangled up with her favorite pink blanket, was sprawled over most of the couch. And Belle, as well, since her legs were tossed over Belle's lap.

His daughter didn't budge as he walked in the room. She was asleep.

"Did your trip go well?" Belle's voice was soft.

He finally let himself look at her. Only long enough to see that she was wrapped in a bulky white robe that was falling open at the base of her long neck. "It went. City seems to get busier every time I drive down there. You probably can't wait to get back there, I suppose."

"That's the plan," she agreed evenly.

He eyed her for a moment. She hadn't said anything, but she had to think his place was stuck somewhere two decades past.

God. What a mood he was in. "How long's Luce been asleep?"

"Since Ariel got her legs."

He glanced at the television. Judging by the stack of DVDs on top of it, he knew this movie hadn't been the first they'd watched. *The Little Mermaid* might not be recent, but it'd been Lucy's favorite Disney flick since the day she first saw it. "She hasn't made it through that video without falling asleep since she was little."

"Didn't hurt that she worked pretty hard today."

"You told me you'd be doing all the same exercises she does, right alongside her."

"Yes. But I'm not working at a disadvantage the way she currently is."

Memories of Lucy growing up battled for space in his mind against memories from his own youth. He'd believed none of the Days had been affected by the accident. God knew, Gus Day had never said a word of it during the few times he'd tried contacting Cage afterward. Now, he knew Belle had been hurt, as well. He dropped his envelope on the ancient coffee table and leaned over the couch.

Belle sucked in her breath, unable to prevent the reaction when he moved so suddenly. But he gave no notice. Simply slid his arms under his daughter, hands impersonally skimming Belle's thighs in the process, before lifting Lucy's limp form easily against his chest. She swallowed and tried not to be obvious about clutching the comforting folds of her robe together over her legs. She needn't have worried what Cage would think, however, since he was already carrying his daughter down the hall toward her bedroom, the pink blanket trailing around his long legs.

She'd seen his expression one too many times when he looked at his daughter. Naked devotion.

On the television, Sebastian was beseeching the prince to kiss the girl, and Belle hit the remote, stopping the singing crab midnote. She was tidying up the scattered napkins and loose kernels of popped corn from the coffee table when Cage returned. "Did she wake up?"

He shook his head and closed his long fingers over his envelope before she could move it out of her way. "Except for the nightmares, it takes something cataclysmic to wake her up in the middle of the night."

She wasn't sure if it was censure she heard in his voice, or not. But they hadn't discussed Lucy's bedtime, so she could honestly say she hadn't deliberately flaunted his rules. She also could honestly say that standing there with him in the hushed light of the snowy television screen seemed suddenly, abruptly, far too personal. As he was fond of pointing out, she was there to do a job. Wondering what in the package—with its embossed return address for an attorney in Cheyenne—was responsible for the tense muscle flexing in his jaw wasn't part of that job.

"Well. It *is* the middle of the night." She lifted her cupped hands a little. "I'll just throw this stuff away." But he was pretty much blocking the way to the kitchen because there was little room to maneuver between the couch and table. She pressed her lips together for a moment, awkwardly waiting for him to shift aside. When he finally did, she hurried past him and dropped her handful of trash in the garbage can beneath the kitchen sink. She rinsed and dried her hands, then remembered the bowls on the table and started for them. But Cage beat her to it, handing her only the empty one even as he shoved his other hand in the leftovers.

"Luce didn't put so much parmesan on her popcorn this time," he murmured before popping some into his mouth. "It's still edible for once."

Belle pushed her lips into a smile. Maybe he was oblivious to the fact that she was wearing her robe, but she was not. And the popcorn he was devouring hadn't been Lucy's, it had been hers. "Yes. Well. Good night." Gloria Day had drilled manners into her daughters, prompting the polite words when her most immediate desire was to simply run up to the safety of her bedroom. He, however, didn't return the sentiment and she thought he wouldn't as she headed into the hall.

"Belle."

Why did he only know her name when his home was

bathed in midnight shadows? She caught her hand around the door jamb. "Yes?"

"Thanks for watching Luce today."

It really was the very last thing she might have expected from him. Surprise softened her for a moment until she gathered herself. "You're welcome."

He nodded once, and that seemed to be the end of it. Of course, he was plowing through the remains of her popcorn as if he were starving. "Did you eat dinner?"

He'd leaned one hip against the counter, cradling the popcorn bowl against his stomach. "This is fine." Which was no answer at all.

"There are leftovers in the fridge."

Information that didn't seem to fill him with glee.

"I made some hamburger-casserole thing," she added. "Didn't have a name, but Lucy said it was one of her favorites. The recipe was in the recipe box in your cupboard." It had taken her a while to gather her nerves to even open the little metal box that was crammed with yellowed newsprint recipes as well as neatly hand-printed recipe cards. It was in keeping with the other aging, but homey, touches the house still possessed.

"That was my mother's recipe box."

Exactly what Belle had assumed, and why she'd hesitated. "I hope you don't mind. Anyway, that's what I fixed. It has hamburger and carrots and potatoes and—"

"Yeah." He set aside the bowl and watched her, his hooded expression too shadowed to read. "My mother used to fix it for us. It was my father's favorite, too."

And wasn't that a handy way to put a stop to their awkward conversation? "There's plenty left for you," she said and continued down the hallway to the staircase.

Upstairs in the bedroom, she felt an urge to call her sister, but didn't. Just because she was having a hard time sleeping under Cage Buchanan's roof didn't mean she needed to share the problem by interrupting Nikki's sleep, as well.

She tossed her robe over the wooden chair in the corner and climbed into bed before snapping off the lamp sitting on the nightstand. Every time she closed her eyes, though, she saw Cage in her mind's eye. Striding toward the house, lean hipped and long legged in worn jeans, his cowboy hat set on his bronzy head at a no-nonsense angle. Wolfing popcorn. Carrying his daughter.

She scooched down the bed. Scrunched up her pillow this way and that. Turned from one side onto her other.

Then sat bolt upright when she heard the brisk knock on her door. "Yes?" Oh, stupid, Belle. She should have gotten up and put on the robe. Instead, she sat there in bed, tangled in sheet and quilt while the bedroom door opened and Cage appeared.

She couldn't summon so much as a coherent thought or word as he entered the room, walking right across to her.

Then he suddenly knelt, one hand braced on the mattress only inches from her bare knee. The mattress dipped and the springs gave out a loud moan.

For some reason, she felt as if they'd been caught doing something…intimate.

"What—" Finally her tongue loosened. "What are you doing?" But his head just kept going lower.

She leaned over, grabbing the sheet up against her chest, flinging it more fully over her leg to see him actually slipping beneath the high-set bed. "Looking for the boogeyman?"

He had a small can in his hand, she realized. "You creak." His voice was muffled.

"Only in the mornings when I first get out of bed," she muttered.

She heard a soft spraying sound, followed by a hint of an oily scent. Then he was pushing out from beneath the bed again, and levering himself to his feet. "The bedsprings."

"I noticed."

He headed to the door. "So did I."

A statement that was disturbing only because it made her wonder what he was doing on his side of the wall that he could hear *her* bedsprings creaking. Did he listen for her as closely as she listened for him, hoping to avoid running into him? Bad enough to know she hid out in this very room early every morning until the sounds of him moving around in his room, then showering in the bathroom, were long gone.

He stopped at the door and glanced back. The light from the hallway spilled around his broad shoulders. "And, so you know, you don't have to keep hiding the scars on your leg."

She blinked.

"If Luce sees that you're self-conscious about yours, she's going to be the same way about hers," he continued abruptly. Then he closed the door.

Belle flopped back on the bed. The bedsprings gave one halfhearted creak, then were silent.

Of course. His only concern was Lucy.

Chapter 5

"Did you ask your dad yet about having a birthday party?"

Lucy shook her head, apparently too intent on painting her toenails—pink, of course—to answer. They were taking a break from studying and Lucy was sitting on the floor in her bedroom, leaning over with the polish brush.

"Why not?" Belle tucked the tip of her tongue between her teeth watching the way Lucy compensated for her injured knee. Lucy was unusually limber, which in general was a plus, but occasionally—when she would ordinarily be forced to make her leg try harder—she could work around it. Which was something she nearly always did. Even though she'd made faces and grumbled about their actual therapy sessions in the five days since they'd begun, she hadn't been completely obstreperous, which Belle had initially feared. What interested Belle even more, though, was the fact that when she was just going through her ordinary day Lucy accomplished ever so much more. Unconsciously.

Lucy still hadn't answered her question, though. "Hey

there." She leaned over, looking into Lucy's absorbed face. "Why haven't you asked him, yet? You said yesterday that you were going to." And the day before that, and the day before that.

"He won't let me have any boys come and if no boys come, then none of the girls will want to come, either."

"Do *you* want boys to come?" Belle idly plucked a bottle of clear polish out of Lucy's collection and shook it a few times before unscrewing the top.

"Anya's gonna want Ryan to come."

Belle flattened her hand on the top of a teen magazine and began stroking the clear polish over her fingernails. Ryan, she knew, was Ryan Clay. Her nephew by virtue of her mother's marriage into the Clay family. "Okay, so I know what Anya wants, but what about you?"

Lucy straightened, and lifted one shoulder as she put the cap back on her polish and tossed it back in the pretty, lacquered box that contained her modest assortment of polishes. "I dunno."

Belle switched hands to paint the rest of her nails. "My old boss used to call me *bulldog*," she murmured. "Because I don't give up very easily. So why don't you just tell me what's really holding you back on having a party? Otherwise, I'll just have to keep asking."

"Bulldog?" Lucy looked skeptical. "You're making that up."

"I can call Nikki and she'll tell you I'm not. She's Mr. Reed's assistant, and he tends to give everyone a nickname."

"How come you don't still work there?"

"Oh, I'll be going back," Belle assured her with a blitheness she was far from feeling. "I'm sort of on vacation."

"So, you won't be at my school next year?"

Belle shook her head.

"Then how can you tell me we'll work on something other than dancing for the talent contest?"

"We've got the rest of summer vacation to figure it out for you."

"But then you'll be leaving."

Belle heard loneliness underlying Lucy's matter-of-fact tone. And why wouldn't she be lonely? Living on a remote ranch. No company other than a dog, a television and videos, a horse she wasn't supposed to go around and a father who worked from sunup to sundown. Other than the day he'd gone to Cheyenne, Cage had been noticeably absent around the house.

He'd even stopped complaining that Belle was cooking meals for his daughter, and had stopped coming in, himself, to make sure Lucy had lunch. "Yes," she finally answered honestly. "I'll be leaving. Because you're going to be running circles around me by then and you won't need me anymore. But we'll still be friends, sweetie. You can call me anytime."

"Do you and Nikki live together in Cheyenne?"

"Lord, no. I love my sister, but we'd drive each other mad in two days flat. We're only a few blocks away from each other, though. She has this beautiful town house that she's been decorating herself. I have an apartment that is completely standard issue. Well, I *had* an apartment." She hadn't renewed her lease when it expired, because she'd been in Weaver, by then. Instead, with the help of Nikki and some friends, she'd moved her few personal items of furniture into the little house in Weaver where she was staying. "I'll have to find a new place to live when I go back there." She smiled, determined to cheer the solemn look from Lucy's face. "Maybe your dad will let you come and visit me there, even."

"Really?"

"Of course."

But Lucy's sharply hopeful moment was brief. "Dad won't let me, anyway."

Belle stopped fanning her hands and tested the polish. Dry. "Enough of that. Your dad seems pretty willing to do back flips for you."

"He won't let me go see my grandparents."

"He said he would think about taking you to Cheyenne to visit your grandmother this weekend."

"My other grandparents. The Oldham side." Lucy dropped the lid back on the lacquered box and lifted it onto her legs. Her hand smoothed over the fine surface. "My grandmother sent this to me a few months ago. Dad nearly had a cow."

"Maybe he's not comfortable with his little girl being old enough to wear nail polish. Dads can be that way sometimes." Hers certainly had been.

"That's what *he* said."

"Well. There you go." Belle's mind was busy, turning over the notion of Lucy's maternal grandparents. The only thing the rumor mill had produced on them was that they were wealthy. "Have they invited you to visit or something?"

Lucy shook her head. "Not really. I just—we've talked a couple times on the phone. Dad doesn't know, though."

Belle wished Lucy hadn't imparted that little tidbit, but the girl was continuing. "They live in Chicago. They're the ones who sent me Satin, too."

The horse that had thrown Lucy.

"Isn't Chicago where that performing-arts school you were interested in is located?"

"Yeah." Lucy leaned her head back against the foot of her bed. "Guess it didn't matter that Dad wouldn't let me go on that field trip there. Even if I could have gotten to visit the school during one of the free days, they wouldn't want me like this."

"Satin hadn't thrown you yet when the field trip was

scheduled. Even so, it doesn't mean the school wouldn't want you when you *are* ready again," Belle pointed out.

Lucy just shrugged again. Then she set aside the lacquered box and turned, pulling herself up onto the bed. She grabbed the crutches propped beside her and braced her weight against them to push to her feet. "Even if I earned a scholarship, he wouldn't let me go." She slowly clumped out of the bedroom.

This is what she got for becoming personally involved with a patient, Belle thought, watching the girl leave. Instead of just being concerned with rehabilitating a body, she began wanting to fix everything else, too. And while she didn't know whether or not Lucy would be better served by going to a private school so far away from home, she *did* know that Lucy was uncommonly talented.

She slid back into her shoes, grabbed Lucy's discarded tennies, too, and went after her. "Come on," she said when she found Lucy leaning against the kitchen counter, staring out the window. "We've explored all over the Lazy-B this past week except for one place." She waved Lucy's shoes. "Sit and put these on."

"There's only one place we haven't gone."

"Right. The stables."

"Dad doesn't think I should go down there."

Belle nodded. "Unsupervised," she improvised, remembering Cage's words. But Lucy's mood had been in the dumps long enough and Belle was tired of trying to catch Cage to talk to him about her observations where his daughter was concerned. Including her suspicion that Lucy's reluctant attitude toward her recovery was somehow related to the horse that had thrown her. "His point is that he doesn't want you trying to ride yet, and I agree with him. Your muscles are nowhere near ready for the strain of a horse's girth. But visiting is not riding. And you've got more horses than just Satin, right?"

Lucy looked vaguely skeptical, which didn't do a lot for Belle's tinge of uncertainty. But it was the middle of the afternoon. If Cage's habit held, he wouldn't make an appearance until it was nearly dark. It wasn't that Belle intended to get away with something. She'd let Cage know, after the fact, that they'd visited the horses, and that doing so had lifted Lucy's spirits. If he had a quarrel with *that,* she'd deal with it.

She was suddenly impatient to get going before she lost her nerve, and crouched down to tie Lucy's shoes, herself. And when that was done, she brought out the wheelchair that was mostly stored in the corner of the kitchen these days. "You can ride this time." The stables were considerably farther out from the house than the barn was. "Bring the crutches, though."

Lucy looked relieved to shift into the chair. She propped the long crutches against the metal footrest and her shoulder, and they went out through the front, to use the ramp.

The summer afternoon was hot, and Belle was perspiring by the time she'd pushed Lucy all the way to the stables. "Too bad you don't have a swimming hole around here," she said as they entered the shade of the stable. "We could use a little cooling off." She doubted that Cage would grant Belle permission to take his daughter out to the ranch her mother lived on with Squire. The Double-C had a great swimming hole.

Maybe she'd look into driving Lucy into Braden. The town was some distance from Weaver, but there was a public pool there. And swimming would be good for Lucy's leg.

"That's Rory," Lucy pointed out as they passed an SUV parked in the space of what would be two stalls and came to the first horse. "He's older 'n I am."

The big buckskin stuck his head over the rail, nudging at Lucy's outstretched hand. "I should have brought carrots." She braced the rubber tips of her crutches against the hard-packed earth that formed the aisle between the stalls and stood. Belle stepped around the chair and slowly walked down one side of the aisle with Lucy. At each stall, they stopped. Lucy greeted the horses as if they were long-lost friends.

It was practically heartbreaking.

Then they got to the last stall in the row.

Satin, Belle immediately knew. Aptly named because she'd never seen a more beautiful black. It was as if Black Beauty had stepped right out of the pages of the classic novel. "Oh... my," she murmured. She'd been around horses her entire life as a pleasure rider, but she'd never seen such a magnificent animal.

Lucy was hanging back slightly but as soon as she realized that Belle noticed, she tossed her head and continued forward as if her hesitation had never happened at all. "Satin Finish," Lucy said. "He's seventeen hands. Sired out of Knotty Wood. He was a Triple-Crown winner."

Belle started. "A *racehorse?*"

"Satin's never raced, though." Lucy started to reach for the horse, but stayed the movement, never quite touching him.

What on earth was a horse bred like that doing on a working cattle ranch? Belle found it unfathomable. "He's quite a gift. Is he being ridden at all?"

"No, and he's not going to be."

The deep voice was flat. But the fury in it was unmistakable, and Belle nearly jumped right out of her skin. She was faintly aware of Lucy reacting similarly as they both whirled around, feeling caught and guilty as sin, in the face of Cage's towering disapproval.

It wasn't directed at his daughter, though. His fiercely blue gaze rested on Lucy for only a moment, obviously seeing that she was perfectly fine, before settling on Belle. "What...the... hell...do you think you are doing?"

She very nearly quailed. She'd known she was taking a chance on angering him. But Lucy's recovery mattered more.

She clasped her hands together behind her back. She could feel Satin's huffing breath at the nape of her neck. "I asked Lucy to introduce me to her friends here in the stable."

"Lucy, go wait for me in the truck."

"But—"

"*Go.*"

The girl sidled along the row until she passed her father, then she quickly swung herself down the aisle to the dusty brown pickup truck Belle could see parked at the end.

Belle started, watching the girl's movements. The moment they heard the click of the truck door closing, Cage stepped toward Belle and she nervously took a step back, only to feel the iron rails of the stall press against her shoulder. Satin began nibbling at her ponytail.

She shifted, quickly pulling her hair out of the reach of temptation. She was undoubtedly safer with the horse's attention, though, than with Cage's.

"The first day you came here," he said, his voice deadly quiet. "What about our conversation that day did you not understand?"

"I'm not a horse thief." The stab at lessening the tension failed miserably.

"You'd be better off at the moment if you were. You could steal *that*—" he jerked his chin toward Satin "—and I'd applaud you all the way to the state line."

Belle stiffened her spine. "So what are you going to do? Glare and stride around all heavy booted and macho? For heaven's sake, Cage, did you even notice what Lucy did a few minutes ago?"

"I *noticed* she was ten inches away from that spawn of a horse," he snapped. "He's unpredictable. I don't need to worry about something else taking my daughter away from me, too."

"She put weight on her foot!" Her hands clenched. Unclenched. "What do you mean, *too?*"

He glared at her, his jaw flexing. "Satan—"

"—Satin."

"—*Satan,*" he repeated, "threw her once. She's a good rider, and she could have been killed."

"But she wasn't," Belle reminded him slowly. "And if you hate the horse so much—think he's such a danger even when he's not being ridden—why is he still here?"

He turned away from her as if he couldn't stand the sight of her. "Lucy would hate me more than I hate that horse if I got rid of him."

His admission was so raw it tore at her. She pressed her lips together for a moment, scrambling for the objectivity that she was supposed to have. "Lucy says that she wants to get better. But something is holding her back during her sessions, Cage."

"And your answer to that is tempting her back onto that horse."

That horse nickered softly and tossed his head, brushing hard enough against Belle's shoulder to make her stumble forward. She caught herself before she knocked right into Cage. "I wasn't doing anything of the sort," Belle defended. "And Lucy doesn't want to get *on* Satin, anyway."

"She bugs me about it constantly."

"Then it's an act!"

"You can't tell that."

"I can," she assured evenly, "as easily as I can see that she's deliberately holding herself back in our sessions. And if you weren't so intent on avoiding me, I'd have talked to you about all this already!"

His expression was plain. He didn't believe her.

Frustration churned inside her. "You'd see it, Cage, if you took more than five minutes out of your day to spend with her. I know why you avoid me, but to avoid Lucy, too, is ridiculous. When you and I first met, I thought you were just a stubborn dad who wasn't ready to let his child go off on a field trip so far away from home."

"That field trip to Chicago was planned a year in advance, and Lucy knew all along I wasn't going to let her go." He leaned over her. "You were interfering then and you're interfering now."

"Well, maybe you *need* some interfering around here! You know, half the population of Weaver considers you an ogre, but I didn't want to believe it. Goodness knows, the people around here have known you a lot longer than I have. So maybe they're more accurate than I am! As far as I'm concerned, keeping the stable off limits to Lucy because you're jealous of a horse given to her by her grandparents isn't overprotective or stubborn. It's cruel."

She brushed past him, knowing the words shouldn't have left her lips, but there was no way to retract them. Instead, they lingered there, silently following as she strode out of the shadows into the lengthening afternoon light.

He'd fire her now, for sure. And maybe that was just fine with her.

But she stopped, seeing Lucy sitting in the truck, her young features pinched into worried lines.

Belle veered back toward the vehicle, propping her hands on the opened window. "Don't worry," she said huskily. "It's me your dad is angry with, not you."

"He better not fire you," Lucy said, throwing her arms around Belle's neck. "I'll hate him forever if he does!"

Belle smoothed her hand down Lucy's gilded head. "You're not going to hate him." She'd once told her father she'd hated him, with devastating results. "And he hasn't fired me." Yet. She didn't even dare look over her shoulder to see if he was bearing down on her to deliver that very coup de grâce. But, of course, she had to.

She looked back.

Cage was still standing by Satin's stall, his hands braced

against the top rail, his head lowered. Strudel danced around his legs for a moment, but he didn't even seem to notice, and eventually the dog skittered away from Satin's vicinity to jump at a woven blanket hanging off a high hook.

Belle pressed her cheek against Lucy's blond head and closed her eyes, but Cage's image was seared into her mind, as clear as a painting.

Man at end of rope it was titled. And it made her heart simply ache.

"It'll be okay," she murmured to Lucy. If she had more guts, she'd approach Cage. Apologize. Try to make amends. Again. Either he'd fire her or he wouldn't, and that would be the end of it.

He still hadn't moved.

And she wasn't brave enough, after all, to take a dose of his bitterness, no matter how deserved. "I'm going to drive back into town," she told Lucy. It was a few hours earlier than she would have left for her weekend off, but just then, the idea seemed prudent.

Lucy caught her hands. "Are you going to come back?"

She forced a smile. "Monday through Friday. That's the deal."

She looked back again at Cage. Belle simply had to believe that things *would* work out.

For all of them.

Chapter 6

She was out in her yard, hunched over a lawn mower.

Cage parked across the street next to the sidewalk bordering Weaver Park and the school and cut the engine. He unhooked his sunglasses from the rearview mirror and slid them on. But his gaze didn't waver from Belle Day puttering about in her small front yard.

Annoying. Interfering. Too sexy for such a scrawny thing. He'd expected those things when he'd hired her, because he'd thought those things from the first day they'd met when she'd cornered him about that damn field trip.

So, he'd expected all that. Been prepared for all that. Been ready to have the daughter of a man he'd hated for longer than his adult life living under his roof because he was beyond desperate to prove to a passel of lawyers that nobody—not even two people rich enough to buy heaven—could provide a better home for his daughter than he could.

He *hadn't* been ready for his daughter to become the woman's champion. Hadn't been ready for Lucy's tearful accusations—when he'd discovered her actually doing her small exercises on her own without him having to get on her case about it—that he'd scared off Belle Day for good. Damn sure hadn't expected to come after the woman, two days later hat in hand.

She was sitting on the grass now, banging at the mower. The metallic noise rang out, sounding out of place in the morning air.

He got out of his truck and crossed the empty street. Down a few doors, a trio of kids played in a picket-fenced yard. The other direction, a teenage boy was slopping a sudsy rag over a shining red car.

He couldn't ever remember feeling as young as they looked. Or as young as Belle looked, for that matter, though he knew she was only a few years younger than he was.

Maybe that's what a man got for inheriting an adult's responsibilities when he was sixteen.

He rolled the sleeves of his shirt farther up his arms as he stepped up on the sidewalk. He could hear Belle muttering colorful curses under her breath. It was almost amusing. "What's the problem?"

She jerked, craning her head around. A tangle of emotions crossed her face. "Won't start." She turned back to the mower. The ends of her ponytail flirted with the faint breeze, dancing around the waist of her faded jeans.

Cage walked around to the other side. Splotches of black grease covered her hands. A few more clangs rang out courtesy of her banging. "That helping?" His voice was dry.

She angled him a look as she tugged up the halter strap of her red bikini top. "Does it look like it? What are you doing here?" Her chin set and she looked back down at the engine. She had a smudge of grease on her collarbone, now. "As if I can't guess."

He bent his knees, hunkering down next to the mower. Better to look at the engine. He slid the wrench out of her unresisting fingers. Just because he was there didn't mean the words weren't sitting in his throat fit to choke him. "I brought Luce into town. She's at Emmy Johansson's."

"Stored there all safe and sound where I can't lead her down danger's path?" She grabbed the wrench back from him. "You're all dressed up. You're going to get greasy."

A clean gray shirt and black jeans was dressed up? She must really think he was a hick. "Luce told me you weren't going to let her ride."

"I told you that, too." She unwound her crossed legs and knelt, leaning over the mower as she strained to remove the housing.

God. He had a straight view down her lithe torso and she had no clue whatsoever. Her nipples were as hard as—

He looked across the street to the park.

She huffed and sat back down on her butt, stretching out her legs. "This is hopeless."

Hopeless was getting the branded image of her breasts out of his head. "She also implied you wouldn't be back on Monday. Give me the wrench."

She eyed him. "Is that the newest euphemism for telling someone to go…soak your head?"

"I heard that Colby's has an open-mike night on Saturdays," he said blandly. "You can try out the stand-up comedy there."

She flipped up the wrench like a one-fingered salute. "And take away your spotlight?"

"Funny." He didn't go to Colby's and they both knew it. Next to Ruby's Diner, Colby's was the best stop for buffalo wings, beer and gossip. He preferred beef, didn't drink beer or anything else alcoholic and couldn't abide wagging tongues. He grabbed the wrench. Studied the mower for a moment then easily unfastened the housing and set it aside.

"Show-off," Belle muttered.

"You're welcome."

She snatched the wrench back once more. "If you've come to fire me, just get it done and over with. As you can see—" she waved her hand beyond the mower to her slightly overgrown grass "—I have things to do." She tugged at the halter strap again and leaned over the mower. She stuck her fingers here and there, poking and plucking and he knew she didn't have a single clue what she was doing.

Irritation rippled along his spine. "I didn't come to fire you. I told you what Lucy said. I came to make sure you didn't quit on me. Don't stick your finger in there." He pushed her hands out of the way, but she didn't move so easily. And now, his hands were as greasy as hers.

She swatted at him. "It's *my* mower!"

He closed his fingers around hers. "So I should just sit here and let you ruin the chances of ever fixing it?"

Her eyebrows peaked. Their fingers felt glued together by the sticky grease.

Heat collected at the base of his spine, shooting right up it, threatening his sanity. He let her go.

She sat back, her wrists propped on her knees, gooey fingers splayed. "Well." Her voice was a little husky. "There's a concept."

"My daughter is not a bloody lawn mower. And you need a new spark plug."

"I *know* your daughter isn't yard equipment." She shook her head, looking disgusted. "So, you came because you're afraid I'm a quitter."

"Are you?"

"I don't quit on people I care about," she said after a moment.

"Admirable. What about Lucy?"

She huffed. "I care about *her*."

"And not me."

Her eyebrows rose again over brown eyes that looked too vulnerable for comfort. "Wouldn't that be the height of folly?

It really must have frosted your cookies when Days began moving to your neck of the woods, instead of staying nice and faraway in Cheyenne. Do you loathe the Clays, too, since Squire had the bad form to marry my mother?"

"Does that mean you're in Weaver permanently?" She started to reach for the housing, but he beat her to it, mostly out of pity for the equipment. In seconds, the mower was assembled.

"No," she said fervently. "Believe me, I cannot *wait* to go back to my job at the clinic in Cheyenne. If you didn't live out on the Lazy-B like some hermit, you'd probably know that. As a topic for gossip, I'm as much fair game as anyone else who lives here." She stood and started to grab the mower, but stopped, looking beyond him with a grimace. "Oh, great."

"Problems, Belle?" A cheerful female voice assaulted them.

Cage looked over and saw Brenda Wyatt practically skipping down the sidewalk, she was in such a hurry to get the latest scoop. "Speaking of gossip," he muttered under his breath.

"Nothing major," Belle assured the woman, ignoring him.

"Anything I can help with?" Brenda stopped shy of stepping on the grass, her eyes curious and sharp as a hungry bird.

"Not unless your husband has a spare spark plug for this thing." Belle nudged the mower with her tennis shoe.

"Well, I'll just go and see." Brenda's gaze rested on Cage for a moment. He could practically see the speculation turning inside her head. Then she smiled again, and hurried back toward her picketed yard.

"Now she's gonna feel compelled to come back, you know."

Belle's smile was mocking. "So? Nobody's asking you to stay. Consider your brief presence here your good deed for the day. It'll provide hours and hours of entertainment for Brenda."

"Is this what it's gonna be like now if you come back to the Lazy-B?" He still had some doubts that she'd return, because she hadn't actually said she would. "Open warfare?"

"You're the one who declared it, Cage."

"Thought you wanted to maintain some civility for Lucy's sake."

"All I was trying to do was help. That's all I've ever wanted to do. But you've either treated me like a leper or a liar. I'm sorry for the past, Cage. More than you can possibly know. Maybe you think you're being disloyal to your father's memory, or to your mother, by employing the enemy. But your father is gone and your daughter is very much here. I *want* to help."

"You think I don't know that?" He nearly choked to keep his voice down. Brenda was jogging back down the sidewalk, waving something in her hand.

"Here you go," she said gaily, trotting up to them. She dropped the small box in Belle's hand.

"Thanks, Brenda. I'll replace this for you as soon as I can get over to the hardware store."

Brenda nodded. "Sure. Sure. Whenever." Her gaze bounced eagerly between Cage and Belle. "So, how is young Lucy doing? Such a terrible, terrible tragedy."

"Good grief, Brenda. Lucy's not paralyzed," Belle countered.

Brenda's smile stiffened. "Well, of course she isn't. And it's so nice of Cage to give you a job, too, after all that—" she waved her hand "—messiness you had in Cheyenne."

Save him from catty women. He took the box and pulled out the spark plug, kneeling down to replace it. "Isn't that your youngest crossing the street, Brenda?" He knew it was because she brought her trio of brats to every school meeting he'd ever had to attend.

She turned around. "Timothy Wyatt," she yelled, dashing after the boy. "You get out of the street this instant!"

"Nothing quiet about living down the street from the Wyatts," Belle murmured.

"Wouldn't think so." When the spark plug was in place, Cage rose. He primed the engine, then grabbed the cord and gave it one good pull. The engine turned over and ran, smooth as butter.

Belle's hands closed over the handle. "Thanks. I, um, well you should go on inside and wash your hands at least. So you don't get grease all over you the way I have."

Looking at her various splotches of grease only meant letting his gaze wander back to the vicinity of her bikini top. Not a good idea. He nodded and headed up the narrow, flower-lined walk while Belle busily pushed her mower over the postage-stamp-size lawn.

Inside, the house was small. Newer than his place, but much smaller, and that was saying something. When he'd come here to ask her in person to take the job, he'd stood on the little porch. Both times. He hadn't wanted to go inside her house any more than she'd been prepared to invite him inside.

He'd thought then, and he thought so now, that the small house was hardly the kind of place where he'd have expected Gus Day's daughter to live. The man had been the most prominent attorney in Cheyenne.

He went into the kitchen—a straight shot through the small living room—and washed up at the sink there. She had little pots of daisies sitting in the window next to a small round oak table. Photographs were stuck all over the refrigerator door with funky magnets.

He didn't particularly want to see all the mementos of her family. Her friends. He looked, anyway.

There were no photographs of her father that he could see. Just her with students he recognized from the school. With kids of all ages, many who were members of the Clay family. Several with a woman who looked a lot like Belle, except for their coloring. Probably the sister.

He leaned closer to one photo. Belle, grinning from ear to ear, a mortarboard on her head and a diploma clutched in her hand. She looked young and carefree. Not much different then she usually looked now.

He'd finally gotten his college degree when he'd been twenty-five. Five years ago now.

He straightened and headed back out, just as she was coming in. Bits of grass clung to the legs of her jeans and he stopped short when she suddenly leaned over, whipping them down her legs, kicking them free to leave on the porch. "Get the grease off?"

He was long past the teenage kid who'd been struck dumb by the seductive efforts of an older blonde, but right then Cage felt just as poleaxed by Belle as he'd been by his first experience with any woman. Only now he knew how high the cost could be.

"Cage?"

The rest of her bathing suit—cut like snug boxers—was modest by current standards. But it still showed enough.

She glanced down at herself, grimacing. "Sorry. I should have warned you." She walked past him to the kitchen.

He could probably span her waist with his two hands. The swells of her breasts—the pink-tipped visions he wouldn't be getting out of his head anytime soon—would fit the palms of his hands. And her hips…

He heard the rush of water when she turned on the faucet and shifted sideways a little. He could see her vigorously scrubbing her hands and arms with soapy water. When she was done and dry, she grabbed a long-sleeved white shirt off the coat rack by the back door and slipped into it. The tails hung around her knees. It was obviously a man's shirt.

"Warned me?" Whose shirt was it?

"The scars. Well, you've seen a little of them already."

Right. Scars. They were there all right. But it wasn't the scars that had made his jeans so damn tight he could hardly move without making the problem obvious. "How long did it take you to recover?"

She flipped her ponytail free of the collar and padded into the living room, not looking at him.

Good thing.

"I'll let you know when I'm finished." She was leaning over, busily stacking together the magazines scattered over the top of the iron-and-glass coffee table. The shirt crept up the back of her insanely perfect thighs.

Was she doing it deliberately?

He ran his hand around his neck. He was driving Lucy down to visit his mother that afternoon. Even thinking about his daughter and his mother didn't alleviate the knot inside him.

Belle straightened and turned, her faint smile rueful. "Almost two years, actually. Recuperating put me behind a grade in junior high school. Hopefully, if we get Lucy's test scores high enough, she won't have to deal with being held back. I had to work with a tutor, too. In high school. All three years, to make up time. So my twin sister wouldn't graduate ahead of me."

He'd had enough reminders of her family. "Do you always strip off in front of strange men?"

Her dark lashes dipped for a moment, then she eyed him with wide eyes. "Why, yes, I do, Cage. I thought you knew that about me." She propped her hand on her hip, but her face was red. "And are you still going to keep calling me Miss Day even now that we know each other so well? Having seen me in my bathing suit, the way you have, that is. Why, we just might have to get married for the scandal of it all."

"You've got a smart mouth."

"The better to eat you with, Goldilocks," she muttered, turning away.

He nearly choked, but she was oblivious.

"I'm allergic to grass, okay? And my jeans were covered with it." She didn't look at him as she returned to the kitchen once more. Apparently, her bravado went only so far.

He followed. "Then why mow your own grass if you're allergic?"

"Well, who *else* would be doing it?"

"Hire someone."

She gave him a cross look. "I could say the same to you, then you would have some *time* to give to your daughter when she needs you. What *is* your real name, anyway?"

"What?"

"Cage isn't your real name, right?"

"No."

"Kind of an odd nickname."

"So?"

"So…how'd you get it? I'm sort of surprised it's not *rock,* because sometimes you act as if you're living under one."

"Calling me a snake?"

Her expression stilled for a moment. "No, actually. I've met one of *those.* Was engaged to him, actually."

Despite Cage's aversion to gossip, he'd heard the brunt of Belle's story. Was the former fiancé the owner of the shirt? Dammit. He didn't want to wonder. He damn sure refused to care.

"I paced," he said abruptly. Anything was better than thinking about how Belle came by the shirt she wore with such casual sexiness.

She looked blank.

"When I was a kid and indoors, I paced. Back and forth like I was in a cage."

"Ah." She yanked open the refrigerator and pulled out two longnecks. Extended one to him.

He shook his head.

"Seriously?"

"I don't drink."

She shrugged and put the beer back, then came out with bottles of water, instead. She handed him his, then leaned her shoulders against the fridge, opening her water. She tilted her head back and drank deeply, then capped the bottle again, resting it against her abdomen. "So, you like being outside better than inside, ergo, *Cage*. The pacing thing, by the way, seems to be something you got over. I've never seen a man who could be so still as you are. And you don't drink. What else is there about you that the Weaver grapevine hasn't already published? Ah. How ironic. Back to the beginning, again. Your real name."

"It's…unique." His voice was clipped. He strongly considered dumping the cold water over his head. Nearly anything would be preferable to the unacceptable thoughts running through his head.

Her eyebrows rose. "You're actually giving a hint? I'm amazed. Something unique. Unique for the English language? For a man? What?"

"Are you going to be at the Lazy-B tomorrow morning, or not?"

Her eyes narrowed in consideration. She tapped her finger against her water bottle, drawing his gaze for too long a moment. Then, her finger stilled midtap, and her cheeks colored, her gaze flicking to his, then away.

So, she wasn't as unaware as she'd seemed.

If it were anyone other than her, he'd do what nature intended. He'd step up to her, press her back flat against that photo-strewn refrigerator, kiss her until neither one of them knew their own names—real or nick—and tug away that bathing-suit top to see if her nipples tasted as sweet as he feared.

And she still hadn't given him an answer. "Miss Day?"

"One condition," she said after a moment.

"What?" He wasn't agreeing until he knew what sort of string she was dangling.

"Well, maybe more than one."

His molars were nearly grinding together. "What?"

"Not treating me like the enemy is probably more than I can expect. But you can at least stop acting like I'm some schoolmarm and call me *Belle*. You don't freak out if we visit…*visit*…the stable. *And* you suggest to Lucy that she have a birthday party."

"A party?" He eyed her. "Lucy doesn't want a party."

Belle *tsked*. "You may be able to spot a faulty spark plug, Cage, but *I* can recognize a lonely girl when I see one. Besides, she and I have talked about it. She wants a party but she figures you'll refuse to allow it."

"If she wants a party, fine."

"With boys?" Her eyebrows rose a little.

"What?"

"Loosen up, *Dad*," she said evenly. "Your daughter is a teenager, and teenagers do generally have some interest in the opposite sex, if you can remember."

He remembered all right. He remembered where his thoughts had been when he'd been thirteen-fourteen-going-on twenty. "I remember what teenagers do with the opposite sex." Same damn thing he inconveniently thought of nearly every time he set eyes on *Miss* Belle Day. "I remember what I was doing when I was barely seventeen. Conceiving Lucy."

Belle's lashes lowered for a moment and when she looked up again, he knew that statement hadn't been some big revelation for her. Of course not. She may have lived in Weaver for only six months, but that would be long enough for a town where gossip vied with ranching as the number-one occupation. "I seriously doubt you were just out sowing your oats," she said after a moment. "Your dad had died. Your mom was critically injured. You had the responsibility of the ranch on your shoulders. You were alone, and you probably needed someone. Badly, I'd imagine."

He'd had responsibility for the ranch since he'd been younger than that. "I had a hard-on for a sexy blonde I saw dancing at a rodeo," he said flatly. Understanding, sympathy or anything of that ilk were not things he wanted from Belle. "Fortunately, I've learned how to ignore wanting things that aren't good for me."

She flushed, obviously realizing where the pointed comment was directed. Too bad he could see the way that rosy color drifted down her throat, to her chest. Because it made him wonder how far the blush went.

She set aside the water bottle and clutched the shirt together with both hands. "Well. Anyway. Your daughter and her friends are more interested in holding hands and getting up the nerve to dance with a boy than…anything else. You agree and I'll be there tomorrow morning."

"She can have a party."

"And?" Her eyebrows rose expectantly.

His jaw felt tight. "You can visit the horses, but I'd appreciate it if you'd wait until I could be there, too." It was the most reasonable he could be.

She inclined her head. "And?"

And. Always another *and*. "And if I'd had a schoolmarm who looked like you, I wouldn't have been ditching classes to sleep with a wannabe dancer named Sandi Oldham." He reached out and brushed his thumb over her soft lips, watching her eyes flare. "Believe me, Miss Day. Some things are better left alone."

Chapter 7

Belle's second drive out to the Lazy-B was accomplished without a deluge of rain.

Instead, she had to deal with a deluge of nervousness that put her misgivings on the first trip to shame.

The drive took much less time, courtesy of the dry roads, as well as her familiarity with the route. So, it wasn't even lunchtime when she closed the gate behind her and drove up to the brick house.

Strudel was again lying on the porch, but he popped up and scrambled down the steps to greet her when she climbed out of her Jeep. She laughed a little, scrubbing his neck as he jumped up on her. "What'd you eat this time that got you banished from the house?"

The dog panted and rolled his eyes in joy.

"Strudel." Cage's voice from the porch wasn't loud, but the command was unmistakable. "Get off the woman."

The dog went back down on all fours. Danced around in circles. Belle ducked back into the Jeep to grab her suitcase.

She felt some sympathy for the dog. There was enough adrenaline jolting through her system that she could have run in mindless circles, too.

She hadn't really expected to see Cage just yet. Running even a small ranch offered enough tasks to keep ten men busy, much less one. But he *was* there, and she'd have to suck it up. Just because she'd spent the rest of the previous day and night preoccupied with the things he'd said…the way he'd *looked* at her…

She realized she was still standing there with her rear hanging out of her old Jeep. Hardly conveying a composed demeanor. She yanked out the suitcase and closed the door. Cage had moved down the steps and was heading her way.

"Where's Lucy?" A nice touch of brightness in her voice. Not too shrill. Not too desperate. First order of business with the girl was to find out why she'd implied to her dad that Belle was prepared to quit.

"Talking to Anya on the phone about the birthday party. You were right."

Hallelujah. One good deed accomplished. Though she was surprised that he so easily acknowledged it. She hastily surrendered her suitcase when he reached for it. Easier than fighting over the thing.

He looked amused, as if he recognized her scrambled thoughts. A disturbing idea. She reached back inside her vehicle. "I nearly ran into the mailman on the road here," she said. "Thought I'd save you a trip."

If she hadn't imagined the glint of humor in those eyes that rivaled the sky for color, it disappeared when she held up the bundled newspaper and envelopes. He silently took the mail and turned back to the house.

Belle sighed at the slap of the wooden screen behind him. "Why, it was my pleasure, Cage. You're *so* welcome." She followed him up the steps where the ramp still blocked half the width. If she did her job well enough, he'd be able to dismantle it for good. Once inside the house, she heard Cage's footsteps overhead and knew he was putting her suitcase in her room.

Lucy was sprawled on her bed in her downstairs room, the phone apparently glued to her ear. She waved and smiled widely when Belle stuck her head through the doorway. She pressed the phone to her shoulder. "You're back!"

"Yes," Belle said arching her eyebrows. "Apparently, that's some big surprise."

The girl had the grace to look somewhat chagrined. "Well, now you know my dad really wants you."

Belle tucked her tongue between her teeth for a moment. She knew what Lucy meant, though the words suggested something quite different. "Finish your call," she suggested. "Then we'll get down to business."

Lucy grimaced. "You're not, like, going to take it out on me by making me do some really hideous exercises or something, are you?"

Belle smiled wickedly.

Lucy groaned. When Belle turned back to the staircase, she heard Lucy giggling into the phone again, though. Obviously, she wasn't too fearful of Belle's retribution.

She dashed up the staircase. Sure enough, Cage had put her suitcase on the foot of the bed, and she unpacked again, as quickly as she had the previous week. After all, her clothes took up no more space now than they had then.

She closed the door long enough to exchange her jeans for a loose pair of shorts, then put on her tennis shoes again and went back downstairs. Cage was in his office. She could see a wedge of his shoulder through the doorway.

Fortunately, the clump of Lucy's crutches coming along the wood floor put the kibosh on any notion she might have been entertaining of going toward that office. What would she have said, anyway?

They were who they were and never the twain would meet.

A shiver danced down her spine and she looked up at the ceiling. Maybe the place was developing a draft.

Right. Blame your nerves on phantom drafts. That's a sane thing to do.

"Belle?" Lucy was standing nearby watching her. "Something wrong?"

Belle shook her head. Then did a double take. "Good grief. You're wearing…blue."

"And you're wearing yellow. Call the newspapers. Come on. Just don't torture me too bad, okay?"

There were already filled water bottles in the refrigerator. Belle hid a smile at that. The prep work had to have been Lucy's doing, because she just couldn't envision Cage taking the time to fill water bottles. She grabbed two, and they walked outside, crossing to the barn. They'd only made it halfway when Strudel came tearing after them. He ran to the barn, then back, barking gleefully.

"That dog needs antidepressants," Belle said as she pushed open the barn door.

Lucy laughed. "Dad found him on the side of the highway last winter. He's a happy dog."

"So I see." It should have been harder to envision cranky Cage stopping to rescue some cold, shivering puppy. But it wasn't hard, and the image burned bright in her mind.

Then Lucy flipped on the sound system that Belle had left there. Debussy soared out, startling the images from Belle's head.

Good thing.

Belle dragged the blue mats into place, then Lucy dropped her crutches and inched to the floor, balancing her awkward position with no small amount of grace.

"You're going to dance on the stages of New York one day," Belle murmured. "Specially if you work as hard on your recovery as I know you can."

Lucy flushed. But she looked pleased by the idea. "My mom is a dancer. Did you know that?"

"Yes."

"That's why she's not here, you know. Because she went to Europe to be a dancer."

Belle knew what it was like to strive for a career, but privately, she couldn't imagine leaving behind her own child. "Do you hear from her?"

"I've got copies of programs from her shows," Lucy said, not exactly answering as she reclined again. She lifted her uninjured knee up to her chest, then slowly straightened it, her toes pointed, knee nearly resting on her nose.

A program was not a phone call or a letter, Belle thought. And because she was too curious about the role that Sandi Oldham played in the Buchanans' life, she kicked off her shoes.

"All right," she said briskly. "Let's get you warmed up. We have a lot to accomplish today. After we're done in here, you have a history test to pass."

Lucy groaned.

Standing just outside the barn door, Cage watched Belle and his daughter. Even Strudel sat quietly for once, leaning heavily against Cage's leg, occasionally slapping the dusty ground with his feathered tail. Lucy started out muttering and outright complaining about every single movement Belle put her through. But he never noticed a single sign of impatience in Belle. She was calm, encouraging, humorous. No matter what Lucy threw her way, she maneuvered his daughter into accomplishing whatever task she'd set out.

And eventually, Lucy was grinning as often as she was groaning.

Even though he had a million and one things that needed tending, Cage stayed there, out of sight, for the entire session.

Only when Belle was helping Lucy get her leg situated in the whirlpool afterward did he finally turn away.

Belle might be a Day, she might be a pure source of frustration for his peace of mind, but where Lucy was concerned, Cage felt as if he'd finally done something right.

There was no way a judge could come along now and say that *anyone* could provide better for his own daughter.

Cage's satisfaction lasted well into the next week. And when it ended, it wasn't even because of Belle Day. It was because of his daughter.

He watched her from the door of his office. Watched her long enough to know she hadn't just gone in there for a piece of paper or some such thing. Not that he'd really believed it, given the fact it was nearly midnight.

He leaned his shoulder against the doorjamb. "Who were you calling?" His voice was mild, but she nearly jumped right out of her skin, casting him a guilty look that made his insides tighten.

"Nobody."

He pointedly looked at the telephone situated two inches away from her twitching fingers. "Is that their first or last name?"

She glared at him for a tense moment. Then her face crumpled and she burst into tears and snatched her crutches, racing past him. A few seconds later, she slammed her bedroom door behind her.

He let out an exasperated sigh. The kid had been moody as all get-out for days. He strode after her, only to find she'd locked the door. He rapped on it. "Luce. Unlock it."

"Leave me alone!"

"Who were you talking to on the phone?"

"I *said* leave me alone!" Her muffled voice rose.

He knocked harder. "Open the damn door."

"Cage?" Belle darted down the stairs, peering at him over the banister. "What's wrong?"

"Nothing that concerns you."

She straightened so fast her hair danced around the shoulders of her white robe. "Pardon me." She pivoted on the stairs, going up even faster than she'd come down. Which was saying something.

He jiggled the knob. "Unlock it, Luce, or I will."

The door yanked inward. Lucy glared at him. She was sitting in her chair. "I don't want to talk to *you*. I wanna talk to Belle."

Sixty-three inches of not-so-little girl knew how to pack a punch. He eyed her for a long moment. She eyed him right back. God help him, she was the spitting image of the woman who'd borne her, but he knew she got her attitude straight from him. "Who were you talking to on the phone?" If it was the Oldhams, he was going to have the bloody phone disconnected.

"I don't have to tell you!"

He lifted his eyebrow. "Oh?"

She exhaled loudly. If she could have managed it, he was pretty sure she would have stomped her feet. Instead, she wheeled her chair sharply away from the doorway. "I wanna talk to Belle." Her voice was thick with tears again.

He shoveled his fingers through his hair. "She's your physical therapist," he said flatly. "And it's the middle of the night."

"She's also my *friend*."

While he was only Lucy's dad. And no matter how much he needed to keep Belle Day firmly in one slot, she kept slipping out of it.

He watched Lucy surreptitiously swipe her cheeks.

Dammit.

He went upstairs. Stared at another closed door for a long moment. Then knocked.

Belle opened it so fast, he wondered if she'd been standing there waiting for the opportunity to gloat. Only he couldn't detect any complacency in her expression. She just looked soft. From the top of her rippling brown hair to the tender toes peeking out beneath her long robe.

He was being punished for something, surely. Why else would he be surrounded by females he didn't know how to handle?

"Lucy wants to talk to you."

She tightened the belt of her robe, clearly hesitating.

"What are you waiting for? Yes or no?"

Her soft eyes cooled. "I'm waiting to see if you keel over, because I'm sure you must be choking on coming up here to pass that on."

"If you don't want to go down, say so."

"Given my continued presence under your roof each week, I'd think it would be clear by now that I'd do just about anything for Lucy."

"And nothing for me."

Her eyebrow rose and even though he could practically tuck her in his pocket, she managed to look down her nose at him. "As if you'd accept…anything." Her lips twisted a little and she planted her hand in the center of his chest, pushing until he moved out of the way.

When he did, she slid past him, a wisp nearly smothered in white terrycloth and topped by wavy brown hair.

He followed her downstairs. Told himself he imagined the oddly sympathetic look in her eyes in the moment before Lucy shut the door. Females on the inside.

Him on the outside.

He scrubbed his hand down his face and returned to his office. His desk was a jumble of papers, books and a hackamore he was repairing. The telephone sat smack in the middle of it all.

Who had she been calling? If it were just her friend, Anya,

Luce would simply have told him. He'd have been irritated that she was up so late—and on a long-distance phone call, yet—but hardly enough to inspire that reaction. He rounded the desk and sat down. Leaned back in his chair.

Across from him, pinned to the wall, were all of Lucy's school photographs. But he didn't need the pictures to remember every single moment. The missing teeth. The crooked ponytails. The grins.

"Are you all right?"

His gaze slid to the doorway. Belle stood there. Arms crossed, hands disappearing up the opposite sleeves of her robe.

"She called the Oldhams, didn't she?"

Belle looked startled. "Her grandparents, you mean?"

"What did she tell you?"

"Don't bark at me. The only thing I know about her grandparents are that they've sent her some gifts. Dance programs of her mother's."

"Gifts including that horse." That horse that Belle insisted on letting Lucy visit. He'd gone with them once. Been frustrated as all hell to see that Belle had been right about something else. Lucy might talk a fast game about wanting back on Satin, but she was definitely afraid.

He looked up at Belle, sidetracked a little by the gleam on her lips when she moistened them. "Yes," she admitted. "Lucy…mentioned it."

He propped his elbows on his desk, crinkling letters and invoices. "Then what *did* she tell you?"

She looked down the hallway for a moment then stepped more fully into the confines of his office. There was no chair for her to sit. "She didn't tell me she'd called her grandparents tonight."

Which didn't mean that Lucy hadn't made the call. She thought he didn't know about the other times she'd called.

"Then what's she going on about?" Having to voice the question stuck in his craw big-time.

"We, um, we need to go into town tomorrow."

"For cake mix and candles already?"

Her cheeks were pink. "Well. We could do that."

"I find it hard to believe she's going berserk at midnight over a cake she doesn't even need for weeks yet. It's not like she's going to be troubled over picking a color for the frosting. It'll be pink. Or pink."

"She's not upset about her cake."

"Then what?" He pushed away from his desk only there was no room to pace in the small room. Not unless he wanted to go near Belle, and he didn't want to do that.

Because getting *near* wasn't remotely as close as he wanted to be. And knowing it just pissed him off even more.

"There's something else you need to know." Belle was looking anywhere but at him. "Lucy didn't even want to tell you, but I said she really needed to."

His neck tightened warningly. "What?" His voice was harsh and Belle took a step back.

"Nothing bad," she assured quickly.

"Nothing bad that has her sneaking in my office to use the phone when she's supposed to be sleeping? If she wasn't calling her grandparents, who the hell was she calling?"

"Evan Taggart."

He stared. "What?"

"Who," Belle murmured. "But she didn't get hold of him, anyway, because his parents answered the phone and said it was too late to talk."

"At least Drew Taggart has some sense," he muttered. "So she was upset because she couldn't talk to some little kid."

"Evan's in her grade, Cage. She…likes…him. I think the Taggarts have been out of town on vacation or something. She was making sure he knew he was invited to her party."

He absorbed that.

"But that's not the real problem."

"Then what the hell is?"

"Would you calm down?" She moistened her lips. "Seriously, this is nothing for you to be freaking out over and—"

He grabbed her shoulders. "What...is...it?"

Her lashes lowered. "Well, actually, Lucy got her first period tonight. She's too embarrassed to tell you. And that's why we need to go to town tomorrow. Because I wasn't exactly prepared for this, either."

He sat down on the edge of his desk. "What?"

She tugged her belt tighter. "Judging by your expression, I think you heard me just fine."

"She's only twelve!"

Belle quickly pushed his office door closed even though she knew the barrier wouldn't completely buffer Cage's raised voice. "You want to argue Mother Nature with me? She's all but thirteen, and regardless of *what* her age is, this is happening." She almost felt sorry for him. He looked positively shell-shocked. But sympathy didn't quite douse the sting of being put in her place by him.

"Your daughter is growing up, Cage, and you better start getting used to the idea, or you're going to be dealing with a lot of episodes just as pleasant as this one! The poor thing is being ruled by hormones right now."

He was silent for a moment. Then he held out his hands, cupped palms turned upward. "When she was born I could hold her right here in the palms of my hands. She was that small." His fingers curled and he dropped his fists. "Lucy's always been able to talk to me."

So much for holding on to her indignation.

She impulsively caught his hands in hers, smoothing out his fingers from those tense fists. "This isn't about you, Cage.

It's about her. She's no more used to the things that are going on inside her—emotionally and physically—than you are."

His lashes lifted and his eyes met hers. She was abruptly aware that holding his hands wasn't just a matter of trying to extend comfort.

It felt intimate.

It felt addictive.

She started to pull away. But his thumbs pressed over her fingertips, holding them in place. She could feel the calloused ridges as he slowly brushed over her fingers, grazing over her knuckles.

Her lips parted, yet her breathing had stalled.

They were so close she could easily pick out the black ring surrounding his blue, blue irises. Could have counted each black lash that comprised the thick smudged-coal lashes he'd passed on to his daughter. Could have touched the nearly invisible scar on his chin just below the curve of his lower lip.

She realized she was leaning in, and shock jerked her back, hands and eyes and traitorous hormones and all. Was she no better than Annette Barrone?

He wrapped his hands around the edge of his desk on either side of his hips. "Put whatever you need in town on my account," he said after a moment. His voice was low.

She nodded and started backing out of the office. Bumped into the door that she'd closed. Heat stung her cheeks as she fumbled for the knob. Thankfully, the door opened. Escape was near.

"Belle."

She really felt safer when he called her *Miss Day.* Did he know how close she'd come to leaning forward those last few inches and pressing her lips to his? "Yes?" Lord, she hoped not. Her humiliation would be complete.

"Thank you."

Her knees threatened to dissolve right there. She nodded quickly and poured herself out of his office.

She hoped to heaven that he couldn't see the way she had to wait until she stopped shaking at the foot of the stairs before climbing them. She hoped to heaven that when she did go up the stairs, she'd remember somewhere along the way that Cage Buchanan was off limits.

He blamed her father for the accident that stole his parents. He didn't know—couldn't possibly—that it was Belle's fault that she and her father had been out at all on that icy road that long-ago night.

Chapter 8

Cage saw her coming. There was no mistaking the sheaf of brown hair streaming back from her as she leaned low over the horse, seeming to race with the wind. Belle was quite a sight. Three weeks had passed since that night in his office. Three weeks of relative peace and quiet. Except for the nights, spent wakeful and alert with her only a room away.

He propped his wrists over the end of the posthole digger and watched her closing the distance between them. Anticipation tangled with wariness and it wasn't a combination he particularly welcomed.

At least she wasn't foolish enough to be riding that satanic horse. No matter how well Lucy was doing after working with Belle all this time, he'd have still probably fired Belle for it.

The horse was a line he wouldn't let anyone cross.

He leaned the digger against the truck and shoved his wire clippers back in his toolbox, then sat on the opened tailgate and chugged down a half a bottle of water, waiting.

Because sure as God made little green apples, he knew that Belle Day was gunning for him.

He heard the hooves pound and wouldn't allow himself the luxury of looking away as she neared, slowly reining in the animal. She looked fragile as she dismounted, but he knew only too well that she was nothing but muscle and nerve under those body-skimming clothes she wore.

She flipped the reins around the side-view mirror of the truck then lifted her hand, shading her eyes from the noonday sun as she looked at him. "As usual, you're a hard man to track down. Gone before breakfast. Back after dinner."

"Where's Lucy?"

"Emmy Johannson brought Anya out to visit now that she's back from visiting her father. They're eating lunch right now. Emmy's going to give Lucy a piano lesson, too."

"Then what's wrong?" He pulled a fence post out of the truck bed and shoved it into the hole he'd already dug, then pushed at it with his boot, aligning it. "And why didn't you drive?"

She propped her hands on her narrow hips and tilted her head. Her long hair flowed over her shoulder and her eyes glanced at him, then away. It had been that way for days. Weeks. Looking, but not looking.

Wanting but not touching. At least on his part, anyhow.

He kicked the post again.

"I'm not unfamiliar with horses," she countered. "I've been riding all my life. And I wasn't foolish enough to ride Satin. Though I did notice you're letting him run at least."

He hated the horse because of what he stood for and how it had hurt his daughter. But he wasn't cruel enough to keep the animal penned in a stall forever. He pushed the post once more, still not satisfied with the way it stood. "I'd have preferred you ask me, first."

She huffed a little then walked around him. "Fine. I will, next time." She grabbed the heavy post beneath his hands and put her shoulder against it, nudging it in his direction. "Centered?"

He narrowed his eyes, studying the top of her dark head for a moment. "Yeah." He made quick work out of filling the hole again then quickly fastened the barbed wire back in place when she moved out of the way.

She flipped her long ponytail behind her shoulders and pulled a long, thin envelope out from behind her. He barely glanced at the envelope, distracted by the wedge of skin she displayed when she'd flipped up her shirt to pull out the envelope tucked against her spine beneath it. "This looked important. A courier brought it out."

His stomach clenched as she extended the envelope.

He slowly took it. Eyed the embossed return address.

"Do you want to talk about it?" Her voice was surprisingly diffident.

"No." He folded the envelope in half then pushed it in his back pocket. If he had to read a letter that he was another step closer to losing custody of his baby, he damn sure didn't want to do it while Belle Day was standing there to witness it.

But she just stood there, though, hands clutched together. "Is there anything I can do?"

"No." Not unless she had about fifty grand lying around unused. He figured it would cost at least that much to get Sandi to back off. Either the money would go in her pocket, or the lawyer's. He turned back to the truck. Hoisted the next pole over his shoulder and moved down to the next hole.

"Cage, if you have some legal problem, my family might—"

"No." He didn't like feeling as if he'd kicked a calf when she paled a little and pressed her soft lips together. But he didn't have it in him just then to apologize.

"Well, then do you think—"

"Dammit to hell, Belle, I said no."

She winced. "You don't even know what I was going to ask!"

He exhaled roughly. Shoved the post into the ground with a vengeance. "I don't want your help. God knows I don't want your family's help. I don't want anything." Except her body. A problem which was becoming more evident by the minute. "Satisfied?"

"The Clays are having a party," she said stiffly. "They wanted me to extend the invitation to you and Lucy."

He looked up into the sky. He'd never had much against Squire Clay or his sons. The boys had been ahead of him a few years, but they knew each other passably. Didn't mean he wanted to sit down with tea and cookies across the table from Squire's wife, Gloria Day.

There was probably a special place in Hades for him, but he just couldn't look at the woman without thinking about his own mother, and what Gloria's husband had done to her. Call him a miserable puke, but there it was.

"What's the party for?"

Her brown eyes widened a little. Surprised that he'd bothered to ask, no doubt. "Angeline's birthday. She's Daniel and Maggie's oldest. The party is a week after Lucy's, actually."

He'd seen the girl. Dusky skinned. Pretty as a picture. All he knew about her was that her natural parents were dead and Daniel and Maggie had adopted her a long time ago. "Take Lucy."

"Really?"

He *really* wished she'd go on her way. The letter was burning a hole in his butt. "If she wants to go."

"Well." She brushed her hands together, obviously surprised. "This is wonderful. We'll be swimming. The Double-C has a great swimming hole, you see, and—"

"—and I don't have time to stand around shooting the

breeze," he said flatly. "So why don't you go back and tend to what I *am* paying you for?"

Her chin lifted a little. "Keep up with the ogre routine, Cage. One of these days you'll have it perfected and maybe even you will forget it's an act." She strode over to the truck and snatched the reins. With a move he admired whether he wanted to or not, she slid onto the horse's back. In a flash, they were racing away.

When she was out of sight, he let his eyes rove over the land around him. When he'd inherited it, the Lazy-B hadn't been much more than a chunk of dirt from which his father had scratched out a meager living.

Now, it was prime. As was his stock. Prime enough that he knew he could get a decent price if he asked. God knew, he'd gotten more than a few offers over the years, specially from the Clays who ran the biggest operation in the entire state.

Problem was, Cage didn't want to sell.

But he didn't want to lose his daughter more.

He pulled out the letter and looked at the envelope. Delivered by a courier this time. Was that a polite word for a process server? He didn't know.

He went over to the truck. Sat down on the ground beside it in the shade and was glad there was no one but the birds sailing overhead to know his hands were shaking as he tore open the envelope.

The letter was brief. The missive unmistakable.

Sandi hadn't been bluffing. The Oldhams wanted Lucy in their family fold. And Sandi was using her parents' significant wealth to make it happen. He hadn't buckled to her, so she'd sicced her parents on him instead. And now their personal requests to see their granddaughter—denied by him—had become a legal challenge. For custody.

He leaned his head back against the truck and closed his eyes. And there was no way the attorney he'd been able to afford would be up to fighting the half-dozen attorneys the Oldhams had pitted against him. Even if he sold the ranch to pay an attorney of that caliber, there was little chance he'd win.

They were the Oldhams of Chicago. Bank president. Society matron. Old money, older reputation. Everything that Sandi had shunned when she'd been twenty years old. Everything she'd warned him about when she'd convinced him that telling her parents she was pregnant would be their biggest mistake. And back then he'd been more interested in keeping Sandi from doing something stupid to end her pregnancy than to argue the issue of informing *her* parents about the baby.

Obviously, it suited Sandi now to have her parents on her side. He pinched the bridge of his nose, fleeting ideas of taking his daughter and getting the hell out of Dodge hovering in his mind.

But he'd never been a runner. If he had been, he'd have run hard and fast from the responsibilities of a ranch and a child when he'd still been pretty much a kid himself.

He thumped his head back against the truck.

Lucy deserved more. She deserved every single privilege that came with being the only Oldham grandchild.

But lying down without a fight just wasn't something he could do.

"Cage?"

He pushed to his feet and pushed the papers into the envelope as he looked across the truck. Belle was back and he'd been too preoccupied to hear. "What?" He slammed down the lid of the toolbox, the envelope safely inside. If she asked him again about it, he was going to rip something apart.

Her hand was shading her eyes. "What were you doing? Hiding?"

No matter what, the idea had appeal. Take Lucy. Hide. Try

and forget the turmoil caused by various members of the Day family. "Forget something?" She couldn't have made it to the house and all the way back again in the amount of time that had passed.

She slid off Dexter's back and tied him loosely, again, to the truck's side mirror. "Figured Lucy wouldn't be finished with her lesson yet. And she needs some time to just hang with Anya, anyway. Are there more gloves in that toolbox?"

"Why?"

She shrugged and walked to the truck bed herself. "Because I don't want to get blisters."

He stepped in her path before she could flip open the toolbox. "Caused by…what?"

She pointedly looked at the posts stacked lengthwise in the bed.

"I don't want your help." Her body? That was something entirely different.

God. He needed to get out of Weaver more often. There were plenty of women he knew around the state who were more than happy to spend a few recreational hours with him. Women who didn't want or expect anything more than what he was willing to share. Intelligent, independent, warm women, who never thought to—or wanted to—interfere in his life.

"Yes. You've made that abundantly clear," Belle said evenly. "The gloves?"

He frowned down at her, but she didn't come close to taking the hint. She just looked up at him, head tilted to one side, eyes squinting in the sunlight that turned her dark brown eyes to amber-stained glass. "You need a hat," he muttered.

"Well, it so happens that I don't have one of those, either." She lifted her shoulder, barely covered by the narrow strap of a snug gray shirt. "Just so you know, if I *do* get blisters, it's going to be hard for me to work out Lucy's muscle spasms, but—"

He nudged her aside and flipped up the toolbox, blindly grabbing a pair of leather gloves. He slammed the lid back down and slapped them in her hand. Then shoved his own bloody hat onto her head. "You're a pain in the ass, you know that?"

"I believe you've expressed that sentiment, as well, even if you haven't used those particular words." She nudged back the hat so it wasn't covering her eyes. It was too big for her.

But damned if she didn't look cute.

Bloody hell.

He yanked on his own gloves and reached for the posthole digger. Pushed it at her. "Know how to use one of those?" Maybe it would shut her up. Keep her from looking at him with those big brown eyes.

She rolled her eyes. A habit picked up from Lucy? "Yes," she drawled.

About as well as she knew how to fix her lawn mower, he figured. He shouldered a heavy post and headed away from the truck. She hurried after him. Five minutes, he calculated, and she'd be all too ready to go back to the sanctuary of the house.

Only five minutes passed and she showed no sign of stopping. Even though the ground was harder than stone and the muscles in her arms were standing out as she struggled.

He swiped his sweaty forehead with his arm. "Give me that."

"I can do it." Her voice was gritty.

"Maybe," he allowed blandly, "but why would you want to?"

She tossed her head, her tied-back hair rippling. "God only knows," she muttered. She wrapped her fingers freshly around the long wooden handles. "Maybe because I still haven't gotten over needing to prove that I can." She lifted the digger and slammed it back into the earth. The sharp edges of the shovel finally bit. "Ha!" She pulled apart the handles, catching a small amount of dirt between the blades, then dropped it to one side.

There was such satisfaction in her sudden grin that Cage stepped back and let her work. Sweat was dripping from her forehead by the time she'd dug the hole deep enough for the post and tossed aside the digger.

"You gonna plant the post, too?" His voice was dry.

She shook her head, leaning over, arms braced on her thighs. "Wouldn't want you to start feeling wimpy," she said breathlessly. "Oh, God. Now that's some serious work, isn't it? No wonder you never have to touch the weights in the barn." She straightened, only to tear off her shirt and wipe her face with it.

He nearly swallowed his tongue, though the sport bra she wore was made of some thick gray stuff that was about as erotic as wool socks.

He had an unbidden vision of Belle wearing nothing *but* wool socks.

He shoved the post in place, backfilling the hole. "Now that you've played at manual labor, mebbe you could get back to your *real* work?" And leave him alone with his frustrating visions, fueled by the memory that wouldn't die even after all this time of her perfectly formed breasts.

She pulled off his cowboy hat and lifted her hair from her neck, stretching a little. "Everybody needs to play now and then," she said, her eyes slanting toward him. "Even you."

He grunted and turned away from the post. More importantly, he turned away from the sight of her, stretching like some sort of lithe cat. "Consider this my back nine."

"Do you golf?"

He looked at her.

Her lips twisted ruefully. "Suppose it's hard to golf, when there's no course around here."

"Suppose it's hard to golf when there's no time," he corrected.

"Do you even *know* how to play golf?"

"Do you?"

She shook her head.

He smiled a little despite himself and headed for the truck. Dexter had his nose buried in the grass, and didn't even lift his head when Cage passed him.

"You didn't answer," Belle said, following him.

"Observant of you."

"Afraid I might bandy about the news of your golfing prowess around Weaver?"

He spotted the tool chest in his truck bed and the brief spate of humor shriveled.

"Go back to the house, Miss Day," he said flatly, and plucked his hat out of her fingers. "Playtime is over."

She blinked a little. "Maybe if you *indulged* in some playtime, you'd start sleeping at night." She grabbed up Dexter's reins and smoothly swung up into the saddle.

As she rode away, he thought he heard her mutter. "Ogre."

Chapter 9

"Range of motion remains severely limited despite marked increase in muscle tone and—" Belle stopped writing when she heard the scream.

Another nightmare. The third since the afternoon Belle had ridden out to see Cage.

She pushed back from the kitchen chair, concern propelling her down the hall even though she knew in her head that Cage would beat her to Lucy's room. Sure enough, he was striding into his old bedroom, and in the half light, she watched him sit on the side of Lucy's bed.

She hovered there for a moment, then turned back to the kitchen and her notes. She sat down, staring at the report that she made out each week charting Lucy's progress. But her mind was still stuck on the picture of Cage with his daughter.

She'd seen him helping Lucy with her exercises a few days earlier. And had hidden out of sight, so as not to interrupt the moment. And, maybe, to absorb the knot of emotion the sight had caused inside her.

She pressed her lips together now, as unsettled as she had been then, and hurriedly shut the file folder.

She needed to talk to her sister. She and Nikki had been missing each other's phone calls for too many days now.

Her cell phone was upstairs in her room, but when she headed for the stairs, the sight of Cage standing in Lucy's doorway stopped her in her tracks.

"She's asking for you."

Belle paused, trying to read his expression. Should she refuse? Make some attempt at sliding back into the professional role she was supposed to be occupying?

She nodded silently and headed toward Lucy's room. Who was she trying to kid? Her professionalism where this family was concerned was nonexistent.

She slipped past Cage into the bedroom, casting him a quick look.

His face was hard.

She ducked her head again and crossed over to Lucy's bed, sitting in the same spot that Cage had. Lucy's hair was tumbled, her face glistening with sweat. Belle snatched a tissue from the box on the nightstand and pressed it to Lucy's forehead. "What's wrong?" Lucy shifted, looking past Belle.

She looked back to see Cage watching from the hall. At their attention, he turned on his heel and went into his office. The door shut after him.

Softly, quietly. Controlled.

Belle chewed the inside of her lip and focused once more on Lucy. "Are you sick or something?" They'd already survived last month's first-period episode. Lucy, fortunately, had adjusted quickly enough.

Belle wasn't sure she could say the same of Lucy's father.

"I have a charley horse in my leg."

"Same place as before?" If the nightmares were frequent, the muscle spasms were more so. Nearly every day the girl had been plagued with muscle spasms in her calf. Lucy nodded and Belle pushed aside the bedding, reaching for Lucy's leg. She gently began massaging, and determined immediately that if Lucy'd *had* a charley horse, it was long gone. She kept working her fingers into the muscle, though. "Another bad dream?"

Lucy made a noncommittal sound, remembering to offer a wince now and then in honor of her phantom cramp.

"Want to talk about it?"

Lucy merely turned her cheek into her pillow.

"I used to have a recurring nightmare." Belle shifted so she was sitting more comfortably, and continued working Lucy's leg. "From when I was hurt."

"In the accident where my Grandma was hurt?"

"Yes."

"It was pretty bad, huh."

It took no effort at all for Belle to recall the excruciating details. Which she didn't want to do. "Yes. Anyway, I was in the hospital for weeks, too. Like you were after Satin threw you. Fortunately, I didn't need surgery like you did."

"How old were you?"

"Thirteen. I had nightmares for a long time after that."

Lucy's face was a canvas of shadows.

"I didn't dream about the accident, though. I kept dreaming that everyone I knew and cared about was walking. On a street, in a store. The places changed sometimes. But they were walking. And I couldn't keep up. Couldn't make myself take one single step no matter how hard I tried. I couldn't run, much less walk, after them. I couldn't walk *with* them." Her fingers slowed. "Of course, when I was awake, I knew that my family and my friends weren't leaving me behind, but when I was asleep?" She shook her head.

"But they stopped. The nightmares. Right?"

"Yes, they stopped."

Lucy looked at her. "When?"

"When I started talking about them." She waited a moment, hoping Lucy would heed the hint. But the girl remained silent. "Charley horse gone now?"

Lucy nodded.

"Good." She tucked the covers back in place and headed for the door. "G'night, sweetie."

"Belle? Could you—"

She stepped back to the bedside. "Could I what?" she prompted gently.

"StayuntilIgotosleep?" The words came out in a rush.

Belle's heart squeezed. "You bet." She pulled up the small pink chair that was crammed in the corner and sat beside the bed.

Lucy scooted further down her pillow and turned on her side, facing Belle. "Are you going to be here for my birthday party?" Her voice was little more than a whisper.

"If you want me to be."

Lucy nodded. She closed her eyes.

In minutes, she was asleep again.

Belle sat there a while longer, her thoughts tangled. When it seemed clear that Lucy was sleeping soundly, she quietly moved the chair back to the corner and left the room, pulling the door partially closed.

Cage's office, when she peeked around the doorway, was empty. But she didn't have to look far to find him. It was the middle of the night. Naturally, he would be sitting out on the porch, his long legs stretched out in front of him, his eyes staring into the dark.

She pushed open the screen to see him more clearly, but didn't go out. "Lucy's asleep again." Her heart ached a little, because she knew it had to sting that his daughter had turned to her again. "It's not my imagination that her nightmares are coming more often, is it?"

The shake of his head was slow in coming.

"Have you—" Lord, she didn't want him berating her for being interfering again "—um, have you told her physician that she's plagued with them?"

His gaze slid her way. Unreadable. He nodded. Shifted, crossing his boots at the ankle. The pose ought to have been casual. Relaxed.

Belle knew better. She also knew better than to probe for the reasons causing *his* habitual sleeplessness.

"She also asked if I'd stick around for her birthday party." Better to get that out now. The party was scheduled for Friday night, after Belle would have ordinarily left for the weekend.

"Damn straight," he murmured. "It was your idea in the first place. Least you can do is play chaperone."

She absorbed that, alternately glad that she wasn't going to have to butt heads with him over the matter, and unnerved that she didn't.

"Then you can kiss her wounds when the party is a bust," he added darkly.

"It's not going to be a bust."

"There's no room for a bunch of kids in this house."

"We'll figure it out. Maybe use the barn."

He shot her a look.

"I'm serious. Crepe-paper streamers and balloons. Plenty of soda and munchies. It'll be fine. In fact, it was Lucy's idea. She mentioned it earlier this week. We've already bought the decorations and stuff. We'll just put it all up in the barn instead of the house."

Cage ran his hand through his hair, finally showing some emotion. Chagrin. "Might as well. *This* place is a mess."

Belle chewed the inside of her lip. She was not going to be charmed by the dusky color running under his sharp cheekbones. If he hadn't been so ornery about her helping with some of the household tasks, the house *wouldn't* be quite as unkempt as it was. "Hard for one person to do everything," she said pointedly. Running the B. Raising a daughter on his own. Taking care of their sturdy, little brick home.

Cage hadn't responded—either to agree or disagree. And standing there in the doorway was making her feel out of place. She started to turn back inside.

"What if nobody comes?"

His gruff comment jangled in her head for a tight moment before her brain engaged her tongue. Instead of stepping inside, she stepped outside the screen door, her fingers holding the door long enough to let it close without a sound. "That won't happen, Cage," she assured quietly. "They are Lucy's friends."

"Their parents aren't mine."

She swallowed, pressing her lips together for a moment. She watched the bevy of moths beat themselves against the glow of the porch light. "Only because you won't let them be. The only reason people speculate so much about you is because you hold yourself apart from them."

"I don't like everyone knowing my business."

"This is a small community. That's bound to happen no matter what you like or don't like. And if you weren't so…standoffish—" She waited a beat at that, sure he'd cut her off. But he didn't. "Maybe people would surprise you. Maybe they'd accept your need for privacy more if you were more accepting of them." Which, even to her, sounded convoluted.

Disregarding the wisdom she was not displaying, she crossed the porch and sat on the low rail, facing him. The night air was cool on her bare arms but she knew if she went in for a sweater, the moment would be lost. "In any case, despite the fact that you hold others at a distance, Lucy hasn't. People in Weaver care about what happens to her, and they'll want to celebrate with her, too. Everyone who was invited accepted weeks ago. You can't really think that they'd blow her off now right before the party."

He looked far from convinced. "It's late. You should be in bed."

Her cheeks warmed, despite the cool night air. "You get up even earlier than I do. I don't know how you do it, frankly. I was still up so I could finish my report and get it in the mail to Lucy's orthopedist. Otherwise I'd be sawing logs by now."

"Lucky you." He leaned his head back against the chair, watching her from beneath lowered lids. "Did she tell you what her nightmare is about?"

Those thin slices of blue—pale even in the subdued porch light—were unsettling and she looked down at her stockinged feet. Two inches from his boots.

She curled her toes down against the wood porch and shook her head. "She'll talk when she's ready, I imagine. Same way she puts effort into her therapy only when she's ready."

"She's been doing her exercises on her own on the weekends."

"I know. I can tell when we work together each Monday. She's still not making the progress I would have hoped." Belle wasn't sure what made her admit that to him. It wasn't that Lucy wasn't progressing at all.

"And what did you hope for? To have her dancing on her toes by Thanksgiving?" He sat forward suddenly, elbows on knees, fingers raking through his hair.

If she lifted her hand, she'd be touching the bronzed strands springing back from his forehead. She pressed her fingertips harder against the wooden rail beneath her. "Maybe not by Thanksgiving," she admitted. "Now, Christmas?" She shrugged, smiling a little, even though they both knew Belle would be long gone before either holiday.

"She's on crutches. Not walking on her own entirely,

but given what the doctor told us after the accident—that she might not walk that well again, ever—I think it's pretty amazing." Then he glanced up at her, the corners of his lips turning up.

The surprise of that half smile had her nearly falling backward off the rail. She jerked a little and he shot out his hand, grabbing hers. "Thanks." She hoped he'd blame her breathlessness on being startled.

"I don't need you breaking your neck on top of everything else," he muttered.

So much for him nearly smiling. She wiggled her fingers, drawing attention to his continued hold and he released her.

Her wrists still felt surrounded by a ring of warmth as she scooted past him toward the door. Asking him what caused *his* sleeplessness would be pointless. Foolish.

She still wondered.

A lot.

She opened the door and quickly went inside. "Good night, Cage."

Not until she was nearly at the foot of the staircase did she hear his quiet reply. "Good night, Belle."

She tightened her grip on the banister and forced her feet to the first riser. And the next. It was frightening how hard it was to continue when everything inside her was tugging on her to go back out there. To keep poking and prodding as if *she* could break through his barriers.

Crazy. That's what she was.

She passed Cage's room, carefully averting her eyes from looking inside, and went in her own room. She'd barely climbed into bed—which had been squeaking again for a solid month despite Cage's efforts shortly after she'd arrived—when her cell phone gave a soft squawk.

She grabbed it off the nightstand. "Nik?"

"I've been calling you for hours."

Something inside her went on full alert. "What's wrong?"

"Who said anything's wrong?" Nikki's voice was tight. "I've left you a half-dozen messages."

Belle flopped on her back, covering her eyes with her hand. "I'm sorry. I should have tried harder to reach you. Oh, God, Nik. I don't know what I'm doing here. Why I thought I could…make up somehow for the past."

"Scott's been released."

Her thoughts floundered. "What? Oh. Well, good. Then his wife won't be making the staff there miserable."

Nikki was silent for a long moment. "Okay, catch me up here, Belle. When you said make up for the past, I thought you meant proving to yourself that you had what it took to be a good therapist. After Scott blamed you because he wasn't ever going to be able to get back to football—"

"Scott hasn't even been the last thing on my mind," she murmured truthfully. And it was a relief to know it. "I wanted…I very nearly…I wanted to kiss him, Nikki. Taste him. Breathe him in. More than once now."

"Scott…oh, no." Dismay colored her sister's voice. "Please tell me you're not talking about Cage Buchanan."

"Okay, I'll tell you that," Belle whispered after a long moment. "But I'd be lying." She waited for Nikki to say all the things that were running through her own mind.

Don't get personally involved with patients or their families.

Don't get personally involved with a man who loathes your parentage.

Don't get personally involved period, end of story.

Nikki said none of them. She merely sighed. "Oh, Belle."

And with that soft, sympathetic murmur, tears stung Belle's eyes. "He's a good man, Nik. And he loves his daughter so much it is heartbreaking and beautiful all at the same time."

"What are you going to do about it?"

Her fingers plucked at the quilt. Had Cage's mother made it? Was quilting just one more thing that had been amputated from her existence the night of the car accident? "There's nothing *to* do. He didn't hire me out of personal interest, after all." Far from it. "I'm here because of Lucy. I just need to focus on her and everything will be fine."

The words rang a little too hollow, and Belle was grateful that her sister refrained from observing it. "So, why the half-dozen messages to call you back, anyway?"

"I quit."

The words made no sense at first. "What? Oh, hell's bells." She sat forward on the bed, pressing the phone tighter to her ear. "Why? Alex refused to give you the raise you deserve, didn't he? Is he out of his tiny little mind?"

"I never asked for the raise." Nikki's voice sounded thick and Belle realized her sister had been crying. She felt like a selfish witch for not having immediately noticed.

"Then why? You love your job." She heard Nikki sigh shakily and her nerves tightened. "Nik? What's really going on here?"

"This is harder to tell than I thought it would be."

"Nikki, you're scaring me. What?"

"I'm…um…I'm pregnant."

Belle blinked, staring blindly at her fingers that were clenching a handful of quilt.

"Belle?"

She scrambled. "Since when? Are you feeling okay? Have you been to the doctor?"

"Almost six weeks ago. Yes. And yes."

"Six weeks…God, Nik, I didn't even know you were involved with someone."

Her sister made a watery sound. "Well, that's just it, isn't it. I'm *not* involved."

"Then how—"

"The usual way."

Belle swallowed. Her sister didn't indulge in casual sex any more than Belle did. "I'm coming down to see you."

"No. You have a job there."

"Then I'll come on the weekend. Don't try to put me off, Nicole. I'm not going to rest until I've seen you in person. Have you told Mom?"

"No. And you better not, either."

"She's going to have to know sooner or later. Angel's party is a week from Saturday. You're going to the ranch for it, aren't you? Mom's going to know something is up."

"I'll deal with next week…next week. Look, Belle. We're not sixteen years old anymore. I just…need some time before I tell her."

Belle chewed her lip. Her sister had always been the one with straight As in school. Who'd never taken a single step off the line of excellence and responsibility. It was Belle who'd been the one to bumble through life. Not Nikki. "What about the father?" She pushed at her temples. "And why quit your job now? You're going to need your medical benefits…unless, do you already have someplace else you're going to?"

"No."

"Then why quit? I can't believe Alex let you go after all this time. Does he know? Is that why he allowed you to leave? There are laws, Nikki—"

"The only one who knows is you. I needed to tell someone or I was going to go mad."

"I have a million questions, you know."

"I know. Can we just deal with them another day?"

"Yes." Her sister was pregnant. And Belle hadn't felt a hint of it. "You're sure you're feeling okay?"

"Tired. Otherwise, fine."

"And you're done talking for now," Belle surmised.

"Yes."

Her eyes stung. "I love you, you know. No matter what goes on. You're going to be a great mother."

Nikki's soft laugh was watery, but it was a laugh. "You'll be a great aunt."

"I'm coming down this weekend," Belle reminded, half warning, half reassuring.

"G'night, Annabelle." Her sister hung up.

Belle stared at the small phone in her hand for a moment, then tossed it aside. She pushed off the bed, and left the room, her mind too busy to rest.

The house was dark now, Cage's bedroom door closed. She let herself out the kitchen door and was halfway to the barn before she realized she hadn't put on her shoes. Her soles prickled, but she didn't turn back.

Inside the barn, she blindly selected a song on her iPod, which was still in the player, turned it down from Lucy's preferred roar, and dragged out a floor mat. An hour later, she was still at it. Two hours later, her muscles were screaming and her hair was clinging to her sweaty face and neck. Her mind was still teeming, but at least she'd managed to numb the questions into submission. She blew out a long breath and dropped down onto the incline bench, closing her eyes.

Maybe she'd just sleep right there.

"Get 'em worked out?"

Numb enough not to be startled when Cage spoke. She looked at him. "What?"

"The demons," he said.

Not in a dozen workouts. "I thought you'd finally gone to bed." Maybe he had. He wore an untucked white T-shirt now with his jeans, instead of the chambray shirt from before. "Don't you *ever* sleep?"

He ambled closer. Handed her a small towel off the stack

she'd kept handy since she'd come to the ranch. "This is usual for me. Not for you."

She took the towel and pressed the white terry cloth to her face. She'd sit up just as soon as she had the energy. "My sister quit her job." She winced behind the towel, wishing she'd kept her mouth shut. But she supposed it was better than blurting out Nikki's *other* news.

"She works at the same place you did, doesn't she?"

"Huffington." Belle dropped her arms, the towel clutched in one hand. Cage was standing near the foot of the bench. "She was the boss's right hand, in fact."

"Afraid that means you're not going to be welcomed back to the clinic with open arms when your…leave…is over?"

Forget aching, tired muscles. She popped off the bench. "No. The thought hadn't even occurred to me," she snapped. "Not that I expect you to believe that I—a *Day*—could be concerned about something outside of myself." She brushed past him, hating the way her voice shook. But his arm shot out, his hand wrapping around her arm.

"I'm sorry."

She shivered. Wanting badly to blame it on the night air drifting over her sweaty body. Knowing it was just as much because of the gruff tone in his voice and the way his knuckles were pressing against the side of her breast.

She tugged away from his hold, that wasn't really a hold at all when he let go of her so easily and she was grateful she hadn't betrayed the way he made her feel.

Without looking at him, she walked over to the sound system. Flipped the power, cutting off Paul McCartney midnote.

"I'm sorry, too," she whispered.

About so many things.

She walked out, leaving Cage standing there in the barn, surrounded by weights and mats and bars and balls, all procured with the intention of helping Lucy walk and run and dance again.

Just then, however, it felt to Belle as if she and Cage were the ones in need of walking lessons.

Chapter 10

"What are they doing in there? I've only been gone ten minutes."

Belle looked up at Cage and shot out her arm, barring him from barreling into the barn. "They're dancing," she said, taking an extra step to keep her balance. She didn't have to keep her voice lowered. There was no possible way the kids inside the barn would hear a word they said outside the barn. The music was too loud.

"I don't *want* them dancing."

A sputter of laughter escaped before she could prevent it. "Don't be such a grouch." Belle wrapped her hands around his forearm, digging in her heels. "You agreed to this," she reminded.

The lights from inside the barn were dim, but the moon was full and bright. Easily clear enough to see his expression as he looked from her hands to his arm. Belle hastily released him and circled her fingers against her palms. For days now, she'd managed to keep her thoughts right where they belonged.

At least she had while she'd been awake.

Sleep? That was a whole other kettle of tuna.

"Just peek in then," she allowed. "See for yourself."

He angled his head so he could see through the open barn door without drawing attention to himself.

Belle chewed the inside of her lip, waiting. She knew what he'd see.

And she knew the moment he *did* see, for his hand suddenly flattened against the weathered red wood and he exhaled slowly.

His newly turned teenage daughter was dancing with a boy. Crutches and all.

"That's Drew Taggart's boy."

She swallowed, an image of Cage's face so close to hers flashing through her mind. "Yes."

"He's got his arms around her."

"Well," Belle smiled gently, "in a manner of speaking, he does." The truth was, Evan Taggart looked as if he was half-afraid to touch Lucy and Lucy looked as if she was equally unsure of the entire process. But they were surrounded by fifteen other couples in exactly the same situation and nobody was making a move to change it. "She was afraid everyone would dance except her." She leaned her shoulder against the wall, watching. "I think they're doing pretty well considering she's still using her crutches."

Cage shifted, moving behind her. A shiver danced down her spine that she couldn't hope to blame on anything other than him. He propped his hand above her head and leaned closer, obviously trying to follow Lucy and Evan's lurching progress around the balloon-bedecked interior.

She felt surrounded by him.

And because it wasn't entirely unpleasant—well, not at all unpleasant if she was honest with herself—she focused harder on the kids. She'd agreed to help chaperone this shindig. She couldn't very well do that when she was preoccupied by the wall of warm, male chest heating her back.

She felt parched but her trusty water bottle was empty, and she was afraid if she stuck her head in amongst the dancers to get another drink, the boys and girls would retreat again to their opposite corners the way they'd been for the first hour.

"Thirteen," Cage murmured. "I guess I blinked."

"They do grow up fast. Every time I turn around my nieces and nephews have grown a foot." She glanced up at him, only to find his focus not on his daughter, but on her. She forgot about being amused right along with the art of breathing.

For days she'd worked so hard at forgetting…things. And now, all that hard work was for naught. "Arnold," she blurted.

His gaze didn't seem to stray from her lips. "What?"

"Your name." A naughty breeze skipped over them, splaying her hair across her cheek.

He caught the strands, brushing them back. "I told you. It's unique."

Arnold wasn't the current rage, but it wasn't unique. She cast her mind about, but coherence was annoyingly elusive. "How long is it?" Why did he still have a lock of her hair between his fingers?

His eyebrows rose. "Excuse me?"

She turned, facing him. Putting some necessary space between them. Shoving her hair behind her shoulders. "Letters. Syllables."

"Six. Two."

Easily as tall as some of her stepbrothers. Tall enough that she could wear heels and press her lips against the curve of his brown, corded throat.

Her face went hot and she hoped to heaven that the moonlight wasn't bright enough to reveal that. "Six letters," she murmured. "Two syllables." Though she'd bet his height *was* right around six-two.

"You're shivering."

"No, I'm not." She quickly turned back around, looking inside the barn. The music had changed. Most of the couples still danced. Not Evan and Lucy. But the boy was handing Lucy a cup of soda, his expression verging on adoring.

"You are." Cage's hand cupped her shoulder.

Belle closed her eyes for a moment. "It's the breeze," she lied.

He didn't reply. But he lowered his hand. And she heard the scrape of his boots on the gravel and turned to see him walking toward the house.

She blinked. Well. Okay. So her imagination was running riot again.

She turned back to watch the goings-on inside the barn. As Murphy's Law often proved, just when the boys and girls were starting to really have fun, it would be nearly time for them to leave. The boys, at least. The girls were staying for an overnight.

She tilted her watch to the light. Less than an hour and the rides would start arriving. Even with carpooling, there were several cars needed. Given the surprising occurrence of a party being held on the Lazy-B, the adults who'd brought their sons and daughters had admirably contained their curiosity. But she'd bet her paycheck that once they were back in town, the phone lines started buzzing.

"Here."

She nearly jumped out of her skin. Cage had returned. And he was tossing a plaid wool jacket over her shoulders.

Gads. It smelled like new-mown hay and fresh air with a dollop of coffee. It smelled like *him*. She clutched the collar with both hands, keeping it from sliding off her shoulders.

"Thanks." The thing did nothing for her shivers, however. And the faint twist of his lips implied that he knew it.

Particularly when he scooped her hair free of the jacket and let it drift over her shoulders. "You don't wear your hair loose very often."

She hurriedly turned back to watch the youths. "No." It came out more of a croak, and she felt her face heat. "It gets in the way." That was better. A little less amphibian.

"Why not cut it?"

She shrugged. The slick lining of the jacket slid over her bare shoulders. Proving that she really was losing her mind. It was an ageless woolen jacket with a crinkling, polyester lining, for God's sake. Not seductive lingerie. "Lazy, I guess." She shoved her arms through the sleeves. The cuffs hung well below her fingertips. She probably looked like a clown. Hardly seductive.

Which she wasn't aiming for anyway. Right?

"You, lazy? That what gets you outta bed to jog around this place nearly every morning?"

How could the man be aware of things occurring when he was out doing the rancher thing? She marshaled her thoughts with some difficulty. "Easier to pull it back in a ponytail than mess with some shorter style. And the weight keeps the waves more or less controllable."

"Ever had it cut?"

"Of course." She had it trimmed regularly. "Never more than an inch or two, though. Cage—" She turned to face him, only to find whatever she'd planned to say flying right out of her head.

He'd sifted his fingers through the long ends of her hair. "Whose shirt was it?"

"Hmm?"

"The shirt you put on that weekend I came to your house." His fingers trailed along her jaw. Came perilously close to her lips.

Her mind was five steps behind the times. "Umm, I don't—"

"Hell with it," he murmured. His hand slid behind her head, cupping her nape, tilting her head back.

Belle froze, disbelief warring with anticipation. She wasn't sure which would win out, but it didn't matter, because Cage lowered his head and pressed his lips against hers and her senses simply exploded.

Her hands were pressed against his chest. She could feel his heavy heartbeat. She knew there were good reasons she should be pushing him away. Knew it.

She just couldn't manage to put her finger on one of those reasons right at the moment.

And then she stopped worrying about it altogether as the taste of him overwhelmed everything else.

Somehow, his arms had circled her, beneath the jacket. Her thin shirt was no barrier against his fingertips, which strolled up and down her spine. She shivered again.

"You're not cold." She felt his murmur against her lips. "No."

The moment she answered, he took advantage, his tongue finding hers. Her knees dissolved. Had she ever felt a kiss down to her toes? Beyond? She arched against him, arms snaking around his shoulders, fingers seeking the shape of his head. Her muscles liquefied even while white-hot energy blasted through her.

Her head fell back as his mouth dragged over her jaw. Found her neck. Overhead, the stars whirled. Pounding music throbbed in the air, vibrating through their bodies.

This was not effective chaperoning, she thought hazily. "Cage—"

His mouth covered hers again, swallowing her halfhearted stab at sensibility. And when he finally did lift his head, she gave a soft moan of protest.

He made a rough sound and pressed her head to his shoulder. "This is a bad idea."

She nodded. Her fingers were knotted in his chambray shirt as surely as his fingers were tangled in her hair.

He muttered an oath. Tipped her head back. She didn't know what to say. Then he swore softly again. Pressed a hard kiss to her lips, before deliberately stepping away.

She swayed a little.

"I don't have time for this." His voice was quiet. Rough.

And even though his expression was as ragged as his voice, the words stung. "You kissed *me,*" she reminded. "I wasn't chasing after you."

His gaze angled her way. "Did I say you were?"

"You—" No. He hadn't said that. But she'd been accused of chasing after Scott—which she hadn't been—but the humiliating memory of it lived on. And there was still the tacit warning he'd given her when he'd told her why Lucy's last therapist had been sent on her way.

"No." She raked back her hair, dismayed to see her hands were shaking.

Giggles gave them a very slim warning before a gaggle of girls darted out of the barn. They nearly skidded to a halt as they spied Belle and Cage. "Oh, good." Anya Johannson was the tallest of the three. "Lucy wants to cut her cake now. Is that okay?"

Belle couldn't prevent her quick glance at Cage. "Sure." She found a smile from somewhere and pinned it on her face, answering when he seemed to have no inclination to do so. "Good idea, actually," she went on, glancing at her watch as she followed the girls inside. "The boys will be leaving soon." And come morning, as soon as she could, she'd be leaving, as well, for the weekend.

She had a date to buttonhole her sister for some answers. She'd talked to Nikki on the phone twice since her sister had dropped the news. Nikki had been frustratingly closemouthed. She'd even warned Belle not to come see her.

Fat chance.

Cage followed her into the barn. He lit the candles on the cake and the kids sang. Lucy blew. Belle cut. Kids ate. The barn was filled with chatter and laughter. The time passed quickly enough, before the first headlights bounced over the ground outside the barn announcing the arrival of the first ride. But it seemed to Belle that the minutes crept because every ticking moment of them she was excruciatingly conscious of Cage's presence.

He didn't have time for "this." Did he honestly think that *she* did?

After what seemed an eternity, he disappeared along with the last of the departing boys, leaving Belle to deal with getting the girls settled. No small task. But she finally got the girls staying behind bedded down snug as bugs in Lucy's bedroom. They easily covered every spare inch of floor and bed space. When she finally closed the door on their whispers and giggles, she was vaguely surprised that some of them hadn't decided to bunk in the shower.

She was in the kitchen, trying to restore some order when Cage reappeared. She ignored him and continued tying up the trash bag that bulged with discarded plates and cups. She started to take it outside, but he silently took the bag from her and went out himself. When he came back, her hands were buried in soapy bubbles, the sleeves of the jacket rolled up to her elbows.

"When I asked you to stick around for the party I didn't mean you had to pull maid duty."

"When it comes to my pitching in around here you've made your feelings abundantly clear." She rinsed a pretty glass bowl that was probably older than she was and carefully set it down on the towel she'd spread on the counter.

"Yet you continue doing whatever you want." He scooped

up the last few pretzels in a bowl before she could dump them out and plunge the bowl into the hot, soapy water.

"Yes, well, maybe I think you have enough to deal with without having to wash a few dishes."

"I don't need anyone's pity."

"Fortunately you don't have it." Her voice was stiff. "Nobody would be so stupid as to offer it, believe me. So why don't you go sit out on the porch again. Do whatever it is that you do when most normal people are sleeping."

He crunched through the pretzels. Deliberately set her aside then picked up the stack of remaining dishes and shoved them in the sink, splashing suds over his arms and chest.

He looked so much like a boy having a tantrum that she couldn't help the bubble of laughter that rose most inappropriately in her.

He glared at her.

She bit her lip, composing herself, and picked up a clean dish towel. Began drying the dishes. After a moment, she heard him sigh. "Lucy looked like she was having a great time." His voice wasn't quite grudging.

"Yes." She opened an overhead cupboard and began stacking the dishes inside. But when she would have dragged over a chair to reach the highest shelf, Cage took the glassware from her and did it himself.

It was positively domestic.

Utterly surreal.

"How long were you and Lucy's mother married?" She nearly chewed off her tongue, cursing her lack of discretion.

He pulled the stopper in the sink and watched the bubbles gurgle down the drain. "Why?" His voice was tight.

"Curiosity," she admitted huskily. She knew what the man tasted like now and her curiosity could no longer be contained.

He was silent for a long moment. Then seemed to shrug

off his reticence. "We were together, more or less—usually less—for about seven months. She never lived here at the ranch."

Belle frowned. So little time. She wanted more details, but she'd already asked questions she shouldn't have. "You were really young," she observed instead.

"Old enough to get a marriage license. Sandi was nearly twenty-one."

Older than he was, then. She tried to picture him as a teenage groom. Had he been reluctant? Insistent? Blinded by love for the woman who was carrying his child—a child who would be living, breathing family for a boy who'd lost so much?

She folded the towel he'd discarded into neat thirds. Then thirds again. "You don't sound as if you're still nursing a broken heart. That's what some people say, you know. To explain why you don't date anyone from town."

He snorted softly. "Some people. Suppose you believe everything you read, too."

She shook her head, all too aware that he hadn't actually denied it. "How'd you meet?"

He turned around, crossing his arms over his chest, an action that only made him seem even broader. The man was both mother and father to his child, and she'd never met anyone more masculine.

She quickly unfolded the towel. It would never dry with those tight folds. He was watching her, and she hastily draped it over the oven handle.

"Want to make sure there's no hidden wife in the wings when we end up in bed together?"

She went still, emotions bolting through her. Foolish of her to assume that *her* personal business had remained personal. After all, if Brenda Wyatt knew about the debacle with Scott Langtree, then she'd have undoubtedly informed the rest of the Weaver population. Which apparently included even a reclusive rancher who was, himself, the brunt of considerable conjecture.

"I guess you've listened to your own share of gossip. And, just for the record, you and I are *not* going to end up in bed together."

He lifted an eyebrow, his gaze dropping to her lips.

She flushed, heat streaking through her with the tenacity of a forest fire. "I don't sleep with men I don't love." She didn't care if she sounded prissy or not. She was old enough to know what she did and did not want. Wasn't she? And meaningless sex was not something she'd ever wanted to indulge in.

Only it wouldn't be meaningless, would it?

"Did you love him, then? The guy of the white shirt? Keep it as a memento before you decided he was a snake?"

"You're really preoccupied with that shirt," she murmured, trying to banish the whispering thought of meaningless versus meaningful. "If you must know, I think my stepbrother Tristan left it behind a long time ago when he and Hope were dating. It's her house, you know."

"There's not much else that's sexier than a woman wearing a man's shirt and little else. But no man wants to see a woman *he* wants wearing another man's shirt."

Well, that was blunt. The man went for days, *weeks*, without hardly saying a word, and in one evening he'd kissed her silly *and* admitted to wanting her.

She snatched up a bottle of water. Fiddled with the cap. Put the bottle back on the table for fear she'd just spill it over herself.

"Must be inconvenient to want something you despise," she murmured. And wished like fury that she didn't want, so badly, for him to deny it. She wasn't supposed to care how he felt about her. She was only supposed to get Lucy back on track, and maybe, just maybe regain some of her professional confidence in the process.

That's not all you want.

She ignored the little voice.

Cage still hadn't responded and she felt something foolish inside her wilt.

Exactly what she deserved for getting too involved with her patients.

Cage isn't your patient.

A muffled shriek of laughter startled her. The girls, of course.

She brushed her hands down her thighs. "Well. Good night, Cage. Try to get some sleep for once."

He remained silent. Big surprise.

But she felt his gaze on her as she left the kitchen and padded up the stairs.

It wasn't until she closed herself in the relative safety and solitude of the bedroom next to Cage's that she realized she was still wearing his jacket.

She lifted the worn wool close to her nose and closed her eyes, inhaling the faint scent of him while impossible images danced in her mind.

The truth was, it would be a miracle if any of them slept at all that night.

Chapter 11

"Got a problem?"

Belle pressed her forehead to the steering wheel for a moment. She'd gotten up early, knowing Lucy and her pals would still be sleeping, and hoping Cage would have been doing the same.

Foolish of her to think that of a man who never seemed to sleep.

She looked sideways at him through the opened window and dropped her hand away from the key. She'd been trying—and failing—to get the Jeep started. The engine kept dying. "What gave it away?"

The corner of his lip lifted and her stomach gave a funny little dip. She quickly looked down, but the sight of his long fingers absently brushing through Strudel's ruff was no less disturbing.

"Pop the hood." He gestured toward the front of her vehicle and the unbuttoned denim shirt he wore rippled, baring a slice of chest. "I'll take a look," he prompted when she just sat there like a ninny. The sideways look he cast her had her stomach dancing again. "Unless you've got a wrench handy somewhere and plan to attack the engine yourself with it?"

"So funny." She flexed her fingers, blocking out the insistent and too fresh memory from the night before, and pulled the lever to release the truck's hood.

She'd feel better—about everything—once she saw her sister. She drummed her fingers on the steering wheel for a moment, then climbed out and went around to stand by him. She braced herself for Strudel's loving assault, but Cage said a quiet word that had the dog settling on his haunches.

She looked under the hood, managing not to skitter away when he shifted, closing the distance between them. But he merely reached into the engine.

She watched him fiddle with this, tinker with that.

She could have been staring into noodle soup for all the sense it made to her.

Then he straightened. His fingers were covered with black smudges. "Try it again."

She blindly climbed behind the wheel once more. Automatically turned the key as she'd done a million times before. Thank goodness for habits because the sight of his chest, up close, was still occupying her retinas.

The engine started, spat a little then settled in with a purr.

"How does he do that?" she asked no one in particular. "Thanks," she said loudly.

He shut the hood and brushed his hands together, watching her through the windshield. "You should get it into the mechanic soon," he warned. Then the corners of his lips quirked up a little.

For a moment she simply forgot how to breathe.

Then he waved and headed back to the house. Strudel bounded after him.

Belle sank into her seat, her breath coming out of her with a little *whoosh*. She was actually trembling.

Her purse suddenly chirped and she nearly jumped out of her skin. She grabbed the thing from the passenger seat where she'd dumped it, and dug inside for the ringing cell phone. She barely had the presence of mind to look at the displayed number.

It was her mother.

Belle swallowed and quickly pushed the phone back into the depths of the purse where it continued squawking.

Guilt congealing in her stomach, she eyed the purse, then quickly shoved it behind the seat and turned up the volume on the radio until she could no longer hear the summons.

Giving the brick house another last look, she pulled the Jeep around and drove away. The sooner she got to Cheyenne to see her sister, the better.

A nice plan.

She still believed it had a chance of working, too, even when—two hours later—she was at her little house in Weaver, trying to figure out how to borrow a car because her Jeep was still sitting on the side of the highway where it had given out.

Handy that one of her stepbrothers was the sheriff. Sawyer had driven her the rest of the way to town and assured her that he'd have the Jeep towed in for repairs. Even more fortunate that he'd received a call and hadn't had time to stick around and chat when he'd dropped her off at her place.

It had been easy to love her stepfamily. They'd all welcomed her and Nikki with open hearts when Gloria married Squire. But she wasn't ignorant of their ways, particularly the men.

Steamrollers, all of them.

But none of them had anything on Gloria. She'd wrapped them all, to a one, around her finger without so much as turning a hair. And even though there were plenty of Clays around who would lend Belle a vehicle so she could drive to Cheyenne, there was no way she could count on that information not getting back to Gloria. And given the fact that Belle hadn't been back to Cheyenne in months, she knew her mother would be suspicious about Belle's urgency in getting there, now.

Weaver didn't possess anything so convenient as a car-rental agency, either.

She tried calling Nikki, hoping she could convince her sister to drive *to* Weaver, but her sister wasn't answering *her* phone, either. Probably hiding out from it, much the same way Belle was.

Hoping she wasn't creating a bigger mess, she quickly dialed the Lazy-B. And much later that afternoon, Belle sat alongside Cage as they drove to Cheyenne.

Too bad Lucy had fallen asleep. She'd chattered nonstop for a solid hour before succumbing to the after-effects of her birthday party. And Belle could only stare out the window at the scenery whizzing past for so long when it did nothing to keep her thoughts safely occupied.

She glanced back at Lucy, sprawled on the rear seat of Cage's SUV. Deliberately waking the girl so she'd start gibber jabbering again would be selfish.

She faced forward. "Thanks again," she murmured. "For letting me hitch along with you." Even though Cage had begun taking Lucy again on the visits to see his mother, she still felt presumptuous. And warily surprised that Cage had readily offered to drive to Weaver and pick her up before making their trip. It would be evening before they arrived. "I guess I really lucked out in catching you and Lucy before you left."

His sideways glance touched on her and it was like being physically dipped in something warm. Something intoxicating.

"We weren't planning to go this week," he said after a moment. "We'd barely started getting Lucy's friends rousted out of their sleeping bags when you called."

She stared. "Then...why?"

"Obviously you're anxious to get there. And Luce always likes visiting my mother at the care center."

She absorbed that. Kept waiting for some dark comment, some grimace, some *something* from him to remind her of the reasons his mother was in the care center in the first place.

But there was nothing at all conveying that in his expression.

There was nothing but a long, slow look from eyes that should have been too pale to have the singeing effect they did.

She swallowed, and trained her own gaze front and center, straight out over the hood of the vehicle. "I see." But she didn't. Not really. "Well. Thank you."

"You're welcome." His tone was dry.

She looked back at Lucy. "*She's* not used to so little sleep at night."

"Wouldn't matter if she'd slept twelve hours." He smoothly passed a slow-moving semi. "For driving company, she's a bust." His lip quirked. "She passes out as soon as she hears the sound of the tires on the highway. Always has."

Oh, Lord. She was staring at the slashing little dimple that had appeared in his lean cheek. She blindly began fumbling in her purse. "Guess she finds it a soothing sound."

"Guess so. When she was a baby, I could get her to sleep sometimes by strapping her in her car seat and driving down to the gate. You mining for gold in there?"

She closed her hand over an object and pulled it out, relieved to see it was something useful. "Just these." She shook the little tin, making the mints inside rattle softly. "Want one?"

"Is that a hint?"

She flushed. The man tasted better than any mint. "No."

He chuckled softly and held out his palm.

She dropped a mint in it, and popped one in her own mouth

then put the tin back in her purse. As a distraction it had been much too brief.

"Did you have to drive her around a lot?" She sounded a little frantic, and swallowed. "To get her to sleep, I mean," she added much more calmly.

"Enough."

Which only made her wonder more how he'd managed at such a young age. "You didn't have any help with her?"

"There was an insurance settlement," he said after a moment. "Eventually, anyway. It came through about the time Lucy was born. Got my mother settled in the care center. Hired a few hands for a while. High-school kids who needed to earn some extra cash."

"*You* were a high-school kid," she murmured.

"Honey, I was born old."

Honey. Nearly every male in the entire state called women that. It meant nothing.

It…meant…nothing. Any minute now, he'd start calling her *Miss Day* in that stubborn way he had.

"You're not old," she dismissed.

"Why? Because you're less than a handful of years younger than me?"

He was teasing her. She scrambled through the surprise of that. "I'm certainly not about to think I'm on the cusp of being old," she said lightly. "Besides. I think *old* is more a state of mind."

"Spoken with the blitheness of someone who hasn't had her child look at her with rolling eyes."

Belle smiled and glanced back at Lucy. Sound, still. "She *is* pretty great."

"Despite me," he murmured.

She flushed again remembering her statement—a serious statement—to that very effect. She turned a little in the seat, facing him. "I still don't understand why you wouldn't let her go on that field trip, Cage." Her voice was low. "If it was a matter of cost—"

"It wasn't." His voice had gone flat as the look he gave her.

She nodded, even though she didn't necessarily believe him.

"I didn't want her in Chicago."

She tugged at her ear. "What are you going to do the next time a field trip comes up? Each class tries to take a cultural trip each year. They're often out of state."

"As long as it's not Chicago."

"Because of her grandparents, or because it's where that private school she's interested in is located?" She straightened in her seat again, certain he wouldn't respond to that.

"Take your pick," he said in a low voice. "I'm not going to lose my daughter to either one."

Her lips parted, but no words came for a long moment. "You could never lose Lucy, Cage. She loves you too much."

But his lips twisted and he said no more.

The sun was setting by the time they hit the outskirts of Cheyenne. Belle pointed out the directions to Nikki's place.

He stopped at the curb in front of the town house. "Looks dark."

Truer words. There wasn't a single light burning from the windows of Nikki's home. Even the porch was stone-cold black.

Lucy, awake since they'd hit town, hung her head over the seat. "Was she expecting you?"

"She knew I was coming. She's probably just out getting a bite for dinner." Belle smiled with more certainty than she felt. "Don't worry. I have a key." She grabbed up her purse and pushed open the door with more haste than was dignified. There was nothing about the trip that hadn't been disturbing. Not sitting alongside Cage. Not listening to the things he'd said. Not speculating about the things he hadn't. She slid off the high seat. "Thanks again for the lift."

"Wait."

She halted long enough to see Cage scribbling on the back of a small piece of paper he pulled from the console.

"Here." He held out the note. "That's where we stay when we're in town and my cell-phone number. Call."

It was more an order than a request and her spine stiffened. "I appreciate the ride, but really, Nikki's car is in *much* better shape than mine. I'll be back at the Lazy-B on Monday as usual."

"Oh, please, Belle. Drive back with us tomorrow. She could even come with us to have supper, right, Dad?" Lucy smiled hopefully.

Despite Cage's knowing expression, Belle couldn't make herself disappoint the girl entirely. She plucked the note from his fingers. "It's really not necessary," she assured. And probably not wise. Being cooped up again in such close quarters. And Lucy wouldn't be much of a chaperone, given Cage's warning that the girl hit the *z's* on any road trip.

"Then we'll wait with you."

"Excuse me?"

Cage's face was set. "You heard me." He turned off the engine.

She made a soft sound, not sure whether she was charmed or exasperated. "It's not as if you're dropping me on some dangerous street corner. This is my sister's home in a perfectly respectable neighborhood."

"Humor me."

She tossed up her hands. "Fine. Whatever. I'll *call*."

"Good." He started the vehicle once more. "We'll wait until you get inside."

Obviously, arguing would be pointless, so she headed up the geranium-lined walk, digging through her purse again. Fortunately, Nikki's house key *was* still on Belle's key chain, and she fumbled only a little in the dark before pushing open the door and stepping inside. She flipped on the porch light and waved at the idling vehicle.

He didn't drive away until she'd closed the door.

Belle leaned back against it, listening to the soft rumble of the departing truck. Then she flipped another switch and warm light pooled through the entry from the two buffet lamps Nikki had situated on a narrow foyer table. Even though she knew her sister wasn't there, she still walked through the place, upstairs and down, calling her sister's name.

There was a folded note on the kitchen table with Belle's name written on it. She dumped her purse and Cage's note on the table, picked up Nikki's and read.

"If you're here, then you didn't listen, and I love you anyway. I'm okay, but I'm not ready to talk about any of this yet. I'll see you at Angel's birthday party. Love, Nik."

"Well, fudgebuckets." She dropped the note and it fluttered to the tabletop, rustling the scrap of paper that Cage had insisted she take. The hotel name and phone number were written in bold, slashing strokes.

No nonsense. That was Cage Buchanan.

She wandered back into the living room and threw herself down on her sister's squishy couch. That day's newspaper was sitting on the coffee table. Proof that Nikki hadn't been hiding out for too long.

She sat forward and pulled the paper closer. Flipped it open to the classified section and ran her eye down the rental listings.

Several in the right area of town, conveniently located nearby the clinic. Decent rent. Good space.

She flipped the paper over, folding it in half.

Perfectly decent rentals and not a one of them held any appeal.

Or maybe it was the fact that moving back to Cheyenne—as she'd always planned to do—was no longer as appealing as it had once been. Because every time she contemplated it, her mind got stuck over a sturdy little brick house and the bronze-haired man who lived there.

"Oh, Nikki," she murmured. "What kind of messes are we getting ourselves into?"

She went back into the kitchen to use the phone there, and dialed the number Cage had left. She nearly lost her nerve as it rang. But on the third, he answered.

"Hi," she greeted. "You guys still up for some supper?" *Say no. Say yes. Better yet, just shoot me now and put me out of this insane misery.*

"Find your sister?"

She crossed her fingers childishly. "Yes. Well, no, just a little crossing of our wires. So…have you fed Lucy, yet?" She could hear the girl in the background, asking Cage if it was Belle on the line.

"In the thirty minutes since we dropped you off?" He sounded amused.

Only thirty minutes? It seemed longer. She tucked a loose strand of hair behind her ear. "I'll take that as a no. If you, um, want to come back here, I can throw something together."

"No." His answer came a little too fast and some of her nervousness dissolved in favor of humor. She cooked regularly for Lucy, but she knew there wasn't much of anything that she'd left that Cage had tried. He'd labeled her cooking as inedible from the get-go and hadn't changed his opinion since. "I mean, Lucy's begging for pizza. I imagine if you flash those Bambi-brown eyes of yours at the cook, he'll make you some wheat-vegetarian thing."

Bambi eyes? She glanced in the window-fronted cabinet above the counter. And shook herself when she realized what she was doing. "All right, but I'm paying. Hey—" she was prepared for his immediate protest, and spoke over it. "It's the least I can do, given the chauffeur job you took on."

"Then breakfast is on me before the return trip," he said after a moment.

Her imagination went riot. Oatmeal and raisins, she thought desperately, trying to counter it. A useless endeavor, it seemed, since her imagination was most definitely in the driver's seat.

"Belle?"

"What?"

"I said we'd be there in twenty minutes." His voice was dry and she had a terrifying suspicion that he was perfectly aware of the reason for her distraction.

"Right," she said briskly. "I'll be ready."

She hung up and sat there in the kitchen. Then, realizing how time was ticking, she darted upstairs. Nikki had been moaning over Belle's lack of interest in fashion for years. If her sister weren't so stubborn, she'd undoubtedly have enjoyed the sight of Belle rummaging through her closet.

With a bare five minutes to spare, she stood in front of Nikki's mirror. Cowardice accosted her. She rarely wore dresses and she'd never filled out one the way her sister did. But before she could change back into her jeans and T-shirt, the doorbell rang.

Her nervous system went into hyperdrive. She looked longingly at her jeans.

The doorbell rang again.

She could almost hear Nikki's musical laughter in her head.

"I'm ready," she called out, clattering in the unfamiliar heels down the steps, the skirt of the floaty sundress flying around her ankles.

She skidded to a stop on the tile at the door and blew out a deep breath. She'd be composed if it killed her.

Then she opened the door and silently blessed Nikki and her well-endowed closet when Cage's eyes sharpened, taking her in from head to toe, a look so encompassing that it made her skin feel too snug.

It was *not* a bad feeling. At all.

"I'm ready," she said again.

She just wasn't quite ready to admit to herself what she was ready for.

Chapter 12

"So. You do eat junk food." Cage watched Belle across the red-and-white checked tablecloth. The jar in the center of the table glowed from the lit candle inside it. The place was redolent with the smell of sausages, onions and garlic.

Nirvana.

And there Belle sat, looking like some fairy-tale fantasy with her long, waving hair providing the dark cloak around that surprising dress. Innocence and seduction all rolled into one intoxicating woman who was eating her wedge of pizza—the real kind, not some bastardized "healthy" version of it—backward. From the crust to the tip. Licking cheese from her fingertips. Gustily working her way through a healthy helping of pepperoni, black olive and mushroom.

She'd raised her eyebrows at his comment, a mischievous dimple flirting from her smooth cheek. "Call the health-food police," she challenged.

Lucy's elbows were propped on the table, her chin on her hands. "Belle's cooking is good, too, Dad," she said loyally.

"That's all right, Lucy," Belle assured her easily. "Your dad doesn't have to try my cooking. Some people are afraid of—"

"Eating birdseed?"

"—trying something new," she finished, her eyes laughing.

"I'd sooner eat Rory's oats."

Belle smiled, obviously not offended. "Might be good for you," she suggested blandly, and lifted the remains of her pizza slice.

He watched her work her way toward the tip. Given the presence of his daughter, he tried to pretend that Belle's obvious relish of her food was not turning him on. "Why start with the crust?"

She glanced from the remaining wedge, little more than a glob of gooey cheese on her fingertips, to him. "Saving the best for last," she said, as if it ought to have been obvious.

His mind, and his damn body, took a left turn at that, right down horny lane. What other kind of "bests" would Belle savor right up to the end?

He grabbed his iced tea and chugged the remaining half glass.

Belle was eyeing his plate where an untouched slice still sat. "You weren't very hungry?"

There was hunger and there was hunger. And he was damn near starved. "Guess not."

"Whenever I take more than I can eat, Dad tells me my eyes were bigger than my stomach."

"Well, right now, your eyes look in danger of falling asleep." Belle finished off her pizza slice, her own lashes drooping. But it wasn't tiredness on her face.

It was an expression of utter bliss.

Cage pushed back from the table. "I'll be back." He ignored the surprised looks—in duplicate—they gave him and headed toward the front of the crowded, cozy pizza joint, maneuvering his way through the line of people waiting for a table, and escaped out the front door.

He hauled in a long breath of cool, evening air, willing his body back under control. If he'd been a drinking man, he'd have found the nearest bottle of single malt and admired the curves of that.

But he didn't drink. There'd already been one Buchanan who'd done more than enough of that. And even though Cage knew his dad's habit hadn't contributed to his death, there'd been plenty of times it had contributed to Cage taking over the reins of the Lazy-B while his dad *was* alive.

He moved out of the way for a family to get to the door and walked along the sidewalk bordering the restaurant. Through one of the windows, he could see Lucy and Belle at the table, dark head and light, angled together companionably. The waiter stopped by the table and Belle smiled up at the kid.

Jesus.

He let out a harsh breath, walking farther, around the corner of the building and away from that winsome sight only to stop short.

Everything hot inside him froze, stone-cold at the sight of the woman standing there, eyeing him with considerably less shock than he felt.

Thirteen years—minus about six days—had passed since he'd laid eyes on Sandi Oldham. Then, her hair had been a wild mane around her shoulders, her cheeks smudged with running mascara. Not because she'd just handed over their baby to him for good, but because her credit-card limit had been reached and she wasn't able to buy the plane ticket to get her to Brazil where there was some dance troupe she wanted to get hooked up with.

Now, her gold hair was pulled back in a sophisticated-looking twist at the back of her head, and her face was cruelly perfect.

"What'd you do," he asked after a moment. "Hire someone to follow us?"

Her eyes flickered, and he knew he was right.

He also knew he had a piece of legalese that said she had no right to be around the child she'd borne but had never mothered. He turned on his heel, but she jogged on treacherous heels until she stood in his path.

"Wait."

"Get out of my way, Sandi. You have something to say, say it through your parents' lawyers. God knows, they have enough of 'em." He kept moving.

She shifted, walking backward, still trying to block his way. "Cage, wait—"

"No." He had to remind himself that—whatever his personal feelings were for her—she was equally responsible for the existence of Lucy. Wishing her back to the far corners of the earth had to suffice.

He brushed past her. She smelled as expensive as she'd ever smelled. Only he wasn't a seventeen-year-old kid still reeling from his parents' accident, and that expensive scent that once had him salivating only made his head ache now.

Give him rainwater fresh.

"Cage." Her voice followed him. "I'm sorry. I didn't want it to be like this."

He frowned. Turned on her, incredulous. "Just how the hell did you think it *could* be?"

She approached, her skinny boots clicking like gunshots on the cracked sidewalk. "You surprised me, coming out of the restaurant like that. I just want to see her, Cage. She's my daughter, too."

"And she wouldn't even exist if I hadn't dragged you, kicking and screaming out of that doctor's office before he performed the abortion." He remembered the day clearly. More missed school, in too many days of them after the accident, when he'd had to fight everyone to keep hold of what was left of his life—the ranch. Finishing high school had seemed the least of his worries when there'd been people intent on putting him in foster care somewhere. As if he hadn't already had a man's responsibilities on the Lazy-B. He'd hated people getting in his business ever since.

So he mostly avoided people when he could.

"I was young. Scared," Sandi said. She moistened her lips, looking vulnerable.

He wasn't fooled. There'd been nothing vulnerable about Sandi. Not from the get-go. And, in physical years at least, he'd been younger than she.

He knew in his bones that she hadn't changed her spots in the years since. He'd be damned if he'd lose his daughter to her after all this time, but even more, he'd damn Sandi to hell for all eternity if she hurt Lucy.

He'd already cursed her parents there and back again for that horse.

"I don't give a f—," he reined in his anger. "You signed away your parental rights a long time ago," he reminded her flatly. Right along with signing the divorce decree. He may have been still a kid, and he may have done some stupid damn things along the way, but he hadn't been a complete fool.

She didn't try to deny it, at least. "I know she's inside with that woman you hired." Sandi looked toward the restaurant door. "Belle Day. Nice work, that, Cage. I must admit, I was surprised to hear that name in connection with you."

His fingers curled into fists since he couldn't very well wrap them around her neck where they ached to go. He was glad the windows near the corner didn't afford a view of the table where Belle and Lucy still sat. "Don't go there, Sandi," he warned softly. If she thought she'd already won, she was sadly mistaken.

She angled a look his way. A look that may have acquired some subtlety over the years, but was still purely calculating. "You should have taken me seriously months ago, Cage. All I wanted was to have a relationship with my daughter. But no. You had to have her all to yourself. And now," she shook her head, looking regretful. "You're paying the price. Because now, you have to deal with my parents."

There was nothing but truth in her words and they still sounded vile. Then she reached out and touched the collar of his shirt, her fingertips slowly moving down the buttons. Her head tilted back and she looked up at him. "We can still work something out, Cage. You have to know that I've been desperate. Otherwise I'd never have brought my parents into this. I told you long ago what they were like. Always controlling everything with their money. I don't want Lucy subjected to them, either, but if it's the only way I can see her, then—"

He wrapped his hand around her wrist, trapping her fingers. "What, exactly, are you suggesting?"

She leaned in another inch. "You're the only one I ever married, Cage."

He watched her about as closely as he'd watch a coiled snake. A snake could be taken care of with a well-aimed, sharp shovel blade, though.

"We were still kids and marriage was your price," he reminded. No matter the struggles his parents had faced before his family was destroyed, he believed in family. To the end of his days. Sandi had given him a family, but she'd never been part of it, herself.

"Maybe marrying you was one thing I did do right," she whispered. "You're looking good, Cage." With her free hand, she reached up and brushed her fingers through his hair. "As good as I always expected. And things weren't always bad between us. We had some good times."

He wondered how far she was willing to go in her little pretense. How he could use it to his advantage, turn it against her and get her the hell out of his—Lucy's—life.

"We were wondering what was keeping you."

Cold slithered down his spine at the cool tone and he looked over Sandi's head to see Belle standing on the sidewalk watching them.

Her expression was calm, but he could see the tempest brewing in her dark eyes. "I'll be inside in a minute," he told her. Willed her to turn and go back. To be with Lucy, because there was no contest in his mind with whom his daughter would be safer.

Protected.

It sure wasn't the blonde who'd given Lucy her genes.

And wasn't this a helluva time to realize just how much he *did* trust Belle?

For a tense moment, Belle eyed him. Looked from him to Sandi. Then she turned, her pretty dress flaring around her delicate ankles, and headed back inside the restaurant.

Relief eased the vise inside him, though he was smart enough to know it was only temporary. He was also smart enough to know his relief was only partially for Lucy.

Belle consumed the rest of it.

As she'd been consuming him all along.

He released Sandi's hand and stepped back so she'd get her fingers out of his hair. "Go back to Europe. Or wherever you've been hanging your broom these last years. There's no way you're going to see Lucy." He'd put Sandi over his shoulder and lock her away somewhere and take his chances with the law over it, if it came to that.

"You're going to regret this, Cage. It'd be easier to deal with me than my parents."

He eyed her. Even though he'd known it in his head, it was still a relief to realize that—face-to-face with her—she left him cold.

"I'll take my chances," he said.

She stared at him for a long moment, lips tight with displeasure. Then she muttered an oath and turned toward the parking lot. He watched her climb in an expensive sports car and didn't go back in the restaurant until she'd driven away with a squeal of tires and a grinding clutch that was criminal in such a vehicle.

Inside, he paused among the throng still awaiting tables and consciously tamped down the anger burning inside him. He caught their waiter and paid the check, then headed over to the table where Lucy and Belle waited.

"Ready?"

Lucy nodded sleepily and reached for her crutches. Belle didn't look at him as she stood also and gathered up the foil-wrapped leftover slices. "I need to get the check from the waiter." Her voice was still cool.

"It's taken care of."

Her jaw tightened. "It was supposed to be my treat."

He tucked his hand around her elbow—absorbing the fine shimmer that went through them both at the contact—and nudged her after Lucy, who was carefully making her way through the crush of tables, chairs and bodies. "Next time."

She shot him a look. Startled. Maybe tempted despite what she thought she'd seen?

"There's going to be a next time?" Her voice wasn't cool now. It was soft. Wistful.

Just that easily, the frozen wasteland left behind by his ex-wife went molten. His thumb stroked over her inner arm. "What do you think?"

"I thought you didn't have *time* for this," she said, barely loud enough for him to hear over the conversations swirling around them.

But the masses had parted for Lucy to make her way more easily to the door, and he didn't want his daughter going out there without him first.

Just in case.

He reluctantly slid his hand away from Belle's arm and slid in front of Lucy to push open the door. Fortunately, he was parked very near the door, and he had the women stowed inside within minutes. And there was no sign of the Porsche having returned.

"Dad?" Lucy was sprawling in the rear seat. "Can you take me to the hotel first before you drop off Belle?"

He looked back at her. "What's wrong?"

She lifted her shoulder. "Nothing. I'm just tired. And my leg is kinda hurting."

And he wouldn't be leaving her unattended in a hotel room for any length of time. Not tonight.

"It's fine," Belle said softly, brushing his leg with her fingertips. "Go to the hotel."

She pulled her hand back quickly, but the whispering contact had more than done its job. His skin was singing. He grabbed her hand again. Ignoring the way she started when he flattened her palm beneath his and pressed it back against his leg.

The warmth seared through his jeans, spearing upward. He was prepared for that. He just wasn't necessarily prepared to feel that warmth head further north than his crotch. But it did, and it was heading up his chest where his heart beat an oddly heavy beat.

"If Nikki's not at her place yet, I'll just grab a cab ride back from the hotel," Belle added. Her voice had gone husky again.

Lucy looked pale in the dim light penetrating the windows from the parking lot. He gave up the brief idea of simply driving back to Weaver that very night. He turned forward and started the truck.

Belle didn't move her hand away, not even when he needed both of his to reverse out of the parking spot.

He drove back to the hotel, watching every set of headlights that seemed to follow them.

Just because you're paranoid doesn't mean they're not out to get you.

But there didn't seem to be any car paying them particular

ttention. And there was no sign of Sandi's car, either. She'd
obviously had them followed—a task that had to have begun
in Weaver—so there was no point in pretending that the
woman didn't already know where they were staying.

He gave up watching the other cars and concentrated
instead on getting to the hotel.

It was so obvious that Lucy was in more pain than she
let on when they got there, that Cage just handed Belle the
crutches and lifted his daughter in his arms, carrying her up
to their room.

Belle trailed behind them, hurrying ahead when he jerked
his chin at the room to use the key and open the door. She
didn't know what was going on—who the woman had been
with her hands in Cage's hair outside of the restaurant—but
she knew that whatever "it" was, it was important. It was
as if the lines of a familiar painting had changed. Ever so
lightly.

And now she didn't know what she was looking at exactly.

The hotel offered complete suites. Belle followed him
through the living-room area into the bedroom where he
deposited Lucy on the wide bed. She set the crutches within
easy reach, then turned to give them some privacy.

But Lucy caught her hand, staying her. "I've got a charley
horse," she whispered.

Judging by the suddenly tense look in the girl's eyes, this
time it was no pretense. Belle sat on the bed and tugged off
Lucy's tennis shoe, carefully letting her fingers work up the
girl's calf until she could feel what was going on.

Cage sat down on the other side of the bed, his eyes on Belle
as she gently kneaded the painful knot loose. It took a while.
Every time it seemed to ease up, Lucy would move, and another
muscle went into spasm. Belle's hands ached a little by the time
they'd licked the thing for good.

She sat back, realizing the position she'd ended up in on

the bed chasing Lucy's muscle spasms—on her knees, her
sister's pretty white dress shoved inelegantly between her
thighs—was hardly attractive. She slid off the bed, tugging
self-consciously at the dress.

"Here. Can you manage?" Cage handed over Lucy's
pajamas from the small case they'd brought along.

Lucy nodded. She was already half asleep, barely
murmuring a good-night when Cage leaned down and kissed
her forehead.

Belle was in the living area when Cage left the bedroom.
He pulled the door closed, his gaze angled toward her.

She swallowed and moved across the room, looking blindly
out the large window at the end of the room. It looked out
over an oval swimming pool. The pool was lit and it glowed
pale, bluish-white.

Like Cage's eyes, almost.

"So." She turned, hugging her elbows. "Who was the
woman at the restaurant?"

Chapter 13

Belle waited, tensely, as her question hovered in the air. She hadn't even attempted to make the question casual. Had she tried, she'd have failed miserably, making this even more humiliating.

"Nobody who matters," Cage said after a moment.

She wanted to believe him. Wanted to hear that *she* mattered, which was so far out of the realm of their nonrelationship that it scared her. "She looked like she knew you well." The sophisticated-looking blonde had had her fingers in Cage's hair, for pity's sake. Looking as though she was staking her claim right there on the sidewalk outside a bustling, family pizzeria.

He shook his head. As slowly and surely as he stepped closer to her. "She doesn't know me at all. Not anymore."

Belle's heart hovered in her throat, making breathing rather a challenge. She stiffened her spine a little. Brushed her hands down the dress that she'd managed to wrinkle, crushing it the way she had on Lucy's bed. What on earth had possessed her to borrow the outfit from Nikki, anyway? If that smooth blonde was the type of woman Cage preferred… "Well. It's none of my business, anyway."

"You look pretty in the dress," he said.

Was she so easy to read? "I don't need meaningless compliments," she said stiffly.

"You think I don't mean it?" He stepped closer. "Fact is, you look pretty no matter what you're wearing. Red. Gray. White robe. It's all good. Believe me."

Panic streaked through her. She couldn't afford to forget who they were. *Where* they were. "Dagwood," she blurted.

His eyebrow peaked. "Pardon?"

"Oh. That's seven letters." Her feet backed up a step, which only made her bump the large air-conditioning unit attached to the wall beneath the window. Silly of her to have forgotten her shoes in Lucy's bedroom. She'd kicked them off before climbing completely onto the mattress. Another few inches of height on her part would have helped counter the overwhelming, intoxicating size of him.

As if.

"I told you." He stepped closer. "It's unique."

"Please," she sniffed. "Dagwood isn't unique?"

He shook his head, a faint smile hovering around the corners of his lips.

Belle couldn't sidestep him, or move backward any farther. She put out her hand, flattening it against his chest. "What's going on here, Cage?"

"You need me to draw you a map?" He didn't push her hand away. Merely pressed his fingers to her wrist, then slid them along the length of her arm. Curved around her bicep and traveled back again, seriously causing her elbow fits as he seemed to find every ridge and bump, before traveling onward, returning to her wrist.

Shivers danced under her skin.

She needed no map to follow the direction he was headed. 'But...why?"

That hint of a smile left his face. His jaw cocked to one side for a moment, then centered again. "Because what I said last night 'bout not having time for this was bull. And I'm tired of pretending."

She decided discretion was the better part of valor, and lowered her hand from his chest, only to tuck both hands behind her back. Out of his temptation. Out of her own. "Your daughter is in the next room."

He made a nearly soundless, wry grunt. "You think I don't know that?"

No. She shook her head. She didn't think Cage would ever forget his daughter. He was too devoted. It was a significant portion of his appeal.

"She's asleep," he assured her after a moment. "She'll stay asleep unless she has a nightmare." He lifted his hand and she watched it, helpless to move, as it neared her face. When his fingers threaded, oh so easily, so gently, through the waves at her temple and glided through it, her muscles turned to warm, running wax. She felt her head falling back a little, like a too heavy bloom on its stalk, still seeking the sunlight.

He'd stepped closer. She could see the little scar below his lip so clearly. Had he gotten it as a rambunctious little boy? A headstrong teenager? "Cage—"

"I love your hair," he murmured, lifting his other hand to her head, also, and effectively cutting off her ability to think even ridiculous thoughts.

He lifted handfuls of her hair, and let it sift down, watching her from beneath heavy lids. His head drooped an inch closer to hers. "I love that you don't wear it loose very often. Then it's like this—" his jaw canted, then centered again and his hands repeated the motion, lifting her hair, letting the strands rain down "—this private...pleasure only for me."

His voice was too low for anyone to hear except her. And he was maddening her. Seducing her with only his voice. His fingers running through her hair.

She struggled for composure, but the battle was spiraling out of her control. Her fingers tangled in the fabric of the drapes behind her. She was probably mangling the poor things. Better that than letting her hands go where they wanted to go.

Around Cage. Over him. Everywhere.

She lowered her head, her chin dipping. His fingers found her nape. Stroked. Petted.

He might as well have set a live wire to her spine for the sensations he caused. Was causing.

Oh, dear Lord.

"Cage. We…can't. Lucy—"

"Shh." His voice whispered over her ear, followed immediately by his lips as he nuzzled her earlobe. "Just let me do this. For a minute. Or two. Or twenty." He pulled her hair to the other side, smoothing it down her shoulder. Her arm. Over her breast.

Her heart surged against him and her knees nearly collapsed for the pleasure of it. She was drowning in liquid heat.

Then she felt his mouth on her neck. Heard the timbre of his breathing deepen. She started to lift her hands, to touch him.

"Don't touch me." His lips moved against her throat. "It's safer."

She exhaled shakily. He was drifting his fingers through her hair again. Rearranging it around both shoulders. "Nothing about you is safe," she whispered shakily.

"I'm hardly touching you."

Craning her head around until her lips could find his was proving futile. "What you're touching is making me—"

He stilled, one palm cupping her breast through skeins of

hair, the other sliding through loose strands, fingers grazing her nape. "Making you…what?"

She tilted her head back as far as his holds on her hair allowed and looked at him. Full on. Gathered enough strength to speak. Heaven help her, to challenge. "Can't you tell?"

She knew what he'd see. Her cheeks were flushed. Her nipples were so tight they ached. She was trembling from head to foot and all points in-between. Particularly in-between. They were both fully dressed and she'd never been more aroused in her entire life.

She'd never had anyone move her—physically, mentally, emotionally—the way he did. Not even Scott. How would she ever survive if Cage touched more than her *hair?* Just then she didn't think he'd even need to, and wasn't that quite a statement on how much the man affected her?

His lips were parted a little, as if even he was having trouble getting enough air.

It was, she supposed hazily, some small comfort.

"Yeah," he finally said, his voice even lower. "I can see. And I've wanted you looking this way for a while now." He lifted one hand, flattening the drapes as he braced his arm against the window above them. He stepped in another few inches. Until there was no pretending that she wasn't painfully aware of the exquisitely tight fit of his jeans. And the reason why.

"I get only a few hours of sleep at night," he said, "and what I do get is full of this." He pressed gently against her. "Thoughts of you. Me. I'll lie there, hard as a rock, wondering if you're tossing and turning in that squeaky bed because you're thinking—or dreaming—about tossing and turning with me."

She shuddered. His words were too accurate.

He pressed his forehead against hers. She could feel the heat of him, the beat of his heart like some freight train bearing down on them.

Or maybe that was just her blood pulsing through her veins.

"I went into your room last week," he whispered. "You were in the living room with Luce. Working on some math thing you're supposed to be teaching her, but she was practicing piano and I could hear you complaining about the directions in the math book." His fingers strayed to her chin only to slide back toward her ear. Glide through her hair again.

She dissolved a little more. "M-math's not my best subject."

"I was going to oil those springs but good. Not just spray them like I did when you first got to the Lazy-B. But really fix the problem."

She opened her mouth, desperate for some air.

"I didn't oil them," he said. His voice was rougher. "I sat there and stared at that old bed, imagining you lying in it, turning from side to side, the sheets tangling around—between—your legs. Your hair—" he broke off, taking a hissing breath "—your hair spread out all over the pillowcase."

It was as if he'd watched her trying to sleep. Had seen her for himself. Night after night. Week after week. She heard a soft sound, a moan, coming from her throat, and couldn't stop it anymore than she could stop the images he was creating.

Then he twined his fingers in her hair more tightly, tugging back her head until she had to look at him. "Tell me what you dream about at night, Belle. Just tell me. And put me out of my misery. One way or another."

She stared at him, mute. Words dammed up behind her lips, too many words, too little strength to get them out.

He pressed his mouth to her forehead. Tipped her head back. Sifted her hair again through his fingers, spreading his arms wide, luxuriating in the length and weight of it. It slowly drifted, strand by strand, from his long, calloused fingers. His mouth touched her eyes. Her cheeks. Closed with the same exquisite slowness that his hands exercised, over her mouth. Not taking. Not plundering.

Just…tasting. Reveling.

And he trembled. Because of her.

"I dream about you touching me," she mumbled against his lips. Her entire body felt flushed with prickles of heat.

He exhaled and she breathed him in. He tucked her head against his chest, his shoulders curving around her, a world of their own creation right there in that moment of space. Of time. "I dream about that, too," he murmured. "Me touching you. You touching me. Every little touch causing a soft creak in that bed. Every catching breath causing it to moan a little louder."

She gasped, pressing her head harder against him, grabbing his biceps no matter what he'd warned. She was trembling so violently, her legs were barely holding her. "Stop."

But he didn't. "And always, always this hair of yours, a dark river against the sheets."

His hands returned to her head, sliding around, through, shaping her skull, something that shouldn't have been so exquisitely intimate, yet was. And it was sending her right over the edge. "Cage, you're going to make me…ah—" He covered her mouth with his, swallowing her gasping moan.

Then his lips burned to her ear again. "Let it happen, Belle. Let me have this at least. Let me have a little of what you dream. Of what I dream." He stroked through her hair, again. "Maybe you haven't come in that bed, Belle, but I've imagined it."

She whimpered a little at that. At the appalling bluntness of it. At the seduction of it.

"That's why I didn't oil the springs. I've *wanted* it. I've wanted to hear those soft, barely noticeable sounds of you in that bed, and I swear on my father's grave that it's only been you that has caused me to think it. Even if it was only in my imagination."

She shook her head, denial, admission, she didn't know what. All she knew was that he was making love to her, and he was doing nothing but touch her head. Getting inside her head. And it was working.

"I want it now," he repeated.

"Kiss me," she begged, nearly broken with need.

He did. His hands fisted in her hair and his mouth covered hers.

Swallowed the keening cry she couldn't manage to contain as she convulsed.

He caught her around the waist, hauling her against him, absorbing the shudders that quaked mindlessly, endlessly, through her there in that private world. And when she finally came to herself again, when they weren't just a mass of sensation, of emotion, when she could form thoughts, he kissed her again, stifling her embarrassment at her own lack of control back into submission.

And after he'd kissed her long and well, he carried her to the couch and sat down, holding her on his lap. Pressed her tight against him for an aching moment, before she felt the effort work through him to relax his hold.

Then he gave a shuddering sigh and threw his head back against the couch. "Thank you."

She could still feel the shape, the length of him pressing hard and insistent against her hip. Her cheeks felt on fire. And embarrassed or not, she couldn't pretend that she didn't want more. "But you haven't—"

He covered her mouth with his hand. "Don't even say it. Trust me." He blew out a measured breath. "Just sit here with me. It'll go away."

She flushed even harder. Tugged his hand away from her mouth, only to tangle her fingers with his and collapse weakly against him.

"Might take a month of Sundays, though," he warned blackly. "Couple of Weaver winters."

She couldn't help it.

She giggled.

His hooded eyes met hers.

And he smiled. Then he laughed. Out loud. From the belly. A laugh that jiggled its way right through her.

And she knew, in all of her life, she might never hear a more beautiful sound.

Chapter 14

Eventually—when Belle had regained enough muscle an[d] mind control to attempt simple functions—she used Cage'[s] SUV to drive back to Nikki's place. But it had been wrenchin[g] to leave him.

Smart, definitely. But nevertheless wrenching.

She still felt the ache of it when she let herself in with he[r] key, only to choke back a scream.

But it was only her sister sitting there in the living room hunched over a book in the corner of her enormous couch.

Nikki eyed her for a moment, her blue eyes speculative. "[I] hope you've come back to clean up the mess you left in m[y] closet."

After everything, Belle had completely forgotten abou[t] that. "I will. Thanks for the dress, by the way."

"I hope you at least cut off the tags before you wore it. I[t] looks better on you than me, actually. Keep it. Your close[t] will rejoice, I'm sure."

Belle dropped her purse on the coffee table and sat dow[n]

n front of her sister. Grabbed the book out of Nikki's hands
and folded them between her own. "Are you all right?"

Nikki sighed a little. Tilted her auburn head to the side
and studied Belle right back. "Are you?"

She swallowed a little, but kept her composure intact. "I
will be once you tell me what's going on."

"By the looks of it, I'd say you've been playing truth or
dare with someone. Since I know you are beyond being over
Scott, it must be Cage Buchanan. Truth?"

Maybe her cheeks were a little rosy from Cage's five
o'clock shadow, but she knew she didn't look as if she'd just
climbed from bed.

They'd never made it to the bed.

Her face went a little hotter at that. It would be a long while
before she could think about it without being shocked at her
own behavior. At the outrageous and unrelenting way Cage
had played her. And she'd sung.

And she wasn't sure she'd be able to sleep in that squeaky
bed back at the Lazy-B again. She just might have to sleep
on the floor.

"I was with Cage," she admitted. "*And* Lucy."

Nikki eyed her.

"Well. Lucy was asleep in the other room," she admitted
grudgingly. Then gave herself a hard, mental shake. "They
gave me a ride down here to see *you*. My Jeep is currently
kaput."

"Because it's only a hundred years old."

"Not everyone drives around the latest models," Belle
countered lightly, "the way you do. So. Talk."

Her sister swallowed. "I'm pregnant."

Belle waited.

Nikki pushed to her feet, shoving a shaking hand through
her thick, auburn hair. "You'd think I'd get used to hearing
those words come out of my mouth, wouldn't you? I'm

pregnant. I'm pregnant." She shook her head. "Nope. Still freaks me out." Her smile wavered.

Belle hopped up and wrapped her arms around her sister.

"Do you love him? This guy? The one you're not ready to talk about?"

"Do you love *him?* Cage?" Nikki's whisper was ragged.

Belle swallowed hard. But this was her sister. The one with whom she'd shared their mother's womb. They were twins. Different. Alike. But always honest.

"I'm afraid I'm starting to," she admitted. "I can't even imagine going back to Huffington, and that's—" She shook her head, unable to explain. "But I want to know about *you.*"

Nikki sighed heavily. She pushed Belle back and studied her face for a moment. "Later. For now sleep or chocolate?"

Nikki had always been an independent soul. "Chocolate," Belle declared. Sooner or later her sister would talk. "Most definitely."

Nikki turned toward the kitchen, padding along in her bare feet. "Fortunately, in the chocolate area, I'm well prepared."

They ended up falling asleep on the couch facing each other, the carton of Double Chocolate Fudge Madness empty on the bare inch of cushion not covered by their sprawling legs.

Belle woke first and watched her sister sleeping.

Nikki was going to be a mother.

She pressed her palms flat against her own abdomen, and she wondered what it felt like. Not the worry over being a single mom, but what it felt like to have something—a new creation—growing inside.

But thinking about that naturally led to thinking about how one became pregnant, which naturally led to thinking about Cage, which naturally led to Belle not having any hope of going back to sleep.

So she carefully slid off the enormous couch. Nikki sank down a little more, unconsciously taking advantage of the extra space just the way she'd always done whenever she and Belle had had to share the back seat of their family car.

Belle draped an ivory afghan over her sister and plucked the empty ice-cream carton off the couch. Silently gathered up the spoons and napkins and carried it all into the kitchen, tidying up. She flicked on the coffeemaker, then went upstairs, took a quick shower, and changed into the spare outfit she'd brought.

Then she cleaned up the mess—which admittedly was more mammoth than she'd thought—of clothes she'd left when she'd raided Nik's closet the night before.

She left a thermal mug of decaffeinated coffee on the table beside Nikki, and with a matching one in her own hand, let herself out of the house, locked it behind her and drove back to the hotel. She buzzed Cage's room from the lobby as he'd suggested she do before she'd left him the night before.

He and Lucy arrived within twenty minutes.

It wasn't taxing to wait. The hotel had that pretty pool, after all. And plenty of chairs around it that weren't yet occupied at the early hour.

She had her coffee. She had the beautiful promise of an early Sunday morning, with a sky that couldn't be more perfectly blue, and clouds that couldn't be more perfectly like big, squishy cotton balls. She had a year's supply of chocolate circulating in her bloodstream and the certainty that her sister—while still reeling—was, bottom line, as strong as she'd ever been.

And she had the sound of Cage's laughter in her heart.

Lucy swung into view first, her freshly washed hair lying over her shoulders in twin braids. She waved and aimed toward Belle, plopping down onto a chair with no sign of the stiffness she'd exhibited the night before.

Cage followed more slowly, a foam cup eclipsed by his long fingers.

She gulped her coffee, dragging her eyes away from his fingers. And nearly choked on the liquid.

Served her right for thinking *those* thoughts about his wonderfully shaped, perfectly masculine hands.

He gave a crooked smile and sat down in the third chair, setting his coffee cup on the table where his fingers hovered around the rim. He lifted his other hand, and she realized he'd been carrying a blueberry muffin. "Want one?" She shook her head and he handed the muffin to Lucy. "Ever catch up to your sister?"

"She was there when I got back last night."

"And?"

"And…I feel better. Thanks a lot for driving me. Really."

He lifted his coffee, the faintest sketch of a toast in his movement. "My pleasure."

Well. She nervously tugged her ponytail over her shoulder. When his gaze shifted a little, she hurriedly pushed it back behind her shoulder and tucked her hands beneath her legs on the chair. "So. Any preferences for breakfast?"

Cage just looked at her.

Fresh heat streaked through her.

She focused on Lucy and it took no small effort to do so. "Well? What are your druthers, miss? Waffles? Eggs?"

"If we go to Grandma's care center, we could have breakfast there. They always have a huge Sunday buffet. That's what we usually do. Right, Dad? Then we can introduce Belle to her."

Belle absorbed that. She looked at Cage, who had begun studying the contents of his coffee cup. "Yes," he said after a moment. Then his gaze lifted and focused once more on Belle. "Let Belle decide."

Lucy looked hopefully at her.

Belle would have preferred to go anyplace else. She'd have preferred to drive straight to the moon and back rather than go to the care center.

All of which only proved that a coward still lurked beneath her skin. "A *huge* buffet?" she questioned Lucy. "Huge in relation to what? To the number of history papers you've written in the past eight weeks? To the number of birds congregating in that tree over there, hoping you leave some crumbs of your muffin behind?"

Lucy laughed, delightedly. "They have, like, five kinds of eggs. And I *know* you like eggs."

Belle smiled and tugged on Lucy's braid. "So I do," she admitted.

So, after Cage took care of the checkout, they drove across town to the pretty tree-shrouded facility where Cage's mother lived.

Belle's eyes took in every corner. Every sight and sound and smell. She'd feared the place would be unbearably institutional. But it wasn't. It was more like a sprawling, gracious home. The front door was double width and could accommodate wheelchairs, but it was a far cry from some sliding metal-and-glass monstrosity that so many places possessed. Inside, there were plants everywhere. The staff members weren't wearing starched whites.

Cage and Lucy headed down a hall, obviously familiar faces from the greetings they received. The exclamations of how well Lucy was maneuvering with her crutches since the last time they'd been there.

Belle would have followed behind them, but Cage slowed up a little until she walked *with* him.

At least he didn't pretend that this was something either one of them could have predicted when she'd become Lucy's PT.

After a couple turns of corridors lined with lovely artwork and occasional chairs, Lucy stopped in front of an open door. She barely knocked before unceremoniously entering. "Hi, Grandma."

Belle swallowed and hung back. She was used to working with people in all manner of physical conditions. She didn't know exactly what Mrs. Buchanan's condition was, but she knew with certainty that no amount of training could have prepared her for this moment.

And Cage, no matter what, couldn't possibly want her here.

The man she'd thought she'd known these past months surely would be affronted by her very presence here.

But he gave no indication of anything. Unlike the previous night in his hotel room when he'd been excruciatingly verbal, his thoughts now were far too well contained.

Lucy had no similar affliction. She pointed the tip of her crutch at Belle, startling the life out of her.

Belle grabbed Cage's arm. "Look."

"What?"

"Lucy took a step without her crutches," she hissed under her breath. "She's standing on her own."

And the girl had. She was. She continued gesturing with her crutch, an extension of her hand, for Belle to come closer. "Come in and meet my grandma," she urged.

Belle blindly walked into the room. She was still amazed at what Lucy was doing so unconsciously. Fortunately, too amazed to say something that might send Lucy backtracking. And she found herself facing Cage Buchanan's mother.

She was sitting in a side chair, next to a small round table, a book on her lap. A mystery. Belle instinctively knew without having to look closely that the stack of books on the bookshelf beneath the window held books by the same authors that filled the shelves at the Lazy-B. The books Cage read.

The window was open and a slight breeze billowed gently through the delicate white curtains, lightly stirring the bronzy curls of the woman.

She was beautiful. More than the aging black-and-white photos hanging in the house at the Lazy-B could ever have predicted.

A female version of the beautiful son she'd borne. The same color hair, the same breathtakingly clear blue eyes. Her skin was soft, nearly unlined. She wore a simple, pink sheath-style dress. Her feet were tucked into delicate pink pumps. She could have been a perfectly healthy woman dressed for church.

"This is my friend, Belle Day." Lucy introduced her cheerfully.

Belle held her breath. But Cage's mother merely slid her softly smiling gaze from Lucy to Belle's face. Obviously, to her Belle's last name was just a name. Her breath leaked out. She stepped forward, holding out her hand. "Hello, Mrs. Buchanan."

"How nice of you to bring Lucy," she said, squeezing Belle's hand with both of hers. They were soft. Cool. Utterly gentle. Only a close ear would have noticed the halting tempo of her speech. And Belle felt a faint smile on her own lips in return of the one directed so sweetly at her.

Then Mrs. Buchanan looked beyond Belle at Cage. She reached out her hands to him, perfectly friendly. "And who would you be?"

Knowing that his own mother didn't recognize him was one thing. Witnessing it another.

The sadness of it was encompassing. Wide and deep. Belle kept her smile in place only through sheer effort as she watched Cage step forward.

He leaned down, holding her hands, and kissed his mother's cheek.

His knuckles were white.

Belle wanted to look away, but couldn't.

"Hi, Mom." His voice held only gentleness. "We came to have breakfast with you, so I hope you haven't already been down to the dining room."

The woman nodded easily. Cage's greeting had no more effect on her than Belle's had. "I was reading. And nearly forgot to eat." She laughed a little, realizing the book had fallen to the floor and took it when Cage handed it to her. She set it on the table, then rose. She smoothed her hand over Lucy's head, pure delight in the gesture. "You look very nice today, Lucy. Are you getting taller?"

"I'm a teenager now, Grandma. My birthday was two days ago." Lucy swung through the doorway. "Maybe I'm taller 'cause of these tennis shoes I'm wearing. They look cool, don't they? Belle gave 'em to me. For some reason, she thinks I like pink. Do you think they'll have blueberry waffles this week? I really missed them when we were here last time."

Belle watched them go, Lucy's cheerful chatter so natural and unaffected, floating down the hall as they went.

Cage stood beside her. He touched her arm through the filmy sleeve of her blouse. "Are you okay?"

She looked up at him. That he could ask *her* that, when it should be she posing the question to him…she shook her head a little. "I'm so sorry, Cage."

"So am I."

She pressed her fingers to her lips for a moment. Felt the drift of the air through the window. "You know, after the accident, my dad was never the same. He wasn't hurt. Not physically. But…he just wasn't the same."

Cage's lips twisted, but he said nothing.

"He had a massive heart attack three years later. I was sixteen. But sometimes I think he left his heart on the highway that night."

"You still had your mother. Your sister," he said after a moment.

"And you had no one." Her eyes blurred. No family at all. And there was no question that family meant everything to this man. It had just taken her a while to see it. "Your mother—"

"Traumatic brain injury," he said evenly. "The only person since the accident that she remembers from one day to the next is Lucy. We don't know why. Maybe because I've been bringing Lucy here since she was born. My mother functions well. Her speech is good. Her motor functions are good. But she wouldn't remember to look before crossing a street. She wouldn't remember to take off her shoes before getting into bed. She wouldn't remember that a sharp knife would cut her hand."

The tears flowed down Belle's cheeks.

"I took her back to the Lazy-B once. Lucy was five." His gaze turned inward. "The insurance settlement had run out and I wanted her home. Thought it might help. But she never connected. And whether or not I wanted to admit it, I couldn't help her. She needed to be in a safe environment. The ranch wasn't it." He glanced around the room. The walls were a pale pink, so similar to Lucy's at the Lazy-B. Everything about the room was pretty and soft and feminine. "So I sold nearly everything I owned except the ranch and brought her back."

And Belle knew that it had broken his heart.

"It's my fault."

"Right." His expression was plain. He blamed her father. He always had. Even though no fault had ever been officially declared. Gus Day had walked away from the accident, and Cage's family had not.

"I wanted to go on a winter break with a friend of mine from school. They were going to Mexico for a week. And I wanted to go along in the worst imaginable way. I was thirteen and I thought Cheyenne was about the most boring place on the planet, and Mexico—" she shook her head "—well I knew it wouldn't be boring. But my father said I couldn't go, and my mother—as usual—agreed with him. He didn't like my friend's parents, you see. He thought they were…irresponsible. I thought they were a hoot. More like friends than parents."

"Belle—"

"Let me finish this, Cage." She had to finish. If she didn't now, she wasn't sure she ever could. And face-to-face with the reality of what he'd been left with that night grieved her so deeply, she knew she couldn't live with herself if she *didn't*.

No matter if it meant he'd never look at her the same again. He deserved the truth. All of it.

"My father was right, of course, but I learned that only after a while. They were busted for some stuff. Anyway." She knew she was babbling. Tried to focus.

"You don't have to cry about this, Belle. I don't blame you for what happened that night. Maybe I started out that way—hell, I know I did. I resented the fact that you and your sister grew up having what had been ripped away from me."

"But I am to blame," she burst out. "The trip to Mexico. I was determined to go, you see. And Daddy just kept telling me I couldn't go. And I told him that I hated him and would *never* forgive him, and stormed out of the house. I went to my friend's and, even though her parents had to have known I didn't have permission to go, we all headed out of town."

Despite her tears she could see his expression had gone still. Stoic. And her heart broke. For him. For the past. For the future.

"Dad caught up to us after twenty miles," she went on. Pushing the words past the vise of her throat. "If it was even that far. I wanted to crawl in a hole and die of embarrassment when he made the van pull over. Now, I think it was surprising he hadn't just sent the police after us. We were driving back to Cheyenne when the accident happened. I was so angry. I wouldn't even sit in the front with him. I was ignoring him. Lying in the back seat like some…some spoiled child."

She pressed her eyes shut. "If my dad was distracted, if he wasn't paying enough attention, if it *was* his fault, then it was because of me. And even if it wasn't his fault, if it was just the ice, or the snow, or whatever the way I was always told, it was still because of me. Don't you see?" She opened her eyes again and faced Cage. "We were only out that night, because of me."

Chapter 15

Belle stood there, feeling as brittle as the last autumn leaf. Waiting for him to look at her again, for his eyes to go cold and flat. For him to tell her that she'd interfered in his life enough, to get the hell away from his family and stay away. Far, far away.

"Why are you telling me this?"

She stared down at her hands. She *had* helped Lucy. She knew she had. Knowingly or not, the girl had stood squarely on both feet and taken a step without the aid of her crutches. It didn't mean the job was done. But it meant that Belle had helped. Finally.

"Belle."

She lifted her chin and looked up at him, wanting to memorize his face. *Him.* From the top of his bronzed head, over the cobalt-blue shirt that made his eyes even more startling, to the bottom of his black boots. A different pair than what he wore around the ranch. These were newer. Shined.

Because he'd known he was visiting his mother, even though she wouldn't remember him from one week to the next.

"Because I...I'm falling in love with you," she said. And she'd told him the one thing sure to put an end to whatever possibilities might exist for them. "Because you have a right to at least blame the right person." She wiped her cheeks and turned to leave.

He caught her wrist.

The pain sweeping through her was physical. Nearly sending her to her knees. But she stood there, knowing the pain he'd endured—was still enduring every time he came to this comfortable room where his mother's life was contained—eclipsed hers by legions.

"Do you mean that?"

Confusion made her hesitate.

"That you love me," he said impatiently.

Did he want his pound of flesh, then? If it made him feel better, he could have it. And more. "Yes." What was the point of recanting?

A muscle worked in his jaw, more noticeable because his face was pale beneath the tan he'd earned putting in alone the work of ten men on the Lazy-B.

Her wrist was beginning to ache beneath his shackling grip. But she'd have done anything just then to take every ounce of pain he felt inside herself, if only to ease him, somehow.

Then his fingers—as deliberate now as they'd been the night before when he'd sat them on the couch, both of them wanting *more* than they could have in that hotel room— carefully eased their tight hold. He lifted her hand, his eyes downcast.

"Maybe it's time to leave the past in the past," he said, his voice sliding over her, deep and gruff.

"The past isn't bringing Lucy here week after week to visit your mother." It was his present, and his future.

He let out a long, deep breath. "No," he agreed. "But Lucy's happy. My mother is happy. She doesn't know anything else now. She's content. This is what *is*."

He slid his hand behind Belle's neck, tipping her face up. Everything inside her gathered into a hard knot centered somewhere under her heart. He lowered his head, pressed his forehead to hers, eyes shut.

Hot tears burned down Belle's cheeks. She cautiously touched his shoulders. Her fingertips trembling along his neck. Feeling the tension inside him. Not daring to believe that he wasn't pushing her away.

"Maybe it's time I let myself be happy with what is, too."

A shudder of grief was working through her shoulders, no matter how hard she tried to suppress it.

Then his fingers slid under her chin, lifting it and his mouth covered hers, swallowing her hiccuping sob. "Don't cry," he muttered. "I can't take it."

A statement that only had the opposite effect. Belle buried her face against the front of his shirt. He swore under his breath, tugged her over to the chair where his mother had been sitting and sat down, arranging Belle in his lap as easily as if she were smaller than Lucy. His shoulder moved, then he was handing her a tissue he'd plucked from the box on the bookcase.

But the tears just kept coming and he moved again, and she felt the cardboard cube being pushed into her hands.

"Go to it, then," he said gruffly.

She leaned against him, sliding her arm over his shoulder, holding him. The box crumpled between them. His hand moved down her back. Back up again.

And after a long while, Belle felt an odd sort of peace creep through her. She sat back a little. Mopped her face with tissues. Finally looked up into that gaze of his. "What do we do now?"

He was silent for a moment. His fingers toyed with the length of her ponytail, pulling it over her shoulder. And even though her emotions were fully spent, the action felt as if he was spreading a layer of soft warmth over her. "We go have breakfast," he finally said. "And then we go home to the ranch."

She absorbed that. Nodded a little. Step-by-step. "And then?"

"Then we'll see what happens."

"You, um, you still want me to work with Lucy?" Her voice was shaking again.

"Yes."

"Okay." It was more than she could have expected.

"I want you to work with me."

"On…what?"

He leaned over her, catching her softly parted lips between his. First the lower. Then the upper. "Learning how not to be an ogre."

"You're not an ogre," she assured thickly. And hoping that she wasn't making the biggest misstep of all, she pressed her mouth against his.

His arms tightened around her.

"Whoa. Wowzer. No *wonder* you guys are taking so long!"

Belle yanked back at the exclamation. Her lips felt as puffy as her eyes. Her ponytail was askew.

"Caught in the act," Cage muttered against the shell of Belle's ear. She was blushing like a spring rose and he looked past her to his daughter, gaping at them as if she'd just discovered fire or something. "We'll be along in a minute, Luce."

Her eyes were bright. No surprise there. She adored Belle. But he was a little surprised that she didn't seem more shocked. Her head bobbed and she planted her crutches, turning smartly only to take another quick look back at them, a grin already on her face. "Wow," she said again. Then swung right out of sight again.

Belle was scrambling off his lap. "Maybe you should go talk to her, or, or something."

"About what? You think she doesn't know what a kiss is all about? She already told me you made sure she knew the facts of life after she got her period."

Belle gulped a little and looked away. "Well, I wasn't sure you were up to—"

"I told you. Luce has always been able to talk to me." But damned if he hadn't been more than a little relieved when he *had* cornered his girl after that particular episode. Not that they hadn't discussed the facts of life long before then. Lucy was a rancher's daughter, for cripes' sake. She knew how babies came to be.

But it was one thing when it was talking about puppies or calving. It was another thing entirely when it was his *daughter*.

"I'm always underestimating you," Belle said quietly. "Aren't I? I'm sorry."

"For caring about my daughter?"

"I love her, too."

He let the fact of it settle inside him, only to have to acknowledge that it wasn't all that much of a surprise, after all.

"Come on," he said, taking up her hand in his. "Breakfast."

Her fingers slid through his, holding tightly.

And they went to breakfast.

Later that afternoon, Cage dropped Belle off at her house in town since there still was the matter of her Jeep to be seen to. The dropping off took longer than it might have, since Lucy was curious to see where Belle lived, necessitating a brief tour.

By the time Cage and Lucy drove off again, Belle knew that Brenda Wyatt had gotten quite an eyeful, hovering obviously out in her front yard. No way could she have failed to miss the kiss Cage planted on her before climbing into his truck and driving on down the road.

By the time Belle had thrown a hasty load of laundry into the wash and tracked down the whereabouts of her Jeep, her mother was standing on her front step, knocking on the door before unceremoniously letting herself in.

Gloria Clay propped her hands on her slender hips and tilted her auburn head that was only showing a few strands of silver. Her blue eyes were expectant. "Well? Has your phone stopped working? Where have you been all weekend? And *what* is going on with your sister? She's harder to get hold of than you are."

Belle warily dumped the towels she'd taken from the dryer on the couch and sat down beside them. "I went down to Cheyenne." She reached for a towel and spread it out, taking inordinate care over the folds.

Her mother lifted an eyebrow. "And?"

"And nothing. Well. I met Cage Buchanan's mother." The admission came out fast. She felt as if she was ten years old again and she and Nik had been caught sneaking Christmas cookie dough out of the fridge.

"Oh. My." The news was enough to distract Gloria for a moment, but Belle didn't hold out much hope it would last. Gloria sat on the other side of the towels and grabbed one, smartly flipping it into a perfect fold in a fraction of the time it took Belle. Then she rested her folded hands on top of the fluffy terry cloth. "Is she doing well?"

Belle wasn't sure how she'd expected her mother to react. "She looked lovely."

Gloria made a soft *mmm*. "What's going on, Anna-belle?"

"Brenda Wyatt didn't give you the skinny?" She finished

folding and stacked the towels together. Then wished she hadn't finished so quickly.

Her mother waved a hand. "As if I care what nonsense that woman spouts. She's been gossiping since long before either one of us came to Weaver. Managed to cause all tha fuss Tristan and Hope had to deal with when that reporter came snooping for a story about him." She tilted her head a little. "Of course, that all had a rather nice result in the end since they got married because of it and fell in love. Hope's expecting again, you know. Erik's over four now. We were all beginning to wonder if he was going to get a little brother or sister."

A quick rush of pleasure jolted through Belle, right along with a sturdy helping of guilt for keeping silent about Nikki's news. "I didn't know. That's great."

Her mother's blue gaze rested on Belle's head for a moment "Well. Sawyer told me about your Jeep."

"It's been hauled to the garage."

Gloria held out her hand and dropped a key into Belle's "You can borrow this until yours is running again."

"Mom—"

"Don't argue, now. Squire insisted and you know what *he'* like. There're plenty of vehicles to spare around the Double-C You can leave it off again next week at Angel's party if your is done by then. And none of us has to worry about you driving that old thing on those roads out to the Lazy-B. know it was your father's, sweetheart, but even he wouldn' expect you to drive it forever."

Belle shrugged. "I like the Jeep, Mom."

Gloria nodded. "So, does this man mean something to you or are you just using him to get over that fool, Scott? Tha boy had no integrity at all, proposing the way he did when he already had a wife. And *then* blaming you because he didn' recover as fast as he wanted to."

"My feelings for Cage have nothing to do with Scott," she

assured. "I can't believe I ever thought what I felt for him was love." Or let him convince her she wasn't a good enough therapist to help *anyone*.

"Because you know what real love feels like now?"

Belle pulled the stack of towels onto her lap. Put them back on the table. Rose and paced. "What really happened that night, Mom? The accident. Whose fault was it?"

Gloria watched her, a hint of sympathy in her eyes. "Accidents can happen with no one being at fault, darling. And that night was icy. Your father did feel responsible, though. Which is why—"

"Why what?"

But Gloria just shook her head. "Nothing. It's in the past."

The past. "I told Cage why we were out there that night at all."

"I see."

Belle suddenly sank down on the coffee table. "I'm falling for him, Mom. And Lucy. And that brick house with its antiquated furniture and everything."

"And how does Cage feel about you?"

"He doesn't seem to hate me." A miracle she still had trouble believing.

Gloria lifted her eyebrow again. "Is that all?"

She was too old to be blushing, yet she did. "Maybe not. I don't know."

"I imagine you do, but you don't have to tell me all the details," Gloria assured her wryly. "My heart won't be able to take it. Now. It's getting to be supper time. Squire wants ribs from Colby's. Everyone's meeting over there. The entire family. Newt is saving the back room because we'll need all the space to fit. You'll join us."

There was no question in it.

"Where is Squire?"

"Right here, girl," the tall man said, stepping through

the door. He wasn't quite as tall as his five sons, but his iron-gray head ducked a little anyway as he entered. A habit she'd noticed more than once in her stepbrothers, who'd undoubtedly conked their heads on low doorways often enough to be conditioned. "Was just checking the rain gutters on the side of your house. One of 'em is coming loose. If that man of yours doesn't come back to town this week to get it fixed up, I'll have one of the boys come over and take care of it."

Belle just shook her head a little and reached up to hug him. There was no more stopping Squire than there was any of the Clays. The "boys" he'd referred to were all grown men, and gossip in town must have been plentiful indeed if people were already calling Cage "her man."

Once she'd spent a few hours in their company over a half-dozen tables pushed together in Colby's back room to accommodate the mass of Clays who seemed to keep filtering in—she stopped counting after twenty—she felt as if she'd filled up some wellspring inside of her.

That was what family could do.

After supper, while everyone was still passing out hugs and chattering a mile a minute, Belle decided she was not going to wait until morning to go back to the Lazy-B. She had a car—maybe not her beloved Jeep—and no desire whatsoever to sleep in the house of Hope's that she'd been using and every desire to be at the Lazy-B. No matter which bedroom she used.

But her plans were preempted by the sight of Cage, sitting on her front porch.

Her heart kicked hard against her ribs as she climbed out from the back seat of Sawyer's SUV. She was hardly aware of what she said to him, just that she was relieved when he wheeled around and drove back up the street to collect his own family before going home.

She watched Cage stand. He doffed his brown cowboy

at and his hair gleamed a little under the glow from the porch light. He was twenty yards away yet she could feel the intensity of his gaze.

Tension slipped up her spine, fiery pinpricks careened through her nerves. She couldn't seem to draw enough oxygen into her lungs and her mouth ran dry. She moistened her lips, torn between fleeing or standing her ground. But her rooted feet took the decision from her because she couldn't seem to move to save her soul.

And then he took a step toward her. And another. And there was nothing but purpose in his movements, purpose that no amount of pretense could hide.

Her heart climbed up into her throat.

Closer now. She could see the flame in his eyes, otherworldly pale, blue fire. "Luce is over at Emmy's," he said bluntly. "All night."

"Oh."

"You gonna stand there all night?"

"Maybe." She swallowed. "I can't seem to make my feet move."

"Where were you?"

As if he had every right to know. It didn't occur to her to prevaricate. Or even to challenge. "Colby's. The whole family was there. I was going to drive out to the ranch tonight," she admitted in a rush.

"The Double-C?"

She shook her head.

"The Lazy-B."

She nodded.

"Whose car?" He jerked his chin toward the sexy little convertible sitting in front of the house.

"A spare from Mom and Squire."

"I'm glad." He stepped closer. "Was wondering about it." His voice was low. Quiet. "Like I wondered about that white shirt."

"There's no man but you." The admission felt as momentous as dropping a boulder into a still, still pond. And she wasn't at all certain how high the ripples might roll. Or even if she were brave enough to find out. "You've had a lot of driving today, Cheyenne. Back and forth to Weaver. You must be tired."

"Inside?"

She pressed her hands down the sides of her jeans. Then nodded and willed her feet to move, heading up the small porch ahead of him. Fumbled with the lock and then the door. He finally reached around her and shoved it open, then nudged her through, and closed the door with a slam, turning and pressing her back against it, his body imprinting itself against hers.

She went straight past wary to aching. No line, no waiting. "I always wondered what swooning was like," she mumbled, staring blindly up as his weight pinned her. "I, um, I guess you're not that tired after all."

"Evidently." His fingers were busy on the tiny black buttons of her blouse then his hands swept inside, finding nothing but bare skin and the world seemed to stop spinning.

Her eyes nearly rolled back in her head. "Good," she gasped. She tore at his shirt. Made a mess of it since she got it off his shoulders but not his arms. The crispy swirl of black hair sprinkling his chest abraded her breasts. The contrasts between them were inciting. Delicious.

And then she felt the tease of his tongue along her lower lip, and the world wasn't still at all. It was racing, spinning, and the only steady port was Cage.

She shuddered, her fingers clenching his corded forearms. Her clothing provided no protection whatsoever against his searing heat. And, oh, she didn't want to be protected. She ran her hands up his arms, fumbling over folds of cobalt shirt, pressed her fingers into the unyielding biceps, her head falling back at his drugging onslaught. His breath was harsh when he finally lifted his head a few inches, hauling in a ragged gulp of air.

"I didn't expect you to happen." His mouth found her temple. Slid down her jaw.

"I know," her voice was woefully faint. Her fingers walked up his shoulders. Felt the cords of his neck. She felt the brush of silky bronze hair against her chin as his kiss burned along her shoulder blade. Pressed against the pulse beating frantically in her throat. "I didn't, either."

"Don't talk," he murmured, straightening. He tilted her head to suit him. "Just kiss me again."

So she did.

She kissed him until her head spun, until her skin felt molten, and her blood sang. She kissed him until she couldn't think, until the only thing she knew was the shape of him, the taste of him. Until she went beyond fear that kissing him would never be enough to certainty that the fear was irrelevant.

His hands raced over her only to stop and tarry, maddening her with the graze of his calloused fingertips along the bare skin of her back, her abdomen. He lifted his head, and she was conscious enough to flush at the moans rising in her throat when his gaze ran over her, only to stall at the thrust of her rigid nipples through the loosened blouse. His hand slowly drifted from her shoulder, over the push of her breasts against the fabric. His fingertip slid in tightening circles around her nipple, and if it wasn't for his other arm around her waist, her knees would have failed her completely. Then he dragged his finger over the peak, and the sensation was so exquisitely intense, she cried out.

His gaze slashed back to hers as he repeated the motion. She shuddered, mouthing his name.

He exhaled roughly, and covered her mouth again, kissing her deeply. She felt his fingers slide beneath the blouse again, drawing it down, past her shoulders. Off her arms where it floated to their feet. Then his palms covered her flesh.

Belle gasped at the sensations battering her from all sides. His drugging mouth on hers. His clever hands touching her. The unyielding wall of his chest against her. "Hold on," he muttered. Then he simply lifted her off her feet. Her pulse stuttered and she twined her arms around him, burying her face in the curve of his neck. He tasted hot, slightly salty, totally male, and at the flicker of her tongue against him, his grip tightened and his stride faltered. He muttered something under his breath, then moved again. He carried her down the hall. "Where?"

"End of the hall."

His mouth covered hers. Her legs bumped the wall. He swore. She laughed softly. Then he was moving again, turning sideways through the doorway to her bedroom. And even though they were the only ones in the house, he kicked the door shut behind him.

The abrupt slam of wood rocked through her as he let her legs swing down. Closed in her bedroom. Why did it feel more intimate just because he'd closed the door? She shivered.

His hands cupped her face. Calloused thumb slowly brushing the corner of her lips. "Say no now, Belle."

She wanted to feel the hard press of his chest again against her breasts, but he held himself away, touching only her face. "Is that what you want me to do? Say no?" Moonlight shafted through her windows, painting the corner of her bed in its tender light. She reached up, unable to resist, and pressed her palm against the muscle flexing in his jaw. "Are you already regretting this, then?"

"No." He lowered his forehead, pressing it against hers. "But you can still change your mind. Now. If you do later…" His voice was low. Rough.

Her palm slid to his nape, fingers slipping through his silky hair. "I'm not changing my mind." Stretching up, she brushed her cheek along his. Whispered in his ear. "Not now. Not later." Not ever, she feared.

He exhaled sharply, and in less than a breath, there was no space for even a whisper between them as he turned to her bed. Settled her in the center of it. She felt the kiss of air on her abdomen in the moment before his lips displaced it as he drew down her jeans. It was like being dipped in fire. She scrabbled at his shoulders, but he caught her hands in his, fingers sliding between fingers, palms meeting palms.

"Let me." His lips brushed her thigh.

And then she wasn't being dipped in fire, the conflagration came from the inside out. Only when she was gasping, then crying out his name, did he slowly work his way upward. She knew she was shaking, but couldn't seem to bring order to her senses, couldn't seem to grasp anything solid or real, except him.

He caught her nipple between his lips, teeth scraping oh-so-gently. His thigh, hair-roughened and hard, notched between her legs. When had he gotten rid of the rest of his clothes?

Then his mouth slid along the column of her neck. His breath was rough. His heartbeat pulsing hard against hers. He slid one hand behind her knee, urging it higher against his hip and groaned softly as his flesh tantalized hers.

She arched, greedy for so much more, and he laughed softly, turning until she lay over him. She arched against him, so much emotion inside her that she feared she might never recover. "I need you," she whispered.

He went curiously still. "Do you?"

If there were any places inside her that hadn't been softened beyond hope where he was concerned, his tense, urgent expression found them. Her throat went tight. Her fingertips grazed the sharp lines of his jaw, her palm cradled his cheek. "Yes."

She could feel the muscle flexing in his jaw. Feel every muscle he possessed seeming to gather itself. Her heart sped, the world spun as he pulled her beneath him.

"Remember that," he said. His fingers fumbled with her ponytail, and then he was spreading her hair out around her. And when he was done, he found her mouth as he took her. Unerring. True.

She pressed her head back against the bed, hauling in a keening breath, feeling her emotions stripped bare. Wanting the moment never to end, wanting to hide from it forever.

He breathed a soft oath that sounded more like a plea. His fingers curled, but he pressed his hands against her arms, smoothing upward until his palms met hers. Fingers linked. "Open your eyes," he whispered.

Such a simple act. It took all her strength. She looked at him. At the naked desire burning in his eyes, in the tendons standing out of his neck, his shoulders. Pleasure flooded through her and she shuddered wildly, on the precipice of something deeper, stronger than she could have ever suspected. Her fingertips dug into his hands. And he moved again.

"Next time," he promised roughly, "I'm going to make this last all day."

She laughed, but the sound was thick, and helpless tears leaked from the corners of her eyes.

He made a soft sound, almost *tsking,* and drew their linked hands closer to her head, where he caught the moisture with his thumbs. His movements were suddenly, indescribably gentle. "What? Did I hurt you?"

She shook her head. "I feel you…in…my heart." Her voice shook. She pressed mindlessly against him. "Don't stop," she begged.

"Not possible." He kissed her again, conquering her mouth as surely as he conquered her body. Then he tore his mouth from hers, his breath harsh, and the sight of him, muscles cording, eyes hot with need, sent her that last, infinitesimal distance and she went screaming into the abyss.

He went with her.

Chapter 16

Belle tucked her hand beneath her cheek and lay quietly in her bed.

Early-dawn light was sneaking through the window, slowly creeping over the foot of the bed and the tangle of sheets and blanket. Any minute, she expected Cage to wake.

But for now, for now she watched him sleep. As he'd been sleeping for hours.

His hair was tousled. His lashes thick and dark and still. There was no tension coiled in his long, strong body. There was only sleep.

It was a sight to behold, Belle thought. And difficult not to touch him. Not to let her hands drift over his wide shoulder. Sift through the hair on his chest and feel the slow, easy rise and fall of his breathing.

She didn't touch him, though. Didn't want to break his slumber.

So her eyes traveled where her hands dared not. Her body,

aching in unaccustomed places, her senses, still alive from the feelings he'd wrought absorbed the close warmth of him.

What the future held for them was a mystery. We'll see what happens, he'd said.

She wanted to believe that left an open vista of hope. Needed to believe it. Her gaze drifted over his hand, thrown above his head, fingers lax. Palm exposed. His bicep, a perfect relief.

She closed her eyes, exhaling slowly. There was no objectivity in her appreciation of his male beauty. She couldn't admire him without wanting to touch him.

But he was sleeping. Soundly and undisturbed for the first time in Lord only knew how long. She carefully turned on her back. Then her other side. Gave the small clock sitting on her nightstand a baleful look and turned her face into her pillow. Another few hours and Cage would be wanting to collect Lucy. Champing at the bit to get back to the Lazy-B and the chores that waited for no man's weekend away.

Cage shifted. "Too far away." His voice was husky, full of sleep. A long arm slid around her from behind, easily removing the six inches of space separating them. She sucked in an absurdly needful breath as his hand flattened across her abdomen, pressing her back against him before sliding up and covering her breast. His chest felt hot against her spine and everywhere that she was soft, he was…not.

She snuck a glance up at him, but his eyes were still closed.

She attempted to do the same.

"Quit wiggling," he said after a moment.

Forget another hour of *z's.* "I can't help it," she whispered. "I'm not used to this."

His thumb roved lazily over her nipple. "This?"

Her blood was heating. Collecting. "Waking up with a man," she admitted.

His hand left her breast. Slid along her side, her waist.

Cupped her hip. He hadn't seemed to notice the scars there the night before.

"Are you sore?" He wasn't referring to the long-healed ridges his fingers slowly traced.

"Are you?" she challenged, if only to pretend she wasn't mortified.

His chest moved against her back and she realized he was chuckling, soundlessly. "Cage—"

"Shh. Relax." He pulled her hair aside and kissed her shoulder. Slid his hand along her thigh. Lulling. Drugging. Then his hand was between her thighs. And he sighed, a sound of such deeply basic appreciation that she melted even more. He kissed her shoulder again. "I want you. Every night. Every morning."

She was swimming in pleasure.

"Marry me, Belle."

She couldn't have heard right. "What?"

Then he moved again, pushing her leg forward just enough to find, to take. Sinking himself into her so smoothly, so sweetly and gently that he stole her heart all over again.

"Oh, yeah," he murmured. "This way. Every way. Marry me."

She arched against him, taking him even deeper. Twisted her head, looking up at him. "You can't mean it." It was supposed to be women who got their emotions all tangled up with sex. Love. It was happening to her, for pity's sake. It wasn't supposed to happen to him.

But it was.

And his eyes were dead serious. Passion pulled at him, she could see it. Feel it. But he was…serious.

"I want all your mornings," he said evenly. "All your nights. Say yes." He covered her mouth with his and her heart simply cracked wide.

"Yes," she breathed into him.

His arms surrounded her, holding her tight as he rocked into her.

It felt as if he'd rocked right into her soul.

They showered separately. Not because either necessarily wanted to, but because he did need to collect Lucy and get back to the Lazy-B, not spend another endless session drowning in Belle.

There would be plenty of time for that, later.

Much as Belle would have preferred to sit beside him on the long drive, her hand pressing against his leg as if to remind herself of all that had occurred suddenly and not so suddenly, practicality managed to assert itself and having her own vehicle at her disposal was only sensible.

And it gave her more time to pack a real suitcase. To let…everything…sink in a little more.

Cage Buchanan wanted to marry her. And she'd agreed.

When she arrived at the house, Cage wasn't in sight. But Strudel greeted her, barking and dancing around, and Belle hugged the dog, feeling as thoroughly and utterly content with the world as the dog. She lugged her suitcase in through the front door. Cage wanted to tell Lucy their plans together, so she knew he wouldn't have shared the news yet.

But there was no sign of Lucy in the house, either.

She lugged the suitcase up the stairs. Debated briefly where to unpack it. Settled on the guest room since she didn't really have the nerve yet to make herself at home in Cage's room.

She'd never even been *in* Cage's room. So after she'd quickly unpacked, she went in. Smiled a little at the hasty way he'd made his bed. Couldn't very well lecture his daughter about the habit if he didn't try to make his own, could he?

She walked over and picked up the photo beside the bed.

Lucy. Wearing a fancy little ballet tutu, in midpirouette. Her limbs strong and true, her face beaming.

Belle set the photo back in its place and went downstairs.

Maybe the barn. She'd barely stepped out of the back door before realizing there was a car parked behind the house. A Porsche covered with a fine mist of dust. She eyed it and headed toward the barn.

She hadn't made it halfway when she heard Cage's raised voice, so angry it made the hair on the back of her neck stand up. "She'll have a mother!"

Belle quickened her steps only to stop outside the barn at the sound of her own name.

"Who? Belle Day? Come on, Cage. You really think you can pull that off?"

"She'll marry me."

A ring of amused, female laughter shattered over Belle. "So you'll finally have some revenge. Gus Day drives your parents off a road and finagles out of any sort of financial settlement, but now you're going to marry his daughter and have your hands on his money through her. And those rancher people, too. The Double-whatever. I'm told they are *very* well off. Not like my parents, of course, but—"

"Is it true?" Belle stepped around the corner of the barn to see Cage squared off with the woman from the pizzeria. He looked as if he'd been pulled backward through a knothole. In contrast, the woman looked perfect. From the top of her gilded head to the toes of her white leather boots.

And they both turned and looked at her when her tennis shoes skidded a little on the hard-packed ground.

Her eyes were green, Belle thought dully. And her face was Lucy's. Why hadn't she noticed that before? "Is that why you proposed?"

Cage's filthy mood at finding Sandi in the barn with Lucy when he'd ridden back in after battling with a bawling cow and barbed wire went even farther south. He'd rather battle a mile of barbed wire than have to deal with this moment.

Belle eyeing him, clearly waiting some explanation. Some *something.* "No," he assured flatly.

"Of course it is," Sandi said clucking, her voice dripping kindness. "You swore on your father's grave, remember? Told me all about it," she said to Belle. "How one day he would make the Days hurt as badly as the Buchanans had been." She looked back again at Cage. "Too bad your success doesn't really matter since Lucy's going to be living in Chicago with my parents. Talk about the original rock and a hard place, right, Cage? Which one to let go of. The ranch or the kid."

He was grateful that Lucy was still out of earshot in the stable where he'd sent her to feed the horses as he rounded on Sandi. "Get...off...my...land." His voice was deadly.

Finally, Sandi had the sense to back off. Her sense of self-preservation kicking in, no doubt because he was two inches shy of dragging her off his property by the roots of her hair and he didn't much care if he broke her neck along the way or not.

She strode toward the barn door. "Good luck with him, honey," she advised Belle. "You're going to need it. If you're smart, you'll rethink the whole marital-bliss thing. My parents will drive him up to his ears in hock if he's not there already, then walk away with Lucy as the prize when they're finished with him." She slid a key chain out of her white purse and jangled the keys. "Of course. He'll have a Day around to finally give him his due." Dust puffed a little around her high heels as she strode out of the barn.

Moments later, her car shot past, gravel and dust spewing from beneath the tires.

Belle was staring at him, her eyes wide. Wounded.

He raked his hands through his hair. He smelled like just what he was. A guy who'd been rolling in mud and manure. Dammit all to hell and back again. Their first day under his roof—together—wasn't supposed to be like this.

Sandi was supposed to be rotting somewhere and he was supposed to be able to pick his time to tell Belle about his legal hassle with the Oldhams and not send her running.

"You could have told me who she was."

"She doesn't matter."

"Of *course* she matters! She's Lucy's mother."

"I didn't think she'd have the nerve to come out here."

Belle's eyes narrowed. "Well she did. This is what all that correspondence with the attorney is about?"

"Yes."

Her chin trembled but she collected herself. "How bad is it? Really?"

"Bad."

"And you need money."

"Yes." The word nearly choked him.

"So." Her knuckles were white. "Everything…Sandi— Lucy's mother—"

"Stop calling her that."

"It's true, though. Along with everything she said. It's all true."

His hands curled, impotence raging through him. "No."

"And I really played right into your hands, didn't I?"

He reached her in two steps, grabbed her arms. "It *wasn't* like that."

"Oh?" She was pale. "Then you're going to tell me that you proposed to me because you *love* me? I should have known better. Realized that there was no way you could have changed so much in these weeks, these last few days. Stupid me." She shrugged out of his hold and ran out of the barn, heading toward the house.

He practically tore the screen off its hinges going after her. Followed her up the stairs and into the guest room. She was shoveling stuff into her suitcase.

He grabbed a handful of sports bras and threw them back out onto the bed. "What I feel for you has been coming on for longer than these past few days and you damn well know it. You're not going to leave like this."

"Really? Do you think you can stop me?"

"I love you, dammit!"

Her hands paused. Shook. Then she scooped the contents out of a drawer and tossed them in the suitcase, her motions stiff. Jerky. "And you never once thought, well, hey, I can make use of this woman? Never, not once?" She waited a long beat. "I didn't think so."

Was he damned forever? He grabbed her shoulders. "It was before I knew you. Really knew you."

"And what about my family? What about if we did—" She broke off, her face a struggle. "If I married you. Then what? You're going to accept my mother? My sister? We're all *Days*. They're my family and they're as important to me as yours is to you."

"Jesus Christ, Belle. The past is the past. I know that. And you're in need of leaving it behind as bad as I am."

"Maybe, I am," she agreed.

"Then we can make a new family. Together. Nothing's changed!"

She stepped away from him, her expression closing. "Everything's changed." She flipped the suitcase closed, despite the edges of shorts, shirts hanging out, and dragged it off the bed. "And just to clear things up. I have *no* money to speak of. When my dad died, my mom had to work just like a million other people to keep a roof over our heads. I went to college on scholarships, not on trust funds. *I* work because I need a paycheck. So, I guess I wouldn't be all that useful to you, after all." She walked out of the room. Thumped her way down the stairs.

His hands fisted. He glared at his old iron-framed bed. Kicked it.

It groaned.

He caught up to Belle before she reached her car. "You love me. Need me. You meant those words, Belle. I know you did."

She threw the suitcase into the passenger seat. It bounced

open, spewing its contents. "I'll get over it," she promised thickly, and yanked open the car door, sinking down behind the wheel only to stare at it, mute frustration screaming from her. Her palms slapped the steering wheel and he realized she didn't have the keys.

He blocked her from opening the car door simply by planting himself there. She'd have to climb over the mess of clothes or him to get away. "Don't leave me."

Her head tossed, hair rippling. "Why? Because of Lucy?"

"Because of me."

Her mouth parted. She shook her head. "I don't believe you."

"Goddammit, Belle—"

"Ohmigod." She grabbed the top of the windshield and hoisted herself up in the seat. "Cage. Lucy—"

He caught a blur of motion, the moment seeming to turn to stone in his head. Turning to see what put the horrified expression on Belle's face. Lucy on Satin's back. Struggling to keep him reined in.

He swore and raced out ahead of the horse, aiming straight at him. In some distant part of his mind he heard Belle scream. Maybe it was the horse.

Maybe it was Lucy who was falling, falling. All over again, even before he could get close enough to snag the beast's reins and drag him under control.

Belle scrambled past him, reaching Lucy first. She huddled on the ground, her hands carefully, gently running over his baby. He fell to his knees beside them.

Satin raced off, hell-bent for leather.

Lucy's eyes were open, tears streaking her face. She tried to move and cried out, clutching her leg and Belle hoarsely ordered her to be still.

His daughter glared at him, her face set in rigid lines. "I heard you guys yelling in the barn. You're sending me away to live with them, aren't you? Just like my mother said."

"No. I won't let it happen."

"She told me she was here for my birthday. That she tried to get here the other day, but she was stuck in an airport in France. But that wasn't it at all, was it?"

He shook his head, wishing he'd been smarter, wishing a million things, all of them too late. "I'm sorry, Lucy."

She angled her eyes over at Belle. "Were you really gonna marry my dad?"

Belle didn't answer that. She looked at Cage, but didn't look at him, and it was worse now than it had ever been in the beginning. "I'm calling Sawyer. We need to get her to the hospital but I don't think we should move her." She touched Lucy's hair gently, then pushed to her feet, running like the wind toward the house.

Lucy closed her eyes. A sprinkle of freckles on her nose stood out, stark against her white face. "I don't wanna be a dancer, Dad. I don't wanna be anything like my mother."

He folded her hand in his. "You will dance," he said roughly, "and you will ride and do all the things you love, and you have *never* been like her. And I'm not letting you go anywhere you don't want to go. Clear?"

She started to nod, groaned.

Belle returned, blankets in her arms. "The medivac's on its way. Twenty minutes, max." She knelt next to Lucy, spreading the blankets over her. Held up her fingers for Lucy to count, making comforting noises.

Then the chopper arrived, settling out in the field. Same place as it had done seven months earlier. Only then, it had landed on a skiff of snow.

Cage and Belle ran alongside the stretcher they quickly loaded Lucy on. He ducked low, avoiding the blades that had barely stopped rotating. Belle hung back, already moving away from the clearing. She didn't need to be told there was a premium of space inside the helicopter.

One of the techs was telling Cage to finish fastening

his safety harness. He did so, watching out the side as the helicopter lifted. The wind whipped Belle's hair in a frenzy around her shoulders as they left her behind.

As far as hospitals went, Weaver's was pretty small. Cage had paced from one end of the building to the other about a million times over before Dr. Rebecca Clay finally reappeared after closing herself with his daughter behind a series of doors some bull of a woman in starched whites had dared him to cross.

The slender brunette held an oversize folder in her hands and he knew from experience they contained the X rays Lucy had just received.

The doctor smiled at him and gestured at the row of hard plastic chairs lining a sun-filled waiting room. "Let's sit," she encouraged. "Lucy's doing pretty well. No signs of concussion. I want to keep her awhile just to be cautious. A few days."

He stared, waiting for the big *but*. "What about her leg?"

Rebecca sighed a little. "There are no fractures, which is a good thing. We've immobilized it for now. But she has done some damage. How extensive, I couldn't tell you. She'll need to see her orthopedist. I know you have a perfectly fine one, but George Valenzuela from the Huffington Clinic has agreed to come up and consult, if you'd like. Belle called him while you and Lucy were on your way in. He specializes in pediatric cases. But you don't have to decide anything right now. We've given Lucy something for the pain." She patted his hand. "They're getting her settled in a room. I'll have someone take you to her."

He nodded. An hour later, he was sitting beside his daughter's hospital bed. She was sound asleep, her leg back in a brace similar to the one she'd worn for so many weeks after her first round of surgery.

He called his house but there was no answer. Called a dozen times throughout the night. His house. Belle's house. The cell phone she avoided as often as not.

By morning he faced it.

Belle was gone.

But if she thought things were over between them, she didn't know him as well as he'd thought.

Chapter 17

Cage eyed the row of men. And women. When he'd driven up the circular driveway of the Double-C Ranch, they'd all turned to watch, seeming to form a line. A significant line looking incongruous against the backdrop of colorful balloons tied by ribbons to nearly every stationary object.

"They don't look real happy to see us." Lucy's voice was subdued.

He hadn't figured showing up this way would be easy. "They invited you weeks ago to Angel's birthday party. It's not you they're not happy to see," he assured her. And, he reminded himself, Belle had visited Lucy each of the three days she'd been in the hospital. Avoided him like the plague, true, but she'd come all the same.

The driveway was congested with dozens of vehicles, not all belonging to the various members of the Clay family, he figured. Their reputation for throwing a celebration was well known, and it wouldn't have surprised Cage to count nearly half the population of Weaver as present.

It was the first time Cage had ever been to the Double-C Ranch, though. For any reason.

He didn't bother with trying to find an open place to park. There were none, so he just stopped his truck close enough where Lucy wouldn't have to drag her brace around any farther than necessary.

Even though there was music riding the air, right alongside the distinct smell of grilling meat that would've made his mouth water if it hadn't already been filled with crow, it still seemed as if a silence settled over the throng as he and Lucy slowly crossed an oval stretch of green grass toward that line of people.

"I don't see Belle." Lucy muttered an aside, looking worried.

Neither did Cage.

"Hey, Lucy." Ryan Clay grinned, seemingly unaware of the collective stares of his parents—Sawyer and Rebecca—aunts, uncles and grandparents as he walked into view, a plate in his hand on which a tower of food wavered dangerously. At sixteen, he was the oldest of Belle's nieces and nephews and the brown-haired kid with his father's blue eyes seemed to take the role with due seriousness. "Nice hardware you got on your leg there. Does it come off? 'Cause some of us're heading out to the swimming hole in a while and we wouldn't want you to sink." He jerked his head, assuming that she'd follow.

Lucy cast a look up at Cage. "Go ahead."

She needed no second urging and slowly worked her way toward Ryan.

Which left Cage facing that line of people alone.

He focused on the slender, auburn-haired woman who stood at the center. Gloria Day. Gloria *Clay*. And of all the men there, eyeing him with various degrees of warning, it was facing her that struck him the hardest. He walked closer. Until he could see the strands of silver in her auburn hair and the gentle lines beside her eyes that were the same shape and size as her daughter's, if a different color. They were the lines of a woman who'd done a lot of smiling in her life.

Definitely not in evidence now.

"If you've come to bring your daughter to celebrate with us, you're welcome," she said after a moment. "But if you've come to cause my girl more heartache, you can turn right on your heel and go."

"Give the boy a chance to talk, Gloria." Squire stood beside his wife and Cage could see the speculation in the man's squinty gaze before he turned his focus back to the fat wedge of cake on the plate he held.

Cage pulled off his hat and got to it. "I've nursed a grudge for a long time, Mrs.—" get it right "—Clay. Way back, it was sometimes the only thing that got me through another day." He figured he imagined the speck of sympathy in her eyes before her lashes swept down. "And I'm willing to admit that I managed to make a comfortable habit out of blaming your late husband for things. When you married Squire and moved up to Weaver—well, I let it bug me more than I should have. And I'm sorry for that. For a lot of things."

"I don't need your apology, Cage." Gloria looked up at him. "Nor do you need mine. What happened all those years ago was a tragedy. So, if that's all you came to say, then—"

"It isn't." A lifetime of fending for himself, on his own, struggling to keep what was his clawed at him. "I'm in love with your daughter, Mrs. Clay. And it's the first time I've ever *been* in love. The kind of love that matters. The kind that'll last a person their whole life if they're smart. And up to now, I've pretty much made a mess of it. I know I'm a stubborn man."

"He's right," Squire put in conversationally. "Cussed stubborn. I've offered plenty for that pretty piece of property he's got many a time and it took him until—"

"Squire," Gloria chided. "Hush up."

"What?" He looked around, innocence personified, which nobody bought because Squire Clay's craftiness was too well known. "I'm only agreeing with the boy. He's stubborn." He lifted his fork and pointed before stabbing it into his cake. "But he's got gumption, too. I'll give him that."

Damned if Cage didn't feel his neck getting hot. He'd had a meeting or two with the man over the past few days. But he hadn't bared any more thoughts than necessary and he hadn't said squat about Belle. It wasn't Squire he needed to get square with.

It was Gloria. "And I'm proud," Cage went on, determined to get through this even if it killed him.

"Too proud, I'd say."

He jerked, the sound of Belle's voice ripping a layer of skin off his soul. He turned and there she stood in a skinny red top and narrow jeans. Want slammed hard in his chest and it had nothing to do with the physical.

"You cut your hair."

Her hands flew to the shoulder-length strands as if she wanted to hide that glaring fact. Then she straightened and lifted her chin. "So?"

She'd done it because of him. There was no doubt inside him. And it hurt. Not because he cared if she had long hair or short hair or no hair. But because he knew what she'd been trying to do. Amputate the memory of them by lopping off her hair.

He set his shoulders, his fingers digging into his hat. "I'm *too* proud," he continued evenly. If Belle wanted him to crawl, he'd crawl, but damned if he was gonna enjoy the process.

"And stubborn," she said, crossing her arms, staring down her nose.

He gave her a sideways look. "I believe that's ground I've covered already."

She sniffed and looked away. But her high-and-mighty act was just that. Because he'd seen her eyes. Looking wet and bruised as pansies after a hard rain. Knowing he'd put that look there made him ache inside.

Gloria lifted her hand, sighing a little. "Stop." She stepped forward, breaking the ranks, and continued until she looked right up in Cage's face. "How is your mother?"

It ought to have ripped, that question. And maybe it would have just a few weeks earlier. "She's doing well. Thank you," he tacked on.

"I'm glad. My husband would have been glad. He worried about you and her a lot. He tried to speak with you, more than once, to tell you how sorry he was. But he was also deeply concerned about intruding on your grief."

He hadn't imagined the sympathy in Gloria's eyes, he realized. But along with that was also a vein of steel. He was a parent, too, and he could respect that. He'd messed with her daughter. "I appreciate knowing that."

"He tried to help, financially. The money you thought came from your parents' insurance came from him."

Belle's *"What?"* was an echo of his own.

"I know it wasn't much," Gloria went on. "Not enough to have lasted out all these years for your mother's care. You've done that. On your own, I'm sure. Doing a fine job of it."

"Why are you telling us this now?" Belle stopped beside him, facing her mother. "Why, after all these years?"

"Because I think—" Gloria's eyes were thoughtful "—Cage is ready to accept the truth of it, now. Aren't you?"

He remembered the day the check had come from the insurance. "I fought the insurance company for months," he said. "Trying to get them to settle. They claimed my father'd let the policy lapse. Then I later got a letter. And a check. Saying they'd been in error." The lawyer he'd hired had finally come through. Cage had always figured the guy had kept on the case only so he could collect his contingency fee.

That money had done a lot of things, not least of which was getting Sandi Oldham on that plane to Brazil and out of his life. "The insurance company wasn't making up for an error, like I was told," he concluded swallowing down hard on that. It wasn't an easy pill.

Gloria shook her head. "Given your situation, and what he learned about you, Gus believed that you'd never have accepted the money outright from him. He knew that the only thing you wanted was for your parents to still be with you. And that was something he couldn't accomplish. No matter how much he wished otherwise. I never was sure it was the right way to handle it, but it was Gus's decision and there was no moving that man when he'd set his mind on something." Her lips curved a little. "I know a little bit about dealing with stubborn men," she added.

And the man's actions hadn't left much over for his own family when he'd died not three years later, Cage figured.

"I'm sorry." He was.

Her hand brushed down his arm in a soothing motion. "There's no need to be," she said quietly. Then she stepped back, folding her arms across her chest. Squire was there and she leaned against him. "Not about that, anyway," she said. Her gaze encompassed him and Belle. And he knew that Gloria already knew some of what he'd come to say. He doubted there were many secrets, if any, that were kept between herself and Squire.

He looked down at Belle. "I'm selling the Lazy-B."

Belle sucked in a breath as Cage's words penetrated the glaze she'd been dwelling in for days. "What? Why? To who?"

"Because it's time," he said.

Her eyes burned way deep down in their sockets. "You shouldn't have to sell the Lazy-B, Cage. It's your home. There must be another way to fight against the Oldham's suit."

"I'm not selling 'cause of them. I'm moving Lucy to Cheyenne."

She wrapped her arms around her middle, glancing over

at the girl who was sitting in a lawn chair someone had given up for her, a hot dog in her hand that held nowhere near the interest that watching *them* did. "Have you *told* her that?"

His lips tightened a little. "Don't you want to know why?"

"No," she lied. "Have some food. There's plenty. If you can stand to eat anything touched by a *Day's* hands."

"Annabelle!" Gloria stared at her.

Belle's eyes flooded. Seemed they weren't eternally dry after all even though they ought to have been given the number of times she'd bawled over the past week. And she was making a scene, just exactly what Cage had to hate most of all, airing his personal matters in public.

Particularly *this* public.

"Don't worry, Mrs. Clay," Cage said evenly. "She's not saying anything I haven't thought at one time or another." His jaw slanted. Centered. "And I'm sorry for that, too."

Belle pressed her hands to her temples. "Maybe we should talk about this somewhere else."

"No," Cage said, shocking her silent. "Right here will do. I'm in love with you, Belle Day. I proposed to you once, but I'll keep doing it until you realize I'm not giving up on you. On us. You think I can't handle being a part of your family. Well, I'm here. And I'm not going anywhere until you can start believing otherwise."

She dropped her hands. Stared at him. All conversation had ceased. They could have heard the grass growing if they listened.

"I'm a simple man, Belle. And I don't have a lot." He made a wry sound, nearly soundless. "I've got... baggage." He looked over at his daughter and smiled a little. "And I'm not talking about that one, there, 'cause she's definitely the best thing I have going for me. Which I guess you know better than most. I've spent nearly my whole life fending for myself and opening up about it isn't my forte."

Belle gnawed the inside of her cheek as Cage stepped closer to her. His black shirt rippled in a sudden flutter of wind that tugged the tablecloths and dragged at the balloons.

"We can't change the past," he said. "It shapes us, but it doesn't have to define us. Luce and I are going to Cheyenne because that's where *you're* going."

"Says who?" she challenged thickly.

"That doctor you arranged to come up and consult on Lucy's case. Dr. Valenzuela. He said you're the best physical therapist Huffington's got and was mighty glad you were finally going to be back on staff."

"Well, gee." Her tone was stiff enough to hold up barbed wire. "Thanks for the validation."

"Is this a battle over *your* pride, then?" he asked. "Yes, Lucy can be treated at Huffington. But we're going to Cheyenne because of *you* and it doesn't have jack to do with your job, so get off your bloody high horse!"

She glared at him. "I'm interfering. I'm nosy. I'm riding high horses. What on earth could you possibly want with me, then?"

"God only knows," he said tightly, "because you're a pain in my heart like you would not believe. I married a woman when I was seventeen years old, but she was *never* part of my family. She was never my wife in any sense of the word. You're the only one I've ever asked to be, and you throw it in my face."

"You only proposed because you—" She barely managed to bite back the words. He'd proposed while they'd been making love.

"Because I wanted to spend my next fifty years loving you? Making a home with you?" His voice was rising furiously. "Giving Lucy a brother or a sister maybe? Watching them grow up with your brown eyes and your laughter? Yes, I should have told you about the custody suit. But it didn't have squat to do with my loving you and it still doesn't! Now are you going to marry me, or not? And don't be looking around for everyone's opinion, here. Because this is not between us and them, it's you and me, Belle."

She was shaking. "Could have fooled me," she whispered, "considering the way you're announcing it to all the world, here."

His eyebrows drew together. His tone gentled. He took another step nearer. "You want me on bended knee with all these witnesses to beg? Will that convince you?" He started to go down.

She shook her head and grabbed his arms, staying him. "I've never wanted you to beg," she whispered. "I just wanted you to love me."

"You have that, Belle." He slid his fingers through her hair, drawing it away from her face. "I've worked out this stuff with the Oldhams," he said quietly. "They took Satin back where he belongs."

"But…how? When? Isn't Lucy upset?"

"When you were hiding from me around hospital walls, and not answering your phone no matter what time I called," he murmured. "When it seemed I had to prove my feelings for you didn't have anything to do with anyone other than you. I did exactly what my attorney advised me not to do, and called them myself. And no. Lucy isn't upset. Now that the horse is gone she's stopped pretending she wasn't scared spitless of it. She thought she needed to be ready to ride, but she wasn't. When she is, when her leg is better, it might take a while to get her back in the saddle, but she'll get there with a horse she's not already afraid of."

She could hardly draw breath. "And what about the Oldhams?"

"I should have done it a long time ago. But there's that stubbornness of mine at work again, trying to prove I can do anything and everything better than everyone else. They never wanted complete custody of Lucy. They just wanted to have the grandchild Sandi'd been denying them."

"And you believed them?"

"I did once they faxed me confirmation they'd dropped the suit. Came this morning." He patted his pocket. Pulled out a piece of paper and showed it to her. "If I hadn't been so stuck on pride and just let them visit when they asked, none of this would have happened. The gifts they sent. The horse." He shook his head. "But then we wouldn't have had a reason for *you*." His voice went a little hoarse at that and he cleared his throat. "In exchange, they can come and visit Lucy *at* the Lazy-B and she doesn't have to sneak phone calls to them, anymore."

"Oh, Cage." She could see the relief in his eyes as he slid the notice back in his pocket. Knew how deep the relief ran. "It was that simple?"

"Well." His lips twisted a little, and she knew then that it hadn't been quite so simple. "In this case it's the end result that matters," he said. "So you see. I'm here strictly on my own. No agendas. Nothing. Maybe nothing is the word you need to focus on, though. I've got some prospects once I finish the sale of my place and get my neck out of debt. It won't be like running my own spread, but I—"

"*We*," she corrected huskily, catching his hand in hers, pressing it against her face. "We, not I, Cage. That's what families are about, aren't they?"

"We," he repeated slowly, as if he were testing the taste of it. The weight of it. "I guess they arc. So is this a yes, Miss Belle Day? No changing your mind, no turning back. Will you marry me?"

She nodded. A tear slid past her lashes and his thumb caught it.

"Mrs. Clay?" He raised his voice, never taking his vivid gaze off Belle's face. "Do I have permission to marry your daughter, or not?"

"I guess you'd better," Gloria said faintly. "Or we might have a revolt on our hands."

Belle slowly looked past Cage's wide shoulders to see a horde of expectant faces. Her mother. Her sister. And then there was Lucy, who looked ready to vibrate right out of her shoes.

"Welcome to the family, son," Squire said blandly.

Cage's lips tilted and his eyes met hers. "I love you, Belle."

"I love you, too, Cage."

"So hurry up and kiss her already, 'cause I want to go to the swimming hole with Ryan and his friends," Lucy said loudly.

"She has kind of a smart mouth sometimes," Cage murmured. "Don't let it scare you off."

"Not in this lifetime," Belle promised.

"Now," Squire said. "About the ranch. Some details we gotta—"

"Hush up, Squire," Gloria chided.

He grunted.

"Don't let them scare you off," Belle whispered back.

His hands held a fine tremble as he cupped her face in them. His eyes gleamed. "Not in this lifetime," he promised.

And at last, Belle believed him.

Then he wrapped his arms around her and kissed her.

And neither one heard anything further.

Epilogue

"Howard. Gorgon. Beowulf." Belle kept her voice low and watched Cage's lips turn up at the corners. Three months had passed since the day he'd shown up at the Double-C. Three months during which she found every opportunity to make him smile. She loved that smile.

She loved him. And each day that passed, she loved him more.

"Unique," he whispered easily, shifting in the folding chair. He looked over his shoulder, but there was still no sign of the bride and groom. "I hope our wedding doesn't last this long," he murmured. "I should have brought a book to read or something."

She contained a laugh. "You've been friends with Emmy Johannson for a long time. You *should* be here for her wedding. She and Larry are probably getting some pictures taken. They'll be here soon enough. Here. You can finish my punch." She nudged her cup toward him.

He took it. Drank it down. Even though he seemed calm,

she knew he wasn't entirely comfortable. Emmy and Larry's wedding wasn't as large as theirs was shaping up to be, but it *was* well-attended. Since he'd proposed, he'd been a more frequent sight in Weaver, but this was the first time they'd attended such a thoroughly social event.

"Come on," she wheedled, tilting her head a little. Sliding her fingers inside the cuff of his handsome gray suit. "We'll be married soon ourselves and you *still* won't tell me your real first name. Don't you think you're taking things a little far? When we pick up the wedding license I'm going to find out, you know."

He caught her exploring hand, lifted it and kissed her knuckles. "I never kept it secret from you, Belle."

She sniffed, but they both knew it was more for effect than anything else. Then Hope—who was a teacher like Larry was—and Tristan rejoined the table. They'd been dancing.

Hope let out a breathy laugh. Her pregnancy barely showed yet, but she was the picture of health from her toffee-colored long hair to her gleaming violet eyes. "Lucy must have worked really hard to be ready for today without needing her crutches. She and Anya look so pretty in their bridesmaid dresses."

"Too grown-up if you ask me," Cage murmured, looking over to where his daughter stood. Lucy and Anya—dressed in matching long red gowns—were surrounded by friends. Many of them male. He looked over to Tristan. He and Hope already had a five-year-old son. "If you two have a girl, you'll know what I mean."

Tristan grinned. His fingers looped through his wife's. "I've got nieces," he said. "So I already have an idea." He looked at Cage. "How's it feel to be partners with Squire?"

"He takes some watching." Cage looked amused. "He's got Double-C hooves grazing on Lazy-B land now."

"You'll buy him back out again," Belle assured. Knowing that Cage one day would. He was simply too proud not to. She understood that now. Understood so much about the boy e'd never really been allowed to be. And she was eternally grateful that he hadn't sold the Lazy-B outright. Not even to her stepfather who was currently circling the dance floor with her mother.

A commotion near the door of the church hall brought their attention around. Emmy and Larry had arrived. They didn't form a traditional receiving line, but went around to greet their guests in their seats. When the couple reached their table, Cage stood and gruffly bussed Emmy on the cheek and shook Larry's hand. "Congratulations."

Emmy beamed at Belle. "I know *you're* the one to get Cage here. Thanks."

"He wouldn't have missed Lucy being a bridesmaid," Belle assured. And Emmy had been one of the few people in Weaver he'd peripherally let into his life in the first place. It may have been more of necessity than anything else since he'd helped so much with Lucy over the years, but she knew he was happy for Emmy and Larry.

"Anya's so excited about going to New York with Lucy and the Oldhams next summer. I don't know which thrills her more. Seeing a Broadway show, or riding on the plane there." Emmy squeezed Cage's hand briefly. "Thanks for including her."

"Thanks for letting her go."

She smiled happily and with Larry's arm around her, they moved on to the next table.

Belle leaned toward Cage. "You've known Emmy since you were kids. Does *she* know your real name?"

The DJ had switched tempos and a slow sexy tune wailed from the speakers, heavy on sax and bass. Cage held out his hand for her. "You know my real name. Come on. I know you want to dance."

She did. But she'd been content to stay by Cage, believing he'd have no interest in it. She put her hand in his and he took her into the center of the swaying couples, ignoring the surprised looks they received. Then he pulled her into hi arms. Two seconds later, she knew he wasn't just a shuffle your-feet dancer. He knew how to dance. Properly.

"Don't look so surprised," he said after a moment, his eye smiling. "My mom made sure I learned a long time ago. Di you think Luce gets her coordination all from Sandi?"

Belle shook her head. "She gets her heart from you," sh whispered. And right now, *her* heart felt so full she was afrai it would start leaking out her eyes. "And how would I know your real name? You've only told me it's unique. What an I supposed to—" She broke off, suspicious at the glint o humor in his eyes, and realization finally dawned. "Oh. Nc No way."

"It's an old family name," he said gruffly. "And I know it's—"

"Unique," she inserted. "All along, you've told me. You name is actually *Unique*." She laughed. Pressed her lip together and giggled some more. "Please tell me we don' have to stick with the family name when you and I star having children," she finally managed.

"You don't have to do anything," he assured. "Except le me love you for the rest of my days. You're my life, yo know," he whispered softly, for her ears alone.

She twined her arms around his neck and it didn't matte that they were in the middle of someone else's weddin; reception. Her heart *did* overflow.

That's just what happened sometimes when a woman foun everything she'd ever wanted with one very unique man.

"And you're mine, Cage Buchanan. You're mine."

* * * * *